American Fiction

volume 16

American Fiction

volume 16

The Best Unpublished Stories
by New and Emerging Writers

Bruce Pratt

Editor

Ann Hood

Judge

©2017 New Rivers Press
First Edition
Library of Congress Control Number: 2016960013
ISBN: 978-0-89823-360-5
e-ISBN: 978-0-89823-361-2

Cover and interior design by Phuriwat Chiraphisit

The publication of *American Fiction Volume 16* is made possible by the generous support of Minnesota State University Moorhead, the Dawson Family Endowment, and other contributors to New Rivers Press.

MINNESOTA STATE UNIVERSITY
MOORHEAD.

For copyright permission, please contact Frederick T. Courtwright at 570-839-7477 or permdude@eclipse.net.

New Rivers Press is a nonprofit literary press associated with Minnesota State University Moorhead.

Nayt Rundquist, Managing Editor
Kevin Carollo, Editor, MVP Poetry Coordinator
Travis Dolence, Director
George McCormack, MVP Prose Coordinator
Thomas Anstadt, Co-Art Director
Trista Conzemius, Co-Art Director
Thom Tammaro, Poetry Editor
Alan Davis, Editor Emeritus

Publishing Interns:
Laura Grimm, Anna Landsverk, Mikaila Norman

The *American Fiction* Volume 16 Book Team:
Quinntineous Fenger, Mindy Kraft, Mikaila Norman, Rachael Wing, Taylor Brown, Joan Dalence

∞ Printed in the USA on acid-free, archival-grade paper.

American Fiction Volume 16 is distributed nationally by Small Press Distribution.

New Rivers Press
c/o MSUM
1104 7th Ave S
Moorhead, MN 56563
www.newriverspress.com

Contents

Editor's Note

In four years as editor of this anthology, I've read over twenty-six hundred submissions. Fewer than one hundred have been published, and only twelve have been awarded cash prizes by our judges.

Simple arithmetic indicates this contest's competitiveness, and the acclaim the anthology has received—including a gold medal and a silver medal from Midwest Independent Publishers Association—is a testament to the quality of those stories that make each new volume.

At the conclusion of my initial readings of this year's submissions, I had selected fifty-eight stories for further consideration, and, because I, too, am a writer, the task of selecting the twenty published finalists was a lie-awake-at-night challenge. I had opened each file for the first time with the distinctly optimistic hope that the story would grab and hold my attention from the first line to the last.

During the difficult selection of the twenty finalists, I endeavored to read no more than a half-dozen or so stories at one sitting, so as to never be fatigued by the process, and I strove to give each of the authors the respect I would expect editors to show my work.

As has been my custom, I used no screeners and did not read the cover letters and biographical data provided by a submitter until after I had decided whether or not to accept his or her story. When I did peruse those writing and publishing credits, I discovered that among the stories not selected for publication were many pieces that had been shortlisted for prizes from distinguished journals and reviews. It is no stretch to assert that we received enough well crafted stories to publish two excellent volumes of fiction.

As I made the final selections, I searched for stories that revealed rather than tried to develop character, and did not wander or stumble through multiple beginnings. I advantaged pieces about people I could truly imagine over plot-driven narratives that were about the *what* and not the *who* of the story.

Thus, the stories in this volume spring from richly imagined and skillfully drawn characters, whose authors avoided clichés and tired tropes. I was impressed by their originality. They gained traction quickly and kept the reader engaged throughout; in each one, what is at stake is clear, compelling, and believable.

It is inevitably true that my personal prejudices and preferences came into play in the selection process.

I avoided stories that read like thinly disguised and uncertain first chapters of novels, or those that appeared to be sketches for longer works. I passed on pieces peppered with non-English words, where the author showed off personal knowledge that did not benefit or enhance the prose or narrative, nor did I select stories that included every trauma or affliction the author could think to add to the character's sorrows and burdens. Murder, rape, dementia, mental illness, cancer, heart attacks, strokes, sexual and verbal abuse, alcoholism, drug addiction, divorce, abandonment, infidelity, estrangement, and the like have to *count* in a story, and should never serve solely as plot devices—and when all of the above are crammed into one story, it inevitably fails the verisimilitude test.

Editing this anthology is a process of discovery, and this year I was particularly delighted to learn that a writer with no prior fiction publications was awarded first prize by our judge, Ann Hood.

I hope readers will be as enthralled, moved, amused, entertained, and engaged by these stories as I was, and will, as I did, enjoy reading them more than once.

Bruce Pratt
Eddington, Maine
August 2016

Introduction

Ann Hood

I fell in love with the short story in Mrs. Calabro's English class at the John F. Deering Junior High School in West Warwick, Rhode Island, in 1969. I remember where I was sitting—four rows from the back, next to Nancy Lancelotta. I remember that it was a gray day, late autumn or early winter, the sky like dulled silver. And I remember the story—that luminous, surprising, mesmerizing, life-changing story: "The Lottery" by Shirley Jackson. I read its opening sentences: "The morning of June 27th was clear and sunny, with the fresh warmth of a full-summer day; the flowers were blossoming profusely and the grass was richly green. The people of the village began to gather in the square . . ." And I did not look up again until I read its last sentence: "'It isn't fair, it isn't right,' Mrs. Hutchinson screamed, and then they were upon her." In less than seven pages, Jackson had created an entire world, had brought me into that world, tossed me around, and left me in love—with her and "The Lottery" and the bright jewels we call short stories.

I was lucky enough to come of age as a writer during the renaissance of short stories in the '80s. Back then, *The New Yorker* published two short stories a week. I could feast on Raymond Carver, Mary Robison, Deborah Eisenberg, Ann Beattie, Antonya Nelson, and, eventually, Lorrie Moore and Julie Hecht and George Saunders, and, always sprinkled throughout, John Updike and Jamaica Kincaid and Richard Ford and Alice Munro.

William Trevor said the strength of the short story "lies in what it leaves out just as much as what it puts in, if not more." Unlike the novel, where we get to embellish and digress and explore and go on and on, the short story demands both a kind of restraint and an opening up of the imagination, the acrobatic skill of balancing how much to omit and how much to give the reader. Those writers I so revered in the '80s—Minimalists, they were called then! If ever there was a misnomer that is one!—developed a style in which what was omitted, the blank spaces, was as powerful as what they gave us. I learned to write short stories by imitating them, often erring on the side of too little information and context and then slowly adding this detail, this flashback, this scene, until finally getting that perfect balance, that thing we call a short story.

It was with great pleasure and admiration that I read the stories for this contest. How I marveled at these writers and their attention to all the seemingly small things that are knitted together to create a story. It was Frank O'Connor who said that short stories are about little people, and his words came to mind as I read "Puro Yakyū," the third-place winner. Our main character is a hotel maid whose days are made up of "the mundane tasks of sweeping, folding, and scrubbing." But through her point of view, a whole world is cracked open. Woven into this world is baseball and family and love—an ordinary character made extraordinary by the magic of the short story.

The teenaged main character in the second-place story, "Meredith's To-Don't List," hears that cracking open. "Everything will sound like it's cracking," she notes in the story's breathtaking climax. Meredith is displaced from her home in Texas to cold Minneapolis, trying to figure out how to fit in there and in the larger upside down world. Told in second person, the story is like the prodigy child of Stuart Dybek and Lorrie Moore, accomplishing what George Saunders tells us a short story can and should accomplish: "When you read a short story, you should come out a little more aware and a little more in love with the world around you."

Years ago I had the great fortune of hearing one of my favorite short story writers, Grace Paley, give a lecture in Bennington, Vermont. In that lecture she said that no story is one story, rather "Every story is two stories, the one on the surface and the one bubbling beneath. The climax is when they collide." To me, a short story that does this, and does it well, is a terrific short story, and the first-place story, "Forgive Me, Father," manages this so deftly that the reader can only wonder at the writer's skill. The story explores adolescence, faith, religion, friendship, family, love, betrayal, and John Stamos with compassion and humor and intelligence.

In his essay "On Writing," Raymond Carver tells us that the short story writer must use his talent and intelligence and all that is within his power to show the reader what things are really like out there and how he sees those things—"like no one else sees them." Perhaps this is the sign of a good story: It reveals the world to us in a way that we have never seen it before. Get ready. These stories do just that.

Hand Picked

Forgive Me, Father

Tamar Schreibman

When I was twelve, church was a place of transformation. You stepped up the brick stairs and through the yawning wooden doors and down the red carpet that rolled out like a giant tongue splitting the cold floor in half. Inside Our Lady of Mercy, with my best friend Colleen Brennan and her family, the words to all the songs were in English and everyone said hallelujah with their heads held high as if they meant it. Here, there were no temple sisterhood ladies lingering in the purple-carpeted lounge after the service with lipstick-stained Styrofoam cups full of Sanka, hoping to get a minute or two with the rabbi, my father. Nobody stopped talking when they saw me and then asked me questions about my bat mitzvah plans or our summer vacation or my great grandma in New Jersey, as if this knowledge of my family would somehow bring them closer to God. At church, nobody watched to see if I knew every word of every prayer, sang every song, or had a pleasant expression on my face. I read along when I felt like it; I kept quiet when I didn't.

At church with Colleen and her family, I felt free to be a better version of myself, quieter, less fidgety, more accepting of all God's creatures, even my sixteen-year-old sister Ruth, who laughed too loud and talked too much. Ever since I could remember, my older sister had been tearing the pages out of my books, drawing with a Sharpie on the faces of my dolls and stuffed animals, cutting holes in my clothes, locking me in closets, biting me. Recently, she had kicked holes in her bedroom walls. These violent outbursts didn't happen very often, maybe two or three times a year, and my parents chalked it up to sibling rivalry, a lack of impulse control, teenage hormones. Ruth was *different*, my parents would sometimes say, but they focused on her average grades, her pretty face, her lovely singing voice. You were either *normal* or you were *retarded*, and Ruth was not retarded because she was not in special ed. Sometimes I would catch a glimpse of my Ruth-shaped mouth in the mirror, or hear in my own voice the Ruthy way I said "that's so cool" when I didn't know what else to say, and for the rest of the day my stomach would hurt.

The first time I walked into Our Lady of Mercy and saw the giant crucifix hovering above the altar, it was May 16, my bat mitzvah exactly one year away. I had seen Jesus before, on the gold crucifix that Colleen wore around her neck, that miniature Jesus whose tiny head I longed to rub like a genie and make a wish. But this Jesus was so big you could see his ribs protruding, and the cloth he wore around his waist was slipping so low that his belly button was visible, and you could almost see his private parts. His wavy hair was matted down, his back arched, stomach concave, lips slightly parted, eyes rolling back in his head. As they filed into the pews, people paused and gazed up at his bearded face and then crossed themselves before sitting down in their seats, their own faces solemn, calm, blissful, like the angels in the stained glass window scenes. Nobody seemed to think it was rude to stare at Jesus in all his private agony. It didn't seem right to me that they should be so happy about someone they loved so much dying a horrible death, yet I wished

I could share in this belief that brought them so much joy. As I stared up at Jesus, I imagined all my pettiness and hostility and jealousy, all my guilt and frustration and fear, dissolving in the sweet musty scent of the yellowing pages of the hymnal books and faded blue Bibles, and a simpler, purer, happier me emerging in the incense-filled air.

After Mass that first time, Colleen's parents took us to the Ground Round for onion loaves and cheeseburgers. It was pouring rain, and we all got soaking wet running from the parking lot. Mr. and Mrs. Brennan held hands as they ran and gave each other high fives when they got inside the door like high school kids. Mr. Brennan asked the hostess for towels with a charming smile and not a trace of the New Yorky Jewish self-deprecation that was my father's trademark, just confidence and gentle assertiveness—a person who knew exactly how to make everything okay and could be counted on to always do so.

The waitress brought us a basket of peanuts and encouraged us to throw the shells on the floor.

"I totally caught Kevin Fahey staring at my butt when I got up to take Communion," Rosemary, Colleen's older sister, announced. Mr. Brennan chuckled and Mrs. Brennan rolled her eyes and laughed. In my family, we always said "tushie" because my parents thought "butt" was crass, but Colleen and Rosemary didn't have to be careful with their words.

"Maybe he was just lost in prayer," Mrs. Brennan said, but she was smiling and one of her eyebrows was raised. Rosemary raised an eyebrow too, then ate a whole peanut, shell and all.

Mr. Brennan gazed out the window at the rain coming down sideways, hitting the windows in loud slaps. "The sky sure looks green," he said.

"Do you think there is going to be a tornado?" I asked, always hopeful for drama in the form of weather, eager for proof that the world was really out of control—not just the world I lived in, but the entire universe.

"I doubt it," said Mr. Brennan. "But what do I know? We didn't have tornadoes in Connecticut where I'm from. Just hurricanes." He turned to Colleen and Rosemary. "Did I ever tell you girls about the time when my great uncle Trip sailed from Sag Harbor to Block Island during a hurricane?"

"Yes, Dad," Rosemary said. "About a million times."

"Well, he nearly died but it was his favorite story. He used to tell it whenever he wanted to make a point that his wife, my aunt Diana, was a worrier. Which she was. Though to be fair, he was damn lucky to survive, the crazy old coot."

Everyone in my family was a worrier, and nobody knew how to sail. (Although I had taken a couple lessons on a Sunfish the summer before at Jewish sleepaway camp in Wisconsin where my dad was the resident rabbi.)

"Your uncle Trip was certainly a character," said Mrs. Brennan. She was wearing a bright green sheath dress and her fingernails and toenails were painted pale pink. She kept touching Mr. Brennan's forearm, wrapping her slender fingers around his wrist. Mr. Brennan ordered a beer, which arrived in a frosted mug. My dad always asked for water with lemon and extra ice, and I couldn't imagine my mom wearing colors other than black or gray or khaki. My mother always wore lipstick and was pretty, but I wished that she and my dad knew how to be fun and breezy and light together. I wished Ruth were thin and smoked clove cigarettes like Rosemary.

"Everything A-Okay, Scout?" Mr. Brennan asked when he saw me staring at his beer mug. I looked up at him, pressed the corners of my lips into a smile and nodded, then popped an entire peanut in my mouth the way I had seen Rosemary do. It tasted salty and a little sweet, and it took a long time for me to chew.

After that first Sunday, I became a regular at Mass, and so began the era of my religious immersion. Every Friday night, as we had done my entire life, my family had Shabbat dinner before going to temple. Then, on Saturday night, I'd sleep at Colleen's and go to morning Mass with her family on Sunday.

"Are you sure you want to spend your free time going to *church*?" my mother asked me once. Several times when I was leaving for Colleen's she muttered under her breath, "I just don't understand," but, as was her usual manner, she didn't confront me directly. Her disapproval was more of a feeling in the air, or a faint smell that you could pretend you didn't notice, and then it would fade.

My father apparently thought it was a phase and that the best strategy was to ignore it, because one night I heard them arguing about it in their room after I went to bed. It was a humid mid-August night, seventh grade just around the corner.

"It's fine, Arlene. If we ignore it she will get tired of it, come to her senses."

"But it's just so weird. And so public! The rabbi's daughter—at church week after week."

"I'm not concerned," answered my father. "She's having her bat mitzvah in less than a year. That's pretty public, too."

More whispering, words I couldn't understand because their voices were so low. Then: "Hank, she should know better. You always make excuses for her. How is she ever going to learn?"

And I knew from their words and tone that they weren't talking about my churchgoing anymore. They were talking about Ruth. I climbed into bed, thankful that I had plans with Colleen soon, hopeful that I would be able to avoid finding out what it was Ruth was doing that my father was making excuses for.

The next day was a Friday, which meant it was time for Shabbat again. On Friday afternoons I usually hung out at home because my mother needed my help setting the table. Shabbat dinner was special—that's what my parents said. A time-out from the routine of our daily lives, a time to enjoy being a family. In our house we believed that saying things made them true. I love you. We are having fun. Ruth is funny and smart and a little unusual. Ruth is just being Ruth.

I was lying on my stomach on the scratchy, white living room couch, listening to Diana Ross and Lionel Richie singing "Endless Love," feeling nostalgic about a great love that I had yet to actually experience. Ruth came in and sat on the backs of my legs, which felt like they might snap under her considerable weight. She was staring at me with wide searching eyes. Her face was round and pale, her eyes tiny, hidden in the fullness of her flesh. I felt my jaw tighten and my fingers tense. She and I had the same bone structure, the same overbite, the same almond-shaped eyes, the same crooked fingers. I knew I should be nice to her because she didn't have any friends, to have *compassion*, as my parents urged, but I closed my eyes and tried to listen to the music, pretending she wasn't there, trying to ignore the aching in my legs.

"I'll get you, my pretty, and your little dog, too!" she cackled like the Wicked Witch of the West.

I tried to kick her off my legs. "Ruth! Stop! That hurts!" Ruth goosed me under the arms, between my legs, laughing a wild laugh with her gummy smile. She wouldn't stop tickling me and I was having trouble breathing.

"Mom!" I gasped and choked.

"Oh, Sarah. It's fine. Go in your room if you want to be alone."

My mother went back to talking in a hushed voice on the telephone while stuffing a chicken with vegetables and thyme, oniony tears rolling down her cheeks. My father was sitting at the dining room table with his legal pad scribbling notes for his Friday night sermon. I went in my room and closed the door, but Ruth followed me, opened the door, and walked right in.

"I don't know why I do that," she said, sitting on my bed too close to me, reaching over and stroking my hair, then taking just a few strands close to my scalp and pulling them out hard and fast.

"Ouch!" I said.

"I'm sorry, I should just leave you alone," she said.

"Just stop it, okay?" I said.

"It must be nice to have friends," said Ruth. "To be thin. Good at stuff. You're lucky, Sarah!" she said, holding my face in her hands.

I was relieved when she said these things. I felt guilty and also happy. I imagined people were filled with stuffing like dolls or turkeys, and fantasized about taking fistfuls of my sister's skin and squeezing until the mushy insides came popping out.

"Did you hear that last night's Cubs game lasted twenty-one innings?" I asked at the table, after we had said the prayers over the candles, wine, and challah. "Colleen's dad told me it was the longest game in the history of baseball." We were using our special silver and china and linen napkins. A white tablecloth covered the dining room table where we sat.

"Can you imagine having the patience to sit through six hours of baseball?" my mother said. "I can't think of anything more boring."

"You know who I think is beautiful? Kate Jackson," said Ruth, apropos of nothing as usual. "She is the prettiest of the Angels, even if everyone says it's Farrah Fawcett. I know I'm supposed to think Scott Baio is cute, but I am more a Pierce Brosnan kind of gal, you know?" she said, turning to me. "Or Ted Danson. I guess I like mature men. They are more experienced, if you know what I mean." She elbowed me. "Wink wink, nudge nudge," she said and made gross clicking noises with her tongue.

My mother was closing her eyes a little, pressing her fingers into the side of her head behind her ear and massaging her hair, the way she always did in the car when she was stopped at a long red light.

"That's inappropriate, Ruth," my father said in the voice he used when he was about to get up from his chair and announce that he had work to do. His lips were pressed tightly together, like he was trying hard not to yell, and he was pressing air into the space above his upper lip so he looked a little like a baboon. He cracked the knuckles of each hand, then let the air out of his upper lip so it made a little pop.

My mom folded her hands and smiled as if she had really exciting news. She took a deep breath in. "Oh, guess what—Judy Silver had triplets this morning!"

"Triplets! I guess Mr. Silver has powerful sperm!" Ruth said.

"Ruth!" my mother said. "That's not the way it works. You know that." Mom picked at wax that had dripped on the potholder from the Shabbat candles. She turned to me. "What did Suzette's letter say?" Suzette was my French pen pal. I wanted to tell my parents that Suzette's family was moving from the countryside to Paris and wanted me to visit once they got settled, but Ruth had already taken this as her cue to start speaking in French. "*La France est un pays merveilleux! Que faites-vous dans la vie? Comment vous appelez-vous? Vous etes-vous plu ici?*"

I noticed a little robin looking at me in the big bay window. It cocked its head like it was trying to make me feel better, and I felt a rush of affection toward it.

"*C'est un plaisir de vous recontrer! Enchante!*" Ruth continued the string of nonsensical French. I catalogued the shapes and colors in the patterned wallpaper—red, yellow, green, and blue triangles, squares, circles, and diamonds.

"*Shhhhh,*" my father said, rolling his eyes. "We are right here, Ruth, no need to shout." She was speaking in English again, about how much she loved Bob Newhart and hated Michael J. Fox. Her voice was getting louder and louder; her mouth was full of chicken as she talked. My parents and I just sat mute and defeated, chewing, not making eye contact. After temple that night, while Ruth brushed her teeth, I snuck into her bedroom and spit on her pillow. It was the grossest thing I could imagine doing and I immediately regretted it. Not because I felt guilty, but because I realized it was something Ruth might do. I couldn't wait to sleep at Colleen's the next night, to be cleansed at church on Sunday of whatever it was inside me that made me like Ruth.

The next night, Saturday, Colleen's sister Rosemary was home with a cold. Most Saturday nights she was with her boyfriend, but that evening after dinner Rosemary lay next to me on the couch in the family room, her legs draped over the side, and did funny impressions of the characters on *Love Boat* and *Fantasy Island*. She introduced me to her favorite snack combinations: Cap'n Crunch mixed into vanilla Häagen-Dazs ice cream; Doritos dipped in sour cream. She had a hearty, deep laugh, and my heart broke when she said, "Toodle-loo! I'm going to take some cough syrup and go to bed," and left me and Colleen in the TV room alone.

Later that night, when Colleen and I were getting ready for bed, Colleen showed me a string of pearl beads her grandmother had given her for her confirmation. She said it was a rosary and it was supposed to remind her of the mysteries of Jesus. "Want to hold it?" she asked. I closed my eyes and ran my fingers across the beads. They were cold and pink and lovely.

"What am I supposed do?" I asked.

"First you make the sign of the cross," she said and she pointed to the top of her forehead, her heart, then her left and right shoulders. I did the same.

"Then you announce the mystery. A different one each day. It's Saturday so you would say, 'The first Joyful Mystery, the Annunciation of Our Lord.'"

"The first Joyful Mystery, the Annunciation of Our Lord," I said, picturing the scene in Colleen's children's bible of an angel telling Mary she would give birth to God's son.

"Then you say three Hail Marys. *Hail Mary, full of grace. The Lord is with thee.*"

I repeated after Colleen, line by line. "*Blessed art thou among women, and blessed is the fruit of thy womb, Jesus. Holy Mary, Mother of God, pray for us sinners, now and at the hour of our death. Amen.*"

I was in a kind of trance uttering the words after Colleen. The parts of me that I usually had to work so hard to hide seemed to be evaporating into the air around me, leaving only my true essence, stripped of all of the Ruthness that usually clung to me. I felt powerful, hopeful, like anything was possible.

After the Hail Marys, Colleen led me through another prayer to say on the large bead.

"If we were doing the whole thing you'd say ten more Hail Marys on each of these beads," she said, touching the small beads. "And then there's one more prayer that you say at the end."

By that time, I had stopped trying to repeat after her and just listened. There was so much to remember. All the prayers talked about fruits of the womb or sinning or death, and one even mentioned the fires of hell. The words gave me a funny feeling in my stomach that I couldn't decide whether I liked or not.

Later, as I lay in my sleeping bag on the floor, I watched Colleen as she put the beads back in the drawer of the bedside table before she crawled into her bed. I tried to remember the prayers as I fell asleep.

In the morning, Colleen's mother called us downstairs to set the breakfast table. I told Colleen that I had to go to the bathroom and I'd be down in a second. Once I heard her in the kitchen talking to her mom, I flushed the toilet and turned on the faucet, staring at my face in the mirror for so long that my features blurred and I stopped looking like myself. I dried my hands on the light pink hand towel monogrammed in dark pink with a curlicue B, and then I slipped back into Colleen's room, slid open the drawer where Colleen had stashed the rosary and stuck it in the pocket of my shorts. I told myself I just wanted to have it for a little while, that I'd sneak it back into her room next week and she wouldn't even notice.

When I joined Colleen in the kitchen to fill the orange juice glasses, Mr. Brennan was already at the table, reading the editorial page of the *Chicago Trib*. Mrs. Brennan was humming as she placed cinnamon apple pancakes onto everyone's plates, then added a little plop of crème fraîche and two links of sausage. Rosemary was drinking a cup of coffee with cream and reading the Sunday comics. In all the time I'd known the Brennans, this was the first time I wanted to get away from them. Through the large kitchen window, the August sun was stabbing me in the eyes, giving me a headache, and I worried that everyone noticed the dark hair above my upper lip. I wanted to be home alone in my own room with the door closed, holding the rosary. I knew I should just go upstairs to Colleen's room to return the rosary before anyone noticed it was missing, but I didn't want to, couldn't.

"I feel kind of sick. I think I'm gonna go home," I said.

"Oh, okay honey, hope you feel better," Mrs. Brennan said, touching my shoulder and then my forehead. "You don't feel warm, but it probably is a good idea to go home and get some rest." She gave me a knowing look that I took to mean that she thought I was about to get my period. It was a look my mother would have given me, and for the first time ever Mrs. Brennan annoyed me.

"Call me later!" Colleen shouted to me as I ran out the door and rode away on my bike. The rosary was still in my pocket when I walked into my house that morning. I had never stolen anything before, not even a pack of gum or ChapStick on a dare. I was giddy about the idea that I was carrying around a secret, and also guilt-ridden. The beads felt bulky and noticeable in my tight-fitting jean shorts, and I kept poking at them so they would lie flat against my hip. My mother was in the kitchen scutting up vegetables for tuna salad. Ruth was parked on the couch in the TV room eating Oreos out of the cookie jar, watching *Grease.*

"Hi." I smiled, determined to be more Christian in character to make up for my stealing. I sat down next to her and thought about touching her knee but didn't.

"Greetings." Ruth didn't look away from the movie, grabbed another Oreo.

I sat on the other side of the couch. Ruth moved closer to me, keeping her eyes glued to the screen. Her asthma was acting up and she coughed loudly without covering her mouth so I could see her tongue and teeth coated in black.

"It's nice to just sit together, you know?" she said in between coughing. "Sisters just watching an old movie and chilling out together. You are my best friend, Sarah. I mean, I know you are my sister, but you are also my best friend."

"Yeah, I know," I said, trying to make it sound like I felt the same way. Without saying that I felt the same way. There was a knot at my core radiating outward like sunshine, but instead of warmth and light and serenity, something cold and dark and unsettling was spreading throughout my body. I sat next to my sister thinking about the rosary in my pocket, wanting to touch it but worried she would notice, while Olivia Newton John and John Travolta danced through the funhouse in skin-tight pants.

When I could no longer bear to watch Ruth stuff more Oreos into her mouth or listen to the smacking sound she made when she chewed, I climbed the stairs to my bedroom, closing the door quietly, hoping Ruth wouldn't come up. She didn't. I sat on my bed and pulled out the rosary. It made smooth clicking noises in the palm of my hand. As I rolled the small Jesus through my fingers, simultaneous currents of discomfort and pleasure shot through my groin, like when I saw blood or contemplated death or climbed rope in gym class. My heart was jumping and my face felt flushed and clammy. I knelt next to my bed and crossed myself best I could, said the first few lines of Hail Mary, then tried to remember what mystery of Jesus I was supposed to say on a Sunday. I tried to remember the other prayers Colleen taught me but I really wanted to have a personal conversation with Jesus, something I'd heard Colleen's priest talk about in his sermons. This idea made me think that Jesus wanted to get to know *me,* the *real* me, the one that nobody in my family seemed to know, the one that maybe I didn't even fully know yet.

"Our Father who art in heaven," I began. "Please grant me . . ."

I was expecting to feel liberated not having to utter the Hebrew words I'd been reciting by heart my whole life, but instead I felt tentative, overwhelmed by the open-endedness.

"Our Father who art in heaven, please grant me . . . happiness."

I was picturing the kind of happiness that I saw on Colleen's family's Christmas cards, on the silver framed pictures all over their house. It didn't feel specific enough to be much of a request at all, but I was frightened to ask for what I really wanted: to wake up one day and not have Ruth for a sister. It wasn't that I wanted her to die, I told myself. I just wished she wasn't there. I tried to imagine my family without her.

I would tell stories at dinner about kids in my class and my parents wouldn't always get Katie Johnson confused with Molly Anderson. They would have heard me when I said I wanted a Schwinn ten-speed, instead of going with the bargain bike they got from a congregant who owned a sporting goods store (a no-name bicycle painted blue with white speckles to look like denim, with painted-on stiches and a real denim cloth seat). There would be less eye-rolling and sighing, more fun and laughter. This is what I was asking Jesus for when the phone rang, the rosary still in my hand. It was Colleen.

"Did you take my rosary?"

"No." I stopped playing with the beads and set them down as quietly as possible on the desk.

"I can't find it anywhere. You were the last person to hold it."

"Did you look under your bed?" I asked.

"Looking now. It's not there."

"Maybe Rosemary took it."

"Why would she?"

"I don't know. Maybe she's playing a trick on you?"

"Well, I asked her and she didn't know anything about it."

"What would I do with it? In case you didn't remember, Colleen, I'm Jewish!"

Silence. I was trying to figure out how I could sneak it back into her room without her figuring out that I had taken it in the first place. I needed to be invited to her house, but she was so mad at me it would never happen. I had gone too far; our friendship was ruined. I wanted to confess everything and beg Colleen for forgiveness but I was too scared. I sat there in silence, focusing all my energy on not crying, staring at my empty hands, at the rosary on the desk next to me.

"I gotta go," I finally said.

And she hung up. I sat for another minute listening to the dial tone before I put the rosary under my mattress.

I called Colleen later that day but nobody answered. I called her on Monday but she said she was busy. On Tuesday when I called, Mrs. Brennan told me to hold on, and then came back a few minutes later and said Colleen would have to call me back. She didn't. My mom could tell something was wrong, and she suggested I go to the pool with Ruth. Instead I called Jenny and Debbie Slovitt. The Slovitt girls were identical twins who lived on my street and whose family went to my dad's temple. We went to the Jewish country club where my dad had a free membership just because he was a rabbi. We charged chicken salad sandwiches and Arnold Palmers to my dad's account, slathered our bodies in baby oil, spritzed lemon juice in our hair, and read *Seventeen* magazine poolside. The twins bickered with each other over who got to sit where and asked me questions I didn't know how to answer, like what was it like having a dad who is a rabbi, and why did God want Abraham to kill Isaac, and do Jews believe in ghosts? I hated the feeling that I got around other Jews, that feeling that they wanted or needed something from me, something they thought I had—knowledge or holiness or some advanced version of Jewishness.

After that day at the pool with the irritating Slovitt twins, I missed Colleen and I missed her family and I missed church even more than before. I missed hearing New Testament stories, stories with clear interpretations about Jesus's many acts of mercy and love. I missed the light streaming in through the stained glass, the plaster statues of saints, the flickering candles in the shadowy space. I missed the giant Jesus floating above the pulpit, reminding me how much I was loved, no matter how repulsive my thoughts or actions.

When school started the next month, French was the only class that Colleen and I had together and I barely saw her. I carried the rosary on me wherever I went, and when I thought no one was looking, I'd move the beads inside my shorts pocket and think of Jesus and his unconditional love. Each night I knelt next to my bed and talked to Jesus. John Stamos would stare back at me from the poster hanging over my desk, his lips curled into a slight smile, his black locks falling into one eye. I knew he was really a soap opera star, but if I squinted I could imagine that he was Jesus.

"Will Colleen and I ever be friends again?" I asked the poster one evening.

"Are you ever going to tell her that you stole her rosary?" Jesus/John Stamos replied. "Are you ever going to return it?"

"Should I?" I asked.

"What do you think?" he asked me, his blue eyes twinkling.

"But it'll just give her reason to hate me more than she already does," I moaned.

"Just be the best person you can be," the poster told me. "That's all you—or anyone—can do."

"But even when I do the right thing, I *think* mean thoughts. I can't stop thinking mean thoughts."

"Do you act on these unkind thoughts or feelings?" Jesus/John Stamos replied.

"No, but my parents—everyone really, except Colleen—everyone thinks I'm so nice, so good."

Jesus/John Stamos shrugged. "So?"

"So. I feel like I am a big liar."

"Everybody feels and thinks things they don't share with the world." Then I imagined that he winked at me, which I took to mean that I wasn't a bad person. As I drifted off to sleep, I said the Shema in both Hebrew and English, ending as always with, "God bless Mommy and Daddy and Ruth and Sarah, and all God's good children everywhere, let there be peace, amen."

After two weeks of praying to Jesus and not getting real answers, two weeks of Colleen walking by me in the hallway without even saying hello, pretending she was deep in thought or talking to someone else, I sought spiritual guidance from my father. It was erev Yom Kippur, the night before the holiest day of the year, the Day of Atonement. I wasn't hungry but knew I would regret it if I didn't eat because after this meal we would not eat again until sundown the next day. After dinner we would go to services, and then we would go to services again the next morning and then again in the afternoon, before we would finally break fast and I would not have to think about fasting again for another year. I moved my food around on my plate, taking tiny bites of brisket and green beans and kugel before I interrupted one of Ruth's monologues to announce: "I have a question for the rabbi." It came out more pointed, less casually than I had intended.

"Yes?" my father asked, matching my formality, seeming amused.

"I have a friend who stole something from another friend. She didn't really mean to, it just sort of happened. And now too much time has gone by and it feels too late to admit it and my friend doesn't know what to do."

My heart was jumping. I felt hot and lightheaded and I thought I might cry. But I needn't have been nervous. Speaking to me as if I were a congregant whose privacy he wanted to respect, my father merely doled out generic advice, without pressing me for more information: "Your friend should ask forgiveness from the person she stole from. Yom Kippur is the perfect time for her to do it! But at any time during the year it's always best to tell the truth even if it's going to be embarrassing or get her into trouble. Because in the end she is going to have to live with herself."

Really? That was all? I wasn't sure whether to be relieved or angry.

"Do I have time to watch *Happy Days* before we go?" asked Ruth.

"Absolutely not," said my mother. "We are leaving as soon as the table is cleared." Ruth stormed away from the table, not carrying a single dish or glass. The line across my mother's forehead got deeper and she looked like she might say something, but then she stacked up the dishes and walked to the sink in silence. My father looked at the clock and said we had to hurry. I cleared my place and then went upstairs to my room and closed the door, putting a chair in front of it so Ruth couldn't get in. I knelt next to my bed and fondled the rosary, gazing at Jesus/John Stamos's faint all-knowing smile, the glow around his face, the love and acceptance and forgiveness. My parents thought I was perfect, but I knew that it was only because they were comparing me to Ruth, only because they weren't looking that hard. But Jesus saw it all, knew me fully and understood; he knew that I wasn't perfect and still loved me, loved me because of it and was going to save me from all my stealing, lying, mean thoughts.

After services that night I couldn't sleep. I saw the light on in the kitchen when I got up to use the bathroom. It was midnight. My father was working at the kitchen table. He wrote all his sermons longhand, pages and pages of blue ink on yellow paper. I hated how he wore a bathrobe and no underwear and kept his legs open so that if you were sitting in the wrong place and he moved his legs you could see parts of him you didn't want to know about.

"Dad, I stole something. I was the one who stole, not my friend. From Colleen. I took her grandma's rosary. I don't even know why . . ." I could hear the blood in my ears, a loud drumbeat, like in a nightmare. "Now she barely talks to me at school and I miss her so much. It's awful."

"Pumpkin face, this sounds very serious but can we talk after Yom Kippur? I'm putting the finishing touches on my sermon for tomorrow morning." He didn't look up from the legal pad. I went back into my bedroom.

"Do you think I am a bad person for wishing my dad had a normal job like a lawyer or surgeon or CEO?" I asked Jesus/John Stamos after I closed my door. I was kneeling next to my bed and the rosary was in my hand.

"It's very human to feel that way. And it is brave of you to admit it," he replied. The chain he wore around his neck hung over the top of his shirt so the silver cross was visible.

"Is Ruth always going to ruin everything?"

"I see good things ahead for you," Jesus/John Stamos told me. "Be yourself. Believe in yourself. Also, try to remember the Ten Commandments. Honor your father and mother. Thou shalt not steal. Et cetera."

I tried to explain to Jesus/John Stamos that I needed the rosary to get closer to him. That I was hoping to return it, I was just waiting for the right moment. But it seemed like he wasn't listening anymore. Instead, I was just sitting in my room alone on Yom Kippur with a poster of Blackie Parrish, making excuses for myself, holding stolen rosary beads in the sticky palms of my hands.

I barely slept that night, and in the morning I was ready for services before my parents or sister. My mom was encouraging Ruth to get dressed and my father was pacing and trying not to yell at Ruth. I was sweating in my navy wool suit and stockings. I hated that I had to get so dressed up for temple when all the other girls from my Hebrew School class would be wearing sundresses with bare legs (some of the boys would even wear jeans), and it seemed that I was the only one who ever had to fast. I lay on the itchy white couch trying to stay cool, already fantasizing about the bagels and cream cheese, whitefish and scrambled eggs and chocolate chip cookies I'd eat when it was time to break the fast, counting how many hours more of fasting there were to go. Hungry, itchy, and hot, I got up off the couch and went to the cool basement to my father's office. I saw a legal pad covered with his illegible scrawl on his big oak desk. I tried to read it but couldn't make out any of the words. I thought about crumpling it up, even burning it. But how would I do that without getting caught or setting the house on fire? Instead, I took it, folded it up, slipped it under my blouse and walked straight upstairs to my room.

"Sarah, you ready?" my mom asked for the third time from the living room.

"Yup" I called, as I shoved the sermon under my mattress where I hid the rosary when I wasn't carrying it in my pocket.

"Where's my sermon?" I could hear my father bellowing from the basement office. "Has anyone seen it? It was on my desk!"

"Ruth! Sarah! Do you know where Dad's sermon is?" My mother's voice was higher than usual. I said nothing. At the last minute I grabbed the rosary from under the mattress, leaving the sermon there, and ran downstairs to put my shoes on.

My dad yelled and stomped and swore, but in the end we had to leave for temple without his sermon. The drive was tense. I looked out the window, studying the faint reflection of my lips and nose in the glass, holding my breath. Wondering what I was doing.

My mother, sister, and I sat in our reserved seats near the front and my father went to his office behind the bimah. My mother kept whispering to me and to Ruth, asking if we knew where my father's sermon was.

I watched families arriving and looking around the sanctuary for a place to sit. Here at Beth Shalom, there was no Jesus for the worshipers to take in. Just my father, sitting in a throne-like chair next to the ark in his black robe, looking far away and smaller than usual, pale, tapping his foot to the organ music. A mere mortal preparing to lead the members of his congregation through an alphabetical list of our sins. I sat there during the service, less bored than usual, watching my father's face for signs of emotion. He had on his I-am-the-Rabbi face, the one that showed nothing. I almost convinced myself that I hadn't really taken the sermon. Finally, after two hours of praying and chanting and singing, of leading responsive reading and directing the congregation to stand up and to sit down, it was time for my father to deliver his sermon.

"Good yentiv," he began.

I was sure he was looking right at me. I sat there frozen, holding my breath, trying to keep the expression on my face as neutral as possible. I could feel a vein in my temple throbbing.

And then he cleared his throat and began his sermon. He began as he usually did with a reference to pop culture. "My family and I went to see *E. T.* last month," he started. (Of course I knew that this wasn't exactly true; my father had gone to see it alone because I'd seen it with Colleen, Ruth only liked romantic comedies, and my mother said she had no interest in a movie about an alien.) But I knew at that moment he was going to do just fine without his notes, that my efforts at sabotage weren't going to work. He didn't falter at all, delivered his sermon as if nothing were out of the ordinary, as authoritative and confident as ever.

I was disappointed, relieved, and overcome with a sense of powerlessness. I tried to hide how upset I was, but tears were streaming down my face and my nose was running. My mom took my hand and squeezed it but didn't say anything.

We were at the conclusion of the service, not much left but a few closing prayers in Hebrew and a final song. I unclasped my mother's hand from my own and took out the rosary. I quickly crossed myself, said the Hail Mary in my head. Then, I prayed out loud but in a quiet voice. "*Our father who art in heaven.*" My mom looked at me confused, pleading with her eyes for me to stop, but I looked down at the rosary in my hands and kept going. "*Hallowed be thy name.*" I heard rustling in the rows near us as people turned around to see who was uttering the Lord's Prayer. "*Thy kingdom come, thy will be done, on Earth, as it is in Heaven.*" Ruth reached over my mother, who sat between us as usual, and gave me a hard painful noogie on the head. My mom whispered "Ruth!" and Ruth quickly put her hand back on her lap. Then my mother turned to me and glared, her face knotted with anger, and something else I couldn't identify. I continued praying. "*And forgive us our trespasses as we forgive those who trespass against us.*" Ruth was laughing now, first a giggle, but soon it escalated into a loud cackle, punctuated by her signature asthmatic hack, deep and disturbing and painful-sounding. Much head turning and whispering in the congregation followed. "*And lead us not into temptation, but deliver us from evil. Amen.*" I knew then, as I finished uttering those final lines, that in the days to come, when people talked about the disruption by the rabbi's daughter during that Yom Kippur service, it would not be me they would be talking about. It would never be me. My hands were shaking and my heart was pounding. I stood, feeling like I might throw up. I put the rosary back in my skirt pocket and walked to the back of the sanctuary and out the heavy door into the bright fall afternoon.

My eyes throbbed and watered as they tried to adjust to the sharp light. I ran the half-mile to my house and stood for a few minutes catching my breath in my driveway. I heard honking overhead and saw hundreds of geese flapping their wings against the blue sky. It seemed to me a giant mess—they were bumping into each other, falling out of formation, pushing ahead of each other and then lagging behind, and all the time there was the wild squawking. I climbed on my bike but at the last minute, instead of going to Colleen's to return the rosary, I followed the geese. I rode and rode and rode, away from my parents' house, away from the temple, away from Ruth, away from the Brennans, toward the skyline of Chicago as fast as I could pedal, thighs burning, the late September wind cooling the back of my neck, forgetting for the moment that it was only a matter of time before I'd have to turn around and go back home.

Meredith's To-Don't List

Eric Vrooman

Don't tell your mom that you eat canned soups and microwave popcorn for dinner because you're only a sophomore and she doesn't get home until 7:30. That maybe if she didn't take so much yoga and work so much, she could do more than leave *The Joy of Cooking* on the counter with a note that says, "Chicken risotto?"

Don't make fun of ice fishing because even the cool kids do that here. And don't ask where the fish go when the lakes freeze because that's a stupid question, apparently. Anna will say, "The bottoms of lakes never freeze, Meredith," as she titrates an acid in her ratty black cardigan and combat boots. "I guess they must not teach that in Texas. Probably because it's related to evolution." Everyone, even Mr. Stendahl, will laugh.

Don't tell your mom that if you got cancer from eating microwaved popcorn and processed foods or whatever, it might not be so bad. You might actually like it. You'd carry a vomit bucket from class to class. In lab, you'd ask Anna and Mr. Stendahl if they know the freezing point of vomit, since they're both so evolved.

Don't start doing your new Minnesota chores just because your mom sees an ad on TV for the LEGO Store at the Mall of America. Every time she sees LEGOs now, she cries.

Don't lie down in the snow when it's almost midnight and below zero— even if you've just spent half an hour on your front sidewalk trying to shovel the ice-prints of your Adidas, which look like trilobite fossils.

Don't vent about your dad's affair and how much you miss your friends in Texas—even if your rescuer pulls you out of the snow, offers to get a torch of some kind to remove the icy fossil footprints, and turns both space heaters in his garage toward you. Even if Angelo and his Rottweilers, Cofi and Reese, are really good listeners. Even if Angelo's mix of Spanish and English reminds you of home.

Don't make fun of head-basket yoga, which is supposed to give your mom the core and posture of African women. You hid your dad's affair from her for three months. You're not in a position to judge.

Don't complain to Angelo about not getting to try out for the basketball team. It costs money and your mom can't drive you everywhere, not when she's working fifty-some hours a week doing in-home speech therapy with kids on the spectrum who need her as much as, if not more than, you. Basketball was something you did with your dad, anyway.

Don't tell kids at school how great El Paso is. People only believe what they see firsthand, and you can't fly them to El Paso. They think Texas is a joke. They'll ask why you don't wear your ten-gallon hat, if you eat beans out of a can on the cattle drives, and if the air smells like taco seasoning.

Don't say "actually" when you're trying to correct people. "Actually" is pretty much like "um . . ." or "duh . . ." and doesn't make a lot of actual sense because pretty much everything is actual. Angelo is right about that.

Don't spend your days at school thinking about things to tell Angelo— the exact wordings you'll use to make school sound awful and you heroic. You'll be staring at the metal pellets in the bottom of your beaker when Mr. Stendahl calls on you. He'll have to repeat the question, "So is density an *intrinsic* quality or *extrinsic*?" and Anna will say, "In Meredith's case, I'd say it's intrinsic."

Don't say, "I'm actually a good student. I got an A in AP English last year. I'm just distracted. I get distracted sometimes." You'll sound pathetic and also braggy, and that will make everyone in class hate you if they didn't already.

Don't spend all your time wondering if a guy likes you—at least not when you're with that guy. When he asks you to pass him the socket wrench, you'll hand him a hammer, and there's pretty much no need for a hammer when working on a car. And later, when he asks if you want to see the car's undercarriage, you'll wonder if that's a romantic act, if you're being asked to look at *his* body somehow. As you lie on the sled with wheels, you'll wonder what to make of the shininess of the new CV joint and the rustiness of the shock absorbers.

Don't tell Angelo about how from your kitchen window you could see the Franklins—actual mountains, not the former landfills that they turned into ski hills here in Minnesota. Or how people don't ever take vitamin D in El Paso. Or how your mom found a LEGO Star Wars toy in your dad's pants pocket on a Tuesday morning and knew instantly that he was having an affair with your piano teacher. How you fessed up—not because you felt it was the right thing to do but because you were so stunned your mom figured it out. And how you knew, as you told her, that your dad was lying to you, that it wasn't just a fling he was having with Ms. Ryan, and that he wouldn't be able to make it right. Angelo will let you talk until you're done, until you've said all you need to say, until you feel empty of thoughts, until you feel hollow. With the way he pauses and then speaks quietly at first, you'll know, or you'll sense, that he's absorbed everything you've said, that he's been filling up with everything you've been letting go. He'll tell you, so quietly that you have to lean closer before the words disperse into the air, how he shared a room with his sister with Down syndrome all the way through high school. How he learned to rebuild the engine of his first car, a 1986 Dodge Omni, with help from his uncle. And how his father later watched this same uncle jump from a two-story building in order to avoid being burned by "the hot"—the tar they spread on flat roofs.

Don't ask a quiet guy like Angelo if he's ever cheated on a girl. He won't answer, and then you won't know if you've offended him into silence or if he's using the silence to hide his answer. You won't feel entitled to ask more questions, like why he never invites you into his house or who Mena is and why you have to leave whenever Mena's on the way over.

Don't wear a coat if you want to be touched or a scarf if you want to be kissed. You'll envy the way Angelo scratches his dogs on their bare bellies, and the way their black gums rise in a pleasure wince. Reese—short for Reese's because he's chocolate-y brown with a peanut-butter belly—will close his eyes, as if he's being transported somewhere else. Cofi's eyes will be open, but unseeing. You'll envy the way the dogs' bodies and Angelo's rise together when they hear a car coming down the alley. You'll follow them into the alley and try to inhale some of Angelo's steamy cold breath through your scarf.

Don't tell a potential new friend that she looks kind of like a Rottweiler—even if you just mean she looks tough, intelligent, and loyal. Before she moves her tray to another table, she'll say, "Well, you look like a lemur without any fur." You'll be holding your tempeh sandwich in both hands, like a lemur might, and, of course, you've always been good in trees, despite being tall and thin. In the bathroom before gym, your eyes will look wet and big and lemury. You'll notice that the mirror is blackening around the edges or maybe shedding some of its reflective pieces like scales. It will look like pieces of you are missing, too.

Don't text your old friends about how you don't have any new friends at school. They'll stop texting you back or tell you that Trina, who took your place at small forward, is "scoring more pts than u did last yr!"

Don't wonder if college might be any different. Kids tear each other to pieces everywhere. They're bred for it.

Don't call your dad or answer his calls, because he's the one who should be punished. He moved in with *your* former piano teacher and her three kids—kids you let play Crossy Road on your phone before lessons, kids who now call him Mr. Dan. You'll wonder if he encouraged you to practice and keep taking lessons because he wanted to see more of her. You'll wonder if he ever really did "see promise in you." You'll wonder if you'll ever play music again or if that part of your life is over now, too.

Don't tell Angelo all the chores you have to do now that *your* dad's out of the picture, or he'll ask you to run an errand for him "while you're at it, *chica.*"

Don't write any more to-do lists because they make you feel good for like one second, but then you never do half the things on the list. Or your mom finds the list and says, "Is Angelo that drug dealer who lives down the alley and leaves his dogs unchained? He's like twenty-three or twenty-four. Why are you buying him tinfoil?"

Don't accuse Angelo of dealing pot and maybe coke or meth, and putting you in jeopardy with the cops or guys like Mena, if Mena even is a guy. You don't have any idea who Mena is, and that itself is a problem, maybe the biggest problem. Don't start accusing Angelo of being dishonest and distrustful just because your mom might be right about him dealing drugs and you didn't see that possibility first. Don't turn your anger over your mom being more perceptive into an anger toward Angelo. Don't ask if he really even has a sister with Down syndrome or an uncle who broke his leg and got permanently disfigured by "the hot." Don't talk so much that the other person doesn't have a chance to answer and then starts to feel like maybe you don't deserve an answer.

Don't just stop showing up at someone's garage after being there every afternoon, and don't hold onto someone's money if you're not going to get them what they asked for. He might not care about the money, because it's hardly anything, but he will care about the disloyalty.

Don't climb out on the sugar maple's longest branch in the backyard with a plastic bag full of snowballs at one in the morning, even if you're feeling really sad, lonely, and lemurish.

Don't shoot a snowball into a neighbor's recycling bin because that bin might fall into the alley and draw the attention of Angelo, even if his garage door is closed and the lights are out. He'll give a special whistle, a whistle you've never heard before. The dogs will sprint into your backyard and claw the tree and jump and bite the air where your legs just were. Your arms and legs will feel too cold to control or trust. Every cold crack will sound like the branch is collapsing. Cofi and Reese will bark like you're an animal they've treed, not someone whose feet they've sat on as they received belly rubs. Not someone who knows and calls their names. You'll wonder how long you'll last with only a few snowballs left, and wet jeans and wet mittens, your arms and legs stretched along the branch. This is actual. This is what will actually happen.

Don't wonder if it was a good idea for your mom to call the cops. Or why it took Angelo so long to give another, different whistle.

Don't wish your dad were here to help, because he's not. He's busy being Mr. Dan.

Don't go over to Angelo's garage a week later, in direct violation of your mom's order and your own promise to her, unless you know whether you're apologizing or expecting an apology. He won't say anything, and he'll refuse to take his change and the tinfoil. Cofi and Reese will get up and then lie back down in their beds when Angelo lowers his hand. They will open and close their black-gummed mouths and slobber as if they're chewing bread. The garage will smell like paint, but the car Angelo was working on, the Corolla, will be gone. It will feel like there is too much space now and not enough for Angelo to do. You'll want to hear your name or *chica* in his voice, but you won't.

Don't cry when your mom makes you microwave popcorn and brings it to you in bed. You'll wonder how she knows that you went to see him, and how you know that she knows. After you and she finish the bowl, she'll give you a paper towel to wipe your hands and you'll wonder why you're always so disloyal to her.

Don't go with your mom to head-basket yoga, no matter how disloyal and lonely you feel. You'll find yourself in a strip-mall studio of women who wear sweatpants with PINK on the butt or blue Indian saris or orange African body wraps, and the floor will be filled with colorful yoga mats and head-baskets and clay pots. The storefront window will glow with lacy frost around the edges. You'll store these details in your mind as if you're going to share them with Angelo later, even though you won't.

When you put on the woven head-basket with the circular two-pound weight inside, you'll feel your spine straighten. Your entire focus will be on holding the basket aloft. You will try to see the basket with the top of your eyes while you listen to the instructor. And then, gradually, you'll be able to look at the instructor and manage to keep the basket aloft. Then you will be able to move your body, a little at a time. Your body's movements will start to feel level and purposeful, and you'll hear the drumming clearly, not just the instructor. Gradually your body will warm and display colors you've been holding inside—pinks and peaches. You'll start to understand how fish survive under many layers of ice. And then your basket will fall, and the weight will roll away and wobble in a circle on the floor.

While you stand still, trying to balance the weight on your head, your mother and this school of older women on their colorful mats will continue to train and stretch for something, individually and collectively. Something that hasn't started yet. Something that will as soon as a whistle blows. But there will be no whistle, just drumming. The drumming will make your skin feel like a percussive surface and your insides feel hollow and full of reverberating sounds.

When the drumming stops, the class will end. *Namaste.* The others will roll their mats, shelve their weights, and stack their pots or baskets. The room will drain of sound, color, and movement.

When you finally remove your head-basket, your feet will step on a light cushion of air before finding ground. Your mom will put her arm around your shoulders, and it will feel like necessary weight.

When you go outside, the clouds will look like they're descending and crystalizing in layers. The air will be thick with snow. You'll wonder if the snow is falling or the air is solidifying. A plane will rumble above, unseen, like a snowplow clearing an icy road.

When your mom releases her arm from your shoulder and leaves you at the front of the car, you'll feel like you might rise into the air if you lift even one foot. You'll wish your coat was made of scales, not feathers. To survive in Minnesota, you need to be hard and heavy. You need to wear dark eye shadow, like Anna, and boots with chains and steel toes.

Everything will sound like it's cracking—the ice on the street as ghostly cars glide past, the glass-lidded puddles underfoot, the tree branches wearing their long white gloves, the big tectonic ice plates in the sky. Everything is cracking. Freezing is cracking. To freeze is to crack. Every molecule in you hardens and breaks, over and over.

Leave this list out for your mother. Do this. Do this because you're not sure what else to do. Leave the list on the kitchen counter next to the cookbook and the microwave. Hold it in place with the empty popcorn bowl.

Puro Yakyū

Steve Trumpeter

Natsuku lingered in Henry Fischer's hotel suite, making minor touch-ups, rearranging the pillows, and re-folding the towels. Though she serviced the other rooms on her floors with detached boredom, his demanded her purest attention. She needed this to feel like home for him, a comforting sanctuary in a metropolis full of constant reminders of the ways in which he didn't belong. She supposed it was some maternal instinct kicking in, this compulsion to coddle a full-grown man, stronger and wealthier than she could possibly imagine.

She strived for small perfections, like moving the television remote to the end table next to the sofa where Henry liked to stretch out and watch ESPN, or making sure there was extra stevia next to the tea cups. She brushed away the few specks of dust that sullied the framed photo of his two young daughters and turned the other picture so that the laser gaze of his wife's eyes would settle on the neon twinkle of the Tōkyō cityscape outside the floor-to-ceiling windows.

He played baseball, a superstar in America who had garnered ecstatic headlines on the sports page when the Yomiuri Giants signed him in spite of the insinuations of chemical enhancement that kept the teams in his own country from offering him a contract. Sometimes he liked to stay up late answering fan mail and signing autographs, so she made sure the desk drawer remained stocked with fresh ballpoint pens and Sharpies she swiped from her boss's office.

One of the other maids called to her from the hallway. "Hurry up, Natsu. I want to get out of here on time for once."

"So go," Natsuku said. "I'm going to finish up here. Clock out for me."

"Murakami-*san* is going to find out, and he's going to fire you."

She picked up a letter from the desk. "Not if you don't go gossiping to the other girls, he won't. Shut the door." She studied the note, ignoring the other maid as if she were Natsuku's own servant. She had little patience for her co-workers, provincial girls whose dreams stretched only as far as the upcoming weekend. It took her a few moments to decipher the message. While Natsuku's English was crisp and practiced, Henry's handwriting wasn't.

Dear Tommy,

Thank you for your letter. To answer your questions, the game in Japan is really similar to the big leagues. The ball is a little smaller and there aren't as many teams, but the rules are the same. We sure do have home runs. In fact, I only need two more to own the single season record over here. Wouldn't that be cool?

I'm happy to sign my rookie card, especially for such a die-hard White Sox fan Glad to see kids still collect baseball cards these days. I used to have a bunch.

I like playing in Japan. They call me "Ryōshi" here, which I'm told means "fisherman" in Japanese. I miss the States, though (especially Chicago). I'll be back next season. Good luck at third. Keep practicing and charge those grounders and maybe you'll be a big leaguer someday.

Best wishes,

Henry Fischer

Clipped to the letter was a baseball card with Henry Fischer's auto-graph scrawled across. The young Henry in the picture—little more than a teenager, really—was finishing a swing, one hand just holding on to the bat, his back foot set at an angle as he squared up to run. The word SOX was printed across his chest in a font that reminded Natsuku of old science fiction titles. This Henry sported a sprinter's build, with lithe, sinewy arms connected to bony shoulders. His calf muscles bulged to nearly the same size as his spindly thighs, and the striped belt that cinched his pants around his hips might have fit Natsuku's trim waist.

It was a far cry from the barrel-chested hulk she knew, the one that had made no move to cover himself three months ago when she let herself in to straighten his room. Her gentle knock had gone unan-swered along with her "housekeeping" announcement. She had barely stepped into the living room before she saw him, his back to her as he stood in front of the vanity drying his hair. When he put down the towel, he noticed her in the steam-fogged mirror right away. He turned, a smirk on his face, and crossed his arms just under his pectoral muscles, his biceps so taut she imagined they might tear through his skin. He was posing for her, she was sure.

Natsuku's gaze lingered for a time that crossed a shameful line, but still she allowed her eyes to drift downward. She should have bolted back out the door, but her feet stayed planted. At twenty-four years of age, she had seen her share of men in such a state, though never a black man, much less such an idealized specimen as this one. Her eyes narrowed and she felt something like hunger spark in her belly and work its way down. If she was to be fired, so be it.

"In or out?" he said.

"In," Natsuku whispered, closing the door behind her. And so it had gone.

She put the letter back on the desk and fastened the baseball card to it, careful not to scuff the crisp edges. She turned the lamp to its lowest setting and straightened the stationery in orderly, ninety-degree angles.

When she cleaned the other rooms in the hotel, she hated this job. The contribution she made was fleeting, transient. She produced nothing. Every task she did was undone within twenty-four hours by people she had been instructed to avoid disturbing entirely. Her role was that of a gentle breeze, barely noticed, unobtrusive. Her work would never endure beyond her, so what was the point? It was only for this room—for Henry—that she hadn't yet quit.

She looked back to make sure the other maid had closed the door as she'd asked, then she opened the bottom drawer of the desk. The unmarked envelope rested right where Henry had said it would be, stuffed with five-thousand-yen notes, twenty of them in all. Natsuku pulled out the bills and tucked them into the pocket of her uniform.

It was quarter to three. Henry's game would still be in the first inning. It'd be a few hours until he returned, but Natsuku had nowhere else to be. She unzipped the back of her uniform and stepped out of her dress, folding it carefully and hanging it in the closet. She crawled into the bed and turned on the TV, finding the game just in time to see Henry get walked on four pitches.

Two days later, Natsuku sat with her father in Kōshien Stadium on the third base side, eight rows behind the visitors' dugout. Her father's seats occupied prime foul ball territory, though she had never managed to snag one thanks to the young salarymen who would hip-check her aside in their scramble for a souvenir whenever a lazy pop-up drifted her way. Neat lines and symbols marked the scorecard in her lap, accurate down to the balls and strikes, just as her father had taught her when she was a young girl. In the top of the seventh inning, Henry's team, the Giants, led the Tigers by eight runs. After Henry's final at-bat, she knew the fans would begin to trickle out.

Henry was on deck, and her cheeks flushed as she watched him. She hid behind dark sunglasses to go with a gray t-shirt tucked in to jeans that hugged her narrow hips and stopped mid-calf. And though she was small, she was well aware that the straight white teeth behind her keep-a-secret smile and the heels that lifted her figure into its cosmopolitan posture made her stand out in a crowd. But to him, she would be swallowed among a sea of fans that coalesced into an anonymous mass of black hair and narrow eyes. Still, she slouched in her seat and kept her sun visor pulled low. To find her at a Hanshin Tigers game—a three-and-a-half hour train ride away from the hotel in Tōkyō—would give him the wrong idea. What they had only existed behind the door to suite 4211. Natsuku would have known this even if Henry hadn't made it explicit. This suited her fine, as she was a woman with secrets of her own. There were the ones she kept from Henry, like the fact that she had knocked too softly to hear, knowing Henry would be in his suite when she first barged in on him in all his glory, or the fact that she had grown up in Takarazuka, just a few kilometers from this stadium, a lifelong Tigers fan since the time Henry was playing A-ball in some one-stoplight town in eastern Iowa. Or the one Natsuku hadn't told her father, that she was ignoring the beer girls with the mini-keg packs strapped to their backs because she was carrying a superstar slugger's baby.

Her father, Kaoru, sipped on Yamazaki whisky, his clipped gray hair peeking out from under a stiff Tigers cap. "Ryōshi-*san* might get something to hit," he said. He pointed at the rookie reliever who had been brought into the game to chew through meaningless innings. "This pitcher wants to make his mark. He'll throw strikes. Just watch."

"He should," Natsuku said. She marked an American-style "K" in the box for Tsuji as he trudged back to the dugout, chagrined at having chased a slider that started low and ended in the dirt for strike three. "He deserves a chance."

"This chemical-juiced *gaijin*?" her father said. "He deserves nothing. He sullies the game with his selfish play. Look at the shift they give him. All he has to do is poke it down the third base line and he'd have an easy base hit. Have you ever seen him sacrifice himself to advance a runner?"

"Have you ever seen anyone hit a baseball like he does?"

"No. Never."

"Sneer at him all you want, Father. You have to at least respect his talent."

"It's not pure."

"Neither is walking him just to deny him a chance at the record."

"Hmm." Kaoru folded his arms over his chest.

Two more *hōmuran* and the record would be Henry's, his legacy etched into history alongside the likes of Nomura, Nagashima, and Harimoto, the legends whose names floated on her father's reverent whispers throughout her childhood. And secret or not, she had installed herself as Henry's center, his muse. She had earned her share of this new piece of history that might, for all she knew, endure forever.

Henry Fischer kneels down outside the batter's box to scoop a handful of dirt, rubs it between his hands. It feels as alien as everything else in this country, powdery and fine like whole wheat flour. In the stands, a handful of fair-weather fans murmur a chant for the visiting slugger—*Hōmuran* Ryōshi-*san*—hoping a glimpse of history-in-the-making might ease the sting of their team's blowout loss. He glances down the third base line, but the coach no longer bothers with complicated signs for Henry. He simply puts his hands together and chops them across his body. Swing away in any language. No sense trying to hide it; it's what Henry is here to do.

He steps to the plate and takes a few swings, then watches the pitcher begin his routine. Back home, Henry knew them all; he spent hours studying the scouting reports, the statistics, the trends. But Henry plays the game here like sandlot ball. Grip it and rip it. Wait for your pitch and knock the cover off the sonofabitch. Too many pitchers with names full of Os and Ks and Ys and Zs. He can't keep them straight. Easier to just see the ball and react.

He has been walked twice so far, two runs scored, but this is a new pitcher, a late-season replacement brought in for mop-up duty. Henry watches him shake off his catcher's signs twice. Maybe this rookie has something to prove. Maybe he'll finally get something to swing at.

Henry knows about a dozen words in Japanese. *Ryōshi* means "fisherman," which is the nickname they gave him when he first started mashing moon shots under the Tokyo Dome. There's *konnichiwa* and *sayonara*, *dōzo* and *arigatō*. He can get to the hotel where he lives, ask someone to point him towards the can, order udon and maki rolls and beer, though the latter is against team rules. *Yakyū* means baseball. He knows how to say "yes, coach" though he usually just refers to his manager as *sensei*. And then there are the two words he hears the most whenever his name comes up: *hōmuran* and *gaijin*. One for the home runs he's hitting at a record-setting clip and one for the reason he isn't seeing very many hittable pitches these days.

"It's not a race thing," Natsuku insists. "Some people just want to keep the record held by one of their own." It's a sentiment that sounds very much to Henry like a race thing.

The kid finally gets the sign he wants and starts into his windup, swinging his arms high and twisting around to face the center field wall. When he finally uncorks the pitch, it looks like a headhunter as it shoots out of his hand, but Henry picks up the spin that will render it harmless. He leans back anyway as it dips toward the plate, missing high and inside. A message pitch for sure. A din rises from the stands, like a crowd in the schoolyard about to see a fight break out.

He steps out of the batter's box and pretends to collect himself, then stares down the pitcher who is again shaking off his catcher. Henry tenses up his shoulders, digs his back foot a little deeper, brings the head of his bat a little farther back. An experienced pitcher would recognize him for the slavering dog he is right now, but this one has no idea, thinks he has Henry's knees shaking. Again with the twister windup, and this time he parades the baseball right down Broadway, as if the sheer moxie of the pitch will sneak it right past. Well, Henry has his own message to deliver. He uncoils and sends number 55 screaming for the right field bleachers.

One more *hōmuran* and just over a week to hit it, and then back to "The Show," this season a speed bump.

Natsuku had hoped to attend the other two Tigers-Giants games in Hanshin over the weekend, but the oppressive heat of July and August had lingered into September this year, and her father had offered up his seats to his underlings at work. He said he preferred to watch the games on television from the air-conditioned comfort of his own living room.

"What if we miss Ryōshi-*san's* record?" she asked. "Aren't the great moments of the game best remembered when you're there to live them?"

"Of course," Kaoru said, slicing a daikon into a pot of miso for their breakfast. "But this isn't such a moment. This hero of yours is little more than a *ronin*. He will serve his year in exile as an invading mercenary, then be back in the States as soon as the ink is dry on his new contract. And you're crazy if you think he'll see anything within a meter of the strike zone for the rest of the weekend."

Natsuku stood next to him, conscious of the timer for the rice that simmered on the stove. Ever since she was a small girl they had cooked together, the two of them, learning each other's rhythms as they danced around the small kitchen, punctuating their conversations with warnings of hot pots and sharp knives. Even now, with Natsuku only visiting on the occasional weekends and holidays, these motions remained fluid and natural, like infielders turning a graceful double play.

Another of the secrets she harbored from Henry: her mother had disappeared without a trace during the autumn festival when Natsuku was only six years old. Her memories of that day surfaced in a wash of disparate images and fragments of feelings. The mild rebelliousness of standing on the pavement of a busy highway that had been cordoned off for the festival. Street performers juggling knives in the middle of an impromptu circle of onlookers. Pants and skirts she didn't recognize everywhere she turned her head. Holding the sweaty hand of the policeman who knocked on their front door when he brought her home that evening. And the one that nagged at her the most—the faintest wisp of a barely believable memory—the chopsticks her mother wore to fasten her hair in a loose bun atop her head slowly bobbing away until they were lost amidst the throng.

But in the years since, Natsuku had stopped dwelling on these memories. Her mother had been declared dead, and she was pleased to think of her as such. Truth be told, she barely remembered her mother's face, even despite the pictures that adorned her father's home. The fuzzy recollections from her girlhood contrasted with the hard evidence displayed on her father's desk and bookshelves, so she had decided long ago to dismiss the conceptions she held about who her mother might have been. Few of the woman's features had been passed to Natsuku's own face, and her femininity obscured enough of her father's features that when she looked in the mirror, she saw no trace of her lineage, only herself.

So why did her eyes now linger on these pictures of her mother, the ones that usually blended into the background like innocuous wallpaper patterns? As if she didn't know.

Kaoru snapped his fingers and pointed at the rice. "Your head is somewhere else," he said. "And you took a day off of work yesterday. Have you become such a Giants fan, living in Tōkyō, that you will burn your vacation days just to see them flog a team that has no shot at the championship?"

"I need to tell you something," she said.

"At last. Should I sit down first?" Kaoru poured the miso into bowls and stirred the rice. "Let us at least enjoy a hot breakfast while you bare your soul."

"Just now, I realized that in all these years, I never pondered how you felt about Mother's disappearance. It must have been painful beyond words for you."

Kaoru shrugged and waited for her to continue.

"It can't be an easy thing, to raise a child on your own. Yet, I never felt that I suffered for lack of a mother."

"I am . . ." Kaoru made a small coughing noise and put a fist over his mouth. "You were your father's girl from day one."

"I'm pregnant, Father."

Kaoru placed the bowls on the kitchen table and carefully folded the napkins before arranging them next to each table setting. "Impossible. My daughter—who fled this humble home for the city lights of Tōkyō as soon as she finished school—is a virgin. Pure as the snow."

Natsuku smirked, surrendering to the notion that she could not play coy with the man who had nurtured her through every significant step of her life.

"And the father . . . ?" he said. Kaoru let the question linger in the air as though it were a riddle to be puzzled over.

Natsuku couldn't meet her father's eyes. "He gave me some money to do what must be done."

"I see." Kaoru stirred the miso soup in his bowl, stared at it as though he were trying to divine answers from the milky swirl. "And what is it that you want?"

Natsuku put a hand over her belly, still flat and firm. "I wish the circumstances with this man could be different."

"You love him, then?"

"No, but there are things about him I love. He is like no one I'll ever know again. Strong and fearless, but far from home. He has a family of his own. I told him I would arrange everything. I was supposed to see a doctor in Tōkyō yesterday."

"You don't have to explain yourself to me. I know you didn't come here for that."

"He will return home soon." Natsuku bowed her head and tried to fight back tears. "I don't know how this is supposed to work. I certainly can't afford a baby in the city on a maid's pittance. I don't know why I didn't go to the doctor."

"You don't have to do anything."

"But I do. I thought this man had it in him to make me a part of something I could only dream of. He felt like a way to go beyond the meaningless life that seems to be laid out in front of me. I don't know how else to explain it. I'm sorry, Father."

"You are my legacy, Natsu. You have nothing to be sorry for. And don't ever think your life is meaningless. You are my only daughter. You mean everything. Everything I ever dreamed of awakened in you. Now eat your breakfast. There is a game this afternoon, and our Tigers may still be able to spoil a shot at the playoffs for these Giants you have come to cheer for."

Natsuku nodded, though she would give anything to see the Tigers lose. If the Giants pulled off a playoff spot, her farewell with Henry could be put off a little longer. But Henry went 0-for-1 that afternoon in a Giants loss that featured a swing-for-the-fences strikeout in Henry's only official at-bat to go along with four intentional passes.

"It's a hallowed record," Teru says, handing Henry a jersey with a Masahito corporate logo emblazoned across the chest. He is Henry's agent's right hand in Japan—Stanford educated, with a thick goatee that, in this country, might as well be a barbed wire tattoo or an AC/DC t-shirt for how it proclaims his American cultural hijacking. And despite the exuberant handshake-hugs, Henry can't shake the feeling that Teru doesn't much care for him. "Don't take these walks personally. I represented Tuffy when he was here. Same thing happened when he got up around fifty homers. Cabrera, too. You get to the playoffs, bro, and you'll get something to hit."

"Those homers won't count."

"Not for the record, no." Teru helps Henry with the shirt. "But walks lead to runs. Runs win games. You want to be King Shit up in this motherfucker, dog? Deliver the Giants a championship. They'll fucking enshrine you."

Henry manages to button the jersey, but he feels like an overstuffed burrito, where one move will end up with him spilling out of the uniform. Like everything else in this country, this wardrobe is not designed for someone his size. The rest of the team is at the Sapporo Dome, running wind sprints, fielding grounders, working on bunting. No game today means the team will put in a solid eight hours of practice, even at this late stage of the season, but Henry's contract is clear when it comes to the amount of drills Henry Fischer requires. Instead, he is using the break in his schedule to film a commercial for a potato chip or a fuel-efficient car or an energy drink—nobody's bothered to fill him in on the details. All he knows is that he must stand in front of a camera and swing a baseball bat. For his trouble, he'll be rewarded with a check for ten million yen, a number that looks much more modest when converted to American currency, but still a nice haul for a few hours of waiting around.

The set is dressed to look like an alley, and dancers in baggy jeans and oversized jackets limber up while the production crew mills about. Henry stretches with the bat while Teru converses with the director.

He wants to text Natsuku and make sure everything went okay with the doctor, but an abortion is not a subject he's keen to broach. He'd rather not even think about it, though he has little power over what pops into his head in the empty moments. This is the kind of situation he should let Teru handle. Have him meet her in a dark restaurant armed with a sizable check and a non-disclosure agreement while Henry hightails it over to the Park Hyatt for the last week of the season. But she isn't that kind of girl, and the truth is, he doesn't want to abandon her. He's swinging the bat better than he ever has, and even Henry can admit that Natsuku gets some credit for that. While it's tempting to think of her as some sexual psychiatrist who keeps his head clear and his gait loose, really, she's the closest thing he's found to a teammate since he put on a Giants cap. Her passion for the game rivals anything he's seen on the field. From the get-go, the way he connected with her sometimes reminds him of how he connects with pitches when he's truly locked in, turning those baseballs into shooting stars, blazing wishes in a shallow arc over the outfield walls. And gone just as soon, little more than a beautiful memory.

He imagines Natsu alone in her apartment in the aftermath of what they'd done and stops twisting. The bat slips from his sweating hands, and his cheeks burn. There are other ways this could have gone, and he has to stop his mind from wandering down that path.

He exhales a few sharp bursts of breath, then picks the bat up again and takes a few practice swings. He hasn't talked to his girls in at least a week or his wife in even longer, but his phone is in the dressing room. It doesn't matter anyway, because he can't remember what time it is back home in Miami. Either very late or very early, but not a time when pleasant conversations take place. Back home, his phone would always be within shouting distance. He'd have a whole entourage to tend to his needs, and if they weren't real friends, at least they'd be smiling faces to shoot the shit with. It isn't the language barrier or the insular racism of the Japanese people that is making this season such a slog. The isolation is the culture shock he hadn't braced for. If it weren't for Natsuku, he'd have no need to speak a word outside of the ballpark or a restaurant.

When they are finally ready to start shooting, Teru relays the director's instructions to stand on his mark and wait for the signal. A hip-hop beat blares over the PA and the dancers cross their arms over their chests while they bounce and sneer at the camera. The director points at Henry, and he takes an upper-decker hack that results in an explosion of flashing lights and alarm bells. The director shouts something that apparently means "cut," and Henry is shooed off the stage. In his place, a man in a gorilla suit sporting a cap similar to Henry's begins jumping up and down as the cameras roll.

"Do I even want to know?" Henry asks.

Teru and the director exchange a few words. "Apparently," Teru says, "the boldness of Masahito's new wireless data network has unleashed your inner power, allowing you to lead the young people to new achievements in the LTE data sphere."

"My inner power is a goddamn gorilla?"

"Bro, gorillas are mad strong."

"This fucking country." The jersey is made of cheap fabric and tears easily as Henry pulls it off. He marches to the dressing area, finds his phone and calls up Natsuku's name in his messaging app.

"C U Thurs?" he types.

Then he calls his agent back in Chicago, where Henry doesn't give a wet fart about what time it is. "One more homer and I'm coming home," he says as soon as he hears the groggy greeting from his agent. "Fuck this blacklist. Find me a team."

She returned to work on Tuesday while the Giants were on the road in Ōsaka, grateful for the chance to occupy herself with the mundane tasks of sweeping, folding, and scrubbing that made up her days. Gossiping with the other maids whiled away the daylight, leaving her with quiet evenings in her own apartment to ponder her consequences and watch Henry get walked, stalled at 55 home runs. The few pitches he saw worth a cut, he whiffed at so hard she expected to see—as her father was fond of saying—the pitcher's cap get blown off his head with the force of the breeze. She wondered if he ever thought of her when he was on the field, perhaps during his slow trot around the bases after a home run.

When Henry returned late Thursday night for the last homestand of the season, he only texted her that he was tired, and he would see her on Friday. But the manager had kept him out of the lineup on Friday—a chance to rest for the final weekend, he had claimed—and Henry was taciturn. He wouldn't touch her, and he feigned sleep rather than staying up to watch highlights on TV as was their custom.

Then, on Saturday, he had gone hitless, and Natsuku scowled at both his on-field performance—his impatience had him swinging at garbage—and his moodiness during the moments when they should have been making the most of the short time left to them. The Giants' playoff chances had evaporated after dropping four of six games on the road trip, and though the record still loomed over them, she had hoped Henry might relax under the lowered expectations. But the embers of his bitterness still smoldered long after the last out had been tallied.

He slouched against the headboard as she leaned back against his shoulder and let his thick forearm drape around her like a shawl. "The game here isn't any more pure," he said.

"What do you mean?"

"All these intentional walks—there's no baseball strategy to it. All I've gotten since I've been here is spite. People look at me like I'm some kind of ape in a baseball uniform. You people call it *Puro Yakyū*, but I don't see what's so *puro* about it."

Natsuku rubbed the top of his hand and imagined wearing it as a baseball glove that might fit her own tiny hand. "*Puro* only means professional."

"How do you say 'pure,' then?"

"*Junsui*," she said. "In this context."

"All this time, I thought it they were calling it *puro* like they'd perfected the sport." Natsuku felt the press of Henry's stomach as he chuckled at that. "Have you ever been to America?"

She shook her head.

"That's too bad. Your English is amazing."

"Are you inviting me?" she teased.

Henry's arm tensed, and Natsuku no longer felt his breath on the top of her head. She jabbed her elbow under his rib cage to regain his attention.

"You haven't asked after me," she said. "Don't you want to know if I'm okay? An abortion is not an easy thing for a girl to go through by herself, you know." Henry winced at the word, as if she'd insulted his manhood.

"You seem fine," he said.

"Would you notice if I weren't?"

"Are you doing okay?"

"I didn't go through with it. I changed my mind."

Henry got up from the bed and put on a pair of shorts. "I have a family back home."

"I know."

"Christ, Natsu. I swear to God, I can't figure out what you're after. I've thought about it; I really have. You're not just some groupie. You're not hounding me for money. You know you're going to be on your own with this kid. What is it that you want from me?"

Natsuku took in his sculpted body, the severe topography of his muscles, the nuances of his face. She wanted to preserve this vision of him, like she should have done with her mother as she receded into the anonymity of that festival crowd years ago.

Henry no longer belonged to her. He was a free agent now.

"I only want for you to hit one more home run," she said. "Nothing else."

"We're not talking about baseball."

"What else is left?"

"The baby. You. Me."

Natsuku giggled. She didn't mean to; it only slipped out. "The record will be your legacy," she said. She patted the bed next to her, and Henry sat. "You must forever think of me as some small, vital part of it. Just as I will think of you and your home runs as a small, vital part of mine." She brought his hand to her belly and rested it there. "It will be a boy," she said. "Ryōshi. He will be a right-handed pull hitter with power to the gaps. I can already tell."

Henry sits by himself in the dugout as his team shuffles off the field in the second inning. He's always hated the designated hitter role because he can't be immersed in the game when he's not fielding his position. Sitting on the pine until his turn in the batting order comes up disrupts the rhythm of the game he's played his whole life. But watching the Giants give up run after run in the first two innings makes him glad he can hide in the dugout as the crowd boos a miserable end to a disappointing season.

On the other side of the field, the Swallows buzz in their dugout as they prepare to take the field. Henry wants to duck back into the clubhouse and check his phone. His agent had texted him this morning that an offer for next season from the Astros might find its way to the table, and while he doesn't relish the idea of spending the next summer sweltering under Houston sunshine, another season banished from the big leagues would be worse. But since today is his last chance at claiming the record for himself, he doesn't want to do anything that will earn the ire of his *sensei*, who would jump at the chance to find a spiteful excuse to bench him.

He's due up to lead off the inning, so he tightens his batting gloves and steps into the on-deck circle to take some swings while the pitcher tosses his warm-ups. He'll probably get three, maybe four chances today, and then that'll be it for his year in exile. It'll either be back to the big leagues, or he's going to hang up his spikes.

The pitcher, Tokoro, is a veteran, too, with a crafty sinker and a fastball that's lost a bit of zip. He nods at Henry as he digs a groove into the mound. This could be his last hurrah, too, a final start to cap a long career, and Henry's heartbeat quickens as he realizes that Tokoro has no intentions of shrinking from a challenge on his last day as a ballplayer. The old timer rises to it and strikes out Henry on three pitches, all mighty whiffs. But then in the fifth inning, down eight runs with nobody on, Henry gets a hold of one, and though it's not the record he dreamed of as a boy, it's a record nonetheless. Now it's his shadow the ballplayers in this country will stand in during their finest seasons. He wonders if the record will endure to the next generation.

He breaks into a home run trot, but he's taking it slow. He wants to extend the moment as long as he can. The number 56 flashes on the scoreboard and a smattering of cheers reverberate off the roof of the dome, but they die down as soon as he steps on home plate. He gets a high-five from the batter on deck, but there is no swarm of teammates pouring out of the dugout to congratulate him. He allows himself a glance toward section 117, where he has reserved a seat for Natsuku. It is the first time she has asked him for a ticket. His eyesight is perfect, and he can see her up there, still standing. She is clapping and cheering for him, and he can even make out the tears streaming down her cheeks. She really is beautiful.

By the time he is back in the dugout, the next batter is already in the box, taking a ball low and outside. Henry does not get a curtain call, so he heads for the locker room, knowing he won't get another at bat.

After the last out is recorded, the Swallows storm the field to celebrate the playoff spot they have just clinched, and the Giants watch with hanging heads, ashamed to see a visiting team invading their home field to celebrate. Henry has already packed the contents of his locker in a duffel bag. He wonders who caught his home run ball and if they might try to exchange it with him for some autographed Giants memorabilia, but he supposes that is unlikely. It'll probably fetch a decent jackpot on eBay. Maybe he can track it down for Natsuku someday—something to give to her boy that he might pass along to his own son or daughter and so forth. It'd make a nice souvenir, though Henry supposes she already has her souvenir from Henry's record-breaking lost season. By the time the rest of the team files into the locker room, Henry is halfway down the tunnel to the player's parking lot where Teru is waiting in a Mercedes with a first-class ticket to Miami.

When Natsuku let herself into suite 4211 that night, it took her a moment to realize Henry was gone. He had never accumulated much in the way of personal effects outside of the clothes in his closet and the toiletries in his bathroom. Despite her best efforts, she had never been able to make this a home for him. The bed was still unmade, and wet towels were strewn about the carpet. Empty hangers littered the floor and the dresser drawers gaped open.

She wanted to call up some fury at him for leaving so abruptly, no proper good-bye, no half-hearted promises to keep in touch, but there was none to be had. Nothing here had been permanent for him aside from the record, which was really little more than an abstraction. Natsuku knew she was included in that transience. This was a hotel—by design a temporary stop on a journey. It was no final destination, not even for Natsuku, who already had slipped her letter of resignation under Murakami-*san's* door. In a few weeks, she would say good-bye to her roommates and the city and head back to Takarazuka, where her father had offered spare rooms for her and the baby in such a way that he had managed to make her feel like she'd be the one helping him by returning home.

While she didn't think of her mother often, sometimes she was powerless to prevent the emptiness of these hotel rooms from stirring up those feelings. The tousled sheets on an empty bed, the smushed, sunken imprints on the pillows, the splashes of water around the sink and shower, the paper cups in the trash cans—they all called her attention to the fact that people had been here who no longer were. She knew nothing about these ghosts. These empty spaces and remnants left behind only offered insinuations of lives being lived elsewhere. And now she could add Henry to that. What had he left behind but impressions and a record that amounted to little more than a statistic in a game overflowing with them? He could keep the record, it was a mark in a book that would someday be erased. She had kept for herself the part of Henry that would endure beyond either of them.

On the desk, there were no final messages left for her, only an unstamped letter addressed to Tommy Nichols, back in the United States. He hadn't even bothered to seal the envelope—it was just like him to assume that someone else would take care of anything that didn't impact his ability to launch a baseball into the cheap seats. Natsuku took out the letter, the same one she had read ten days ago. She slid the baseball card out from the folds and looked again at the photo of Henry. Another picture of someone who looked nothing like the person that lived in her mind. She put the autographed baseball card in her pocket and said, "Sorry, Tommy." Someday, when the time was right, she would show it to her son when he asked about his father and explain to him the story of the scrawny slap hitter who had grown into a titan, taking his place among legends. She would tell him how his mother had nurtured the purest virtues of that greatness to course through his own veins and done what she could to filter out the rest. "You are my legacy," she would say.

She returned the letter to the envelope, and dropped it on the desk. Someone else could clean up the rest.

Youth

Fox

William Burleson

M ost days Fox hung around outside Paul's Superette after
school like all the other kids. The treeless corner of broken
pavement and street lights was the natural place for guys to
hang out, Paul's being the only business around for several blocks, and
there was nothing else to do. Fox seemed popular among the horde of
teen boys and, rarely, teen girls, their faces reflecting our written-off,
forgotten inner-city neighborhood—poor white kids, lots of Mexicans,
a few black kids from a nearby high rise, and a selection of new immi-
grants of all shades from places I had never heard of. I went to school
with Fox. Not that we were pals or anything, but I knew him from
homeroom. He was an Indian kid, high cheekbones, crew cut, tough—
even at sixteen his shoulders filled out his t-shirt like Adrian Peterson;

51

he would laugh at my jokes, and we even talked a couple times about the Vikings and other guy stuff. Being friendly sometimes might explain why he saved me one day.

Paul's, a dirty, creaky, poorly-lit corner stop, had two aisles of dusty cans that never sold and two aisles of pop, beer, candy, and chips that did. I sat on a stool behind the cash register watching *30 Rock* on a tiny old TV, putting in two hours a day after school so the owner, Perwîn, could do errands and have dinner. It wasn't much of a job, but then few fifteen-year-old boys in my neighborhood had jobs, so ten bucks a day in cash seemed like fat city.

George and his younger brother Andrew came in, Andrew texting as he walked, George scanning the store like a lion in the Serengeti. They both wore baggy pants hanging down their asses, George in a San Jose Sharks cap just so and Andrew a Minnesota Wild. George was in my grade and square-framed and Andrew one year behind, taller than his brother but more angular. Both of them were bigger than me. A short, husky kid, as in fat, I never played sports, trying instead to pretend to be the artist type with a few Goth details—studded belt, black t-shirt and pants—as much as my ma would allow. It didn't work. No one confused me with cool.

George went to the candy aisle and Andrew the chips. They moved in a way that I knew, and I stood up trying to watch. They came back to the front, George holding a giant-sized Snickers bar up, and said, "Hey, Moose, put it on my tab." George and most of the neighborhood kids called me Moose, which rhymes with my name, Bruce, again probably because of my being husky. Andrew laughed, eating out of a bag of Doritos. They stood there in front of me. They could have walked out, and there would have been nothing I could do to stop them, but instead they stood there, taunting, shit-eating grins on their faces.

"You gotta pay for that stuff," I tried.

George ripped open the wrapper and took a bite out of the candy bar. "Hook me up, bro," he said, looking through me. He had these eyes that were not quite right, not quite true, seemingly focused on something a long way away. I heard kids say his dad slapped him stupid and now his eyes are out of alignment like a car's front wheels after driving over too many railroad tracks. Andrew stood there. He never talked, at least not that I ever heard.

"Hey, dude, I'm going to lose my job."

"So?" He bit off some more Snickers.

"Come on, man. Perwîn will be pissed."

"Who the hell is Perwîn?"

"You know. The owner."

"Paul? How's he going to find out?"

Those guys had been a pain in the ass ever since we moved there—sayin' shit, giving me a look—and I put up with it, but now I had a job and I knew they'd be back every day, for sure, if I let them get away too easily. "I'm going to tell him. I'm telling Perwîn."

The smiles disappeared. "You're going to do what? Did you just say what I think you said?"

Mrs. Rodriguez walked in, bell jingling above the door. She waddled in pushing a square wire basket with two wheels for her usual carton of cigs and two twelve-packs of grape Fanta.

"*Hola*, boys. Bruce, would you please give me a hand?"

I said "Sure," overjoyed by the interruption. I went to the pop aisle and got her twelves.

She eased her way to the counter on her tree-trunk legs. "George," she said, understanding there was no use addressing Andrew, "Would you tell your mother that I have some black beans and rice to drop off? I hope you all like it. Do you boys like black beans and rice?" Their mother had been sick with something, but no one knew what.

George said "Yes, ma'am," all polite.

I deposited the pop in Mrs. Rodriguez's basket and returned to the register.

"Bruce, I need to play my numbers." She pulled a folded up piece of paper out of her purse, carefully opening it.

Then I had a stroke of genius. "I'm sorry, Mrs. Rodriguez. I'm just finishing these guys up." I rang up the jumbo candy bar and the Doritos and told them the price. Now they were in a jam. No way could they leave without paying with Mrs. Rodriguez there with their mom on speed dial. They looked at me with blood in their eyes, George finally fishing a crumpled up five out of his pants pocket and laying it on the counter. I made change.

They left, looking back at me all the way, as I got her carton of Marlboro 100s and put it in her basket. Pretty smart of me, yes sir.

I walked out the door at seven with no coat, it being a warm October evening. The usual group of kids was standing outside, a couple with long boards, a couple smoking cigarettes, and George and Andrew.

George sat on the retaining wall at the end of the building texting, Andrew doing nothing. Andrew pointed at me, and George looked up. "Hey, Moose." They hopped off the wall and walked toward me, pulling up their baggy pants as they walked.

The other boys stopped everything, ready for some action.

"Oh, no." "Oh, yeah." "Watch out, Moose." "Emo goin' down."

I stopped. What else could I do? George got up in my face, looking down on me with those weird eyes. He pushed me with one hand. I moved back a step.

"Moose, I'm going to Fuck. You. Up." He pushed me with both hands. I almost fell down but regained my balance. I was like a stunned bird, waiting for the cat to come in for the kill. I had to pee.

Out of nowhere, Fox ran in, grabbing George by his shirt, practically lifting him off the ground, running him backward all the way to Paul's Superette, pinning him against the wall. It took everything George had to squeak out, "Fox—"

"Leave that kid alone," Fox said through his clenched jaw. "He's not bothering you."

I didn't know what to do. No one moved. I looked at Andrew standing by me; he seemed to know even less what to do.

"You got that? Huh?"

"Yeah, man, be cool."

Fox looked him square in the face, teeth gritted, every muscle flexed.

George looked at Fox, then to Andrew—no help there—then around at the others, who were all saying and doing nothing. He looked anywhere but in Fox's eyes.

Fox smiled. Just like that, smiled, and put George down. He laughed. "Come on, man." He slapped George's shoulder like they were best friends. George hesitated, and then took the gift of face from Fox and laughed also, if a bit too slowly, finally chucking Fox on the arm in return.

Fox put his arm around George's shoulder and they returned to the group smiling as if they just got off a roller coaster together. No one seemed to notice me standing there.

The next day in homeroom I told Fox thanks.

"For what? That? Last night? What are you doing messing with George and Andrew for, anyway? Those fuckers are serious."

We sat by the window in the old wood-floor-and-chalk-dust classroom. The homeroom teacher was late again. Most of the thirty-five other kids sat quietly, only because it was 8:00 a.m. and no one had gotten enough sleep to misbehave. I changed the subject. We laughed about what an odd guy Perwin was. Bald guy, walked like he had no knees. Funny accent, we didn't know from where. We talked about not much of anything. We had in common that we didn't have dads around and both of us lived in shitty apartments. Fox had dreams, though. He told me about playing football—tight end, linebacker—and how he hoped to get a scholarship one day. He could get a scholarship. He was that good.

"I don't know anyone who went to college," I said.

"Me neither." He looked out the window, red and gold leaves on the trees. Then, "So what? I'm going. You wait and see."

I didn't care what Fox said—I appreciated him saving my ass.

That would be the last time I would see him there, in that room or in school. The next day when he was gone I assumed he was sick. The day after, too. All week. After three weeks, I figured he moved away. Kids came and went all the time. Moving here and there, city to city, parents getting a job, losing a job, going to prison, and kids going to live with their aunt, their grandmother, on the street. I missed him. I had hoped we could become friends.

George and Andrew didn't go anywhere, though. They were still outside of Paul's most evenings as I sat behind the counter watching TV. They left me alone; still, it made me uncomfortable to see them there before and after work and from my living room door.

We lived right across the street from Paul's Superette. My mom and I moved there after she and dad got a divorce two years before, my dad being a "no-good worthless bum." She told me I should watch out, or

I'd grow up just like him. The apartment was all we could afford, given my mom worked in a nursing home kitchen and my dad rarely paid up on time. From my living room I had a bird's eye view of Paul's—the shabby, run-down wood-framed building, paint peeling from the graffiti-tagged, windowless wall, backlit plastic sign's faded message about RC Cola, and the boys in front of it—from the window of our second-floor apartment. Well, not technically a window—sliding door to a little deck in danger of falling off the building.

It was out my living room door, February, four months after I had talked with him in homeroom, that I saw Fox standing with about six other kids in front of Paul's. He was on crutches. Because he was wearing a bulky black winter coat, it took me a minute to register that he was missing a leg. The sight made me cringe. What happened to his leg? I looked at him for a while, horsing around, whacking kids in the ass with an aluminum crutch. At one point, a black kid grabbed the end of the crutch and twisted it away from Fox. Fox dropped the other crutch and hopped on one leg after the kid, everyone laughing, especially Fox. Finally they stopped, and the kid handed Fox back his crutch. Fox braced himself on it, reached down, and picked up the second crutch off the snow.

I told my mom I was going to the store for a Coke. She gave me a ten and asked me to bring back a pack of generics and to not forget the change.

I walked a wide perimeter around the group of boys. Fox saw me and swung his way over on his crutches. His leg was missing all the way to the top.

"Yo, Bruce.'Sup?"

I asked him how he was doing.

"Not bad. Considering."

The other kids ignored us. Two black kids looked at another guy's new iPhone 7 while a white guy in a light coat shivered by the retaining wall, smoking a joint, paying no attention to anyone.

"Bone cancer."

I let that sink in. Who ever heard of bone cancer? Breast cancer, sure. Lung cancer—that killed a great uncle of mine. But bone cancer? What color ribbon is that?

"But I'm okay now. The leg's not coming back, though." He said it was hard getting used to the crutches, but he's getting better at it. "I guess it'll be hard to get an artificial limb, given it's cut off right at the hip. We'll see, though. Maybe someday they'll implant one or something. I'll be a cyborg." He appeared to enjoy the thought.

We talked more, pretty much about nothing. He seemed like the same Fox as always—quick with a smile. I couldn't tell anything was different if I didn't look down. But I did look down. I said I needed to get the smokes and go home.

Fox hung around a lot after that. He apparently didn't go to school, and I would see him hobbling around the neighborhood, hanging out in front of Paul's, hanging with the other neighborhood boys. He would come in the store sometimes when I worked and we would talk a little. One time, I asked him about his mom.

"Oh, she's okay," he said, absentmindedly picking through a plastic bin of key chains on the counter. "She got pretty freaked out when I had cancer."

I scratched my earlobe, looking at the floor. It was the first time he had mentioned the cancer since that one day. I asked him what he meant.

"She blamed herself. Said it was because she didn't take care of me right. I said, 'bullshit, ma, bullshit. You did alright by me. It just happened, you know, it just happened.'"

I wondered if my mom would blame herself if I lost a leg. I wondered if Fox actually said *bullshit* to his mom.

Then one day he quit coming in. Again I wondered if he moved, maybe back to the reservation because his mom wanted to take better care of him or something. I asked a couple of the guys outside if they knew anything—they didn't—but one tall Mexican kid knew where he lived. He told me he was a block and a half away in an old duplex with a busted front porch hanging off at an angle. After work one day, I walked by but didn't see anything. The house was dark and the curtains were closed.

When I got home, Mom was putting plates on the kitchen table. She asked me where I had been. I told her how I hadn't seen Fox and thought I'd walk by his place.

"That one-legged kid?"

I said "Yes."

"Maybe it's for the best. I think that kid is trouble."

I asked why.

She put the bucket of KFC in the middle of the table. "I don't know. But I've never met an Indian who wasn't."

On a warm May day, Fox reappeared. I was leaving Paul's, and there were seven or eight boys hanging around enjoying spring, all that energy bottled up for months, just waiting for an evening like that. I saw baggy-pants George and Andrew first. They looked at me, but as usual it was as if they didn't recognize me, or at least didn't care about me. In the center of the group, a guy in a wheelchair with a Twins cap had his back to me. I didn't recognize Fox at first. Then I did, and I felt cold down my back. I started walking on home but instead circled back.

"Bruce! What up, B?" he wheeled over, the gang not following. He had no legs. I must have been staring. "What's the matter? Never seen a guy without legs before?"

I asked him how he'd been.

He said, "Sucky—lost my other leg. More cancer. Turns out one leg wasn't enough. Now I'm getting chemo. Blows, man." He took his hat off, showing off his hair in patches. He laid his hat in his lap. "Check it out." He popped a wheelie, rocking back and forth in his chair.

The guys laughed and hooted.

"Watch out for hills." "Build this boy a ramp." "Mark Zupan wannabe." The kids laughed, but Fox didn't seem to care.

George said with more spite than humor, "Fox is a Special Olympian. Special, as in short bus special."

"I got this thing all tricked out. It's a racing chair." All black metal, nothing extra to add weight, wheels at an angle. He looked like he could stay up forever.

When I got home, Mom was cooking dinner. I leaned on the counter in the kitchen where I could see, through the doors, the boys in front of Paul's. I told her about Fox. "Right there, Mom. Across the street." I pointed.

She turned around, still holding a jar of Prego. "Where?"

"In the wheelchair."

"Oh. Isn't he kinda young to already be losing limbs to diabetes?"

I was going to correct her, but I was more interested in watching Fox horse around with the other guys, chasing, spinning in his chair.

As quickly as he came back, he was gone again. This time, I caught on that it couldn't be good news. Again, no one seemed to know anything. I even asked the homeroom teacher, but he didn't remember Fox at first, and when he did, he said he had no idea.

Spring turned into summer. And what a summer. I turned sixteen. I kissed a girl—or, more accurately, she kissed me—at a barbecue at my uncle's. She was a neighbor of my uncle's out in the 'burbs. Kissed me behind the tool shed. She had black lipstick and nail polish and said that she thought I looked like Brian Eno, whoever that is. I had my first drink of beer, appropriately enough from Paul's. I drank it on the Fourth of July at the lake in the afternoon. And now, strangely, I had become friends with George and Andrew. It started because they discovered I was happy to sell them beer and cigarettes. They took advantage, and eventually they even started talking to me. They would hang around, chatting about cars and who fucked up who. Andrew still never said anything but otherwise seemed to be normal.

"Yeah, Moose," George said one day, looking at me with his wandering eyes. "Our mom died."

No one I knew ever died before. I didn't know her either, but I knew George and Andrew, so I kinda did. I didn't know what to say.

"Yeah, she had a bad liver. She looked like shit at the end, all yellow." We stood there, not looking at each other. "You know what really sucks? Now I have to count on my old man. Dang. Messed up, that's all."

Andrew nodded.

"All I have is my mom; my dad disappeared in the spring to avoid paying child support," I said.

"Maybe we should introduce them." They both laughed. "No, I wouldn't wish my old man on anyone."

That night, George and Andrew waved me over as I left the store. With their approval, I found myself getting to know all the neighbor kids for the first time, the start of many hours standing out there laughing and horsing around in front of Paul's. It felt good. I had become one of the guys. Funny, I spent so much time worrying about those two that it never occurred to me that they probably never gave me a second thought. Now I was alright by them. Go figure.

Every so often, I would roll by Fox's place, but I never saw him. Although, one time I might have. Someone looked out the window, but when I stopped the face was gone. Could have been a cat, too; maybe I just wanted to see Fox's face.

End of summer, late August, I sat on the couch in the living room playing my Xbox. No, not an Xbox One, an old Xbox 360 that Mom found at the Goodwill. Went fine with our nineteen-inch analog TV. I was playing *Madden NFL 12*, Christian Ponder was letting me down again, when I glanced out the living room door. There, in front of Paul's, the usual five or six guys stood around, plus a wheelchair. Whoever was in the chair had on a stocking cap, and even though the chair looked completely different than before, I knew it had to be Fox.

I watched for a while. The chair looked heavier and moved around mechanically. No wheelies. The guys surrounded him, talking and laughing. I didn't know what to do.

Finally, I drummed up enough courage to cross the street. At first, I stood a bit on the outside of the group, not sure. He had his back turned and didn't know I was there. George and Andrew stood next to each other, arms crossed, in front of Fox. Andrew looked up at me and elbowed his brother.

"Hey, Moose. Come over here, man. Fox's back," George said.

The wheelchair whined and turned around. "Bruce. 'Sup, man?" He sounded hoarse. Fox had no eyebrows. He looked gray, hollow, eyes yellow. That's what I noticed first. Then I noticed he only had one arm. His right arm was missing at the shoulder.

The sight freaked me out inside, but I held it together and said, "Hey, where ya been?"

"Hospital, mostly." He went to a rez hospital because he could get free care there. Plus, his relatives thought the fresh air would do him good. "Yeah, more cancer. Got my arm, as you can see. It better leave this last one, that's all, it better leave this last arm." He looked deadly serious saying it.

"Dude's being dismantled," George said, without a hint of humor. Everyone else laughed, including me. Including Fox.

"Check out the chair," Fox said. "It's pretty cool. Goes fast too. Turns in circles." He demonstrated it for us, spinning it around in place.

The guys approved. "Check it." "Fuckin' thing's fly." "Sick."

"You're like a top, man." George laughed. "My cousin has a lawn-mower that can do that."

Fox stopped spinning, facing me. Big smile. Missing limbs and all, he was still Fox.

"What do you think, Moose?" George asked, standing behind Fox.

I stood in front of him after all those months. "Happy to see you, man."

"Boy's a freak, that's all. Ya know? A freak," George said.

All the guys were silent, watching. Fox's smiled dropped. George moved even closer behind the chair.

George's eyes seemed even more catawampus than usual. "What would you do if you lost your legs and an arm? What would you do, Moose?"

What was I supposed to say? "I don't know."

"Shit, man," George said, talking like Fox wasn't even there. "Fucking shoot me, okay? If I ever end up like that, shoot me. Sneak up behind me and cap me in the brain, okay?"

A couple of the guys chuckled and muttered, "Doin' a favor." "Livin' like that."

Fox looked hurt, more hurt than pissed.

What should I say? "Pity, man."

"No shit, Moose. Pity. One-armed freak. Don't know how he can do it. That's all."

More laughter, louder this time. Fox looked hard into my eyes, hard enough I couldn't look back for fear of getting burned.

"Yeah, man," I said. "I think it's the diabetes." I laughed, looking at the other guys for approval. Some of them laughed, also.

Fox looked down in his lap. Someone behind me said, "Diabetes, yeah." Someone else said, "Oh, no."

George smiled. "What's that, Moose?"

"Diabetes. I bet it's really the diabetes. My mom says it's the diabetes. Not bone cancer at all. How could Fox have cancer? It doesn't make sense. Can't be cancer." I tried not to, but my eyes began to water. "No way. Not Fox. He's tough. Toughest guy I know. Can't be cancer. He's . . . he's . . ."

"He's fucked up, that's what. Injun's fucked up." George laughed. He looked down at the back of Fox's head. "Yeah, Fox, you don't have much to work with anymore. Did they save your dick? Or did they amputate that, too?" George said. Andrew laughed. Now no one else did.

"Dick's fine, George. You want to suck it for me?" Fox said without turning around.

The smile fell off George's face. "What did you say?"

"George, suck my big Injun dick. You know you want to."

George backhanded Fox on the side of his head from behind, hard, stocking cap flying off, revealing his bald head. Quick as lightning, Fox grabbed George's arm as it went by. George was surprised and off balance, and Fox pulled him down with his one hand, their heads now next to each other's for just a beat. George looked shocked. Fox bit George's nose; he screamed, partially muffled by Fox's face. Fox didn't let go, neither with his hand nor his jaw, as George recoiled back, lifting Fox out of his chair, now hanging off George, who continued to scream. They fell backward, boys clearing out of the way, giving space, no one helping George. Fox lay on top of George, who punched Fox as best he could, considering he was flat on his back on the ground. Fox let go of George's nose, head lifting up and smashing down on George's skull already on the pavement. George quit punching, his eyes rolling back, mouth open. Fox reared up again, and again smashed George stupider that he already was. He was out, knocked out cold. It all happened in a matter of seconds. Teeth clenched, Fox propped his torso up on his one elbow on George's chest, surveying his work.

Andrew, with his long legs, kicked Fox in the side, knocking Fox off balance, rolling him off George. Andrew tried to kick Fox again, but Fox caught his foot with his one hand, and they had a tug of war with Andrew's Converse.

"What are you kids doing?!" Perwin stood in the door to his store, then walked stiff-kneed over to the crowd. "Fighting? Get out of here, punks! You hear me?"

Andrew looked at Perwîn, looked at his brother on the sidewalk, looked at Perwîn, and took off running. The other four guys took the cue and scrambled out of there themselves, sure that there would be trouble with one boy unconscious on the ground and a one-armed, no-legged boy out of his chair next to him on the pavement.

Perwîn looked at me as if to ask *what the hell?* He ever so carefully, stiffly, bent down and looked at George. "I better call 911." He eased his way back to standing and went back to the store.

I walked over to Fox. He was breathing hard. I bent down, grabbed his hand, and helped him to a sitting position on the ground. "I'm sorry, Fox. I'm sorry." My chin quivered.

"Help me, Bruce."

I got down, wrapped my arms around him, and lifted him into the chair. He didn't weigh much at all.

My junior year I still worked at Paul's. October, the days short, leaves blew against the door, and Perwîn had me sweep them up with a broom into the trash whenever there wasn't anything else to do. It seemed stupid, but whatever.

I heard an electric wine. I straightened up and turned around.

"Bruce. 'Sup?"

I hadn't seen Fox in over a year. And, yet again, no one seemed to know where he went. He looked the same, maybe more pink, maybe more thin, but with hair on his head. He also had no arms at all now.

"I missed you, man," I said.

"Missed you too, bro." We stood there, me with my broom and dustpan, Fox strapped in his chair with a black stick to control it in front of his face. "Lost my last arm."

"Yeah. See that." I shivered. No coat on, just a black t-shirt, and it was getting cold, sundown already. The neighborhood felt quiet, neighborhood guys nowhere to be found. We asked after each other's families, school, football.

"Bruce, I'm going to go to college, man." He smiled that Fox smile. "Maybe not a football scholarship. Baseball, maybe. Play second base. Not *at* second base, *as* second base." An old joke, but that didn't keep us from laughing like we were stoned. "No, really, I've been homeschooling. I'm going to graduate and go to college."

I thought how if I would ever know anyone who went to college, if anyone could make it, it would be Fox. Then we talked about the fight. "Man, you fucked George up."

"I hear his eyes are straight now," Fox said.

"I haven't seen George or Andrew since."

"Good. I don't think I could take him any longer."

I laughed again, but this time, it came out as crying. Fox saw that.

"Check it out," Fox said. He used his mouth to push the black stick, driving the chair forward and back, spinning around and around.

Old as Rain

Josephine Cariño

I'm eight or nine or so and you're old as rain. Inside, not out. Outside, you're the same as me. Mudpies in the rain. We scoop grit up, get dirt under our nails, our claws, our talons. After school—throw them at windows and doors. I think you are swell. Go through bramble woods, behind sheds, away from swings. Dark trough of mud; it's in us. Rain pelts hard, typhoon overhead. Blow blow wind. No nuns, priests, teachers berating, saying: Sing your hymns, clean your hands, kneel, say your prayers, do your formulas, all in dark hallways. Always dark. I think I am a brown kernel of mud. Just. Like. You.

No, Mama says. Don't go over to his house. Don't you know? His father's not his father. Bastard child, dirty child. But friend, Mama. No. Well, I think—. No. Don't think, just do. So I sneak out back on Sunday after Mass. Oh, Heavenly Father, forgive us our trespasses. Scale the cement wall, rub rough knees, hike up my skirt. Bloody gash. Waiting on you. By hedge pots an old Buddha, his eyes closed, balls on his head, a funny cone. Cloth draped over his chest, feet, legs. Stares at me. Waiting on you still. Then you come with a—a car. Toy car. Zoom zoom. Racetrack on the cement. And let me? No. Let me! Grab past straggly arms. Sticks in the ribs. Sharp, ouch, you hurt me. No. You. Don't.

I scream bastard dirty child, slap you, slap me, scratch. Dirty child, dirty dirty you. Yaya comes running, yanks my hair, my shirt, smacks me on the chin and I spit. Who let you in? Out the gate. Before. I. Call. Your. Mother. Heathen child. Rough push, hands clasped on shoulders, march march to the gate. Before I go, I kick. I run. Up the road to chickens in the backyard. Want to guzzle down a Coke but—oh, Mama.

What have you done to yourself? All bloody. What a mess. Scraped your knees, your cheek, where have you been, I told you not to go there, you ungrateful little girl. I'll take you away, take you overseas, teach you some manners. Make new friends. Better ones.

I'm nine or ten. You're still old as rain. Older than, even. Only I can see. And I see clouds under the engine's rumbling blades. Spinning, *wheee*. Flying over mountains. Rain underneath, like you. Only I can see. I send you pictures of crepe myrtles, purple pink white, by the sidewalk. No mud here, I can't reach. Hi, hello there, nice to meet you. What's your name? It's—oh, well I live there. Go to school. Lessons, recess. Whistle blows, time to go in. Lessons. Then peanut butter jelly sandwich, banana, carrot sticks, cheese, milk. Time to go home, see ya tomorrow.

Dream. Dream of mud streaking your hands. Dream of slapping earth wet with teardrops God cried. Dream of grassy sticks and stones, break your bones, only you laugh and shout: hallelujah, praise be to God. Dream of a happy boy, you. Dream of guzzle guzzle neck and muzzle. And we fly like birds, whip whip through branches. Away from peanut butter.

Years go by and by and by until. I stop writing back. And here we are, I'm twenty, are you old as rain? Maybe not. Maybe I only thought. Yesterday Mama said sit down, here's a clipping. From a paper someone sent. From back home. Ah. Yes. Didn't you know him? Yes. I. Did. Shot himself in the mouth and head, so sorry they don't know. Why. I didn't know. No. Eyes filled with mud. So sorry. You okay? Like a typhoon's overhead but in me. Wind blow blow. Get up, slam the door, into rain, not a monsoon but still warm. I make swirls in the ground with sticks. Who are you? Where did you go?

Hands plunge deep into brown slime, guck, worms. Grab handfuls in the pouring rain. Wait until cars pass—throw, slap slap. Slammed brakes. I run mad, dash like mad. Out he comes! Yells, Hey you! Run wicked fast but not really. Really, still a child. Lungs burn and out comes breath like razors. Into woods behind sheds I wait under shadow branches until he passes. Me holding still as Buddha in the back. Only this time. I cry.

How can someone disappear. Like. That. Like a rainbow's shimmer. Color that spangles bright light. Clouds hide it. Or, the sun goes away. My fault. You bastard. Bastard child. Heathen for you only. If, only if. I had stayed. But couldn't, no. Still. Breath catches under sobs and I'm a wailing baby. Like babies we were, in a crib where they toss scraps of trash. Kernel of mud mine. Kernel of mud yours. Now gone.

You, old as rain now, older than. Younger than. Timeless. I want to have that. But nothing can bring it back; there's only mud. I wonder, I wonder if you could. Or would. Bye. Bye now. I stand, wipe grime on jeans sopping wet. Squish squish underfoot. Sneak in the back door. A Sunday after Mass. Wash off brown from face, hands, shirt. Where'd I go? Oh, just around. Back. Around and back. Once again. Big circle, one big. Circle.

The Devil's Age

Robert Johnson

Put an axe in a lazy man's hands, Danny Baker figured, and he can't help but chop. It's the smoothness of the handle, the weight of the head, the sharpness of the blade. Likewise, put a bat in a boy's hand and he wants to take a cut at a ball. If he's a real boy, that is. He wants to take a hard cut at a fat pitch, the same way he wants to put his shoulder beneath a guy's ribs on the scrimmage line and feel them break like damp sticks.

"You can't be surprised Mitch went a little wild," Danny said to his wife, but Helen buried her face in her hands. She hadn't said two words since the call came the night before. He groaned and stabbed out his Pall Mall so the ashtray clattered across the table and onto the floor. Normally she'd be on her knees in an instant to clean up the mess, but now she didn't move. Like everybody else, she was waiting to see what he'd do next. Nobody had asked—they were all too chickenshit—but if they did, he'd say the boy had to face the music like anybody else. A marshal's son was no different.

Mitch was seventeen, raw and spiky as barbed wire. Sixteen, and you're still a big mama's boy. Eighteen, and you're out of school and thinking about a full-time job. Seventeen is a goddamn no man's land, the devil's age. Anything can happen.

"I'll find him," Danny said. "I'll bring him home." He wanted to grab Helen's wrist and make her look at him but thought better of it. Instead he stood and walked from the kitchen onto the back deck, where he lit another cigarette and surveyed the October morning. A frost had come down hard overnight, and the pine trees at the edge of the yard were ashy white on their bottommost branches. He sucked in the smoke and let the cool poison do its work. He'd fix this. A broken furnace, a seized axle on a Chevy short bed, a rash of upended tombstones in the town cemetery—give Danny Baker a problem, and he'd find the cause and bend it to his will.

He walked to the pole barn where his pickup was parked and his tool collection overflowed the work bench: a sledge hammer from his year on a rail crew, a wood plane with a burled walnut handle, a giant hex wrench used on Chicago's Clark Street Bridge. In the empty stall, a Chevy engine block hung naked from a hoist. It had come from the machinist the week before, and it gleamed like the day it left Detroit. Its eight cylinders were bored to five thousandths of an inch clearance, its valves shone like new quarters, and its head was milled clean of every trace of crud and heat so the surface flashed like a mirror. He had planned to teach his son to rebuild the engine from top to bottom— pistons, rings, crankshaft—and together they would drop it into the teal blue '57 Bel Air.

The car, if accounts were to be believed, Mitch was driving the night before.

Danny Baker pushed the block so it swayed gently on its chain, casting a shadow like a giant horse's head on the concrete floor, then he stepped to his pickup and lifted his bulk onto the front seat. He was forty-three years old and tired to the bone. His khaki shirt stretched tight across his stomach and the plantar wart on his foot hurt against the clutch. He yanked the truck into reverse and backed onto the road. He'd fix this. Of that there was no doubt.

When he turned onto Sellersville's Main Street, he felt the eyes on him, but when he met people's glittering stares, they looked away. Chickenshits. A crowd of loafers gathered in the alley between Newell's Hardware and the bank, where one of the hardware store's windows was covered with plywood and the pavement was littered with broken glass. Big Chet Newell had a new pane coming later that morning, and with his man in the hospital, he'd need someone to help him install it. Danny Baker made a note to be there when the window arrived.

Until then, he had other things to do. Ahead was the fire station, with the marshal's office and jail cell in the basement and a hitching rail behind it for the Amish. There, Samuel Troyer and his son Marvin waited by the family buggy, Sam's big red sorrel tied fast and blowing steam from its nostrils. Danny Baker parked and descended the three steps into his cramped office, where he fell on the swivel-backed chair and lifted his boots onto his desk. Only then did he look to see that the Amish man and his son had followed and stood waiting with their hats in their hands. Samuel Troyer was ruddy and barrel-chested and, though it was Wednesday, dressed in a formal straight coat. His eyes were fiercely blue and his bald pate gleamed where the sun rarely touched. His beard bloomed downward to cover his sternum and was reddish-brown like the horse tied up outside.

Danny Baker blew smoke at the ceiling. "Sam, I won't say I'm glad to see you."

"Yah. I wish it was not—"

"Marvin, do you know what it means to be an accessory to a crime?"

The boy's face was pale and sprinkled with acne, and he wore suspenders over an aqua shirt. When he opened his mouth his voice was a whisper. "I don't think I—"

"Speak up, boy," Danny Baker said. "I'm in a bad, bad mood."

Marvin lowered his eyes and studied the brim of his straw hat. When he spoke again the words were husky. "I don't know what that means, no."

"It means that—even if you weren't inside the hardware store last night, even if you didn't make a run for it like Mitch and your brother

Lloyd, even if you turned yourself in—you still acted as a lookout and might be charged with a felony and go to jail. Do you understand my meaning now?"

The boy swallowed. "Yah, I guess so."

"Do you have any idea, Marvin, what a sixteen-year-old boy would face up in Joliet? Do you have any idea what those men would—"

"He knows he's in a world of trouble, Dan," Sam Troyer said. "You'll get nowhere scaring daylights out of him."

Danny swung his boots to the floor and pounded the desktop so hard a calendar jumped from the wall. "And you'll get nowhere by telling me how to do my goddamn job. Your son and mine are violent criminals now. Their lives will never be the same."

"That may be true for your boy," Samuel said calmly. "It ain't true for mine."

Just like the Amish, Danny Baker thought. Huddled against the world, simple as the cows they milked by hand, their women dressed like crows, yet there was a smugness to them that begged to be squashed. He looked at Marvin. "I've known your pa forever," he said. "Since we were boys playing softball. He's always been more sure of himself than he has a right to be."

Marvin made a choking sound. "Are you going to shoot my brother?" he whispered. He was staring at the Colt revolver strapped to Danny's side. "When you find him? Are you going to shoot Lloyd?"

"That's up to him," Danny Baker said. "That's up to him and Mitch."

"Every boy has a crazy time," Chet Newell said. He knelt to hold a dustpan as Danny swept broken glass into it. "You and me were no different, the scrapes we got into."

Danny leaned on his push broom and looked up the alley toward Main Street, where the crowd of gawkers peered back at him through the dust he'd made. Anybody worth a damn was at work by now. "I appreciate you saying so, Chet," he said. "But this isn't stealing watermelons."

"No. In fairness, it's not. Even so—"

"A man was hurt."

Chet stood, groaning from the effort, and dumped the shards into a trash bin. "Ah, Toby'll be OK," he said. "He got his bell rung is all."

The two men entered the hardware store through the side door, and Danny Baker began scraping old putty from the window frame while Chet Newell fetched a handful of glazier points to hold the new glass in place. Danny tried not to look at the stain on the floor boards near the shotgun case.

"Mitch is a good boy at heart," Chet Newell said. "Not like that Lloyd Troyer. He's a bad one, that Lloyd." He reached out a big paw to cover Danny's hand holding the putty knife. "As long as Mitch pays damages, Dan, I won't be pressing charges."

"It's too late for that," Danny Baker said. He freed his hand and resumed his work. "There was a witness. A man was assaulted during a burglary attempt."

"Toby'll be okay," Chet Newell said again. He laughed weakly. "Might've knocked some smarts into him."

Marvin had taken the family buggy into town, he'd told Danny that morning, and was playing pinball at Schott's on Warren Street, when Mitch and Lloyd pulled up in the teal blue Chevy and honked until he came outside. Mitch told the younger boy they needed help with a project, and he said it in a way that meant he wouldn't be refused.

"You don't say no to Mitch," Marvin had said. "I would have done anything for Lloyd, but I was afraid to say no to Mitch."

"What do you mean you were afraid?" Danny asked.

The boy had looked at his feet. "Everybody is, I guess."

Danny thought of those words as he puttied the new glass into the frame. Twice Chet Newell said, "Okay, Dan . . . that's good enough," but Danny Baker couldn't leave a job done half-assed, and he smoothed the seal until it was a perfect forty-five all the way around.

As he stood to inspect his work he heard Chet say, "I bet this was Lloyd's idea all along. These Amish boys and their wildness. I bet it was Lloyd who hit Toby."

Danny Baker turned to face him in the dimness of the shuttered store. "It wasn't," he whispered hoarsely. "Marvin saw it from the window. It was Mitch hit your man. Lloyd was jimmying the gun lock, and Toby came out of nowhere with a ball bat and didn't see Mitch in the shadows, and Mitch took the bat from him and smacked him across the skull." He brought his hands to his cheeks as if not believing his own words. "He hit Toby so hard he dropped like a sack of cement."

"Ah, God," Chet Newell said. "Ah, God."

"This was all my son's idea," Danny Baker said. "Marvin said they were going to sell the shotguns for amphetamines and beer."

"Ah, God," Chet said again.

When Danny Baker let himself out the side door and walked up the alley to Main Street, the idlers waited there. Men on disability, others never the same after France or the Pacific, a few who couldn't hold jobs and relied on their wives to take in laundry. The group parted as he approached and most cast their eyes downward, though one or two stared at him brazenly. He walked up to the boldest and said, "I'm guessing you have something to say."

"Some of us are wondering, Marshal," the man said after a moment's start, "if you have any leads." He glanced at the others, then turned to Danny again. "This sort of thing won't be tolerated in Sellersville." His eyes were pink, and broken veins swirled down each side of his nose and joined at the tip. He reeked of whiskey at eleven in the morning.

"If I had any leads, do you think I'd be sweeping up glass in an alley?"

"Be that as it may," the man said. "Some of us can't help but wonder—"

"You can't help but wonder if I'm giving this my full attention because my son was involved."

"Well, some of us . . ."

Danny Baker felt suddenly happy. "Go ahead." He smiled and drew so near their chests all but touched. "Tell me I'm not doing my job because of Mitch."

The man's mouth opened and closed several times, but then his face fell, and Danny Baker brushed past him to his truck.

Two hours later his tires rumbled over the truss bridge east of town, where the creamery and feed mill and cemetery gave way to Amish country. The October sky was intensely blue behind clouds the color of gun metal. Farms stretched away on all sides—houses tidy and square, cotton dresses billowing from clothes lines, vegetable gardens plowed under until spring. Unhitched buggies stood in the barnyards, and unbridled horses watched from the pastures. Sam Troyer had told him that no Amish family would knowingly hide the fugitives, though Danny Baker answered that there were enough sheds and outbuildings scattered about the countryside to conceal a Chevy Bel Air, and enough Amish boys who knew the suspects and might be thrilled to abet them.

"You don't know the Amish," Sam had said. "This isn't a time for law-breaking." He was referring to *rumspringa*, when Amish teenagers spent a year or two "running around" before settling down to join the church.

"I know them well enough," Danny had answered. Every season he picked up some seventeen-year-old for drinking or pot possession, only to see the same boy in town a year later—a bonneted girl at his side, a wispy beard on his chin, a pink infant against his chest.

Now he drove the dirt roads and peered behind latticed corn cribs and stone silos and wagons stacked with hay. He had alerted police as far north as Napier and as far south as Cairo, though his gut told him Mitch and Lloyd were still nearby. Once he caught a flash of blue through some trees, though it turned out to be a pond behind a milk house, reflecting back the sky.

He had gone earlier to Decatur to see Chet Newell's man in the hospital. Toby had been awake and sitting up, though his head was wrapped in bandages, and an amber liquid seeped through them where the bat had cracked his skull. He'd been kicked by a horse as a boy and was subject to spells, and the medication he took to subdue them caused him to push out a blue-gray tongue and lick his lips constantly. He winced when Danny Baker opened the blinds.

"Back among the living, I see," Danny Baker had said.

Toby lifted a hand as if to wave off a gnat. "It ain't nothing, Marshal. I've had worse headaches." He put a finger to each eyelid and massaged them gently. "This one's a doozy, though."

Danny Baker found a glass of ice water on the bedside table and held the straw to Toby's lips. "I guess those morons didn't know you had a cot in the back."

Toby laughed and winced again. He laid his head on the pillow and worked his tongue for a while. "It's awful nice of Mister Newell to let me help at the store," he said at last. "I let him down, though, didn't I?"

Danny felt an unfamiliar itch at the back of his throat and swallowed it down. He put a hand on the man's shoulder. "No sir, you didn't. You did exactly the right thing. You didn't let anyone down, Tobe."

Toby looked up at him. "Mister Newell called right before you came. We had a talk." He worked his tongue furiously. "Don't you worry, Marshal. I don't remember a thing." He reached to squeeze Danny's hand. "Mitch is a good boy at heart."

As he drove the roads east of Sellersville, Danny Baker tried hard to believe him. Mitch had never been an easy one, there was no denying it. As a toddler, he'd shown rages so fierce he ran blindly into walls. Danny knew only to hold him in an iron clasp until the fits passed, though Helen's touch sometimes calmed the boy.

"Go ahead, spoil him," Danny would shout as she hurried away with the child. Once when Mitch was three and kicked at him in anger, Danny grabbed his collar and the seat of his pants and threw him like a sack of meal onto the couch. Each time he tried to escape, Danny muscled him into the cushions again. Over and over it went—twenty, thirty times—until Mitch surrendered, his body exhausted, his face scarlet with fury.

Helen had cried that Danny was only making things worse, but he knew he was teaching the boy about an ordered world, one with limits and consequences, and the sooner Mitch understood its makeup the better.

"That's the way my pops raised *me*," he'd said. Rather than break him, his father's discipline had only made Danny stronger, the way fire hardens steel.

The old man had scorned tenderness, despised waste, hated the idea of someone doing a job for him that he could do for himself. Once when Danny's mother was home alone, an encyclopedia salesman with a mustache like Errol Flynn appeared at the house and convinced her that every boy needed a broad outlook on the world if he was to make something of himself, and she plundered her mean savings and bought a set. When her husband came in that night, he opened the front door and tossed each of the gilded volumes, one after the other, into the yard, where the pages soaked up rain and mud and burning sunshine for a week before he allowed his wife to clean up the mess.

Yet hard as he was, the old man could do anything. Let a tire on the Studebaker go flat, and he submerged it in a horse trough and followed the bubbles to the leak. Let a birthing heifer go full breech, and he buried his arm to the shoulder and wrestled the calf ass-end into the world. By the time Danny was ten, he could hand crank the old Allis-Chalmers tractor to life on a winter morning. By the time he was twelve, he could roof a shed with cedar shingles he'd split himself.

That's all I ever wanted for Mitch, Danny thought, as he combed the hills and swales for his son. *To teach him what's what.* Say what she might, Helen couldn't accuse him of ignoring the boy. When Mitch showed an interest in baseball, Danny volunteered to coach his Little League team. When he asked to go fishing, Danny taught him to tie his own flies. On his sixteenth birthday, Danny bought him a Winchester twenty-gauge pump and took him to the skeet range, where Mitch blasted clay pigeons from the sky.

Yet in each case, the boy's passion had died before it could flower. He'd shown a knack for the Winchester, exhaling before his shot and leading the clay target even after he'd fired, but the few times they'd gone hunting and a living, breathing rabbit broke from wintry scrub, he forgot all he'd learned. A panic would seize him, and he'd throw the gun to his shoulder and let go wildly, gouging the earth with buckshot a yard behind the fleeing animal.

"What the hell was that?" Danny Baker said once after he'd killed the rabbit himself with his twelve gauge, but Mitch was already stalking away, leaving Danny to fetch the creature from a red pinwheel in the snow. "Get your head out of your ass," he shouted at his son's retreating back.

"Don't fret," Chet Newell had said later that spring. "When the worm turns, he'll make you proud."

By then Mitch was seventeen and spending night and day with the older Troyer boy, Lloyd. When summer came, they passed hot afternoons at Stone Lake, where they misted their hair with lemon juice so the sun would bleach it blonde. The juice didn't take for Lloyd, but Mitch's curls turned nearly white, and he wore skintight jeans and sleeveless black t-shirts and a rawhide braid around his throat.

"Just look at him," Danny had said to Helen. "He's a hoodlum, a good-for-nothing." She'd begged him to wait out the phase, even after tales of fights—a meanness in their son that frightened even older boys—began to reach their ears.

"He can be the sweetest child you ever saw," she'd said, "but when someone pushes him, all he knows is to push back." Danny had felt her sideways glance as she said it, but he scoffed and shook his head.

When the teal blue '57 came up for sale and Danny found that its straight-six engine had bad compression and leaked oil, he snapped it up for a song. He saw himself and the boy changing the engine mounts and dropping in a rebuilt V-8, passing tools back and forth, hands foul with grease, knuckles bloody from when a wrench slipped off a head bolt.

"You won't be sorry," he'd said after he'd parked the car in the pole barn. He lifted the hood and leaned in, snuffing like a chef over a pot roast. "Any man who doesn't know the internal combustion engine regrets it sooner or later." Mitch had lolled beside him, chewing a thumbnail and tapping a foot on the floor, but he kept the old crankcase filled with oil while they waited for the new engine from the machinist, and sometimes Danny came home to find him soaping down the Chevy in the driveway.

Danny looked up to find himself crossing the bridge back into town. A moment of vertigo came over him—he'd been so lost in thought he'd forgotten where he was—and he remembered something Sam Troyer had said in the office that morning. When Mitch and Lloyd had peeled from the alley and raced out of town, Marvin first stood at the corner to watch them go, then waited for men to appear so he could tell them what happened, then climbed into the buggy, pointed the sorrel's nose east and lay down on the seat and cried.

"How'd you get home like that, boy?" Danny had asked.

"*Ach*," Sam Troyer had answered for his son, "the horse knows the way."

Now Danny shook off his dizziness and squinted at the sun, deciding it was after three o'clock. He was starving—he hadn't eaten since the day before—and he drove to the house for a sandwich. There, Helen met him at the back door and told him Chet Newell's man was dead. An autopsy would say for sure, but the doctor surmised that the injury

Toby had suffered years before had created a swollen place that had never fully subsided, and the blow from the bat had caused it to weaken and finally give way.

"He went to sleep and never woke up," she said, and then, "Oh, Danny." She stood on the deck—the deck he'd built ten years before, while Mitch played among the tools and extension cords and stacks of weather-treated lumber—and hugged her bare arms against the October chill. He stared at her, his large hands hanging uselessly at his sides, then walked to the pickup, hoisted his body onto the driver's seat and drove away.

Samuel Troyer lived at the end of a dirt lane, with poplar trees lining the sides and a disordered collection of buildings at the end. As Danny parked, he saw there were actually two houses on the property—a large one from where Sam and Marvin and various younger children emerged to meet him, and a smaller house beyond it, where an old man stood in a doorway and watched his approach. A barn sat on a stone foundation above the houses, and grain bins and sheds lay randomly about. The big sorrel gazed at Danny from a nearby pasture, motionless but for the flicking of its ears. He stepped from the truck and walked toward the main house.

"I don't like the looks of this," Sam Troyer said as the two men came together. He was hatless, his sleeves rolled above his forearms. Marvin stood silently at his elbow, but the other children hung back and stared, their faces smooth and innocent as dew melons. "I'm guessing you have something, Dan."

Danny opened his mouth to speak, but the dizziness from the bridge came over him again. He reached out and gripped Samuel's shoulder, both to steady himself and to pull the man away from his children.

"We need to talk," he croaked. He looked at Marvin. "We need to talk alone."

The two men walked toward the pasture where the sorrel horse waited, and there Danny leaned against the rail fence and tried to clear his head. "Sam," he said at last, "Toby's dead."

"*Ach, Mein Gott.*"

"He's dead," Danny said again. "Our sons are murderers now."

The Amish man's lungs filled like organ bellows, and as he exhaled, he began to mutter words Danny didn't understand. The horse nickered softly and pressed its nose into Danny's chest, and he cupped one hand beneath its silky muzzle and lifted the other to grip its mane, and in that moment he remembered eight-year-old Mitch in the crook of his arm as the two of them looked at the Sunday comics—*Blondie, Gasoline Alley, Orphan Annie*—and Mitch reading the words aloud because he was a good reader and Danny was not, and Danny squeezing a fistful of the boy's hair the way he now squeezed the sorrel's mane, and the urge coming on him to squeeze harder and harder until Mitch whimpered and squirmed, and then Danny, letting go and stroking his son's hair smooth and being proud of the boy's toughness and the clever way his voice went high or low depending on the character he was imitating.

Danny pressed his face into the horse's neck and, for the first time since he was a child, let go a half dozen hard, choking sobs. The sorrel tried once to pull away, but Samuel Troyer clicked his tongue against his teeth and the animal settled, its flank trembling and its giant heart thudding against Danny's cheek. After a while he straightened to rest both hands on the fence. "Sam," he whispered, "it was Mitch swung the bat. It likely won't matter to the law, but Lloyd didn't hurt anyone."

"Yah, Marvin told me."

"As for Marvin, he didn't know what was going on. He told the truth the moment he had a chance. There'll be no trouble on that score."

"Yah, *danke.*"

Danny Baker turned. The Amish man was staring away over the empty fields, his arms crossed upon his chest. "Ah, Sam, we've lost our boys," Danny cried out.

Sam Troyer shook his head. "You don't know the Amish," he said, not unkindly. A tear ran unchecked down his cheek and into his beard. "When Lloyd gets out, however long from now, and if he wants to come home—" He looked toward the smaller of the two houses. "I'll probably be in the *daadiheiser* by then, and Marvin in the big house with a wife of his own." He turned to Danny. "If Lloyd wants to come home, there'll be a place for him at the table. There'll be cows to milk."

Later, as Danny climbed into the pickup to drive back to town, he heard Samuel call his name and looked to see the man walking toward him. He rested his forehead on the steering wheel until Sam reached the truck's window.

"Dan," the Amish man said, "there's something else. I don't know what it means, but Marvin—" He spoke with great sadness. "Sometimes I think the boy's a mite touched, but he thinks the world of his brother Lloyd." A tear spilled down his face again, and he wiped it with the back of a fist. "Marvin has said something to me three times—not once, but three times—about when Mitch and Lloyd drove away from the hardware store last night." He stared at Danny, his eyes burning with a strange light. "He told me that when the car went east out of town, it was *lifted up*. He stood at the corner and watched 'til all he could see was taillights, and then the car was lifted up, he said, like Elijah was lifted up in a whirlwind." Samuel put a hand on Danny's arm where it rested on the window frame. "Dan, Marvin thinks God lifted Mitch and Lloyd into heaven, and that's why you won't find them. I don't know what it means, but three times now he's said it."

The sun was low as Danny crossed the truss bridge back into Sellersville. The clouds had disappeared, and the sky was a hard, twilight blue. He would go home to see Helen, then get on the phone with law enforcement up and down the state. How the Chevy hadn't been spotted yet, he didn't understand, but experience told him nobody ran for long. They always panicked. They always made a mis—

He braked so hard the nose of the truck nearly touched the pavement. He sat in the middle of Warren Street and stared straight ahead, where the town's only stoplight changed from red to green five blocks away, and the white front of Newell's Hardware gleamed beneath it on the corner. He pulled onto the shoulder and turned the pickup's nose east toward the bridge, on the path the fugitives had taken out of town. He looked into his rear view mirror and watched the stoplight change again behind him. An Amish boy standing at the corner of Main and Warren Streets would have an unbroken view to where he sat.

He remembered Mitch throwing the shotgun to his shoulder, losing all acquaintance with his training when a flesh-and-blood target presented itself. Or Mitch casting a newly tied fly into Rat Run Creek and tangling it in a snag and succumbing to a rage so fierce he threw his rod into the water. Or Mitch running the bases like a boy possessed, ignoring the third base coach and tearing for home, where the catcher waited calmly with the ball.

Mitch in a blind panic, driving a teal blue Chevy away from where he'd just beaten a man to the floor with a ball bat.

Danny swore and leaped from the truck and ran to the grassy overhang south of the bridge. There the bank sloped steeply to the water's edge, and he immediately saw fresh gouges on the sandy decline, fresh scars in the stands of milkweed and wild carrot and lamb's quarters, where a car might recently have tumbled, its taillights lifting skyward as its nose plunged toward the dark water.

He shouted and half scrambled, half fell down the bank. Boys had forever used the slope as a daredevil place in the winter, tilting over the bluff on saucer sleds and down to the icy surface, but now the river was swollen from September rains and flowing fast. He reached the water and waded in but was immediately waist-deep, the current threatening to take him off his feet. He lurched to the bank and struggled up the slope again, grasping roots and ragweed stalks. When he topped the bluff, he ran to the middle of the bridge and stared downward. The evening light reflected the sky back to him, but even so he could make out the Chevy's dark shape beneath the surface, its teal blue color obscured by swirls and eddies and the ghostly fingers of underwater plants, and because the Bel Air rested on its roof.

When Helen Baker heard the sirens, she went to the deck and listened, deciding finally that they came from town, not from the country, where Danny had told her the boys were hiding. Someone had had an accident, or maybe there'd been a heart attack in one of the stores.

She went back into the house and sat in the living room. She held a sodden hanky in her fist, though she was done with crying and had begun to bargain indignantly with God. Surely the fact that Mitch had no criminal record would mean something. Surely the fact that he hadn't meant to kill poor Toby would figure into a judge's decision. Surely the fact that her husband was a town marshal and a respected—no, beloved—member of the community would impact what came next.

She gestured angrily to the darkening room. If a miracle allowed for it, if Mitch was ever a member of the household again, things would be different. Danny Baker was a fine man—everybody said so—but he'd never given the boy his proper due. He'd never seen how gentle Mitch could be, how happy he was to have a real friend at last in Lloyd, how the two of them idled around the house when just she was home and joked with her and each other.

She rose and went to the kitchen, where she tidied the countertop for the third time that day. It was then that she heard the sound, a tolling that might have come from a distant church, but more uneasy in timbre and less regular in occurrence. She stepped onto the deck again and saw her husband's pickup truck in the driveway outside the pole barn, its headlights on and pointed into the open barn door. The sound was coming from within, and though she was barefoot, she stepped onto the grass and hurried toward it.

She entered and saw her husband standing in the glare of the headlights and beating the engine block with a sledge hammer. The engine bucked crazily on its chain, its shadow monstrous against the wall as sparks showered down with each blow. Danny was shirtless, and he grunted as he swung the hammer, and in his nakedness, in the chaos of light and shadow, in the sparks that flew, he looked like an ironsmith shaping the Earth's most rudimentary parts.

Then Helen saw that Danny's khaki trousers were soaking wet, as was his shirt where it lay on the concrete floor at her feet, and a terrible truth came upon her, and she began to scream his name. She screamed and screamed, but her voice was lost in the din of hammer on steel and in the echoes that rang against her ears like a cold, rebuking bell.

Sidney's Sound

Corey Mertes

When I was thirteen, a retarded boy moved into my neighborhood. His name was Sidney Happ.

I say *retarded*, but I mean something else, I don't know
exactly what, the politically correct term for it—developmentally disabled,
maybe, or severely autistic. None of us really knew for sure what was
wrong with Sidney. At the time, we said retarded.

I say *boy*, but in fact he was eighteen the year I knew him. In addition
to his other infirmities, Sidney had been diagnosed with epilepsy. To
protect him from head injury in the event of a seizure, he wore a thick
leather helmet that made him look like one of those old-time football
players, like Red Grange. Sometimes we saw him without the helmet.
His hair was thin and showed signs of premature aging. He was a large

boy, packing what must have been two hundred and sixty pounds onto a noticeably bowed frame. If he hadn't stood so stooped over, he would have been well over six feet tall.

Sidney moved into the house where his parents and younger sister lived, close to the park. Prior to that, he'd been in some kind of private home for people who require long-term care; and prior to that he'd been in a public institution. The conditions were derelict there, or so the story goes, and Sidney didn't thrive. So his parents, who, like most of the families in our neighborhood, were getting squeezed by the widening wealth gap, worked longer and harder until eventually they were able to afford the private facility, where they knew Sidney would find life more rewarding. He'd been there two years when the recession began. Sidney's father was an early casualty of that downturn when he was laid off from his supervisor job at a company that sold heavy construction equipment. Before long, the family could no longer afford to keep Sidney in private care. Talk among the stay-at-home moms in the neighborhood, of which my mother was a charismatic figure, had it that Sidney's father refused to send Sidney back to the public facility. Instead, the family committed to somehow taking care of him at home until rosier economic times arrived.

At first they could afford a part-time nurse, who stayed with Sidney during the day while his mother worked and his father looked for employment. When money became too tight, however, they dismissed the nurse, and the job of watching Sidney turned into a family responsibility, most often falling on a grandmother who had recently moved in, presumably for that reason, or to Sidney's fourteen-year-old sister, Meg, when she wasn't in school.

I remember my first sighting of Meg. It was early summer of that singular year. Ten months older than me, she had just finished her freshman year at the high school I would attend in the fall. She hadn't gone to my junior high, so when I watched her approach the park with Sidney in tow, it was the first time I could remember seeing her, even though, as I later learned, her family had lived in the neighborhood since she was a small child. Her hair is what I remember best: blonde, shoulder-length, and straight as the A's she was later famous for in school. She's the first girl I can remember having hips that registered as a body part distinct from her legs and torso.

We were playing football, me and Alvie and Chris and the other boys. We played a lot of football that year. I hung out with kids a little older than I was, perhaps drawn to them, or them to me, because I was large and athletic for my age, later earning a football scholarship to a small southeastern college. We were a good bunch of kids, I don't mind saying, the kind of kids who would allow an oafish, disabled boy to join our game, even if that meant we had to design the plays with his limitations in mind. When Meg asked if her brother could play, Alvie didn't hesitate to welcome him to the huddle.

It worked out great. It was said that Sidney had the mind of a two-year-old. No one knows for sure. He couldn't talk, we knew that. He had a distinctive laugh, his primary way of communicating—a goofy, retarded boy laugh (sorry, that's just what we called it) that made it impossible not to laugh along with him. He laughed especially hard when all the boys from both teams gang tackled him. We did this sometimes even though, under our rules, Sidney, unlike the rest of us, had only to be touched to be considered down since it would have been impossible for any one or two of us much smaller kids to get him off his feet. Sometimes we gang tackled him for fun just to hear him laugh. He would carry us ten or fifteen yards and then fall on purpose and encourage us to pile on. He loved football as much as we did.

Whenever Sidney played, Meg read books on a nearby bench. When she got tired, she would call to him and he would come running. He always did exactly what she said. Around the third or fourth time he played, I can remember wondering about Meg, about her home life with Sidney, about the kinds of books she read. Occasionally she would watch the game, and it wasn't long before I found myself unwittingly trying to impress her. None of my friends had had a girlfriend yet. The few boys my age who had kissed a girl, or just been with one semi-privately, on the fringes of some birthday party or school mixer, were still snickered at by the others, not envied as they would be just a couple years later. Nevertheless, there I was one sunny June afternoon, rising over my best friend Alvie for an impossible catch that left him prostrate, and strutting into the end zone where I did a celebratory dance—so common now at the professional level, though rarely seen back then—with a flashiness I would ordinarily deride and still do today. I recall looking Meg's way and feeling disappointed that she seemed to have missed the show, instead watching Alvie brush himself off and head back to his teammates, saying "My fault. Won't happen again." That was Alvie. He had his head on straight. Normally I would just spike the ball after a touchdown, but Alvie wouldn't even do that. He would lay it on the ground or give it to one of his blockers to spike. Alvie was in high school, a year older than me. He and Meg shared a class called The History of Western Civilization.

One day, a couple weeks after my end zone display, Alvie did something surprising. It was one of those clear, breezy, hot-but-not-too-hot summer days that somehow, in later years, become exclusively associated with youth. It was also the day we first heard what we thereafter referred to as Sidney's sound. Not his laugh, something else: a two-part sound that originated deep in Sidney's throat—from as deep, it seemed, as the innermost mysteries of his soul.

Meg wasn't there that day. I didn't know why her family would trust us with Sidney. We were responsible kids by and large, but as far as I knew, none of us had any idea what to do if Sidney had one of his seizures, which we had heard about but never seen. Sidney was on my team, running with the ball when he was touched down, but he kept going anyway. For fun, the boys on the other team tried to gang tackle him, and when they couldn't get him down, my other teammates, Terry Crouch and Chris Hopkins, and I joined in. Sidney dragged all of us, laughing the whole time. And we laughed too before finally letting go, at which point Sidney, still chuckling goofily, lumbered into the end zone and spiked the ball. His delight was only finally cut short by a blunt appraisal from across the field.

"Pathetic!"

We all turned. We hadn't noticed the five boys approaching, all neighborhood kids a year or two older than us who went to the high school, each from a rougher line. The voice was from their leader, Ricky Sordo, who came by his reputation as a bully honestly.

"How many girls does it take to tackle one retard?"

Ricky's father had been to prison. His mother, a slim, tiny, muscular woman whose gregariousness secured her acceptance among the mothers in the neighborhood despite her former affiliation with her ex, often inadvertently exposed marks of violence, like a burn along her upper back or a neck bruise covered with foundation, rumored to have been inflicted by her never-seen boyfriend.

"*Huh huh huh huh huh*," one of Ricky's cohorts sounded, mocking Sidney's laughter.

I called out to leave Sidney alone, but my bravery had limits. As they advanced, I backed away slowly. Alvie held his ground and kept silent. I might have held mine too, if Meg had been there. It occurred to me that my initial instinct to stand up to them came in part because I'd forgotten that she wasn't.

"What are you going to do about it, sic the retard on us?"

None of us responded. We looked at each other, sizing up our latent combat abilities. Then, out of the blue, Sidney did something really shocking: He picked up the ball he had spiked moments earlier, lowered his head, and ran directly at the bullies, with his free arm rigid in front of him like the ancient halfback he resembled. His targets parted to avoid the onrush, and when he turned in the direction of a pair of them, one of them stuck out his foot to bring Sidney down. It didn't work. Sidney barreled past them, halted himself, turned and came at them again. This time, one of them stepped out of the way before lunging at Sidney's shoulder and ball arm, latching on. That slowed Sidney down; it didn't stop him. Nor was he checked when two others tried to join in the tackle, one at his thighs, the other around his waist. Sidney kept churning his legs and twisting his body violently, like one of our heroes at the time, the great Earl Campbell. When Ricky and the last of his disciples joined in the assault, Alvie and I moved to help Sidney by peeling the roughnecks back. The effort proved unnecessary. Sidney shook them off himself, harshly, one at a time, despite their attempts to punch at the ball, at his stomach and chest—even, I think, once, at Sidney's head. After he stomped his leg free from the grasp of the final boy, a kid named Delbert, lying on the ground, Sidney made his sound: "*Uuuuuuhhhhhhr! Uuhhhhhhhhhrrrrr!*"

He made it with his mouth wide open, his tongue rolled back, and his eyebrows arched and straining over small brown eyes. It was not a sound of triumph. The first part startled us; we thought it was a train. The initial note, which lasted about three seconds, was followed by a brief silence. The second part sounded similar except lower in frequency and longer lasting. It tailed off, as if the train had passed and then disappeared around a bend. Had I heard it several years later, after learning the term in high school science, I would have likened Sidney's sound to the Doppler effect.

"What the hell?" Ricky said, and he and his accomplices laughed. Undeterred, Sidney kept making the noise:

"*Uuuuuuhhhhhhr! Uuhhhhhhhhhrrrrrr!*
Uuuuuuhhhhhhr! Uuhhhhhhhhhrrrrrr!"

The third time, he pointed at Ricky and his gang as though Sidney was the one amused. By then they had stopped laughing.

"Why doesn't he shut up, Ricky?" one of them said, confused.

Ricky's friends stared at him as if they expected him to do something, but for a change he didn't seem to know the proper way for a bully to respond. "Because he's a freak," he said, finally figuring it out.

"Why don't you shut that freak up?" he barked, challenging all of us.

"Why don't you?" Alvie responded. Good old Alvie. We steeled ourselves for an attack.

Sidney continued making his sound while Ricky shuffled his feet and then took a step in Sidney's direction. His friends did the same. Alvie shifted sideways, in front of Sidney, emboldening the rest of us to form a blockade as the bullies advanced. I don't remember who pushed first; there was a scuffle, a brief interlocking of limbs, before Sidney abruptly stopped making his noise.

"Look! Sidney!" Terry yelled. Sidney was having a seizure and had hit the ground hard. The scrum between the rival groups ended.

"What is that? What's going on?" Ricky asked in a worried tone.

Alvie reacted immediately. "Help me turn him on his side!" he cried, rushing to where Sidney lay shaking.

Terry obeyed, and together they rotated Sidney as saliva leaked from his mouth. "He'll be okay, just wait," Alvie said.

Ricky and his companions glanced around nervously, bouncing on their toes, not concerned for Sidney I'm sure, instead worried that authorities of some kind might show up.

"Let's get out of here, Ricky," Delbert said.

Ricky hesitated and then suddenly turned and ran, followed closely by his friends. The rest of us waited out the seizure while Chris sprinted to Sidney's house. By the time he and Meg were rushing toward us minutes later, the seizure had ended. She cradled Sidney's head on the ground until he was calm. When finally we helped him get to his feet, the sun was beginning to set. Meg walked him home. Halfway there, she looked over her shoulder. Alvie, the closest to them, gave her a little wave and smiled.

"Man, Alvie," Chris said once they were out of view. "How'd you know what to do when Sidney went down?"

Alvie just shrugged. We decided there was enough light for one or two more possessions. Only Alvie declined, citing undone chores. In the distance, I could see him turn at the last moment in the direction of Meg and Sidney's home.

Alvie and Sidney had something in common besides their love of football. Like Sidney's father, Alvie's father lost his job during the recession, the month Sidney moved in with his family. Also like Sidney's father, Alvie's dad had a lot of pride. As there were no jobs in his field (he'd been a manager at a box factory, as I remember it), he took the only paying position he could find, as a server in a local pizza chain restaurant called The Italian Garden. Because the place had a pool table, it served as a summer hangout for many of us kids.

One day while Alvie's father was working lunch at The Italian Garden, the main actors from the park episode came together again, purely by chance. Alvie and I were having a slice of pizza at the counter when Ricky Sordo and his friend Delbert came in. The place was crowded, and at first they didn't see us. Through the mirror behind the counter we watched them lay quarters on the pool table and take a seat by the window.

"You want to get out of here?" I said to Alvie.

"Uh-uh."

Something had happened to Alvie since Sidney's seizure. His humility had evolved into something more textured, more dark even—a moodiness or preoccupation that occasionally seemed to border on despair. He didn't confide in me anymore. And he didn't play ball with our gang as much, often citing unspecified "commitments." We were eating in silence a few minutes later when Meg and Sidney walked in. I noticed them first. When she saw us, I was sure I caught a gleam in her eye before she began to steer Sidney in our direction.

I gave Alvie a nudge. "Look who's here."

He looked up. Immediately, his eyes shimmered in a way identical to Meg's. It lasted only an instant, until he realized there might be danger for Sidney with Ricky in the room. With the slightest nod toward the window, he conveyed that concern to Meg. She saw Ricky, and instead of continuing in our direction, sat with Sidney in a booth off to the side, making sure his back was to us all.

During the next few minutes, Alvie repeatedly glanced over his shoulder at Meg. I watched her in the mirror peek our way now and then, unable to tell for sure if it was Alvie or me she was making eye contact with. Alvie and I didn't say a word to each other.

"These haven't been touched, guys," Alvie's father said, rousing us from our trance. "It's on me." He slid two milkshakes in front of us and went back to work.

"Your dad's cool," I said.

"Yeah, cool dad there, Nob." We'd been paying so much attention to Meg that we hadn't noticed Ricky and Delbert approach. "Nob" must have been some disparaging term that Ricky picked up from The Handbook for Bullies. Had Alvie been the target of Ricky's verbal assaults at school? If so, he had never let on. So much about high school, and even about Alvie, seemed intimidating and obscure.

"He's really moving up in the world," Ricky added sarcastically.

Alvie ignored him. He had turned a concerned eye in the direction of Sidney and Meg.

"Why don't you mind your own business, Ricky?" I said.

"What's your problem there, hotshot? I'm just complimenting Nob's cool dad."

Alvie tried to motion inconspicuously to Meg to get Sidney out of there. She saw what was going on and got him standing, but Sidney tracked her gaze and witnessed it too. He wouldn't allow her to guide him away this time; instead, he headed in our direction.

"What's your father doing these days, Ricky?" I said. "Still working for the state?"

I could be pretty witty for thirteen. Everyone knew Ricky was sensitive about his father. His eyes ignited. His upper body tensed. I stood up slowly, my chair screeching behind me. Somehow, with Meg in the room, I knew I wouldn't back off as I had in the park.

"Look who's here," Delbert said, indicating Sidney's approach, momentarily redirecting Ricky's anger.

"Well, well," Ricky said.

"Don't start, Ricky," Alvie said. He readied for a fight.

"I'll start whatever I want, Nob," and with the final word he lightly shoved Alvie's shoulder with his hand, which Alvie batted away. That small sequence triggered an unfortunate chain of events. Sidney took a step forward, and Meg, right behind him, tried to wrap him up with her arms.

"Let him go," Ricky said. "The retard wants to fight."

Sidney shook her off and stuck an arm out, as he had in the park, like Red Grange, with his palm facing forward, a few inches from Ricky's face. He started to make his sound, but Ricky didn't wait for him to finish, he slapped away Sidney's hand. Meg said "Hey!" but before anyone could do anything more in Sidney's defense, Ricky had shoved him backward, hard enough that Sidney tumbled into an empty table and chairs and fell sprawling to the floor.

That did it. Though I had long dreamed of heroics on the playing field, recently the scope of dream-worthy acts had expanded to include less grandiose ones—small gallant deeds in defense of the opposite gender. Sidney—and, by extension, Meg—needed help, so I hauled my arm back with the intent of throwing my first-ever punch. My aim was thwarted. Alvie's instincts were quicker. He knocked me away and with a wild flourish unleashed a punch of his own. Unfortunately, that brief act of pushing me aside had given his mark enough time to react. Ricky ducked the punch and struck back, connecting with his fist on the side of Alvie's head, sending him reeling. Meg, who had knelt down to help Sidney and was holding him to the floor to prevent him from re-entering the fray, reacted immediately.

"Alvie!" she cried.

In an instant, she was crab walking toward him. I lunged at Ricky only to be intercepted by Delbert with a stumbling half-tackle. Freed from Meg's grasp, Sidney got to his feet and charged at Ricky, who, having braced himself for my attack, didn't see him coming. Sidney met him full force, engulfing him in a bear hug that with Sidney's size and momentum carried them both to the floor. Once there, Sidney sat on top of him, pinning Ricky's arms down with his weight. And then Sidney just started belting him, striking wildly at Ricky's head, shoulders, neck, chest.

"Stop it! Sidney! Stop!" Meg cried, cradling Alvie's head. Ricky cried out, too, for help. When Delbert tried to save him, I held him back. After a few seconds, however, the beating became so severe that I not only let him go, I helped him try to pull Sidney away to end the barrage. Sidney would not be moved. He swatted us away like he did on the football field. The brutal scene only ended when Alvie's father and the manager rushed in and dragged him off, kicking and flailing. The entire skirmish lasted, at most, two or three minutes.

A month later, I saw Sidney for the last time, in church. I hadn't seen Sidney or Meg since that fateful day at The Italian Garden. My family arrived early. We sat near the back.

The Order of Services listed the subject of the sermon as "Forgiveness and Grace." Parishioners lined every pew. As was widely known by then, Sidney would soon be returned to the public facility from which his family had once rescued him. The Department of Family Services had conducted an investigation into The Italian Garden incident. Sidney had broken Ricky's nose and jaw. While Ricky was in the hospital, from which he had only recently been discharged, his mother had contacted multiple authorities. Investigators concluded that the Happs had been negligent in their care and were unable to keep Sidney safely at home.

Sure enough, the Happs showed up, and many heads turned. Meg entered first, wearing a blue and white sundress, with Sidney by her side. None of them noticed me or my family as they passed. As I watched Meg search for a seat a few rows in front of us, I was suddenly moved by the reappearance of a long-missing memory. Something about her gait triggered it: a bounce or a spring. I had seen it before. That slightly-on-her-toes carriage, I had seen it years earlier, in that very church, on one of my family's infrequent visits. In our congregation, young children were sent to the playground and basement classrooms during Mass, while teenagers attended the service with their parents. Meg and I must have been there at least once at the same time when we were kids of seven or eight, probably in a basement craft room at Christmas or Easter. I only noticed it at that moment, I think, not previously at the park, because it was the same location. I could recall nothing else about her from that earlier sighting. From that point forward, however—no, from further back even, from the moment she first showed up with Sidney in the park—I would never forget her. I would always keep an eye out for her in the hallways in high school, which began the following week, and always sense, even if I didn't look in her direction, whenever she was near. As her family filed into a pew, she saw me and gave a little wave. But her eyes did not illuminate like I knew mine did, and like hers did at The Italian Garden when Alvie was by my side. I meant nothing to her, that much was evident; she only waved because I was part of the group that played football with her brother. Nevertheless, I recognized then that she was and would always be my first love, forever unrequited.

Alvie's family arrived minutes later. Like the Happs, they were Sunday regulars. Alvie scanned the room when he walked in. When he saw me, he forced a smile. Noticing there were no seats near us, he shrugged, as if to say, *Sorry*, but I could see his relief, and then noticed his restrained excitement moments later when his father pointed out the Happs and directed his family to the row behind them. After some awkwardness about who would sit where, he ended up behind Sidney. Separated from Sidney by her parents, Meg looked over her shoulder at Alvie and they both smiled shyly.

"Today," the priest was saying minutes later, "we transition from God's grace toward us to the grace we extend toward one another and toward ourselves."

I watched them throughout the sermon. Meg snuck peeks at Alvie periodically, trying to be inconspicuous. Her movements were transparent from where I sat, driven as much by compulsion as choice. The priest would begin a parable—"There was a powerful king who had a servant who owed him ten thousand talents"—and Meg would capitalize on the adults' engagement to glance backward. When he would say something that sounded potentially controversial—"Jesus is saying, in essence, 'Peter, you forgive as many times as necessary'"—she would pretend to want to see her father's reaction by turning sideways, then her eyes would give away her real intent, searching behind for affirmation from Alvie, whom, I finally had to admit to myself once and for all, she adored.

I yearned to be in his place. At first, he avoided meeting Meg's glance, turning instead toward his parents to see if they noticed her obsession. Then he would steal a glimpse himself to determine if she was still looking, and if she wasn't, he would stare at the side of her head until she sensed his gaze and turned around again. Finally, once, when she did, he didn't turn away, they locked eyes, and that's when I knew for sure what I had suspected that first day in the park and feared later in The Italian Garden.

Meg's father saw the way they looked at each other too, and smiled a melancholy smile reminiscent of his larger troubles. Only at that moment did I know for certain that she and Alvie had been spending time together privately, that he knew her family and they trusted him enough to have let Sidney play with us without Meg the day of his seizure. Perhaps he'd even witnessed a previous seizure while visiting Meg at their home. In any event, the family knew Alvie would react capably, as he had. The sight of the three of them in that instant aroused in me the first stirrings of a burgeoning transformation. My physical and emotional proximity somehow rendered me capable of understanding something new and significant about my evolving identity—about sacrifice and longing, responsibility and pride, about everything that makes a man different from a mere boy.

The setting appeared suddenly bolder. For the first time, I noted the iconography on the priest's vestments and the colors behind the altar on the porcelain Virgin Mary. I sat up straight, feeling as though a reservation had been made for me for some unique future place in the world, a world of choices and consequences, suffering and rewards.

"God's Word tells us that we've been washed clean with the blood of Christ, and our sins are removed through the atoning work that Jesus did for us, yet we still could kick ourselves for our mistakes."

Though I hadn't been paying attention to the sermon, I could tell the priest was nearing the end, pacing back and forth excitedly, beginning his crescendo. He seemed to look directly at the Happs as he finished up, as though speaking only to them.

"Then we are basically saying, 'I don't care what the blood of Jesus has done. I still hate myself for what I've done!'"

The Happs were riveted, even Meg. I was watching her when she turned toward Alvie again. This time, to my amazement, she had tears in her eyes.

"It's staggering to think such a thing, but that is what really happens when we refuse to forgive ourselves."

At first, I had no idea why she was crying. Alvie was looking away, so she turned back to the priest as he continued his summation. Then, still with a tear in one eye, she turned around again, this time meeting Alvie's gaze, and mouthed what appeared to be the weightiest of words: "I love you."

My heart crumbled. Alvie mouthed something back—"Me too," I assumed at first, although it looked more like "I will" when I thought about it further. With all the bodies between us, and the priest going on so animatedly, maybe I had read my own fears into Meg's words. Maybe she had said something else entirely, not "I love you," but only two words: "Help me."

From the corner of her eye, Meg saw me and knew I had witnessed their exchange. She spun forward, never to know that I couldn't tell for sure what she had said. Alvie turned to see what had startled her. His face seemed older than when he had entered the church. We exchanged nods, smiles, silent acknowledgment of our dimming friendship and our mutual feelings for Meg. The priest brought his sermon to a resounding close.

"Accept His gift with great joy and begin to see your failures as being paid in full by the sacrifice that Christ made for you. Begin to see yourself the same way that the Heavenly Father sees you!"

And then suddenly, on cue, as if to punctuate the idea, Sidney made his sound: "*Uuuuuuhhhhhhr! Uuhhhhhhhhrrrrrr!*"

It was a raucous bray. Everyone was stunned except the priest, who seemed prepared for the outburst. When Sidney finished, without missing a beat Father Kern pointed at him and said triumphantly, "That's a BIG Amen, Sidney!" And then by reflex, every adult called out in unison, "*Aaaaaaaa-men!*"

Not one person under the age of eighteen did the same. Instead, every one of us, me and Meg and Alvie included, having never made, or in most cases even heard, Sidney's sound before, mimicked it as best we could. We did so not mockingly but in spontaneous tribute, expressing our understanding through repetition, the way children are taught.

"*Uuuuuuhhhhhhr! Uuhhhhhhhhrrrrrr!*"

That chorus was followed by a silent, breathless pause, during which, for reasons I cannot explain, I came to understand even more of what previously had been so unclear. Why Meg had tears, for example, when the priest spoke of self-forgiveness. How, in The Italian Garden, having given in to her budding passions by tending to Alvie instead of holding Sidney back, she must now feel guilty about the pounding that impulse allowed her brother to give and for the subsequent consequences for him and her family. How those tears might also be a reflection of her parents' related guilt over their inability to do more for Sidney, a result of their unique combination of burdens. And though I couldn't recognize it then, the seeds were planted too of my later understanding that Meg was learning adult lessons just as Alvie and I were: that with love comes longing; with responsibility, guilt; with anticipation, fear; and with success, the duty of humility.

The moment passed, and Sidney responded to our salute by sounding off again, louder than ever, as if all the pain and complexity and frustration of his condition and all the beauty, injustice, and regret in the world were contained in that complicated roar. Again the teenagers echoed it, and again the priest and adult congregants, by now smiling or laughing out loud, demonstrated their approval with a symphony of *Aaaaaaaa-mens*. And so it went, with the adults Amen-ing, and we teenagers repeating Sidney's sound as if voicing sympathy, at a time of transition in our lives, for a boy who would never change.

Meg and Alvie and I, I noticed, were the first to go silent. It occurred to me that how Sidney's sound was perceived and what an appropriate reaction should be depended upon where you stood relative to it, what point you were at on life's iron curve. In mid-life now, divorced, nostalgic, I still marvel at how little we know about the emotional life of those closest to us, how inadequate we are at expressing what we feel. Alvie and I largely went our separate ways during high school. He and Meg dated for most of it and then went their separate ways too, although I heard they stayed friends. Recently, I searched for them both on Facebook, without success.

In church that day she looked back at him again, no longer teary-eyed. Her beleaguered parents appeared briefly happy as they called out Amen after Amen. In the moments before Sidney's sound and its responses died out, she and Alvie and I just listened, all smiles, reveling in that collective, transitory joy, that celebration of monosyllables, silently wondering what, if anything, would take its place at the end.

Snow Angels

Tatjana Mirkov-Popovicki

In Syria, I had a Barbie doll, a present from my uncle from his trip to Europe. In Canada, I got a Raggedy Ann, a present from Mrs. Ferguson, Alex's mom. Mrs. Ferguson owns the house. She and Alex live upstairs; my mom, dad, and I live in the basement. In Syria, and later in Istanbul, there were so many children, so many people. Here in Canada, it's just the five of us in this big house with a frozen backyard. And still, Alex says there is no privacy. His mother sticks her nose in all of his personal things. That's what parents do in Canada. There were no personal things and privacy where I came from. I never thought about it then, but that was before I was in love. Now I have Alex, and suddenly, I yearn for privacy too. Who would've thought?

I put on my snowsuit and fetch Raggedy Ann from the bedroom. We are visiting Alex's tree house in the backyard.

"Fatima, ver you going again? Outside is frizing," says my father, his English words coming out stiff and lumpy, as if his mouth is full of mud. Mom and Dad learn English in the community center and practice at home, and still they have a hard time remembering and pronouncing words.

"Ven is veding?" asks my mother and she giggles, but Dad doesn't laugh. He frowns and tells me to be back before dark.

The first time I saw Alex, I thought of Dumbo. He wore a puffy sky-blue snowsuit and a hat with floppy ear-protectors. He is twelve, just two years older than me, but he is almost as tall as my dad, and deliciously chubby. Imagine soft rosy cheeks and eyes large and blue like a character from a cartoon. Dumbo. Right away I wanted to hug him. His cheeks got rosier, his eyes rounder. "I'm Alex," he said. "I'm a restaurant critic."

I learned English in Istanbul from a Canadian lady, Miss Barbara. She never mentioned such a thing as a restaurant critic to me. I think that we had restaurants in Syria, but I don't really remember. I was very small when we left. We crossed the sea in a boat and arrived at the refugee camp in Istanbul. I don't really remember much except that there were many boats and people everywhere. I couldn't take my Barbie doll.

There were restaurants in Istanbul, but we didn't get to go to any of them. All we did was talk about the future with other people from Syria. I think that Alex would like Syrian and Turkish food.

Baklava, he writes in his notebook holding a pencil in his mittened hand, sitting cross-legged on the floor of the tree house. The sun makes a single orange stripe across the gray sky, painting the top branches of our tree pink. All the backyards we see from here are empty and white. I crouch next to Alex. Raggedy Ann sits in the corner, slumped against Alex's baseball. She hugs the ball with her left arm, red curls nicely cascading down her body. Alex's snowsuit is a magnetic mountain next to me. I wear a hand-me-down white one, which used to be Alex's when he was younger. Alex is next to me and all around me.

I describe how baklava looks and tastes and he writes it all down in neat, slanted letters. His breath smells of bananas. I lean as close to him as I can, soaking in his warmth.

It's bitterly cold. Rungs to the tree house were encrusted in ice like the frosting on the birthday cake Mrs. Ferguson baked for me last week. She is a professional writer. She writes articles for newspapers and magazines, and she has published a cookbook, which Alex and I sometimes bring to the tree house and read to each other. Alex will one day own a famous restaurant where all the restaurant critics from all over the world will come to dine and write fantastic articles describing the best dishes they've ever eaten in their life. Alex said that I can be the restaurant manager and tell everyone what to do.

The cake had coconut icing on it. We didn't have coconut icing in Syria. For my last birthday in Istanbul, I got baklava from a nice Turkish lady. Her name was Esma. She always gave me oranges and dates and all kinds of trinkets, which Mom then gave to other children in the refugee camp. Many children in Istanbul didn't have any toys. Some didn't have any food at all. Some didn't even have parents.

"Establishment?" Alex looks at me.

"Aunt Esma's kitchen. In Istanbul." I watch him write this down.

"How many stars?" asks Alex. His lips are red and moist, but the little golden hairs below his nose are stiff with white frosting. He looks at me quizzically, his woolly paw with the pencil hovering, ready to draw in one, two, or three stars. Three stars are the best. All entries in Alex's notebook have stars next to them, according to how much Alex enjoyed each meal. McDonalds, Big Mac, two stars. A&W, Teen Burger, two stars (three stars for the root beer). Red Robin, Sizzling Fajita, three stars. I wonder how the Sizzling Fajita tastes.

"Alex?" I watch the black circles in his blue eyes widen as I lean into his face, a banana-flavored cloud thawing frost from his eyebrows. A single drop falls from the tip of his nose onto the notebook, blotching the page.

"W . . . what?" He reminds me of Mrs. Ferguson's kitten when it comes to me, but runs away when I reach to pick it up.

"If I was food, what flavor would I be?"

His eyebrows go up. "If you were food?" He shifts a bit and purses his lips. "How . . . how would I know?"

I want him to answer my question. "Well, Alex." I fix my gaze on him. "You are a restaurant critic. You are an expert. You must have some idea how I would taste if you were to eat me." I flutter my eyelashes, trying to encourage him to think creatively. "Think outside the box." That's what they tell us in the Canadian school when we don't know the answer.

He takes his time, chews on the pencil and looks at the sky. He grins. He wipes the page with his mitten and starts to write a new entry in the journal, three lines below the one for baklava.

Sizzling Fatima, he writes. Establishment: Alex's Treehouse.

He tucks his chin deep into his collar but I can see him grin. He shifts to the side, hiding the notebook from me, so I have to grasp and tug at his arm, leaning all the way over his shoulder to see what else he is writing. He presses the pencil so hard, the letters come out black and large. Slowly and carefully he draws in one star. Two stars. Three, four, five stars. My jaw drops. I stare at him, but he snickers, shuts the notebook, and tucks it behind Raggedy Ann, then he jumps into the snow, ignoring the stepladder altogether.

"Sizzling Fatima," he calls out and laughs. I make my way down and join him, rolling in the snow. We wave our arms and legs, make snow angels, and yell at the top of our lungs. "Dumbo!" "Sizzling Fatima!" "Dumbo!"

It's getting dark and our parents' heads pop up in backlit windows, the house looking like a spaceship, aliens ogling at us before they abduct us and perform their gruesome experiments. One bobbing head on the top floor, two in the basement. Two snow angels in the backyard.

Love Lost and Found

It Formed a Heart

Mike Goodwin

I wanted to be a mother once, but working for a daycare center jaded me. It wasn't so much the work that was slowly killing me, though. Kids were kids; colleagues were colleagues. It was everything else that the job involved: low pay, exhaustion, the walk to-and-from, and the pressure to keep it.

Brian kept telling me he was looking for jobs, but I didn't believe him. It's a slow economy, sure, and we've got standards, too. But the ass indent on my couch told me his job application process seemed a bit too leisurely. I've been down this road before. I was getting tired of taking care of him. I was tired of taking care of everyone.

Recently, a guy at a bus stop offered me money to suck him off. "A hundred bucks," he said. The few seconds I took thinking it over told me a lot about myself in the moment.

"Me and my friend here," he said.

"Like a buy-one, get one? Do I look like a holiday sale?"

"Ho, ho, ho," said the friend.

"We won't take long," the man said. "He won't, anyway. Promise." They laughed. And I laughed. It was all I thought to do in the moment to keep walking home and avoid having them take for free what they were willing to pay for.

A black lab had been sniffing around storefronts and it began following me from an alley nearby, trotting alongside until I stopped to shoo it away. Literally. I took a heel and waved it at him. He sat when I waved my arm around and then he cocked his head at me. I threw the heel back where I found it, on top of an overflowing garbage can. His tail snapped at the ground a couple of times. He gave me a goofy smile, or what looked like one anyway, and when I looked to see for sure that he was, well, a he, I saw a spot of white fur on his belly. It formed a heart.

"I've had enough bad luck with your type." This was the point where he was supposed to bark a couple of times and we'd carry on a conversation that I would make up for us. I fast-forwarded to the end and sighed.

So I took it all as a sign that the world wanted me to fall in love again. I let him follow me home, where I told Brian to pack his shit and leave.

"Wait, where did you get a dog?"

"The same way I got you: He followed me home."

"You're really replacing me with a dog?"

I explored the stacked mess of our hall closet. My hall closet. "Do you even own a suitcase or do you just carry everything around in plastic bags?"

"I patiently wait for you to come home and this is what I get?"

"Oh, I know, the world owes you everything," I said. "We're all indebted to your presence. I should be so lucky to have someone so precious, so unable to work."

"Don't be a cunt."

"We all are, honey. Meeting's on Mondays."

The dog sat between us, panting. I stood over Brian, who remained on the couch until I kicked him in the shin. I told him again to get out. He stood, gave me an "are you serious" three or four times. I opened the door for him. Brian looked down at the dog and shoved him with the heel of his boot, sending him rolling across the carpet, crumbs and dust sticking to his fur. The dog squealed and ran for cover under a metal folding chair at the foldout table where we ate dinner when one of us bothered to make it.

The dog whined, so I pulled Brian by his arm, dragging him to the door, and punched him in the back of the head. He faltered and I slammed the door on him, locking it before he could force his way back inside. He pounded on the door until a neighbor came out and told him to piss off.

"I'm coming back tomorrow for my stuff!"

"Will be outside waiting for you." I leaned into the door and put my ear up to it.

"I want my books back too," Brian said, raising his voice with each sentence. "I want it all back. I'm not messing around! Just open the door!"

"Don't *you* worry about *your* graphic novels, much as I *truly* treasure them." I felt a punch to the door in my shoulder. The neighbor told Brian to leave again. Or else. After a cock-wagging contest—"yeahs," "oh-yeahs," and "yeahs" back and forth, with chests puffed out—the neighbor's wife—or girlfriend, or sister, or mistress—threatened to call the cops, and that was that.

Then the dog barked and it scared me up a wall. "I didn't realize you could talk, buddy." Now I was calling him buddy. We were pals now.

The vet told me the dog had a somatic mutation, that the heart wasn't a sign or a symbol of anything existential. Basically, he told me there was no hope for love in my life, though he had no idea that's what he was telling me.

"Have you tried to find the owner?"

"I only found the dog yesterday. He wouldn't leave my side."

"Make signs and hang them around where you found him. Sometimes a dog gets out without its tag. He doesn't seem to have a chip in him, though, so he might have been abandoned. Can't say for sure."

"You're telling me to use what little money I have to find a dog's possibly negligent owner?"

"We've got paper. We've got markers. We've got tacks. Do what you want. I'm just trying to help," he said. "But if you decide to keep him, it's costly. And then what happens if the owners come across you a month or two from now and think you've stolen their dog? You set yourself up for failure if you don't try."

"In another life, you were a motivational speaker, weren't you?"

"Take it or leave it. At least I'm not charging you for this." And with that, away he went to his next appointment. I apologized to the dog for the doctor's unfortunate bedside manner. I stood up from a hard, plastic chair, and when I moved for the door, the dog cut in front of me and I stepped on his paw. His squeal produced in me a similar sound I hadn't known I could release. I sat on the floor and checked his paw, kissing it several times. He panted. It looked like the dog was smiling, but a lot of them looked that way to me.

A parrot shrieked and squawked in the waiting room when I entered, and it made my request for simple supplies difficult to communicate. I wrote a crude sign that offered vague details of a lost, spotted black lab, writing the number of the veterinary office instead of my own. I didn't want random people showing up to my door for a dog, so I left my information with the front desk. Then I hung flyers on telephone poles on my way home, dog trailing close behind me, and the man from the bus stop catcalled me again.

"He'll chew your balls off," I said.

"I like it rough."

"With dogs? You like it rough with dogs? Because that's what I'm hearing."

The friend had a good laugh, so I made it past them once again without incident. I never really knew with those two, but the more it happened, the less I feared them getting violent. In that way, they were a lot like Brian. They were a lot like many others I had dated, sweet-talking in that dirty way, like their graphic flirtation was all in good fun until it actually worked out for them. It takes a certain boyish charm for that to work, and when it does, I often find they don't know what to do about it from there.

I had kept trying to get the dog to respond to a temporary name that suited us both on the way home. We stopped first at a pet supplies store where I purchased a bone, a thick rope, a squeaking ball, and a leash so I could avoid stepping on him again. I could only think of typical dog names that neither of us seemed to like: Sparky, Rocket, Fido, Spot, Max, Bear, Jack. They all felt too easy, so when we got home, I used commercials as a guide: Heineken. Target. Cap'n Crunch. Pepsi. Verizon. Gillette. None of them worked either. In the end, we settled on Taco. We were getting hungry.

I packed Brian's things a little later. They fit into one box. A large one, but still, I didn't expect that to happen. There were some shirts, comics, an old PlayStation and the games he owned for it, and several DVDs including a few pornos. He had a thing for cosplay and Asians. I had nothing against comics, really, but I couldn't eat Chinese food for a while.

I taped the box shut and left it outside for Brian so he could get it when I was at work. I used the sign supplies from the Vet's office, thought that I should return what was left, and within an hour of thinking about it, the vet called me. It was a fine coincidence. Maybe more, if I could convince myself. He wanted to know if anything turned up.

"In only a few hours? No such luck."

"That mutation might make him easier to find," he said. "Did you offer that as part of the description?"

"Hmm? Mm-hmm."

"Did you get him any food?"

"Shit, no I didn't," I said. "I got a leash though."

"Listen, I'd like to buy you coffee. I could fill you in on how to care for him in the short-term, give you some food that I've got, and maybe down the line we can go over what he needs long-term."

"Well," I said. "That would be nice, doctor." I ran through the internal Rolodex of men that have come and gone in my life. No doctors. This could be nice.

"Tomorrow afternoon good? Across from my office?"

"Does after my shift work? Say around four?"

"Sure does."

Taco sat with me in the activities room. He had been good with the kids, chasing some, and being chased by others. Some yanked on his tail what looked to me a little too rough, but he took it in stride, yanking back from them by pulling away and shaking it off.

When he seemed to tire of the children, Taco sat his butt down on my feet, panting, looking at all the commotion around the room, turning to me from time to time. I gave him an upside-down kiss. My first dog kiss, as far as I could remember. We were a thing now. More than friends. I avoided saying that last part out loud.

Kim, the manager, approached me. "A mother just demanded a refund because her child caught a cold."

"I haven't sneezed in a week."

"Tell me again why you have a dog now? And here?"

"I've heard scared dogs will tear your place apart if you leave them alone," I said. "He seems lonely. I can't leave him."

"Brian can't even manage a dog?"

"I finally kicked him out. Punched him, actually."

"What happened?"

"The dog, I guess."

"Surely there's more to it."

I thought for a moment. "I can only take care of one boy at a time," I said. "This one seems to appreciate me more."

"The dog is a liability," Kim said. "We've got enough to deal with around here. These parents are getting more high-strung by the day. I had a mother in here the other day requesting we put mosquito nets around the entire play area outside. Another one claims her child is allergic to wind."

"I'm in the process of locating his owner. If I can't find anyone, I'll have it figured out. I'm even meeting a handsome vet about it soon. No strange allergies, I'm betting."

"Do what you have to do," she said. "But the dog cannot be inside."

I walked Taco around the building a few times, escorting some of the kids around, too, while waiting for their parents to pick them up. Most were always on time, as the daycare leveled fines—five bucks a minute—for any parent who arrived late. Some of the staff stuck around until six o'clock though, for parents who paid for the extra time.

Usually after work, I'd return home, where Brian might be strumming my guitar along with a Beatles record. He was good, but not that good.

But I still preferred it to coming home and seeing him playing a game or watching a movie, especially one I wanted to watch. We didn't start out that way. He took me to movies before they got too expensive. "It's better to watch at home now, babe!" he'd say. But that wasn't the point. We were always home. Never going anywhere. Always trapped inside ourselves.

Instead, now after work I got to go for coffee. I started my days off with it. Straight black. "Like you like your men," one of my white exes said. A real winner, that one. But ending a shift with it after hearing riotous children all day doesn't do much of anything for me. I was already fried and shaky.

"It's how we meet new people," I said. "It's how we act like professionals. Over coffee. Or we sit alone and contemplate human existence. We blow off steam by blowing off this steam, unless you're too good for that and get one of those iced drinks. We drink those to maintain a sense of superiority over those who don't bother with it. Just don't ever call it a 'hot cuppa.' Don't ever be that person."

"I don't think I've ever said that in my life," the vet said.

"That's good to know. I dated a guy once who said it and it turned me off of coffee for a solid month. What is it about people that ruin things like that? I mean, why can't I continue enjoying a thing just because someone else makes it weird? Am I weird? Am I talking too much?"

"You're just fine."

Dr. Thomas Taylor. Doc Taylor. Tom after he paid for our drinks and a couple of bagels. Prospective husband after he told me to "Love Taco like family, like a child." Philandering husband after his wife called looking for him. Unpleasant option when he told me he was leaving her and it was just a matter of bureaucracy. Disappointing lover when he fucked me too fast at my place. Even Taco was embarrassed, waiting in the kitchen for us to finish. It was the first time he had strayed from me.

"He has separation anxiety," the doctor said. "Make sure you stay consistent with the attention you give him."

I stood in front of the sink, wiping my inner thighs with a wash rag, and asked, "And your wife?"

"What about her?"

"Did you give her enough attention?"

"She's a real battle axe," he said.

"Who says that?"

In that moment, a banging on the door shook the entire apartment. The muffled yelling that Brian projected through the thin apartment walls sounded accusatory, like I had forgotten to pack some of his possessions, or worse. He just kept banging on the door and screaming, "Let me in! I want the rest of my stuff!" I threw the wash rag into a pile of dirty clothes in the corner of my bedroom and put on the sundress I wore to meet the doctor.

Doc looked nervous as I let Brian inside. Taco ducked for cover under the chair again. The boys stared at one another, exchanged "who are yous" before their names, and I let Brian roam around the place looking for his porno, or his comics, or whatever the hell he was looking for. He didn't find it. I knew he wouldn't find anything. There was nothing of value here anyway, including the doctor. Brian left without saying anything else.

"I think I should leave, too."

"Do that."

"Get a microchip in the little guy," Doc said. "Be sure to keep track of him."

He left the door open, and when I went to shut it, I noticed my neighbor and the woman I saw with him earlier standing in the parking lot. They were yelling. She pushed him after a while. Did it a couple of times before he slapped her. She crumpled to the newly paved concrete, holding her face and moaning. I felt sweat accumulating on my lower back. I shut the door, quiet, and locked it the same way.

I needed to sit, so I settled into the couch with Taco for a movie. He fit right into Brian's indentation while I looked through what I owned. We watched *High Sierra*, an old Bogart film my father liked. By the middle, I was finally exhausted, wondering if I was crashing from the coffee, the sex, or everything.

On the second viewing of the movie, when neither of us still really wanted to move, I said, "You could have been an Otis." Taco's ears perked up and he raised his head. Then we heard a light knock on the door.

I expected it to be Brian, tail between his legs, coming to apologize. Instead it was a family: mom, dad, and child—a daughter. It was *the* family.

"Hello," the dad said. "We heard you might have found our dog? Do you have Taco?"

My mouth hung open until I said, "You named the dog Taco?"

"He got away from our daughter on a walk. Is he here?"

I shook my head and said, "That might be the strangest thing I've ever heard."

"So you have him then?"

I felt dizzy and I hesitated. I looked back at Taco, who stared at me with his head cocked. "Describe him," I said.

"He's a black lab with a white spot on his belly," the daughter said. "It's a heart."

"Alright," I said. "Come in."

Taco leaped over the couch and went right for the child. They rolled around the floor and Taco's tail bounced around, beating into the floor and furniture.

"So his name is really Taco?"

"I don't know what we'd do without him."

"He's a real charmer," I said.

"Thank you so much for taking care of him," the mom said.

"It's what I do. It's what I always do."

Each one hugged me as if I was a new member of their family, the daughter holding on extra-long. I was a bit rigid with it. I'm not a hugger. Never have been. Then it was the mom's turn, and over her shoulder I saw the leash and the toys I purchased but never used. I never got any food for him either. The dad gave me a quick one and a hundred bucks for my troubles. Seems like I should have been paid a little more, though. But then I'd really feel like I was for sale. And then the guys from the bus stop would really want in on me.

One Something
Happy Family

Mark Williams

M y friends call me Geo. Short for geography. For the past eighteen years I've taught teenage boys and girls the difference
between an island and a peninsula—in Florida: The Peninsula
State; The Sunshine State; The Orange, Flower, Alligator, Hurricane State.
As a University of Miami Hurricane in 1993, I met my wife, Lucinda, in
a class called Stream Dynamics, the gist of which was that streams are
ever-changing, immeasurable, and dangerous. A lot like marriage.

Two years ago, Lucinda left Foreverglades—the gift shop she manages
in Coral Springs—for her Pilates class and came home late. Two weeks

late. Turns out, she'd been practicing her newfound strength and flex-ibility on her thirty-three-year-old Pilates instructor, Maureen, for the past three months. Things had not been going well between Lucinda and me. Our marriage had become landlocked, and Lucinda found a friendly port.

I don't blame Lucinda. If I had met Maureen first, I might not have come home either. Petite, with fierce green eyes, curly red hair—ripped as a power forward. There she was, standing with Lucinda in my door-way the day Lucinda returned home to Archipelago—our Australian Shepherd—and me. "I miss Archie," Lucinda said as Archie ran circles around us. "Maureen is staying, too."

The following month, while at Furry Friends for Archie's nail trim, I met Chrissie—the translucent, purple-haired, twenty-six-year-old new vet tech. "I love your dog!" she said, gathering his clippings. That night, wearing my checkered Izod button-down, my khaki pants, and Asics Walkers, I took Chrissie to see *Foxcatcher*. The next day she took me shopping at Hot Topic for new clothes.

Six weeks later, Archie needs another nail trim. Nails clicking, he's herd-ing two shih tzus into a corner of the Furry Friends lobby when Chrissie walks in with a kitten in her arms. Immediately, a man about my age, dressed as I had dressed but weeks before—white Bermuda shorts, yel-low polo shirt, and sockless loafers—stands and talks to Chrissie in a whisper. Then, turning toward the door, the man passes by me on my bench. That's when Chrissie sees me, smiles, and shouts, "I love you!"

We'd been dating less than two months—eight, maybe ten dinners, a few movies, and, as for more intimate details, let's just say Chrissie has a way of making me forget where I am. And I teach geography. Still, *I love you?* But in the two seconds that elapse—before the man makes it to the door—I think, *Well what is love anyway, if not the desire to be with someone more than anyone—the isthmus that connects my North America to her South?* Okay, three seconds. "I love *you!*" I shout back to the obvious enjoyment of the people in the lobby. A woman with a corgi-mix breaks into applause.

"I was talking to my dad!" Chrissie hisses. The kitten's eyes grow wide.

"So *you're* the one!" Dad says.

The upshot of this is Chrissie's dad, Phil, is my new friend—runs a little bar in Pompano, called Phil's, popular with Wisconsin retirees for some reason. Chrissie has moved into our guest room with me—across the hall from Lucinda and Maureen. And, thanks to Chrissie, Archie's nails are always short.

But that day at Furry Friends, Chrissie, silver lip ring aquiver, one eye on her father, one on me—the lobby occupants' attention divided fairly equally—says, "We'll talk about this later! Dad, this is Geo."

"Geode?" Phil says.

So I'm in my classroom one spring afternoon, explaining to Parker Parkhurst that, no, after Thor Heyerdal built his bamboo raft, *Kon Tiki*, in South America, he did *not* get so hot he floated to Antarctica to cool off before giving a penguin a lift to Australia, where Thor *didn't* learn the words to "Kookaburra Sits in the Old Gum Tree," and he certainly didn't sing them all the way to Asia. Furthermore, neither did he recondition his soggy raft with fresh bamboo, nor did he drop off a lovesick panda in North America before continuing home to Europe. And his wife did not run away to Africa with Dikembe Mutombo. "It was a *story* to remember the *continents*, Parker!" I say just as my computer *dings* with an email from an old fraternity brother at the U who runs something called the South Florida Technical Institute, SOFTI—a junior college outside of Loxahatchee, thirty miles as the egret flies from the Big O: Lake Okeechobee.

Hey Geo,

In an effort to boost our graduation rate, we've decided to offer a summer course in intro to geography—Atlantic Ocean, Rocky Mountains, that sort of thing. 6:00 to 8:00 Wednesday nights. Interested?

Norman

P. S. Fifteen Hundred

The next thing I know it's June and I'm at SOFTI parked in my Sonata outside a metal building called Ponce de Leon Pavilion, fronted by an algae-filled fountain called, yes, the Fountain of Youth. I'm ten minutes early, time enough to eat a power bar and spoon a carton of yogurt before I'm due in class, when it occurs to me that I don't have a spoon. Plowing through my glove compartment (no spoon), I find the little, red-handled magnifying glass I sometimes use to look at maps. I'm dipping a small magnifying glass into my yogurt when an old security guard pulls up beside the Fountain of Youth in a golf cart. "You're in a restricted spot," he says—fit old guy, in a heavy-set way, chiseled face, gravelly voice: Jason Robards in *Parenthood*, his blue-capped head poked inside my window. "You'll have to move this car."

"I don't have a spoon," I say by way of explanation.

"A spoon?" he says.

The following Wednesday, fountain spluttering outside my classroom window, I spend the better part of three hours explaining Abraham Ortelius' radical 1596 notion of continental drift.

"Abraham who?" Jorge Dominguez asks.

"Ortelius, a Flemish cartographer."

"Say what?" Destiny Patmore inquires.

"Cartographer. A mapmaker. From the French word for map, *carte*," I explain.

"Where's Flemland?" Robby Rickhardt queries.

In 1627, German mathematician Joseph Furtenbach, in an attempt to prove the Earth rotates on its axis, shot a cannon ball straight into the sky. Betting his life that the ball would land slightly to the west as he rotated east, he leapt onto the cannon muzzle. My guess is Furtenbach taught college, that the outcome of his wager was win-win. The ball missed his head by inches.

Exhausted, I climb off *my* cannon fifteen minutes early, trudge past the Fountain of Youth, and, backing out of an authorized spot, bump into the old guy's cart. "Are you okay?" I shout, jumping from my car.

"You again," he says, easing from his cart. "I'll have to see some identification."

If the guy were thirty years younger . . . well, he isn't. And though it's still light enough outside for me to see the age marks on his face—the Orkney Islands mapped on his left temple—he whips a giant flashlight from his cart and shines it into my eyes. I comply.

"Roger L. Bosworth," he says, his flashlight lowered to my license.

"My friends call me Geo," I say, "like in *geography*."

"Harold, like in *Harold*. Harold Kingsley," he says, offering his hand. "I'm off at eight. Wanna grab a beer, Geography?"

"Uh, sure," I say. "Follow me to Pompano—place called Phil's."

"Roger that," Harold says, returning to his cart.

"My friends call me Geo," instinctively, I say.

For the next three months, Harold met me by the fountain every Wednesday after class. Then he'd follow me to Phil's—about a twenty-minute drive from SOFTI—in his Explorer. That first night we walked in—me in my new skinny jeans and black Radiohead t-shirt, Harold in his dark blue security suit and cap—Phil mistook him for *my* dad. "Your old man?" Phil said.

"No, this is Harold. Harold, Phil—my girlfriend's dad."

"You own this place?" Harold asked, knocking on Phil's bar as if it held the answer.

"Last I heard of."

"Ever thought about security?"

"No, not really," Phil said, eyeing Harold in his suit. "How about a beer, you guys—on me?"

"Sounds good. I see you got some Yuengling," Harold said to Phil. "Grab that table in the corner," turning, Harold said to me, "away from all this—*noise!*" as "Blue Eyes Crying in the Rain"—polka style—blared on the jukebox by the bar.

Sitting in what would become our usual spot, accompanied by the clicks of balls on Phil's pool table, I learned that Harold had been a mailman in Kettering, Ohio; that he retired to Florida ("God's waiting room," he called it) with his wife, Pauline, in 2005, and took a week-night job at SOFTI when Pauline died last year ("She didn't have to wait too long," he said). I also learned that Harold, Jr.—Hal—lives in Cincinnati. Never married. Chief penguin keeper at the aquarium in Newport—across the Ohio River in Kentucky. "Did you know there are penguins in Australia, Geography?"

"Geo, not Geography. I *teach* geography. But yes, I did."

"Did you know that when Ponce de Leon first sighted Florida, he thought it was an island?" Harold said, finishing his beer in a gulp. "I better be getting home. My Legs gets restless."

"Try standing up."

"No, Redlegs, my cat. Anyway, I'm good to go."

"Yeah, me too," I said. "My wife will wonder where I am."

"Your wife?" said Harold, lifting his cap, running his hand through thinning gray hair—his ears, which hadn't struck me until now, the size of our St. Pauli Girl Beer coasters. "I thought you said you had a girlfriend."

"My girlfriend's with my wife's girlfriend tonight. They take a Spanish class on Wednesday, the night I teach. We all live together."

"You live together?"

"Yes, with Archie."

"Who's Archie?"

"Our Australian Shepherd."

"A dog, I hope," he said.

At this point I figure Harold's had about enough of me as, that first night, we say good-bye to Phil, step outside, and walk to our cars. "Nice to meet you, Harold."

"Yeah, me too. Next Wednesday we'll shoot some nine-ball," he says, making like he strokes a shot. A leftie.

"Next Wednesday?"

"Okay, see you then," he says, revving his Explorer.

Pulling out of the lot, I take a right onto Cypress and a left onto Atlantic, when, looking at my rearview mirror, I see Harold two car-lengths back, where he remains for three more turns before he pulls into a drive beside a little stucco house one block before I turn into my complex. We're neighbors!

"Hey, Geo," Lucinda says as I walk into our condo. "Maureen and Chrissie got home early. Where've you been?"

"*Buenos noches!*" Chrissie and Maureen shout as Archie herds me toward them in the den.

"*Una extraña familia feliz,*" I say.

"One something happy family!" says Chrissie.

The next few days, each time I passed the little stucco house, I looked for Harold in his sandy yard of colored stones and driftwood, his green

Explorer always in the drive, a small, tarp-covered bass boat beached beside the house. Then, the following Monday, almost nine at night, our phone rang. "Hey, Roger L. Bosworth, it's for you," Lucinda said. "A Harold Kingsley."

"Hello, Harold?"

"Roger, this is Harold. Need some help over here. My Legs died. Can you dig a grave?"

"Sure, I'll be right over. I know where you live."

"I figured," Harold said.

As we jumped into the car and drove a block, I brought everyone up to speed—Lucinda, Maureen, Chrissie, Archie. Widowed, catless security guard I had a Yuengling with, essentially. By the time we stepped from Harold's foyer, he'd been held by three women and sniffed by one Australian Shepherd. "This must be Archie," Harold said, leading us to the kitchen, where Redlegs, a faded orange tabby, lay curled inside a little, cushy bed. "He didn't greet me at the door when I got in. Found him just like this."

"On the kitchen *table*?" I said.

"Could one of you girls grab a pillowcase from the hall closet?" said Harold. "The shovel's on the patio out back. I'll show Roger where to dig."

When Harold went missing—after I'd lost a couple hundred dollars to him at nine-ball; after we'd spent several mornings fishing off Torry Island on the Big O and at least a dozen evenings eating dinner at my place with the girls—I thought about that night in his backyard, when, for each two shovel-scoops of sandy soil I scooped, one slid back down. "Two feet wide, three feet deep," said Harold, porch light shining through his ears.

"Three feet!" I said.

"Alligators. Otherwise, I would've dug the hole myself. I'll be inside."

"Harold, wait. Did you know we're neighbors?"

"Why'd you think I asked for your ID? I wondered where you lived. I've seen you drive by here a thousand times."

"Well, I'm glad you called. Sorry about your cat. How old was he?" I said, resting on my shovel.

"Twenty-three."

"Twenty-three!"

"At least. Pauline found him in her wheel well in December, '92. Now I've lost them both," he said, swatting at a mosquito by his ear. "I'm good to go."

"What about your son?" I said.

"He's chief penguin keeper at the aquarium in Newport."

"That's not what I mean. You have him to live for, don't you?"

"Live for?" Harold said, smacking a mosquito on his forehead. "What are you talking about?"

"You said you're good to go."

"Inside, I meant. They'll eat me up out here."

Still, the whole *good-to-go* thing stuck with me. Take that Saturday in July, the first time we fished Harold's favorite Torry Island inlet. He'd picked me up at four that morning, his bass boat, *The Pauline*, in tow. By the time we drove the sixty miles up 27 through Belle Glade, crossed the bridge, and put in at the ramp on Torry Island, the sun was giving thought to rising. By the time I baited a shiner and wet my line, I could have cast myself into the lake. "It's going to be a hot one," I informed Harold, the sun a giant five ball in the east above his head.

"Sure is," Harold said, steering closer to the shoreline, trolling motor humming. "Did you know this lake is only nine feet deep?"

"Everyone knows that," I said.

"Half the size of Rhode Island?"

"Yes."

"Doesn't seem so big when you look at it like that—shallow, half a Rhode Island."

"I guess not," I said.

"Did you know Roger Williams started Rhode Island, Roger?"

"Jesus, Harold, are you going to fish or what?"

"I don't know. Some days I don't feel like doing anything," he said, just as a gator, maybe six feet long, slid into the water and disappeared beneath our boat. "Did you know that if you shine a flashlight toward the shore at night, alligator eyes light up like headlights?"

"Yeah, one time Lucinda and I went camping in the Glades. After dark, we shined *our* headlights into Florida Bay, not far from Flamingo Campground. Eyes lit up by the hundreds. Crocodiles, I think."

"Must be something to see."

"Yeah," I said. "But I know what you mean. Lots of days I don't feel like doing anything either."

"You? Living like a colony of penguins?"

"Penguins?"

"My son, Hal, says penguins are the most social birds alive. You and all your girls is what I'm saying. Back in Kettering, Pauline and I had six close friends—the Come Double Club, we called ourselves. The eight of us met once a week for Clabber. Now I'm like a hawk, one *old* hawk," he mumbled, easing down the shoreline. ". . . good to go," he whispered.

"So, you mean you want to head back in?"

"What? Ten bucks says I land a crappie before you," Harold said, reaching for his tackle, rummaging through the box—brushing aside a handgun in the mix beneath a drawer.

"You keep a *gun* in there?"

"Yeah, an old Mauser I bought in Bamberg. I was stationed there in '62. Never know when it might come in handy."

And another time at our place—late August. Lucinda sent me for some carry-out Chinese, and I brought home some Harold. I saw him sitting on a piece of driftwood as I passed by his house and asked if he had eaten.

"Today?" he said.

"Yes, today. Tonight, actually."

"Hadn't thought about it."

"Well, get into the car and think about it. Do you like Chinese?"

"I suppose," Harold said, rising from his driftwood.

Soon Lucinda, Maureen, Harold, and I were sharing moo shu this and vegetable that when Chrissie, looking even paler than usual, walked in late from Furry Friends. "Hi, everybody," Chrissie said with uncharacteristic un-enthusiasm.

"Everything all right, Chrissie?" Maureen said.

"I had to stay late to help a rat terrier to the Rainbow Bridge."

"The what?" said Harold.

"One day she'll cross the bridge with her person, when her person dies," Chrissie explained, taking the seat beside me.

"What was wrong with her?" Maureen asked.

"Her age, mostly," Chrissie whimpered, chopsticks trembling.

"Well, you did the right thing," I said, as if I knew anything.

"I hope Redlegs meets me at the Torry Island Bridge," Harold said, opening his fortune cookie. "Then put me in *The Pauline*, set her on fire, and shove us into Lake Okeechobee."

"*The Pauline* is made of fiberglass. I'm not sure she'd burn," I reasoned.

"Nice, Geo." Lucinda said.

"Kerosene," said Harold.

By now it was almost Thanksgiving. Though summer SOFTI had ended three months ago, once or twice a week I still drove into Phil's—where Harold met me after work. But that night, a Friday night, it was after 9:00. No Harold.

"Call him on his cell," Phil said.

"He doesn't have a cell. But he should be home by now," I said, tapping Harold's face on my smartphone.

"You've reached Harold and Pauline Kingsley," Harold's voice said. "Leave a message, and one of us will call you back."

I bet I know which one, I thought, waiting for the beep. *Beep.* "Harold, this is Geo—you know, Roger. Call me on my cell as soon as you get home."

"Not there?" Phil deduced, quartering a lime behind the bar.

Next, I looked up Security at SOFTI. "You've reached Security at South Florida Technical Institute," a woman's voice—smoker, obviously—said. "Office hours are seven thirty to five thirty, Monday through Friday. If the event's an emergency, call 91—."

"They're closed!" I said.

"I'm not surprised. Get your car. I'll close up. Let's go."

"Hurry up wid dem beers real quick, ya know," a customer said at my side.

About 9:30 that night, Phil and I, in my Sonata, pull into Harold's drive: no Explorer; *The Pauline*, unmoved; a faint light coming from two of Harold's three front windows. Walking to the door, we pass the piece of driftwood where Harold sometimes sits. No Harold.

"Harold!" I shout, his front door opening to the pressure of my knock. "I'll go down the hall. You check the kitchen," I say, pointing Phil toward a light above the sink. "Then I'll call Norman."

"Who's Norman?"

"My buddy who runs SOFTI. He might know if Harold came to work."

Finding Harold nowhere, I look up Norman's number on my phone. "This better be good," Norman answers.

"Hey, Norman, it's Geo. I'm trying to find one of your security guards."

"You mean Harold?"

"Yes! How'd you know?"

"Harold *is* our security guard. Lost fifty bucks to him last week. Dolphins-Jets. What's up?"

Unsurprisingly, Norman doesn't know if Harold came to work. "But I do know he meets some guy every Wednesday night to shoot some pool," he says.

"I'm the guy, Norman! Harold didn't show! Isn't there anyone else in your so-called Security Department? Who normally answers the phone?"

"That would be Hilda."

"So call Hilda!"

"Oh, man, Geo, I don't know Hilda's *last* name! Meet me at my office in half an hour. I'll look her up."

"You ever seen a house as neat as this?" Phil says, scanning Harold's kitchen. "It's like no one lives here."

It's 9:55 by my car clock. We're heading north on 441, halfway to SOFTI, when Phil says, "And why are we driving here, exactly?"

"To call Hilda, the other security person."

"Why couldn't your friend drive to school, call Hilda, then give *us* a call?"

Phil has a point, but by now we're more than halfway there, and knowing Norman as I do, it wouldn't hurt for me to do the talking. Once, in college, our American history professor said he'd caught malaria at Guadalcanal. "Does the yellow *ever* go away, Mr. Banco?" Norman said.

Then a few minutes later, my phone rings. It's Chrissie. "Geo, where are you?"

"Your dad and I are looking for Harold."

"That's why I called. Harold left a message earlier and we sort of forgot to tell you."

"Tell me what!"

"He said he couldn't make it tonight."

"Okay, but where is he?"

"Home, I guess. I love you."

If Norman were a peninsula, he'd be Iberia. Iberia at a desk: Spain and Portugal thumbing through a Rolodex the size of Andorra, relatively speaking. "Hilda's got to be in here somewhere," Norman says. Heavier by a hundred-fifty pounds, at least. In college he'd been Italy.

Somewhere in the C's, Norman yanks a card and hands it to me. *Hilda Crump.* I tap Hilda's number in my cell and get the same husky voice I heard earlier. "You've reached the home of Hilda, Bruno, and Juno Crump. I'm not home right now, but Bruno and Juno are, so don't get any funny ideas." *Beep.*

"Hilda, if you're there, pick up, I'm a friend of Harold—"

"Hello."

"Hello, Hilda? I'm looking for Harold Kingsley. Did he show up for work?"

"No. But he called about five o'clock and asked if I'd fill in."

Imagining Bea Arthur in a golf cart, I ask, "Did he say why?"

"He said he needed kerosene. Asked where he could find some. Stop that, Bruno!"

Snarl.

"Kerosene?"

"Said there was something he needs to do. Juno!"

Snarl.

To sum up, Hilda doesn't know what Harold needs to do, what the kerosene is for, or where to find it. "Anyway, if Harold calls, tell him to call Roger."

"Roger that!" Hilda says, so pleased with herself she starts coughing. "Drop it, Bruno!" *Cough, cough.*

Snarl.

"Roger," one might ask, "did it ever occur to you to call the police?"

Fair question. And the answer is, *yes.* But look at it this way: Harold was old, not ancient; held a job, drove a car; told a co-worker, so to speak, he wouldn't be in that day. Oh, yeah, the police would have *sprung* into action. Still, I was worried, especially when Phil and I ran by Harold's house again and not only found the front door—which we had left unlocked—locked, but *The Pauline* missing. And though you're probably way ahead of me on this, this was the time, around 11:00 that night, it also occurred to me that Harold's need for kerosene might have something to do with bridge crossing—Torry Island *and* the Rainbow—with a little help from an antique Mauser. Fiberglass notwithstanding, we had no time to waste. A minute later I gave the girls a call to let them know what's up, and five minutes after that Lucinda, Chrissie, and Maureen were scrambling into my backseat. Archie jumped in front with Phil.

Driving northwest on 27 toward the Torry Island boat launch, I no sooner fill everyone in than Chrissie starts crying. "If I hadn't brought up the Rainbow Bridge, he never would have done this," she says.

"We don't know that he's done anything, honey," Phil consoles.

"Yet," I unsettle.

"Now see, that's the trouble with you, Geo," Lucinda says. "You see the worst in *every* situation."

"You're right. I forgot Harold needs kerosene for his nautical fire-breath-ing act. He's probably on his way to Disney with *The Pauline*. Or maybe his arthritis is acting up and he needs a boatload to rub into his knees."

"And honey!" Maureen says.

"Yes?" Lucinda responds.

"You mix kerosene and honey," Maureen explains. "*Then* you rub it in."

"Never mind," I say. "The point is, Harold misses Pauline; and you can only play so much nine-ball."

"That's the point?" says Lucinda.

"Mostly. Mostly he doesn't have anyone. He's alone in the waiting room."

"What?" Lucinda says.

Looking in my rearview mirror, I see Chrissie in the middle of the seat, wrapped in Maureen's and Lucinda's arms—a white-skinned Hindu goddess off to battle darkness, what with all the arms and darkness. We zip through Belle Glade and, eerily, as we drive onto the bridge to Torry Island, Archie starts to whimper. "It's all right, boy," Phil says. "We're almost there."

When we arrive at the Torry Island boat launch, we find it empty except for two young guys drinking beer and fishing on the pier that separates the ramps. "Hey, guys!" I shout, launching from the car—Archie at my side. "Has anyone put in?"

"Yeah, look at all the trailers," one kid says, taking in the non-existent trailers with a sweep of his beer can. "Is your dog friend—? Hey, Mr. Bosworth! It's me, Robbie!"

"Robbie? Robbie Flemland?"

"Rickhardt!"

"Listen, Robbie, you know the old security guard at SOFTI?"

"You mean Harold? Lost ten bucks to him on the Heat-Knicks game last week."

"Okay, but have you seen him tonight?"

"Nope."

"How long have you been here?"

"Hey, Kyle. How many beers have you had?"

"Eight or ten," Kyle says, shining his flashlight down the shaky shoreline.

"About two hours," Robbie says.

"Robbie," I say, "how long do you plan to—"

"Oh, man!" suddenly Kyle shouts, loud enough to scare the crappie *in* Rhode Island. "Dude, look at this!"

And just as suddenly, I think I know where we'll find Harold.

Abraham Ortelius would be interested to know that Florida was once part of the African region of the supercontinent, Gondwana—itself a part of the *super* supercontinent, Pangaea. When Pangaea separated, Florida sunk beneath the waves and became a part of North America's continental shelf. Seashells and coral rushed in, geologically speaking, and compressed to form the water-bearing limestone beneath the Everglades today—none of which anyone in my car was interested in hearing as we sped that moonless November night past the unmanned ranger station two hours after leaving Robbie and Kyle to their drinking/fishing.

"Spare us, Geo," Lucinda said. "How much farther?"

"Not far. Just this side of Flamingo—where we camped. Remember?"

"I can't see you guys camping," said Chrissie.

"It was a long time ago," I said.

"Not that long," Lucinda said. "Chrissie would have been what, like six?"

Sure the birds were memorable—that time camping with Lucinda—egrets, herons, ibis. The labyrinth of mangrove trees along the estuaries. Alligators that slid into the inland water not far from our canoe. But nothing so memorable as the mosquitos—that December when there had been no freeze. Foolishly, I'd left the tent flap open while Lucinda and I drove to see the bay at night. Nearby campers, foresighted campers—the ones who'd zipped their flaps—must have thought young Lucinda and I were athletes of a sort when we returned: *slap, slap, slapslapslap* and Lucinda shouting, "Geo! Geo!"

"Slow down!" Lucinda said now. "That looks like an Explorer. Its lights are on!"

"That's him!" Chrissie said as we pulled next to Harold's car, its headlights aimed at Florida Bay, "there!"—where, midway between the car and bay, Harold stood inside the beams. As we stepped into the brackish air, Archie ran toward Harold, while from the bay at least fifty pair of eyes shined back.

Wearing his security suit and cap, as though to keep the crocodiles in line, Harold didn't budge until Archie sniffed a pant leg. "Archie?" Harold said, stooping down to Archie's height. "What are you doing here?"—as if Archie might have driven south to fish or bird-watch.

The smart money today has it that the Americas and Asia will drift toward the Arctic Ocean and, a hundred million years from now—give or take fifty million—form the new supercontinent, Amasia, encircled by the Atlantic Ocean.

"It's us!" Chrissie said as, backlit by the beams, we walked toward Harold—Chrissie, Phil, Lucinda, Maureen, and I.

"You owe me fifty bucks for gas!" I yelled. Harold stood and turned.

"Would you look at that," faintly, Harold said. "Fat chance!" he shouted.

Then the five of us joined Harold, and Archie circled us.

Thirty minutes later we squeezed around the picnic table in Harold's campsite, *The Pauline* nearby. "Hadn't camped since I was in the army," Harold said as he fired up his cook-stove for coffee.

It seems the camping bug bit Harold about five that afternoon. Dressed for work, he called Hilda, ate some dinner, and spent the rest of the evening shopping for groceries and tracking down a lightweight sleeping bag, a tent, crushed ice for his cooler, and, with difficulty, a Lucky Craft Sammy lure for largemouth bass and kerosene—for his stove! Phil and I were somewhere between Harold's house and SOFTI when Harold swung by for *The Pauline* and headed south for the Glades. No sooner had he pitched his tent when, two campsites over, he noticed three guys playing Texas Hold'em. Sixty-eight dollars richer, past two o'clock in the morning, Harold jumped into his car to stare at crocodiles.

"After what you said, I couldn't get that sight out of my head," Harold said to me. "Something to see, all right."

One week later, Harold, Phil, and I saw Dwayne Wade score thirty-two at American Airlines Arena in Miami. Phil lost ten bucks to Harold on the over-under. Two days after that, about three o'clock Tuesday morning, Harold called. He said he wasn't feeling so good and asked, "Could you come over, *Geo*?"—the first time he ever called me Geo. My guess is he got out of bed to unlock the door for me. Then, wearing Cincinnati Reds pajamas, Harold crossed the bridge in his living room recliner, where we— the girls and I—found him at rest. South Florida must be full of Harold Kingsleys. But I met this one, a guy who'd moved a thousand miles from home, lost his wife and cat, but kept on living: fishing, shooting pool, gambling, and finding someone to fish, shoot pool, and gamble with. Archie laid his head on Harold's knee.

That Thursday, on the top shelf of Harold's dresser, Harold, Jr. and I found a note attached to a maple box containing Pauline's ashes. *Just put me in a box like this and take us both to Phil's.* Leaving nothing to chance, Harold even insisted on our corner table—where the two maples boxes were to stand. *Then anyone who wants can say a few words. Pauline likes anything by Kenny Rogers. Just keep it down. And spare us both the oompah.*

"I never knew your dad for such a showman," I said to Hal.

"Are you kidding? Did Dad ever tell you how he met my mom?" Hal said, glancing at the box of ashes in his hands.

"Not that I remember."

"Well, he'd noticed her around town. So one day he saw her coming out of work at Sears and, just as she was backing out of her spot, he sped up his mail truck and bumped her," Hal said, giving Pauline's box a thump.

"Really."

That Sunday afternoon, to the muted sounds of "Lucille," "Coward of the County," "Ruby, Don't Take Your Love to Town," and—"The Gambler," we said our words and drank our beers. On that Green Bay Packers off-day, Phil served Brandy Old Fashioneds—a Wisconsin favorite—to the few customers who were there. The rest of us drank Yuengling.

Standing at the corner table, Hal said it had been his parents' dream to move to Florida. "Dad used to say he fought the Cold War twice: two years in Germany, then forty-five winters in Ohio. My dad loved to fish. He loved that old orange cat. But mostly he loved my mother. One day, Dad saw a girl coming out of work at Sears and . . ."

Hal went on to say that he expected Harold would move to Cincinnati after Pauline died. "Then, last summer Dad started talking about these *strange* people he had met. He said they were better than TV. He called you his Florida Family."

One by one, we stood by Harold's ashes. Yuengling in hand, Norman said no one in the history of SOFTI had issued more citations.

Hilda said Harold once found her favorite cigarette lighter by the Fountain of Youth and brought it to her house. "My Rotties took to Harold. That was enough for me," she said.

"The Fountain of Youth?" Maureen and Lucinda, turning to each other, mouthed.

Lucinda spoke of Harold's sense of loyalty and how she could tell he was the kind of man who never took his marriage for granted and "it's a shame more men don't," et cetera, et cetera—plus something about *sarcasm*.

Chrissie said that she loved Harold.

Finally, with Kenny and Dolly murmuring "Islands in the Stream," Archie nudged me forward. Standing in the spot where I had sat those many Wednesday nights, unclear as to which maple box was Harold, I placed a hand on each. "My friends call me Geo," I began.

Bruised People

Elizabeth England

Lulu only gets a quick look at the photo before she's distracted by the heat-pulse from Wilford, the project manager who's begun leaving Peppermint Patties on her chair like dead birds. He sits at her right angle, radiating a longing. Is she available? Is she into older men? Is she someone who will abandon him like his wife did, leaving him with angry children? His interest in her has recently heightened. He's begun asking others about her, passing along these queries to informants who've sent Lulu text messages with crying emojis. These co-workers are sympathetic to both sides, yet they're rooting for Wilford. Everyone wants a happy ending, Lulu reminds herself.

"I'm going for a coffee," Wilford says. "Want one?"

"I'm good," Lulu says.

"I don't mind getting you something," he says.

She looks up and sees damage. His eyes, his hair, his shoulders tilted forward like a mast pulled by a storm. So this is the visual of gutted, she realizes. "If they have any black tea," she says. "I'll take one with milk."

"Thank you," he says and walks purposefully towards the community kitchen.

Once Wilford's gone, Lulu looks at the newspaper photo again and confirms what she already knew but didn't want to know: Billy Gerston is now a famous rock star and is never coming back to her. The photographer has captured everything about Billy that she loved and, unfortunately, still loves. Even though he's awkwardly bent, tying his sneaker, Billy manages to contort himself so his face is in the frame: his sweet good looks, the doll-curls, the chubby cheeks interrupted by the pointed chin. He loves to be loved and the camera is smitten. Despite herself, Lulu's moved by his relaxed smile, the gentle slouch of contentment his lips easily fall into. She glances at the caption and, just like she knew the photo was of him, she knew what the description would say: Billy Gerston and his band now reside in Sacramento, California.

When she gets home that evening, Lulu holds open the door for Rex, Billy's seventy-five pound Labrador retriever. He's a big dog, Rex, with heavy muscles. He lumbers to his bowls: food and water, water and food. The dog looks first at Lulu, then at the door, his eyes moving with consideration from the old snow to her. He knows. He knew when Billy packed the small duffel, said he'd see them in a few weeks, and waved from the pickup truck that he drove to his new home on the other side of the country.

"Yes, yes, yes," Lulu says, repeating the word as if worrying it. "He's left us."

Rex gazes beyond her at the gravel driveway, which hits the paved road in a sharp T. He tenses and sniffs, quick intakes of cool air. His ears prick and then, as a car goes by, they relax. His shoulders resume their slouch, his tail droops, and his body resigns itself to abandonment.

With her coat, hat, and gloves still on, sobs heave out of Lulu as if a freight train is passing through her organs, sticking on her heart, then attaching themselves to her lungs. She kneels next to the dog, rocking, gasping, wrapping herself like a cape around Rex. "I'm sorry," Lulu says. Rex doesn't move; he stays rooted and she leans. The dog takes on all of her. The light outside shifts and the sun appears and then coyly disappears. They sit there until Rex grows rigid, benignly shirking off Lulu. He lifts his neck and tips back his head and howls. He holds this croon on a note, an octave, that Lulu has never heard him reach before. He repeats the song again and again, taking pauses in between to rest. When he's done, Rex stares at Lulu with a stoicism that confounds her. He shakes his body twice, as if ridding himself of not just the moment but of Billy Gerston. He then walks outside to pee.

"So the dog's yours, I guess," Tina says the next day. She's new and young and says this not like it seems or could be, but like it is. "Did he ask?"

"Ask what?" Lulu says, confirming she hadn't just missed the point but a whole generation.

"If you'd inherit the dog when he ditched," Tina says. She files and staples and uses paperclips like the old days.

"No," Lulu says. "I guess not."

They are sitting in the nook with its one window and leafless tree cluster. Tina spreads hummus on a rice cake. "I'm not a sharer," she says, offering Lulu one. "But this situation is extreme." She then smiles and Lulu sees that she's pretty.

"Thank you," Lulu says. "I guess it is."

Rex is at the front door when Lulu gets home. His tail's raised and suspended midair as if he's awaiting an answer: Where has she been? Who was she with? Is she going to leave him, too? The questions exhaust Lulu who, instead of answering, lies down on the couch again with her boots, coat, and scarf on. She sleeps until the heat turns off, the click of the radiator awakening and reminding her that Billy Gerston's still gone.

Wilford bookmarks sites that have to do with excavation, rare books, and home-brewing. He scratches the top of his left hand with his right at least once an hour. He chews gum and catches the air in the wad so it snaps with no rhythm or predictability. He answers his cell phone in a whisper and makes promises he can't keep to the person on the other end, like "I will be there for you always." He rarely does what he says he's going to do and when he does, the staff's caught off guard, which makes a dull job lively. In this way, Wilford's an amenable boss.

Lulu lifts the four sections of *The Sacramento Bee* from her desk and puts them in her lap. The weight of the paper is comforting, like a baby. She has a section system, C, D, A, and B, whose logic Lulu can't explain, and luckily, no one has asked her to; her colleagues are thankful that someone—Lulu—will do this searching for a needle in the haystack so they leave her to it. She eagle-eyes the sections by columns and then she cross-checks horizontally, employing a geometric equation in which the points plotted create shapes in her brain that organize the information. When Wilford leaves their corner, Lulu anticipates his return so she never fully loses herself in what she's doing.

"I know *what* you do," Billy had said. "But *why* do you do it?"

"I like solving problems," Lulu had said.

"Then become a spy," Billy had said.

"I am," Lulu had said. "Undercover."

"Under the covers?" Billy had said, lifting the blanket and looking at her.

"I'm serious," Lulu had said.

"So am I," Billy had said. "Very, very serious." They had made love and Lulu tried not to like it, or Billy, or the small life they had created out of a rental house and used furniture and meals made from this and that. But she had liked it.

Tina disapproves: She doesn't like the way Wilford tells Lulu what to do without asking; she doesn't like the way Marcus, the technology wizard, reboots Lulu's computer once a week without asking; she doesn't like the way Billy has left Lulu with Rex without asking. "It's like the world's sending you a giant *fuck you*," Tina says.

It's snowing again, so when Lulu wakes up she considers staying home, though the prospect of being with Rex all day makes going to the office a holiday. Whenever he can, he lies on her feet, the weight of him almost cracking her. Then, when she gets up, he does too, following her from the bedroom to the bathroom, from the bathroom to the kitchen, and from the kitchen to the bedroom. His walk is slow and considered, but he keeps pace with Lulu. If she looks at him, he turns away as if he wasn't staring at her. When she shuts the bathroom door, he waits, and when she opens it, he looks away. This goes on until she leaves for work.

A week's passed and Lulu is searching for a line mention or a chunky article that could support her not-for-profit's dedication to keeping people safe from the decaying ozone layer. Her feelings about this topic are unpopular, particularly within her company's culture of optimism through knowledge. She doesn't believe any theory or proven fact that she may find in *The Philadelphia Inquirer*, *The Sacramento Bee*, or any other national daily is going to protect anyone from being sizzled by the sun. Still, she's not going to be the buzz-kill that tells her co-workers, particularly Wilford, that the punch is poisoned. Instead, she combs the paper for data.

"I thought I saw something in Sports," Wilford says. He has recently hired a digital team that handles online editions, but Lulu knows that what she does is invaluable, and she isn't, like her co-workers, fearful of being canned. No one can synthesize print like she does.

"Football fields," Wilford says. "The air quality after the turf has been sprayed." Wilford has developed a tic when he talks to Lulu. He doesn't turn around, but his back and ass tense as if he's bracing for rejection.

"Thanks for the heads-up," she says, searching for more pictures of Billy.

Tina and Lulu are sitting on the railing of the porch of the building on Main Street where their office takes over the first two floors. It's a gray New England day with no promise to be otherwise.

"Have you heard from him?" Tina asks.

"Not since the postcard from Baja."

"When did that come?" Tina says.

"Seven months ago."

"Bastard," Tina says, looking at Lulu. "And the dog? Did he mention the dog?"

"No," Lulu says. "I don't think he did."

"Bastard," Tina says again. "Do you want to go dancing on Friday?"

Billy said, *There's no one like you.*
Billy said, *I love you.*
Billy said, *Will you marry me?*
Billy said, *I'll be back in a month.*
Billy said, *I promise.*

The digital team found a miracle, so Wilford springs for champagne and miniature cupcakes, where four equals one. A Teflon company has invented a new form of non-stick that uses the sun's rays like a boomerang. "That's how they explained it to me," Wilford says to the staff of eight, which has been summoned to Lulu and Wilford's shared space. Tina is sitting on the floor, her knitting needles clicking like a metronome. She looks at Lulu and rolls her eyes, mouthing, *What next?*

Billy's underwear lived for four years and two months in the top drawer next to hers, small knots of wrinkled cotton. *This is how I fold*, he said, and bunched them up. She laughed and said, *like this*, folding his boxers, left leg, right leg, then in half. He grabbed the perfect rectangle from her and bunched it up. *Like this*, he said. She laughed and then he smiled and picked her up like a barn post, stick straight, so that her head—she was taller than he was—almost touched the low bedroom ceiling. He carried her to the bed where he undressed her, piece by piece, bunching up her jeans, underwear, t-shirt, bra, and tossing them onto the floor, useless fabric separating his body from hers. *Like this*, he said and then kissed every bit of her.

It's late at night and Lulu's listening to the icicles melt. There's a persistent drumming of the water that keeps her from reading or sleeping, so she packs up Billy's clothes, books, CDs, and bottles of essential oils. Rex watches her standing in the hallway with the closet door open, trying on a motorcycle jacket. "Should I keep this?" The dog stands up and walks to her. He sniffs the waist of the coat and when she lowers her hand, he licks first her palm and then the leather cuff. He sits and waits until she hangs the coat back in the closet. "It's the least he can do," she says. When one box is taped, she carries it downstairs to the front door. Rex curls himself next to the cardboard and rests his chin on his paws. He's still there in the morning when Lulu pours food into his already full bowl.

They go to a bar where live bands play on Fridays. Tina knows everyone, so they get in without a cover, take stools at the counter, and the round is on the bartender. Lulu wears make up for the first time since Billy left. She realizes this when Tina picks her up and says, "I guess I'm an occasion." Is it a date? Is Tina gay? Is Lulu? Rex has begun sleeping in her bed, their bed; the space that was taken up by Billy is now Rex's. Tina kisses a guy and then says, "He's my brother."
      "But not really," the guy says.
      "But not really," Tina says and they laugh.
      When they're alone, Tina says, "Were there clues?" The bartender doesn't ask but just keeps filling Lulu's glass with Malbec. After the third pour, Lulu puts her hand over the top and the bartender holds up his hands as if arrested.
      "No clues," Lulu says. "At least not that I was aware of."
      "No offense," Tina says, standing up and taking lipstick from her back pocket. "But you don't seem like the most aware person." She then uses the mirror behind the bar to run the tube around her mouth. "Ready?"
      They dance as if they're a couple, aping each other in a way that's intimate. Tina sashays her hips and then leans into Lulu and says, "I think Billy is an asshole." She smiles and Lulu feels a part of herself break off and fly away.

That week, *The Sacramento Bee* offers up nothing about Billy. There is, however, a teensy article on D2 guest-written by a local sixth grader about how the Earth's puckering and the rain's not cooperating and the forecast predicts heat and more heat and no moisture for eternity so it's absurd to think that California will be habitable in fifty years.
      "Anything?" Wilford says.
      "No," Lulu says. "Just this." She puts the article on the corner of his desk.
      "You're a miracle worker," Wilford says. He smiles at her, but not at her. In no time, Rex has halved himself. His eyes bulge from their sockets and his hipbones nearly catch on the doorframe as he staggers like a starved war prisoner following Lulu from room to room. He rejects his

dry food, his canned food, his special dog treats made from organic products. Lulu tries meals from her grandmother's recipe book, chicken and lamb with root vegetables and paprika. He looks at the plate with meat swaddled by gravy and mashed potatoes and then walks over to his bowl of kibble with more enthusiasm than he's had in days. Lulu squats down and takes a handful of the dry food and puts it in her mouth as if it were cereal. She's unsure she'll get the stuff down without water or vomiting, but she does and Rex watches as if making sure she's committed to this. "Try some," she says. He noses the small circles, flipping a few from her palm and onto the floor. He licks and licks and chases one or two as they scuttle across the wood but swallows none. He then raises his head to stare at her, his skull visible under his skin.

"He's giving up," Lulu says on the phone to Tina, who is two cubicles away. Everyone in the office is quiet, listening.

"Wouldn't you?" Tina says.

The veterinarian says that Rex is normal, though there's nothing normal about Rex. He sits on Lulu's lap, his head, as hard and small as a coconut, resting in her palm. His eyes close and his paws go limp in midair. The vet runs the stethoscope over his chest, around and around, searching for his heart. They are all waiting for relief: Is he alive or dead? "There it is. Slow and steady," the vet says. She rubs his back and neck in a way that Lulu never does, not rough but not gentle. Rex isn't a baby boy anymore and the vet doesn't treat him like one. When he responds with a groan, she nuzzles up to him, and Rex licks her chin. She laughs and Rex tries to lick her again and this physical playfulness goes on and on with Rex suddenly half in Lulu's lap and half in the vet's. There's panting and low growling before Rex jumps off of Lulu and sits, waiting and wanting for whatever the vet is fiddling with in her pocket. "Is this what you want?" The vet teases Rex, and Rex barks, and the two stare at each other in a taunting, feisty way. When the vet finally offers him a small bone from her pocket, Rex lunges for it, crunching and drooling, sniffing her fingers for more.

Instead of chocolate, there's a note on Lulu's chair from Wilford that says, "Will you go out with me?" They talk about the sections of the dailies; they talk about the color of the shrub that is beginning to bloom outside their shared window; they never mention the note so it sits behind Lulu's computer, read, but unanswered.

Tina's wearing jodhpurs and paddock boots, but when Lulu asks her if she rides, Tina says, "Do I look like a rider?" Tina has begun smoking clove cigarettes and even though they smell good, she has to take her habit outside. They are leaning against the gutter, breathing in clove and wet grass shoots, wearing down parkas. Lulu air smokes and Tina laughs. It's the season where anything seems possible even though it isn't.

Tina asks about Rex and Lulu tells her about his ears pricking forwards at the vet.

"That's sort of hot," Tina says.

"It sort of was," Lulu says. "I was the third wheel."

"You were," Tina says and smirks.

"He's coming back to life," Lulu says.

"Now what?" Tina asks.

Lulu isn't wearing much, a long t-shirt and underwear. The weather has changed, and while yesterday it was winter, today it's summer. Rex sits in the red sling-back chair and watches her uncross her legs. She does it again, cross, uncross, cross, uncross. Rex's eyes move past her calves and up her thighs. When he gets to her face, his eyes stop and he stares at her. He lifts his head and studies. This was a trait of Billy's, the contemplation of her. Sometimes he did it to get her attention and other times, like when he stuffed two t-shirts and his only pair of unripped jeans into a duffel bag and left her with Rex, he would stare to communicate something bad. Any time Billy stared, Lulu would sweat, high on her neck and between her breasts.

Rex is staring and Lulu's sweating. She scoops up her hair and twists until it stays put with a pencil. She tries staring Rex down, making him turn away first, but like Billy, Rex wins because he can look at her forever. Once Lulu has lost, Rex crawls out of the chair and eats his bowl of food and whimpers for more. He is ravenous.

The sky's blue with no clouds, and there's a heat that seems prehistoric. She looks for it, but finds no trace of winter as she loads the car with the seven boxes of Billy Gerston's. He's becoming harder for her to smell and touch, but she can still hear him as if he's behind her, reading a magazine that reflects their shared humor. She both longs for and dreads her eventual non-reaction to a photo in *The Sacramento Bee*. Her nervous system still speeds up when she sees snapshots of him at the farmers' market, a fundraiser for water preservation, performing with one of the big bands he dreamed of becoming. When she can no longer hear him behind her, reading, these photos won't faze her and he will be gone entirely.

Rex starts on Billy's side of the bed, but then stretches himself like Gumby so that by morning he's melded with her. Lulu often wakes up with her fingers wound around his collar holding tight to the leather, spooning with him. Since the vet visit, sometimes, in the middle of the night, Rex's eyes open, his head jerks up, his nostrils flare and he moans softly to the horny terrier down the block. He gets out of bed and paws at the door until Lulu lets him out. In the morning, he's on the porch waiting for her.

She finds Tina sharpening pencils, turning the crank and holding No. 2s steady while the shavings fall into a plastic waste bin.

"That was quick," Tina says. "You and Wilford."

"What about me and Wilford?" Lulu says. They have moved to the coffee machine where they put metallic pods in the dispenser and watch them pop into the garbage post-brew.

"You're going out," Tina says. She pours half-and-half into her mug and walks away.

It's Saturday afternoon and Rex is agitated. He's been living a few nights a week down the block and has plumped up, so Lulu knows someone else is feeding him. There are two young girls who live with the lovesick dog, and they have made it clear that their house is Rex's. "It's okay," Lulu tells Rex. "Thank you for staying, but you can go." He's lying on her feet, and though she's accustomed to the bulk of him now, she nudges him forward. He stands quickly, his body ready to move but his mind hooked on Lulu. She stands, leans down and looks him in the eyes. He stares back and then his eyes move from her to the bathroom, bedroom, bookcase, rug, lamp, his food and water. Lulu gets up, empties and packs his bowls, a leash, and two tennis balls. "Let's go," she says, standing by the door. Rex doesn't even turn towards her voice when she talks to him. He just lowers his chin towards the ground.

"Let's go," Lulu says again.

Rex walks through the open door and leads Lulu towards his lover.

"Did you get my note," Wilford asks.

"Yes," Lulu says, her salad on her knees.

They say nothing for a while and then Lulu says, "Sometime, but not now."

"Fair enough," Wilford says. His back and ass release and he resumes typing. The sound of his finger pads on the keyboard reassure her that he won't take no for an answer.

"Friends?" Tina says, holding out a Chia cow. Its ceramic haunches are covered with a thin green fuzz.

"I thought we already were," Lulu says.

"I like clarity," Tina says. "Speaking of which." She gives Lulu a piece of paper with Billy's band manager's address so now, Tina says, Lulu can mail Billy back to himself.

"Wow," Lulu says.

"The dog has me stumped," Tina says. "Give me some time."

"He's gone," Lulu says. "He fell for a dog down the road and the owner wants him."

"That was easy," Tina says. "Do you want to go get a tattoo for remembrance?"

Lulu shakes her head but accepts the cow and the address. Once the last box gets put in the bin at the post office, she waves and the postmaster shrugs and waves back.

On her desk, there's a picture of Billy Gerston on the front page of *The Sacramento Bee* with a girl who looks like Tina. A yellow Post-It says, "This is not me." Lulu laughs and Wilford says, "Is that a yes?" There is silence and though Lulu listens, she hears nothing.

Damaged

Her Dentist

Yen Ha

S he wakes to the sounds of her husband's fingers laboriously tapping out emails on his phone, one letter at a time. The swoosh
of sent mail chases away her dreams. She turns over to face him,
clearing the sleepiness from her throat.

Can you do that in the living room?

He gets up, throwing off the comforter, eyes focused on his screen
as his forefinger hits the backspace button. She watches him stumble
out of the room. She stays in bed, running her tongue around the rear
of her mouth. The temporary double crowns, in the upper back, are
indistinguishable from her real teeth. In the bathroom, her husband
doesn't bother to gently lift the shower glass door and she braces herself
for the daily harsh scrape of glass edge against tile wall. She listens to

him start the water, and still tucked in bed, she wonders if it will be warm enough to wear sandals.

Last year, midway through the summer at their beach house, an intermittent pain surfaced in her cheek. Occasionally it sharply spiked but when the prickliness grew into a duller, constant ache that lasted half a day, she resorted to painkillers. When she pressed down on her cheek, it hurt more. She avoided pressing down on her cheek, but eventually the ache occurred without any involvement on her part. Instead of coming and going, it came and stayed. She grew tired of taking nonstop painkillers and remained instead in perpetual low-grade discomfort.

She looked up *cheek pain* and *cancer of the face* and *sharp stabbing pain next to the right side of my nose* but didn't find any answers. Her primary care doctor told her it was sinus pressure and gave her a prescription for a nasal spray. The doctor also recommended she use a neti pot to wash out the impurities. The spray and wash cleared out her passages, but they did nothing to alleviate the pain that moved mercurially between a dull throb and a sharp piercing. She couldn't decide which she preferred.

By the time an unseasonably warm fall had left the city, the pain had traveled lower into her jawbone, making her teeth ache when she chewed. She was constantly aware of a faint tenderness in her cheek and developed a habit of pressing on the bone. She dragged a recliner into her home study, separated from the bedroom by a narrow hallway. Sometimes, with her feet propped up on the ottoman, the pain would subside for a moment.

Her doctor sent her to an ENT specialist who recommended she see a dentist. The first time she went to him, dirty mounds of snow lined the streets. She trudged through cold, mud-slicked sidewalks to his office at the back of the ground floor of a residential building. When she walked past the doorman, she said *dentist* and he nodded. She passed old ladies taking a rest in the lobby and boxes of deliveries waiting to be picked up, stacked high on the reception counter. Beyond the doorman, other people stopped to wait for the elevators, but she turned left and walked up two carpeted steps and down a long hallway to the dentist.

She hung her coat on a hook behind the front door. The receptionist greeted her while yelling back to the dentist without moving from her chair. He came out, balding forehead with wispy hair, dark blue scrubs and a face mask pulled down around his neck. He blinked from behind smudged wire-frame glasses perched on the tip of his nose. Gesturing with a hand, he led her back to the exam room, where it was just the two of them in the cramped space. A sagging white laminate cabinet sat next to a window with drawn vertical blinds. The cabinet door lacked a handle and the edges had started to peel. Cables strung through the dropped ceiling tiles connected a computer to the monitor on her right. She placed her bag on the floor against the wall, behind an unused chair holding a lead apron. He clipped a blue bib over her chest and leaned her back, adjusting the light above her. Firm hands gripped her jaw and feeling around the edges of her teeth, he pushed deep into her gum with a finger.

When he took the first set of x-rays, his hands gently turned her face to the left. For the last set of images, he held her hand and showed her where to put her finger in her mouth to keep the tray in place. The x-rays came up on the screen, and he pointed out a massive infection in her sinus that lay trapped beneath her cheekbone. When he explained that the abscess would have to be removed and drained, she could barely understand his raspy voice through the facemask. She listened to him but said nothing, nodding when it felt like he asked a question.

Instead of draining out like it should have, the infection, an opaque darkness at the edge of the root, had puddled above her upper back teeth. She was still picturing the malignant growth harboring undetected beneath her cheek, when she looked up to a long needle of Novocaine.

The old silver on the rear molars flew off in tiny chunks, landing on her tongue. When he got to the wisdom tooth behind the molar, he told her the decay had spread so deeply he couldn't save the tooth. Tilted back, with his hands in her mouth, she barely responded when he said he'd have to remove the tooth. She braced herself for the tugging but it slid out easily. An intensity of agony erupted in her exposed teeth. The infection was an angry mass seeping down into the gauze he tucked into her cheek. Pus spilled out and she shifted in the chair. She could feel it mixing with blood from the gap where the tooth had been. The suction made loud gurgling noises as it worked nonstop to vacuum out the liquid.

He leaned over her to remove the rest of the decay on the molar that remained, his chest inches away. The closeness of his body reminded her of being a child and lying in the dark safeness of her mother's lap to have her ears cleaned. She didn't notice when he switched from the regular drill to a smaller, more bone jarring one. It reduced her entire world to a rumbling that started somewhere in her mouth and extended into her cheeks, her nose, her forehead. The roar of the drill emptied her brain of rational thought. To distract herself from the awareness of time passing, she started counting—one one-thousand, two one-thousand, three one-thousand. When she reached sixty one-thousand she started over again. She was on her seventh round of counting when he finally turned off the drill. She opened her eyes in the sudden silence to his face peering deep into the back of her mouth. He traded his drill for a dental probe to scrape away the last of the decay.

She couldn't believe it was over. Relief spread through her body and the tension she had been holding on to dissipated.

It took the remainder of the winter and all of spring before he was satisfied with the temporary crowns covering the back two, hallowed-out out teeth. When she told him she was leaving for their beach house instead of waiting for the permanent crowns, he said nothing.

She spent her time in the salty ocean air trying not to think about him, her tongue running constantly over the seamless insertion of porcelain, knowing she would have to go back for the real ones. She ate her meals outside on the second-story deck, lying back in the lounge chair and watching the waves crash down. Her husband didn't want to leave the surf that summer. They ended up staying at the beach house longer than usual.

When they have been home for a couple weeks, she calls him. He tells her to come in next Tuesday afternoon. The weather hasn't quite lost its summer heat and, lying in bed, fingers pressed reflexively on her cheek above her jaw, she wonders what to wear for a warm fall day.

Her husband comes into the bedroom, dressed for work in gray slacks and a checkered button up. He addresses her while hopping on one foot, pulling a sock on.

Have you seen my sunglasses?

Did you check the drawer next to the counter?

No, I didn't.

He goes back out into the living room to look in the drawer. She hears him leave, the front door slamming behind him. Getting up, she makes her way to the shower. Picking up the sweats her husband dropped, along with the balled underwear left on the ground, she throws everything in the hamper.

By herself, she spends too much time in the shower. Last year, when the pain consumed her spare moments, she cut her hair short so that she no longer needed a brush, which should have made her showers quicker. Instead, she uses the time she would have saved to stand under the hot water until the guilt of wasting it forces her out.

In front of the mirror, she opens her mouth again to marvel at the bright whiteness of her rear teeth. Before him, she didn't look inside her mouth. Fillings dating back to high school covered her back teeth. Dark patches of old silver crowded in at the sides, tops, and bottoms of her molars and pre-molars, turning the insides of her mouth into a wasteland. Her mom tells her she brings it upon herself with too much soda and coffee, but she prefers to believe she inherited bad flora, that no amount of careful brushing would change the welcoming environment of her teeth to cavities. She never expects to see clean white surfaces in her mouth. She brushes her teeth, pacing back and forth, while picking up more of her husband's crumpled things off the floor.

Dabbing on more under-eye concealer than usual, she picks a heavy foundation and uses a powder brush to add a faint sheen to her skin. She draws in a dark brown eyebrow to mask the thinning hair. She wishes she could see her face with her eyes closed to make sure her eyeliner is on straight, but when she closes one eye to see the other, the closed eye quivers too much.

Her husband has left the radio on, and she follows the trail of lights from the bedroom out into the living room.

She turns off the radio and overhead lights and makes herself a cup of coffee. She places his empty cereal bowl in the sink. At the kitchen counter, underneath the brightness of the skylight, she starts her list for the day. The list spills over onto a second page. She tears it up and starts over in even smaller handwriting. A hotel room needs to be booked for her cousin's wedding next month. Her husband's niece's birthday is coming up and she has to send a gift. She adds a postscript underneath, "nothing pink." Opening the refrigerator to check the contents she writes down butter, eggs, bacon, and beer for her husband. Before leaving the apartment, she checks her eye makeup in the hallway mirror one last time and adjusts the drape of her jacket against the slim gray skirt.

On the way to work, she picks up a croissant and her second cup of coffee. After she has taken off her jacket and put her bag away, her assistant hands her the day's schedule. She checks the last meeting of the afternoon, making sure she has time to get to her dentist. Though she knows the lack of feeling in her mouth does not manifest physically on her face, she dislikes feeling lopsided from the Novocaine, so she schedules him as late in the day as possible.

She stopped asking for Novocaine in college when she overheard a professor saying it wasn't necessary for small fillings. She tried it once and found she would rather bear the temporary pressure of drilling than the discomfort afterward of a swollen mouth. Novocaine numbs her tongue and lips so that when she is told to rinse, she can't keep her lips closed around the water. She has to use her fingers to create a seal. She misses her long hair to hide the childishness of holding her mouth closed with her fingers.

This morning's schedule contains back-to-back meetings. She hurries to the conference room booked for her weekly review with the design team. She leaves one meeting for another. In the hallways, people approach her as she walks to her next appointment. She rattles off answers, not stopping to check if someone is listening.

Use Pantone 17-2031 Fuchsia Rose for the last page of the brochure.
Does Accounting know we only have the budget for billboard ads this month?
Rush the print job for the Jacobs project.
Where are the final mock-ups for the Wythe account?
Has my new printer arrived yet?

Lunch is a salad she eats at her desk. Her assistant orders the same one for her every day—romaine lettuce, a hardboiled egg, alfalfa sprouts, shredded carrots, and mushrooms with a sherry wine vinaigrette. It occurs to her too late that she should have had her assistant order something more substantial today. It will be late by the time she gets home for dinner. Her hand feels along her lower jawbone, remembering the months of procedures that followed the first visit. The infection had trickled down into the crevices above her teeth and they had to wait for it to drain completely. When it had cleared from her cheek, the underlying cavity had dug so deep she needed a root canal.

After the initial winter visit, she saw him every week, sometimes twice a week when he wanted to check on the slow progress of her gums healing. At first, she tried working from her phone while he maneuvered around her, but her arms grew weary of holding up the device. Instead, she closed her eyes and laid there in stillness, tilted back in the chair with her mouth open to his gaze. The only awareness available to her was the pressure of the drill against her tooth, the warmth of his body next to her head and his chair creaking as he leans over her. Winter coats shifted to lighter jackets until she no longer had to use the hooks on the back of the door.

Heavy spring rains drenched the city when he called her in for a two-hour manicuring visit. He filled her with Novocaine so she wouldn't feel the sharp scalpel separating her gum from the tooth, but she could still hear the scraping of the blade against the bone. He tucked a straw in her mouth to suck up the blood. At first she didn't realize how much bleeding there was. It was only when he kept stuffing folded gauze inside her mouth, against her tongue and on the outside, sandwiched between her cheek and gum, that she thought about what the gauze was absorbing. She opened an eye to look when he pulled the wadded cotton from her mouth with fine tipped tweezers. The pads came out soaked in blood. He filled a cup with them. He stripped off the rubber gloves, also covered in bright red. While he rummaged around for clean ones, she cautiously poked around with her tongue. She could feel a crevice running along the sides of her teeth where he pulled back the gum to expose the enamel base.

When the bleeding finally slowed, he stitched her gum together and covered the flap with a soft, pink putty material that adhered to the gaps he had made. If she opened her mouth too wide, it looked like food was stuck to her teeth. She couldn't stop pushing her tongue into the putty covering the stitches holding her gum together. Self-conscious about the putty, she tried not to open her mouth to talk, and when she couldn't avoid it, she casually held up one hand to cover the side of her face where it might be visible. Over the course of the week, as the pain faded, the taste of rose hips flooded her mouth. The pink putty released tiny increments of an artificial scent so small she thought she was imagining it. Her morning coffee tasted faintly of roses.

Before she had left for the beach house, he had begun preparing her teeth for the permanent crowns. The first set had arrived before the spring holidays, but he wasn't satisfied with the way the porcelain sat against her regrown gum and sent them back to be recast. He made her temporary crowns that he adjusted one millimeter at a time. One hand gripping her jaw, he fit them snuggly over her teeth and then peered deep into her mouth to check the fit, running his fingertips along the edge of the crowns, lightly back and forth. The back crown hit her bottom tooth at a less than perfect angle and he removed it to file off a minute portion. He put it back in and felt around again with his fingers where they met her gum line. Summer had begun teasing the city with sultry humidity before he pronounced himself satisfied. He wanted her to come back for the final fitting of the permanent crowns, but she left him for the beach house.

Now, a dry autumnal air trickles through the city, and she is seeing him later this evening. After lunch, she rushes down the hall for another series of meetings. She listens to her directors presenting project updates with one hand pressing down on her check, a reflexive motion. She constantly turns her left wrist surreptitiously below the table to check the time on her watch.

When she leaves she doesn't tell anyone. She slides her laptop into her bag, puts on her jacket, and grabs a scarf for later. At the elevator, her foot taps a short staccato beat. She looks straight ahead, not wanting to catch anyone's eye. She comes out of the subway into the languid afternoon, though by the time she leaves her dentist, the afternoon will have changed to twilight.

Let's take a look then.

Open wide.

Wider.

Turn towards me.

He repositions the lamp overhead for a better view. Strong fingers gently push her lips back. He uses either hand with equal ease. She closes her eyes. She sinks into the sensations in her mouth, focusing solely on the pressure of the drill against her tooth. Pain explodes in her mouth. She breathes into it, narrowing her mind to the one point. She opens her eyes when she feels a shadow pass overhead. She sees the fine hairs of his forearm, muscles slightly tensing as he reaches across her to settle the straw suction in the corner of her mouth. He doesn't have an assistant. Sometimes he forgets about the suction and she reaches a hand up to adjust it herself.

Turn away and close a little.

A little more.

Good.

He tucks a finger against the inside of her cheek and reaches deep back to check, for the third time, the fit of the filling on her back two molars.

Something's not right.

I need more time with you.

Can you stay another hour?

He shifts in his chair to look down at her, tilted all the way back.

She looks for his eyes, the only thing visible of his face, and nods.

He turns toward the counter behind his chair to cut a length of dental cord to insert underneath her gum before casting a new mold. She hears him preparing another dose of Novocaine.

When he turns back with the needle, its tip moist and dripping, her whole body tenses. His fingers wrap around her jaw, gripping her face firmly. His thumb hooks inside the back and he presses down where the needle pierces first. When he finally pulls it out, she breathes and lets her body go. Her mind clears.

He opens the drawer behind her head and rustles around, the metal implements knocking against one another. He sits her up to insert the mold impression. Tucking it in at a diagonal, he runs a finger alongside the gum line to make sure it sits properly. His left hand steadies her jaw as he tugs at the mold.

Don't move.

Give that a few minutes to settle.

I'll be back in a couple.

She doesn't move. She hears him walking into the hallway, leaving her there, breathing through her nose. She focuses on the far wall instead of on gagging like her throat wants to do. She inhales deeply, the air passing through her nose down into her lungs. She exhales and her breath leaves her body to mingle with the room. Her mind empties. She is alone in the chair, breathing slowly in and then out again, waiting for her dentist.

Let's see where we are.

She didn't hear him come back. Instead of sitting, he stands in the space next to her and uses his forefinger to push back into her mouth, breaking the suction of the mold. He pulls it out and examines the contours of her imprinted teeth.

Perfect.

Now he sits as he rotates the mold in his hands, using his head lamp to peer closely at the crevices. He takes a curved probe and scratches at the rough edges.

Next Tuesday I want you for half an hour.

He unclips her bib and turns away to clean the tools in his tray.

She walks slowly to the subway stop, not rushing to get home. The shop lights in the darkening twilight daze her.

Her husband doesn't ask her about her evenings at the dentist. She usually tells him she'll be late and that he should wait for her for dinner, but tonight he has started eating without her, a paper open next to him. At least he has taken out an extra container of soup for her from the freezer. When it has heated up in the microwave, she takes the bowl and sits down across from him at the table. She clears her throat.

Did you ask your boss if you could have time off next month? We need to book a hotel for my cousin's wedding.

I forgot. I'll do it tomorrow.

Can you try and not forget? This is the third time I've asked you. Also the table in the office needs to go down to storage. You said you would call them to come pick it up. It's been a month.

I said I'd do it. I'll do it.

He goes back to reading the paper.

The heat from the broth makes her teeth ache.w She takes a smaller bite, blowing carefully before putting the spoon in her mouth. She cuts a meatball in half and dips the spoon in the soup, picking up some bits of tomato and orzo. She rests the spoon on the edge of the bowl to let it cool down. He looks up.

Did you get me more beer? I'm almost out of yogurt, too.

Yes. I did.

He goes back to his paper. He finishes dinner before her and gets up, the chair scrapping against the floor. He places his napkin next to his water glass and leaves his bowl and spoon on the table.

She tests each spoonful of soup with the tip of her tongue before eating. She calls out to her husband on the couch where he has settled to watch TV.

I told the Sherwins we would join them for dinner next Thursday. They want to try that new Chinese place a couple blocks from your office. You can meet us there after work.

I can't go on Thursday. I'm meeting the guys from work to watch a game. You have to change it. It's the only day they're free.

She feels him frowning from across the room. He doesn't respond, switching between a football game and a movie they saw in the theaters last summer. An explosion followed by gunfire sounds out from the TV. She takes another bite of soup. She can't see the TV from the dining room table but she waits until a commercial before speaking again.

Can you find the itemized receipt from your check-up last month? The health insurance company will freeze the card if they don't have it in the next two weeks. And they need a copy of your physical for their records.

Another commercial comes on. Her husband doesn't stir from the couch.

Did you hear me?

I heard you.

Can you acknowledge that you heard me? Are you going to send me the receipt?

I heard you. I said I'd do it.

Well I wish you would answer me the first time.

There is no response. She has almost finished her soup. After she has cleared the table and put away the dirty dishes, leaving her husband still in front of the TV, she heads into the study. She doesn't turn on the light, using the illumination from the hallway sconce to adjust the angle of her recliner to a horizontal tilt. Shutting the door softly behind her, she lies down in the darkness, closes her eyes and opens her mouth. She pictures the pulsing of blood in her gum flowing from her mouth to her jaw, then cheek, out to the ends of her head and, beating a gentle rhythm, downward through the rest of her body.

Mirrored Reveals

Deena Linett

Mirrored Reveals

Y ou'd think someone would've seen something.

Probably you learn to quit seeing: It's scary or you tell yourself what you see is normal because it's familiar, or maybe you think it's not significant. How could you possibly know?

The thing in the mirror is something. Sometimes it's my own face, or Jade's. Where is it, though? Behind the glass, against the silver? Floating in the air between me and the mirror?

Sometimes I think the thing in the mirror isn't just with me; it could be anywhere—who knows.

Reveals are those three-inch-wide frames on doors and windows. The word comes from the French, and in French chateaux, my mother says, they're sometimes four feet thick—Versailles, for example. This is one of those things you'd never know if your mother wasn't a decorator.

She has great taste, my mother, very dramatic. Theatrical. The door-frames in both our living and dining rooms have mirrored reveals. The living room's a big airy space with a high ceiling and a mirror that nearly covers one wall. The only furniture's a massive sofa upholstered in sea-green jacquard silk and two bamboo chairs. No scattered tables, which makes it impossible to put down a drink—or even a comb. No scattered anything, which may be the point.

A flowering tree shimmers in one corner. No matter where you stand you can see its reflection in the reveals that toss the light around in interesting ways. Sometimes my mother puts a branch of quince or pussy-willow in a tall floor vase with scarlet peonies and sea-green rushes on it in the hallway, and she replaces the tree periodically. That's it, summer and winter. You have the sense you're underwater, occasional streaks of color glimmering in all those mirrors, dark and cool.

The Mask

I always felt safe with the lion mask on the wall at the back of the apart-ment, near our bedrooms. It was our mascot, Jade's and mine, in lieu of a dog or cat, our pet and protector. When we were little our friends said it'd give them nightmares. It lives opposite a window under a ceiling lamp in the broad back hallway, so it's always illuminated. Almost four feet across, it's bright green and blue and orange with red and gold trim-ming. It has red and jet-blue tassels, which, when we got tall enough, we'd flip as we walked past. Its hot-pink tongue hangs out and its eyes are orange glass with pupils painted on, bigger than my fist.

My father, American, white, used to joke about the mask, calling it Mighty Mouth, but never with real derision. Its proper name is Fuzzy-Face in Chinese. My mother's Chinese. She came here when she was twelve, so she's comfortable with things American, and she gave me and my sister a lot of freedom, much more than other children of Chinese parents. My theory is, it depends on when they came.

Jade's theory—she's my twin sister—is that it depends on their sex life. *Jaa-aade!!* She's like that, outrageous. She goes to art school, and mostly, I think, likes to shock people. I'm the "good" child, the law-yer. Twenty-six, we live on our own. Separately. See, this is something Chinese parents would never permit, but my mother's cool.

But nothing—not even Columbia Law School—prepares you for the arrest of your father. On sex charges.

The house, the mask: I felt safe there, I felt they had things under con-trol, my parents. My father's a municipal court judge and a teacher of history at a posh private school. For the municipal court appointment, you need a law degree, which he has, and for the teaching you need a degree in history, which he also has. The story in our family was that he didn't like the competitiveness required for the practice of law—he always said Jade and I were competitive enough for three families. He loved history and loved teaching—that's what he said.

Right now it occurs to me that I don't know anything about him.

The Daughters

He has two daughters, so imagine my horror when he's arrested ("like a common criminal," my mother will say, literally twisting her hands) for sexual misconduct.

With high school girls.

It does something to your soul. Nails, like. Long metal nails.

Your *father.*

Mine.

I read it in the paper.

I mean, my mother didn't call. This is not surprising. In our family the children were add-ons. The central item was the couple, the mother and the father, the man and the woman, the husband and the wife. Some couples are like this; they almost exclude their children. Other couples make family central, and still others—I have noticed this all my life—focus on the children. Often to the exclusion of the father, it has to be said. Which I assume is because on some level the father wants to be excluded—from responsibility, from the messy emotional life of a family.

I wish my father were old enough that I could think this is senility or something, but it's not, and on some level, it doesn't even surprise me. Horrifies, yes. But surprise? I'd have to say no.

Questions

What goes on between them? When it's your mother and father you never ask the question. It'd be like asking why there are air and water. And it'd be beyond awful to blame my mother. I do not. Jade won't either. I know her.

History

When we were children, we called our American parent General Chō. Where this came from—and the rude rebellion it signified—is lost to me.

Was he harsh, dictatorial? Probably, but don't all children see their fathers that way?

I was going to have to call Jade, and I couldn't make myself do it. I kept having this choking feeling, and then I couldn't imagine what I'd say.

She lives with her boyfriend, Erik Standy. She giggles when she says his name; she's got this line—she postures, my sister. I hate her doing it, but I see its value. The negatives: It's affected, says she's some kind of movies-version Asian. She giggles, delivers the line, Erik's a stand-up guy.

Questions, II

Why did we call him a Chinese nickname? For distance? Because he seemed so different from us? I can't imagine.

Green

It took me a couple of hours to stop shaking after I screamed and cried and threw up. Thought I'd never cried before, compared. Out the window: a light sunny afternoon, late March. Colder than it looked, probably, and some of the trees were getting little buds on them. I love the new greens and always try to walk in the parks when spring comes. Jade's a greenie too. She paints nature—abstracted images of weeds and spores and seeds and the tall stalks and plumes of wild grasses. Where did a pair of New Yorkers learn to love all this stuff? Jade says it's in the genes.

Oh shit.

What does this say about our own sexual preferences, proclivities, acts?

If it says nothing, it still says something.

How could I ever be with a man again? Would every penis make me think of my father's?

Sex

It's one of those things—sex is—that you don't have any standards for, and after you've finished all the teen-years' reading, you assume whatever you do is normal. Or I had. Once Mark wanted to do something I didn't and I stopped it. Made him mildly angry but he got over it. I didn't stop to think then about what people do and what's "normal," which of course depends on who you talk to.

Once in college a professor asked us—not only the women—if we'd ever been touched without our permission, and I was amazed to see *all* the guys raise their hands.

Not like this.

I'll never know.

I mean I'll never know what he says to himself when it's over.

I think about that sometimes when I read the papers, about guys who do terrible things to children. What do they tell themselves after?

Now it's my father. "Father." Means the man whose little squirt of semen made you.

Me. I keep avoiding the *me*.

When you're a child, he's one of the big people who gives you things. He keeps you from running into the street and holds you on his lap on the bus and takes you to museums and tells you the names for things. I remember his pointing to a ledge on a building where there were pigeons and—I must've asked—saying they were pigeons, and I remember liking to say it, *Pigeons, pigeons,* entranced for the first time by the way words you repeat several times become pure sound. *Pigeon.* Later I learned the word *pidgin* and then I remember thinking—this must've been third grade or so—that *pigeon* looked like *pig* and like *neon*. A Midwestern farm-child wouldn't have had *neon* in her vocabulary. I had a mad moment of wishing I were a safe Midwestern farm-child whose father drives a tractor.

English is enough to make you give up on language. I remember thinking this, but I must've been much older then. Maybe I was trying to imagine my mother coming here when she was twelve with her sister Jen-li, whose name she gave me. I could not have done it, I sometimes think, move worlds away and lose the language I think in. It would be impossible to learn English with the necessary nuance if I hadn't come to it from birth. I'm not certain of a lot, but I know this. The older I get the more I admire my mother.

As for my name, it's something I wear, like clothes—only I get to choose my clothes. It's not uncomfortable, but it's like a jacket, not against my skin. It's loose, easy enough I suppose, but in some real way I could take it off and not miss it. My name isn't about me, but about my mother's culture—and mine. It's something other people call me. I call myself *me*.

My aunt Jen-li died crossing a street. Confusion. Foreignness.

I look like I could belong in a lot of places, but I don't. I belong here, New York, with the ocean right there beyond all the buildings, and the rivers. Once, in California, I kept getting confused because the ocean's on the wrong side. And also in California, people assume things about you if you look like I do. Jade doesn't mind it so much, but she's more Anglo-looking, with wavy brown hair.

Questions, III

Why?

I Tell Her

General Chō's been arrested. That'd be one try.

Jade. General Chō has been arrested. For sexual misconduct with children.

I called her. We have to talk. Seriously? The question was a way of saying, Will you please be serious here?

She giggled. The only place you see her real feeling is in her painting, and not everybody can see it.

Seriously, I said again, stern.

Okay. Now I heard the waiting in her voice.

Okay, good. Now listen to me: Do not read the papers, just come to Freddie's. Clear your evening.

You need me? She sounded frightened.

I hadn't thought that. Yes, I said.

I still hadn't thought about my mother, who'd need both of us, and when I did, it erupted: God help us.

Freddie's. I faced away from the door. She let me know she was there by reaching over the top of the booth and brushing my hair awry with one hand. Then she plopped down opposite, theatrically divesting herself of all her stuff: backpack, red scarf with yellow polka dots—ketchup and scrambled eggs, it reminded me of—and one with yellow and orange stripes (today only two; she's been known to wear as many as five), her famous long Russian officer's coat, silk jacket. If things'd been different I'd've teased her about the jacket: *Doing your Chinese look today?* But it wasn't that kind of occasion. Terrible word.

You look pretty strung.

I blew air out of my mouth, couldn't speak. I looked past her at the mirror and all the pennants and bottles in front of it. It was way too early for anybody to be here.

Big stuff, she said.

You have no idea.

Start.

All I could think was how there're no tables in the living room. Do you think Ma didn't want anybody to be at home in our apartment?

She stared.

Daddy, I said. How that childhood word emerged from what I'd been thinking I have no clue. There it was: Daddy.

Died? Her face went bone-white.

You'll wish he had, I said. Then I started to laugh, and couldn't stop crying. She came to sit beside me and I felt her arms go around me and I buried my face in my sister's neck and cried.

Answers

You think you can know another person?

You think you can know this? The best answer is, it's part of human experience, and it gets acted out by person X here and person Y there, and one of them happens— in this instance— to be your father.

People say, but they don't know. Nobody knows.

Aftermaths

We wanted to weep and talk but we would have to go to our mother.

I felt as if I'd been beaten up. Everything hurt. My head aches, Jade said, rubbing her forehead with thin paint-stained fingers. I wear long red nails. We don't look so much alike as we used to want to, but we have one heart. We drank a ton of coffee and ate some nachos and cheese, when what we really wanted was to get completely bombed and make believe it hadn't happened. I said this.

Make believe it hasn't happened *yet*, she said.

Which means . . . ?

Right. It would be going to happen sometime.

Like it'd be waiting there, out in the future, like something you walk toward?

Just like, she nodded.

Awfully deterministic, I said.

Right, she said, eyes filling. If it weren't going to happen sometime, why now?

I felt a huge sigh. It was going to have happened sometime. What an astonishing idea.

She was ready to go before I was. You're braver, I said.

He's our father, she said.

I'm the lawyer. I'm supposed to say things like that, I said, thinking of consanguinity tables and posters of the bloodlines of English royalty from my undergraduate years.

We were a good family, I said.

That's dumb, her look said.

I know, I said.

I stood there in my navy jacket while she wrapped herself up in all her stuff: purple-patched black silk jacket, red and yellow scarf, yellow striped orange scarf, the coat.

I don't know how to think about it, I said as we went out into the windy dark.

New York's sometimes a mess down here. Cans and bottles rolled along the sidewalk and banged into storefronts and over curbs. My face felt dirty: grit and paper kicked up by the wind swirled, and the currents plastered some of it against my legs, her long coat. Horns and brakes, trucks clattering, shouts.

Usually I love it, all this noise and filth and clamor. Usually I think it's pure energy, absolutely wonderful.

Think this, she said. He's our father. For the rest of our lives we'll love him and we'll hate him—

And, like a stone from heaven, I thought, What if I have daughters? Because then I knew: it wasn't only high-school girls. I screamed. She whirled and grabbed me.

Jen! What? What is it?

Little girls . . .

Fiercely: You don't know that.

I do. I do know it.

How can you know that? she said, stiff. She had to raise her voice over the wind and all the noise. She felt rigid, holding me in the wind. I remember thinking it was the Russian officer's coat.

I couldn't speak. I was screaming into her coat. She held me as hard as she could and rocked me, smoothing my hair, which was whipping both our faces.

Jen, she said. Don't. Don't.

She said it again. It would go forward with us into all the rest of our lives, into each day, sun and rain and snow, and when we're old. He's our father.

No. No no no.

Yes, she said, like stone.

I thought if I looked behind me—as I walked forward into the rest of my life—if I turned to look, there'd be a slimy trail of something, like tracks of snails.

Like semen.

Right there on the street.

Then she was holding me again, her face pressed against mine, and she was making little sounds like the idea of a song—vague and musical, almost inaudible. She did it for a long time, and finally it wrapped us in quiet.

My eyes felt gritty.

I pulled back to look at her.

We'll *live*, she said.

Spring Beneath Silence

Kenneth John Holt

Mother is lost in the color of her wine glass. Why is it called white wine? It is not white. It is golden in color, particularly when a late afternoon sunlight kisses it from the window, as is happening in this moment. The southwest side of her studio from top to bottom is a bank of several clear glass windows that provide a shadowless wall of soft light to work by until the sun finally dips too low. At this time of day, the sun refuses to be the supporting act. It speaks the truth in direct form. This afternoon it points her toward the colored truth of white wine.

A highlight in the wine glass is blinding. It hurts to look into. She lifts the stem and gives it a wrist action, setting the wine swirling, and lands the glass back down on the same spot upon her drafting table. The highlight has lessened. It is fragmented by the spinning contents but again shines brightly as the wine settles back to its stoic placement within the glass. Mother averts her focus from the accent and follows the path of the hard sun onto the floor, where a shadow has formed a replica of the wine glass sitting atop the table. She is there, too, in the replica. Her etched silhouette is standing beside all the rest. She is almost always standing. There is far too much to get done in a day.

Her boy lies on the clean slate of the hardwood floor just beyond the reach of the direct sunlight. The sharp-cast shadow beside him looks so real that she imagines he could grab the glass and drink from it, but he never would do such a thing. He has a glass of his own. It is in the right place on the floor, since he puts it there himself. His food is there, too. He arranges the food before he eats from the plate. Things have to be a certain way, and for as long as memory will allow, it has always been so with him.

The boy is encircled by the drawings he has made on the floor. Mother freely hands out lightweight tracing paper a few times a day and at each occasion her son starts out by squinting through a sheet around the room. The stock is of the best quality, nearly as clear as anime celluloid. In the beginning she reasoned he might like copy elementary shapes but soon witnessed he fervently works a method all his own. No thought is given to the amount of material he goes through because there's more than enough to go around. She is gifted with art paper at every Christmas and at every birthday, since it is well known that the boy's mother is a successful illustrator. It would be nice if he were like her in this one way. It is her hope to find something in common with him.

She cleans up the drawings when he has made too big a mess and then gives him another dozen sheets to work on.

"Here, let me have those. You know where they go . . . they go into their very own cubby each day. Today is Thursday, child."

There is a new cubby for each new day of the week. At the end of every afternoon, she places his drawings in the proper one for him. All of the papers then go into a special trunk on Sundays so that at the start of each new workweek they can begin once more.

"But first, let's put them here on your desk so you can see how many you've done so far."

Mother bends to pick up the drawn sheets and replaces them with a fresh stack. Her boy wastes no time in spreading them out all around.

It happens every time—he undoes what she has organized. She used to try to help him make the circle he likes, but it is of no use, for only her son knows the exact position and angle each sheet must achieve.

Mother flips through the drawings and attempts to make sense of the lines and patterns. There they are again, the abstract images confronting her. She takes a while studying them and recognizes some continuity in his use of color. The pictures are an unsettling mix of pastel hues running off the end of each paper as though they are meant to exist beyond it. Even better than the color, it is clear to her that he loves shading. He graduates from the blackest black to the faintest gray whisper. In it, she finds a degree of comforting structure. There is some promise in the shading.

She collects all of the drawings throughout their time and sets them neatly onto the low desk she bought for her boy, the petitionary zone from where they pose until transferred into the corresponding cubby at the end of each day. It was meant to be his own worktable, like hers, but he hasn't ever used it. He prefers the wide floor to the desk she has given him. Even so, it does retain a purpose. It now holds the drawings at a height that can be easily seen until he is finished. Mother hopes this will boost his confidence by a sense of accomplishment. A few dozen drawings a session is an accomplishment, even if they don't make any sense beyond that of abstraction, even if they are only lines, patterns, and pastel hues. She then reflects upon the promise in the shading and chooses to view this as progress.

The shadow of the wine glass still shows strongly and reminds Mother it is time for a refill. The kitchen is a half floor up from the workspace. She makes the twelve steps, turns, and holds there a moment, standing, looking out through the bank of windows at the view. The last of the penetrating sunlight has just now gone and is replaced by a skyline tapestry made up of multiple colors struggling for dominance with bleeding cayenne always winning in the end. The studio loft is infused with what is reflected from the sky.

The wine is coming on nicely and she thinks about the many fortunate aspects of her life. She loves her father so and misses his company. He has made much of what is fortunate possible for her. Where would she be without him? She does wish he could visit, but he won't; he has stopped all that. What he hasn't stopped are the deposits into her account each month—a new deposit for each new month. The amount is more than she needs to subsidize her income. It is more than she needs to afford this grand loft with a view. It is more than she needs for the doctors and special educators. It is just plain more, relentlessly coming at her to such a degree that she thinks she might suffocate by the blanket of it. In his absence he sends his wife, her own mother, to visit the grandchild each new day.

Her boy sits upright as his favorite television show begins. She watches him from that high position of the kitchen. The TV stays on all day, as it seems to make him more productive, but he never looks at it until this hour, and it is unclear if he even listens to what is said. The tests have all reached the same conclusion: He does not have trouble hearing, though he hasn't a normative reaction to sound.

This one show has his attention every evening at this same time. It's that old black and white one with Robert Young. Mother used to watch the same reruns as a little girl and now he does the same as a little boy. She has considered there might be a connection in the black and white images, and so she has tried a variety of different black and white programs. None of them lasted very long. Could it be he is somehow attracted to Mister Young? She'd once found a listing for a color TV program starring the same popular actor, but the boy stared at the ground within a minute's time.

The show is finished and her boy returns to himself. She makes the steps downward to pick up the last round of drawings and places them neatly atop the stack on the desk.

"Well, look at that. I'd say you've outdone yourself today!"

She turns off the television, goes to his desk, and shuffles through the papers.

"These are some of your best. You should be proud of yourself."

Her boy takes his gaze from the floor to just beside the television set. This is his usual look. This is where he fixes when the television is off. Sometimes he walks right up to it with an off-center stare, as though what comes from the television might live behind it. She thinks he waits for it to be on again but is mistaken in her assumption.

"Bedtime."

Mother takes him by the hand and they start in the bathroom. Later she rests a book upon his pillow and notices there is just enough of this chapter to get through tonight.

The wine looks quite different in the kitchen light and nearly passes for true white at this late hour. Her favorite place in the loft is the high landing up the twelve steps. She can see most everything from there. The city view has a meditative effect on her and she never rushes her movements while looking out at it. The light of the kitchen spills out, making a pool down onto her workspace. Her drafting table doesn't look so tall from this vantage, but she knows that it really is tall, as she rarely ever sits down. She picked out the twin desk for her boy with the same idea in mind. She thought it would be nice if they both stood while working; she thought it would be nice if they were the same. Thinking in this way, while alone, has the same meditative effect on her.

In the pool, Mother just now sees she has forgotten to place today's new work into the cubby of the day. "Today is Thursday, child," she remembers saying to him. The wine is not at risk while she makes her way down the steps as it is carried in the casual manner indicating an experienced hand.

At each step downward, the scene from the window changes slightly, but it is not as altogether different as a person might expect when moving one's perspective. A highlight from the pool flashes onto an object beside the television as she makes the landing. Something produces a glare at this angle, obscuring any detail of it, and so she goes forward trying to make out its likeness when her foot slides across the floor by rolling on a handful of the boy's colored pencils. The wine is saved but her hip bumps his desk, sending the papers spilling broadly out across the hardwood. She takes a nice hit from the glass and sets it down on her drafting table before getting to the job of the cleanup. Some extra light might be helpful for the task, but her mood is such that it would be considered an intrusion on the musing influence happening near the midnight hour.

Mother circles 'round the far end of the pool made by the kitchen light to avoid her own shadow and finds she can see well enough to do the job. She bends and stops. This is a long pause, a break, the type to which she is unaccustomed, as she takes in what has come up in front of her. Four sheets in a row follow the same drawn line. They marry up nearly perfectly, and it is clear that the muted pastel did want to run off the sheet; it wanted to run onto the next corresponding paper, and there it is. All it takes is a minor adjustment by her and they match, then she sees five or six more that belong together. Mother gets to work organizing the three-dozen sheets of drawings and they line up very quickly. She tries to straighten them out so the edges of the paper all run in the same direction and are framed by right angles, but it doesn't work that way. The image coming together has a circular frame with the papers at a diagonal.

Knowing the papers have to be at a diagonal helps her with the correct pattern. She completes the outer circle of it and this is where the shading really comes into play; it attempts to be a sphere rather than a flat circle, with the outer rim of the blackest black graduating to a whisper of gray toward the middle. Each diagonal sheet has one corner sticking out sharply around the entire perimeter, making the frame look like the sprocket of a bicycle. Filling in the rest is easy once the outer is completed.

It is a human face surrounded by a sprocket. Mother is fascinated by the detail of the image and by the unusual technique used to create it. It is ghostly. The eyes are pure black, with only one speck of white in each center, and its skin tone shows mostly pale cyan with a strong blue taking over in specific contoured areas. The hair blends an even mixture of washed turquoise and hues of magenta, and it moves within the frame, flying away into a measured background. There is more here than just the face standing forward. On the lower end, the backdrop is made up of a row of buildings coming in at different heights, like the result of poor dentistry. They have the same supernatural feel, with black windows filling in, spotted inside their muted pastel framework. It looks like a touch of spilt pea has been added to a bowl of faded pumpkin soup above the buildings to finish a horizon line behind the face. And this completes the picture.

Mother goes back to her wine. She is tempted to wake the boy at this very moment and scold him for playing such games, but she doesn't.

How would she address what is beyond her understanding? The ghostly representation of the image is a bother. It is unnerving to a point that she is frightened. This is it? This is what he does each day while not talking, while not allowing her into his world? Mother tries to conjure up his intention and wonders what other mysteries are held within the many drawings she has collected over these months. An idea comes as she lifts the glass to her lips and finishes. No more wine for tonight; it would only slow down what she as yet to do.

Her boy wakes late this morning. He uses the bathroom and goes directly to his place on the clean slate of the hardwood floor. The television is not on. Mother has decided it will remain off for today in the hope there will be less distraction between them. He sits and finds his glass. He moves it two inches to the right. He then arranges the food on his plate before taking a bite. Mother bends and lands a fresh stack of paper that number one dozen beside him. Her boy spreads the individual sheets into a circle all around his position. He takes a drink from his glass and sets it back down, giving it a small adjustment. It doesn't take him long to finish breakfast. Mother knows to add new items as needed to the plate. It is his custom to graze there throughout the day. It is this way every new day.

The boy does not lie down on the hardwood. He does not begin his drawing. He only stares toward the television, but without any certainty. His off-center look is just beside it and she thinks back to the obscure idea that what comes from the television might live behind it. Mother waits for him to look up at her. She wishes he would notice the far and high area of the window bank featured behind her, the area where the sunlight intrudes on them each late afternoon. This wish is a long shot, as the boy only glances toward her when he thinks she is not paying the slightest attention. She catches him once in a great while when his timing is off by enough to allow for this mistake.

Her tall stance at the drafting table blocks a portion of what she has taped to the window behind her. She notices this, and moves two feet to the right to clear it, and when sliding the table over, her boy was late in returning his stare to beside the television. Mother has caught him in the act of the mistake. So quickly and so easily she has caught him looking her direction. She goes about organizing the things that shifted during the move, staying focused while keeping her boy in the peripheral. She can tell he is pondering the image behind her. He gazes off-center at the television whenever she makes direct contact with him, but then he sneaks a glimpse of what is pasted to the window every chance he gets. They spend all morning long and late into the afternoon playing this game. Mother finally takes a chance by speaking openly about it.

"I can't believe I figured it out. It was quite by chance that I did, really." She's not sure where she is going.

"It's a beautiful, beautiful drawing. I don't even know how you did it . . . so many pieces. How do you keep it all straight?"

Mother looks from her boy up to the window where last night she gathered the three-dozen individual sheets into the completed image. It fills almost an entire window with its size. The indirect soft light illuminates the muted hues and the whisper gray, while blackest black remains opaque. It glows in its unnaturalness and reaches Mother as a daylight haunting. There is something backwards about it. It requires extra effort to hold the black eyes within her lock.

"Are there more? . . . Will I find more of these if I go through the cubbies? I can't imagine what has gone into the trunk for all of these months."

Her boy takes his look from beside the television to the floor at this time. His retreat tells Mother she has gone too far with him. She too would like to retreat and climbs the steps upward to start on the wine. Her wrist action swirls it round. This has brought her back to the blinding highlight of yesterday that was fragmented by the movement of the contents.

Something tells her to walk to the edge of the high landing. It is the sun. The sun has finally dipped too low, setting the image in the window ablaze with its hard, penetrating light. It is painful in its brilliance. Mother forestalls the harm in it by looking downward toward her boy. Her eyes need a moment to adjust, but still, she sees it clearly enough. The wine glass falls from her hand, hitting the clean slate of the hardwood floor, breaking into dozens of pieces. Her boy snaps his head around.

Mother rushes down the steps and goes straight to her drafting table from where she has the best view. The sun has painted an image of the multiple drawings into one likeness on the floor. It is vivid. It is perfect.

She turns and studies the window and sees the image there is reversed. She now understands what is happening. Her boy has created a color negative from the three-dozen sheets of paper, and the driving sun projects the photo-picture of it onto the floor for them to view.

Mother looks to her boy, who, in turn, looks to the object beside the television. She sees that it has been mostly forgotten, and by neglect was pushed to the back of the shelf, nearly disappearing behind the screen. The details within its frame have been replicated in the painting on the floor. The man's face, the coloring, the buildings in the background, and the sky above, are all almost identical in their representation to the real thing. The promise in the shading is there, too, and it reveals an image bound by more than a flat sprocketed circle. It is indeed a sphere—a sun. And she remembers the day when she took this photograph of her boy's father standing before these very windows.

"I want to see him."

"What? . . . Did you say something?" asks Mother.

"I want to see him," her boy says again.

"I want to see him, too," Mother replies. "I want to see him, too.

Endangered Animal Release Specialists

Joe Dornich

M onday morning I hurry to the Intake and Assignment meeting and tell myself this time things will be different. This time my potential and experience will be recognized. This time I will be assigned a high-profile case. Do I think it will be a Tibetan antelope or a Mediterranean monk seal? Of course not, though a girl can dream. Still, after months of Releasing amphibians, really anything from the Mammalia class would feel like a bonus. I just need something to be proud of. Something that will let me feel the work I'm doing here is making a difference. Something I can counter with when Ma cruelly, and inaccurately, asks why I'm wasting my life as an animal masturbator.

I arrive just as everyone is taking their seats and Dr. Farragut is plugging in the projector. When we're settled, and everyone has helped themselves to coffee and a doughnut, Dr. Farragut begins the meeting the same way he has every Monday morning for the last four months:

"How are you, you bunch of jag-offs?"

It's his favorite joke. He *still* thinks it's hilarious. We all offer a pained smile or an obligatory half-laugh in response. All of us except Janet. The fire, and subsequent scarring and deterioration of the muscles, rendered Janet's face incapable of any real expression. Dr. Farragut says the shiny pink scar tissue makes her face look like a glazed ham, which, while somewhat accurate, isn't very nice. Either way, no one expects Janet to pretend to be happy.

I envy her.

Then the lights go dark and the meeting really begins. Our first Intake slide features a long, ashen face ringed in copper-colored fur. Everyone perks up. *Pongo abelli,* or, as he is more commonly known, the Sumatran orangutan, is listed as Critically Endangered. Less than 1,500 remain. This is an extremely high-profile case. Lots of potential press. Lots of potential notoriety.

"I know what you're all thinking," Dr. Farragut says. "*Pongo abelli* is a high-profile case that will garner a great deal of attention. As such, I think it's best if I personally handle the Release of this animal."

No one is surprised. Dr. Farragut always assigns himself the most note-worthy cases. In his office is a framed copy of *Conservation Quarterly.* Dr. Farragut is on the cover with Ozzie, the Brazilian ocelot he assigned to himself and Released to much fanfare. The article is titled, "The Man, and the Hands, That Have the Ocelot on the Rise." Dr. Farragut had Ozzie autograph the cover by dipping his paws in ink, which, to me, seems tacky.

It's not as if I'm not happy for the ocelots. I am. They're beautiful creatures. But it's hard to forget that the day the reporters came and took their pictures and made a big show of everything, I was down in the sub-basement trying to Release an extremely uncooperative poison dart frog.

But still, through it all, I bide my time and quietly endure.

The next slide shows a familiar face. Duncan is a four-year-old speckled bear on Temporary Transfer from the Scranton facility. Dr. Farragut tells us that Duncan has recently been classified as a problem specimen because he attacked his Release Specialist. He tells us this as if we all haven't watched the security footage about a million times.

At first, things seem to be going well. The Release Specialist begins with some lower-abdominal massage. Duncan looks content. Soon, he achieves complete rigidity. The Specialist appears to have a firm, but not too firm, grip and a steady, even rhythm.

It's textbook technique.

But then something goes wrong. It's not clear what. Maybe the Specialist gets lazy. Or over-confident. Maybe he looks the animal in the eye, which is completely verboten.

It's the first thing we learn in Orientation.

Regardless, Duncan leaps from the Release Bay, lands on the Specialist, and pins him to the floor. A muffled whimper can be heard on the audio. Duncan inflicts some minor lacerations to the chest and neck area, and chews off the tip of an ear before the boys from Control swarm in with their tranq guns.

Dr. Farragut reminds us about Duncan's temperament. He warns us to be cautious. Then he assigns Duncan to Janet. I look over to see if Janet is excited or nervous about being given such a challenging animal, but of course I can't tell.

I'm next to get an assignment. I close my eyes and hope for a black-footed ferret, or an African wild dog. I hear the click of the projector. Then I hear Monroe snort out a laugh. I don't even know what Monroe is doing here. He's not a Release Specialist. He runs the Cryogenics Lab. But still, he's here every Monday morning, inhaling the free doughnuts and then sucking the jelly and powdered-sugar from his fingers in a suggestive manner.

I open my eyes. I see a mosaic of black, brown, and yellow pebbled skin. I see two marbled, golden eyes, and the distinctive upturned snout that rests between them. Fantastic. The Puerto Rican crested toad. Another amphibian.

I begin to protest, but Dr. Farragut raises a hand, silencing me.

"Before you start in with the lack of variety in your Release Assignments, or how you feel underappreciated, or how I must have some personal vendetta against you, let me assure you, I do not. Would I love to assign you a pygmy hippopotamus or an African bush elephant? Of course I would. But do you see any African bush elephants around here? Because I don't."

Then Dr. Farragut makes a show of looking around the room, and under the table, as if he has simply misplaced an African bush elephant. Which is ridiculous. They're huge.

"I can only assign what we intake," he says.

I think about mentioning the orangutan, but then I don't.

"Plus," Dr. Farragut continues, "Would you prefer Duncan? Would you prefer the bear that may claw your pretty little face off? Not that I believe that will happen. Not for a second. But it might. And as such, I have to try to minimize risk. I have to try to minimize the collateral damage in a before-and-after type of assessment. Does any of this make sense?"

Janet and I stare blankly ahead.

Monroe devours another doughnut.

Then Dr. Farragut sighs and runs a hand over his hair. Not through. But just over. Dr. Farragut is extremely meticulous about his hair. Every light-brown strand is slicked back into a smooth dome. It reminds me of the shell of the Yangtze giant turtle.

Which is also endangered.

Which is also another animal I'll probably never get my hands on.

"Okay," Dr. Farragut says. "Let's say it's raining. It's raining and I have the option between a work boot and a fancy shoe. Maybe the work boot is scuffed up a bit. Maybe the leather's cracked and the sole is loose. You get the idea. The point is, with this particular kind of weather, there's a chance of some destructive and overall disastrous impact befalling one of my shoes. Again, for the record, I believe that said danger is unlikely. But the potential is there. Puddles and mud and whatnot. And so, should some damage occur, it will be less noticeable on the shoe with the aforementioned wear and tear: the work boot. So Janet gets the bear, and you get the toad, and I have an early lunch."

Then Dr. Farragut slaps the table, stands, and exits the meeting.

I turn to Janet. I wish there was some indication of how she's feeling. She's taking long, audible breaths through what's left of her nose, so it's probably not good.

"Janet," I say, "I'm so sorry. I should have never said anything."

"Unbelievable," she says, standing up so fast her chair rolls back into the plastic ficus. "If anyone in this glorified animal bathhouse is a fancy shoe, it's me."

Then she spins on her heel and storms out of the room.

I spend the rest of the morning looking for Janet. I look in each of the Collection Centers. I look in Processing and Analysis. I check Animal Enclosures and watch Duncan destroy a perfectly good tire swing. I check the cafeteria, and though I don't find Janet, I realize I could have some lunch.

So I have some lunch.

I get in line and am immediately flanked by Rod and Derek, two stooges from Insemination. Rod has porcelain veneers that are an unnatural, glaring shade of white. Derek has a way of working his beach house in Montauk into every conversation. Both think they're better than everyone in Release. Most of Insemination does. In a way, they're probably right. People tend to only care about the aftereffect, the final result. They fixate on the fruit or the flower and rarely give a thought to the seeds that make them possible.

Still, it doesn't help that Rod and Derek are insufferable morons.

"So," Rod says, leaning over as I try to help myself to some corn, "I heard things didn't go so well at Intake and Assignment."

"More amphibians?" Derek says. "Poor girl."

"You know," Rod says, "since you've become such an expert at Releasing amphibians, maybe you could help me out. I've got a trouser snake that could use a Release." Then he smiles and my pupils dilate.

"Or, if you're afraid of snakes," Derek says, "I've got a crotch lizard you may be interested in. I could show it to you this weekend. I just put in a hot tub at the Montauk house."

Then they both laugh and high-five over my head.

I feel like reminding them that snakes and lizards are reptiles, not amphibians, but I don't. It's a sad and pathetic defense. Instead I carry my tray to the corner table and sit facing the wall and eat my stupid lunch.

Things weren't always like this. I used to be a vet. I used to have a job I loved and kind, supportive co-workers. Then one day they were all taken away. My then-boyfriend, current ex-boyfriend, current pile of human garbage, had been stealing my keys to the clinic and proximity card to the narcotics locker. Apparently he'd been doing it for the better part of a year. At first it was just a few pills here and there. But later, as his addiction grew, he was stealing entire bottles. He replaced the missing pills with tic-tacs, never stopping to think that at some point someone might notice that the canine oxycodone smelled like arctic peppermint.

What an idiot he was.

What an idiot I am.

When the police showed up with a search warrant, they found over three-thousand dollars' worth of pills in his tennis bag. Which, now, makes sense since I never once saw him play tennis. He folded right there, went full hysterical. Between wet, stuttering breaths, he copped to everything. Stealing the card. Stealing the drugs. Then he also admitted that he'd been cheating on me with a girl who was addicted to horse enemas.

The entire time he's leaking tears and snot on my good rug.

Though I was cleared on all charges, my reputation and my practice were destroyed.

Sometimes late at night I lie in bed and wonder what my problem is. Why I allowed myself to lose everything to a guy who I knew deep down wasn't good for me. It's not like I saw myself having kids with him. Not really. But, then again, I did spend two of my ever-dwindling childbearing years on him.

I like to think of myself as an intelligent person, but when it comes to men, something just . . . I don't know.

I do know that because of my latest lapse in judgment I am no longer a veterinarian. I am now here, surrounded by frogs and toads, all of us, in our own way, continuing to exist.

I finally find Janet in the Allen Lindstrom Memorial Break Room. Dr. Lindstrom is credited as single-handedly moving the Iberian lynx from the Critically Endangered to the Endangered category on the IUCN Red List.

"Single-handedly." That's one of our little jokes. Because, as everyone knows, Releasing an Iberian lynx is at least a two-handed job.

"Mind if I sit?" I say, and Janet nods to one of the chairs. "I think I owe you an apology."

"No," she says, "you don't. The whole thing was ridiculous. Who screams 'I'm a fancy shoe' at work?"

"Dr. Farragut knows how to push people. He was out of line," I say.

"His entire being begs for tolerance."

"Yeah," I say. "That too."

Just then, Dr. Farragut walks in. "What's all this?" he says.

"We were just talking about work," I say. "Our latest assignments."

"Oh?" he says as he takes a seat next to Janet. "You don't mind if I smoke do you?" Then he leans unnecessarily close to Janet as he lights his cigarette. Her entire body stiffens at the sight of the flame.

Things have been tense between Dr. Farragut and Janet ever since Dr. Farragut learned that Janet and his wife were seeing each other.

"You're not afraid of a little bear are you?" Dr. Farragut says. "Tough gal like yourself?"

Janet stares at the floor for a second and then looks fully at Dr. Farragut. "Every day I see the way people look at me," she says. "The way they stare when they're trying to hide the fact that they're staring. I hear the things people say when they think they're far enough away. When they think they're being quiet. So no, I'm not worried about that bear hurting me."

"That's fascinating," Dr. Farragut says. "Good for you. You know what I'd like to see and hear? You getting back to work. We're on a deadline and that bear isn't going to juice himself."

When I get back to my office there is a message from Ma telling me to hurry home because it's her turn to host the Yellow Hat Society meeting. Then there is another message asking me to stop and pick up some almond milk because a few of the Yellow Hat ladies are lactose intolerant. Then there is a third message telling me to make sure that the almond milk is unsweetened because some of the ladies that are lactose intolerant are also diabetic.

Ma moved in after I lost my veterinary practice. Not out of support. Nothing like that. She moved in when she got evicted from Horizons, her eldercare facility. I didn't even know they could do that. Evict people. But they can. They did.

They called me at work. They said there'd been "an incident." That was the word the woman on the phone used. "Incident." I pressed for specifics, but she was unwilling. When I arrived, I found a stern-looking nurse standing behind the admin desk and Ma sitting off to the side with her suitcases stacked around her.

"What seems to be the problem?" I said.

"There was a minor disagreement about the allocation of desserts which, unfortunately, evolved into an eviction-worthy event."

"I don't know what that means."

"It means they screwed me out of my cake," Ma screamed.

The nurse glared at me, and then continued. "Each night we deliver a fully-prepared dinner to our residents. This meal, barring any specific dietary restrictions, includes a dessert. Last night's dessert was a piece of German chocolate cake."

"Okay," I said.

"Your mother claims that she never received her piece of cake."

"Because I didn't," Ma screamed again.

"I'm sorry," I said. "Please go on."

"We explained to your mother that each meal is plated in our kitchen, and then that meal is cross-referenced by Distribution. This insures that every resident receives the correct meal, including dessert. Still, your mother insisted she did not receive her piece of cake."

Ma's been stubborn for as long as I can remember. When I was nine, she tried to sue the post office because she was convinced the mailman was using our letters to pick his teeth. For almost a year, she carefully inspected each envelope for any signs of oral defilement.

"The disagreement continued until this morning," the nurse said, "when your mother removed her colostomy bag and then dumped its contents in the middle of the TV room, ruining the good recliner."

I looked over at Ma, but she wouldn't meet my eyes. She busied herself picking invisible lint from her slacks.

"Your mother then pointed to the mess and asked us," and here the nurse paused to read from a clipboard, "if it looked like there was any fucking cake in there."

"Well did it?" Ma screamed.

I tried to plead my case. I tried to explain the level of care Ma requires and the amount of hours I work, but it didn't make a difference. They cited their inability to continue to tolerate such toxic behavior. They said Ma had to go.

So I took her home.

We stopped at the Food Farm and I got some things for dinner.

I made up the spare room.

We ate and watched a documentary about Eleanor Roosevelt.

We had cake for dessert.

When I get home, I find a bunch of strange cars in my driveway and the ladies of the Yellow Hat Society gathered in my living room. On paper, the Yellow Hat Society prepares and sends care packages to the troops, but what they mainly do is gossip about other members of the neighborhood. That, and snack on easily chewable food.

I once asked Ma if all of the ladies wore yellow hats to their get-to-gethers. She looked at me with a mixture of disgust and disbelief.

"No," she said. "What kind of stupid question is that?"

Tonight the Yellow Hats are gossiping about Mrs. Edna Peagrim, and why, after living in the neighborhood for twenty-eight years, including the six since Morris died, she is suddenly moving to Fort Wayne. What terrible tragedy is forcing Mrs. Peagrim to spontaneously flee from what is, really, her one and only home? One of the Yellow Hats suspects early onset dementia. Another assumes cancer.

"A bone, or a brain, you know, one of the inoperable kinds."

"They never had kids?" one of the ladies asks.

"No," says another.

"I heard she had one of those barren uteruses," says a third.

"How could she leave?" Ma says. "At this point, we're the only family she has left."

"Then God help her," I say.

Ma shoots me her stink face. The one where she narrows her eyes and sucks in her cheeks. "And what about you?" she asks. "Any chance of you giving me some grandkids before I'm dead in the ground?" Then, to the rest of the group, she says that I scare men.

"My Carissa has that," says one of the Yellow Hats.

"It's that job of hers," Ma says. "I've told her a thousand times that she'll never get a good man when she spends her days surrounded by animal penises."

One of the Yellow Hat ladies puts down her egg salad sandwich and quickly makes the Sign of the Cross.

I leave them to their philanthropy and head upstairs.

I hate to admit it, but Ma's right. Guys are intimidated by my job. The majority of my first dates are like conversational ticking time bombs. We sit there and talk about where we grew up, our childhood pets, our favorite books.

Tick. Tick. Tick.

Then comes the question about what I do for a living, and, *BOOM*, any chance of me not dying alone is blown to smithereens.

Even the guys that persevere and make it beyond the first few dates eventually develop a sad and woefully misguided case of A.P.I.C. Animal Penis Inferiority Complex. Apparently, it's an occupational hazard. As if there aren't enough already. As if Releasing a western lowland gorilla is just a stroll through the daisies.

What can I do? I've tried being honest. They say it's the best policy. But lately, I'm not sure who *they* are, and more and more I seriously doubt if *they've* ever tried maintaining a relationship in this sordid day and age.

But still, I've tried being honest. *Yes*, I've told them, *a Northern black rhino is bigger than you. Because every part of him is bigger than you. Because he's a goddamn rhinoceros!*

But by then I've already lost them.

About an hour later I hear the Yellow Hat ladies drive away. Then I hear Ma call me from the bathroom.

"Get in here and help an old lady out," she says.

Sometimes Ma needs help reattaching her colostomy bag to her stoma, which isn't always easy. Ma can be a difficult patient.

"Careful, careful" she says, before I've even touched her. "How about you wash your hands first?"

"My hands are clean," I say.

"Are they? Because your father, God rest his soul, was the only man I let into my bloomers, and I won't have that purity sullied now by your filthy, wooly mammoth penis hands."

"Jesus, Ma. First of all, I wear gloves at work. You know that. And secondly, the wooly mammoth is extinct."

"Oh?" she says. "So you're not good at your job either?"

The next day is Tuesday, which is the day I push the collection cart around the facility. I collect any extra samples from Release and any leftover samples from Insemination and bring them to Cryogenics to freeze for later use.

When I get there, Monroe holds out one hand, stopping me, and shields his eyes with the other. "Don't tell me. Don't tell me," he says.

Monroe fancies himself something a semen sommelier. He believes he can ascertain the species of any animal just by studying the samples of its Release. He's turned this belief into some sort of obscene guessing game. He's never been right once.

Monroe picks up an extraction container, making sure to cover the label with his thumb. He swirls it around. He holds it up to the light. Then he unscrews the lid and waves the container under his nose. He inhales deeply.

The day he takes a sip is the day I quit. I've promised myself.

"Ganges river dolphin?" he says.

"Good-bye, Monroe."

"No?" He gives it another swirl. Another sniff. "Southern rockhopper penguin. It's a rockhopper penguin isn't it?"

I turn to leave.

"C'mon, don't be like that," Monroe says. "Give me a hint. Is it at least a member of Aves class?"

I can still hear him screaming guesses halfway back to my office.

Sometimes I really hate it here.

In my office, I find Dr. Farragut sitting on the corner of my desk. He's looking at a picture of Ma and me at the Paul Anka show and making a scrunched-up face.

"Can I help you?"

He puts down the picture. "Follow me," he says.

I follow Dr. Farragut back to his office and he tells me to take a seat. So I take a seat.

"I know you're unsatisfied here," he says. "Frustrated. And who wouldn't be? What with week after week of frogs and toads? Toads and frogs. What with everyone referring to you as the Amphibian Milk Maid? Oh. Were you not aware of that? Doesn't matter. That's in the past. Or it can be. But first we have to make some changes. Are you ready for that? Are you ready to address what, as I see it, is our supply and demand problem? Because, to me, we have too much demand. And what is demand as it applies to our situation? Is it people? Personnel? It is. We have too many employees, and not enough quality assignments, and what does that give us? Does it give us a nice, qualified person wasting her time, wasting her talent, Releasing fringe-limbed tree frogs all day? I think we both know it does. And so, I'd like to propose that we lessen our demand. I'm talking about removing some dead weight. Some over-cooked, hard to look at, wife-stealing weight."

I think he's referring to Janet.

"I'm referring to Janet," he says.

"You're going to fire Janet?"

"No," Dr. Farragut says. "Of course not. Not that I wouldn't like to. I'd love to. But I can't. I can't fire her. Not with all of the . . ." and then Dr. Farragut stops and limply waves a hand around his face, ". . . you know. That whole mess. That, plus her sexual orientation, which apparently gives her some sort of protected minority status. Well, it basically makes her unfireable. Nope. I'd catch less hell trying to fire Jesus himself."

"I'm not sure I understand," I say.

Dr. Farragut says that we need a scenario that takes the firing of Janet out of his hands. That puts it above his pay grade. He says we need something that will force her out.

"It's some unpleasant business, I know," Dr. Farragut says, "but what else can we do? Do you see any alternatives? Because I don't. Perhaps, instead, we should focus on the positive aspects. Because, to me, we both win. You get higher quality assignments, which improves morale and makes for a happier workplace. And I no longer have a daily reminder that I've been cuckolded. That I'm a cuckold. Is it cuckold or cuckolded? Doesn't matter."

Then Dr. Farragut says with Janet gone there's some potential wiggle room in payroll. He says he'd be willing to talk to Head Office about getting me a promotion.

"How does that sound, Ms. Assistant Director of Facility Operations?"

A promotion? A promotion would be nice. I think about who this would help. I'd be able to hire someone to look after Ma. Maybe, down the road, get us a bigger place. And me. It would help me. I'd outrank Rod and Derek, which should finally shut their moronic mouths. Plus, AD of Facility Ops is a job title that may not ignite the insecurity of every eligible man.

I think about who this would hurt. Janet, of course. It definitely hurts Janet.

Janet used to be a vet, too. She had a nice little practice in Oyster Bay—nothing too stressful, just a bunch of rich old ladies and their tiny fluff-ball dogs. One morning a woman came rushing in, screaming and wailing and clutching Biscuits to her chest.

Biscuits is her Pekingese.

Biscuits wasn't breathing. His little heart had stopped. Janet tried oxygen. She tried an IV to maintain blood pressure. She tried chest compressions.

Nothing worked.

Then the woman took out her checkbook. She said she'd give Janet ten-thousand dollars if she saved her baby.

So Janet tried one more thing. She tried to shock Biscuits's heart back into action with a defibrillator.

"I don't know what the hell I was thinking," Janet had said. "That dog wasn't much bigger than the paddles."

Janet charged up the machine, shouted *clear*, and administered the first shock.

Nothing.

Then she tried another shock.

It worked. Sort of.

Biscuits sprang back to life, but the electric pulse also set his fur on fire. He leapt from the table and ran around the operating theater. Janet and her nurse ran after him. The curtains caught fire. The smoke alarm went off.

"I finally got him cornered," Janet had said. "I wrapped him up in my lab coat, and smothered the flames. But the sleeve of my shirt must have caught fire. At the time, I was going through something of an experimental phase with my wardrobe. My shirt was this shimmery, faux-silk/polyester monstrosity. The thing went up like it was soaked in brandy."

Janet said the woman never paid her the money, despite the fact that she saved her dog. Despite the fact that in saving her dog, Janet suffered second- and third-degree burns to over forty percent of her body. Janet said that instead of paying her, the woman sued for damages and emotional distress.

"She had the summons delivered while I was still in the burn unit," Janet had said. "They dropped it right on the bed. Can you believe that?"

And I couldn't. I still can't.

I can't do this to Janet.

"You look like you're having doubts," says Dr. Farragut.

"She's my friend," I say.

"And you're concerned about her well-being? Is that it? That's okay. That's a natural concern. But it's a concern that also, I think, comes from a place of limited knowledge. Because, are there some factors you aren't privy to? Are there some elements about Janet's situation you may not be aware of? There are. Did you know that Janet's girlfriend—or whatever it is they're calling one another—runs a lucrative podiatry practice? Yes, indeed. There's good money in feet. Everybody has them. So, financially speaking, I'd say she's good. Plus, if Janet wants another job, she'll have no problem finding one. Because you know what? Not hiring people like her is almost as bad as firing them."

Then Dr. Farragut does a kind of sideways lean and checks his hair in the reflection of his computer monitor. "Why are we even talking about Janet?" he says. "Why aren't we talking about you? About your future well-being? About the wealth of quality assignments that will soon be coming your way? I hear the Guadalupe fur seal isn't doing so well. How'd you like a crack at one of those?"

Then Dr. Farragut points behind him, to his framed cover of *Conservation Quarterly.* In the photo he has a strong, confident smile. Even the ocelot looks happier than I can remember being.

"That could be you in a few months," he says. "Would you like that?"

I would. I know I shouldn't. I know the focus should be on the animals, but after everything that's happened, everything I've been through, don't I deserve a break?

I think I do.

"What do you have in mind?" I say.

"I have a plan."

First, Dr. Farragut announces that we'll have an extra collection day on Thursday. So, on Thursday, I push the collection cart around the facility. I collect any extra samples from Release and any leftover samples from Insemination and bring them to Cryogenics to freeze for later use.

As always, Monroe stops me and examines an extraction container. He gives it a swirl. He gives it a sniff. He guesses at the species of the sample and, as always, he's wrong.

But this time, I tell him he's correct. Monroe is overjoyed. He actually swoons a bit and almost spills the sample. I take the extraction container from him and help him find a seat. I tell him to breathe.

Then doubt creeps in. Monroe questions his ability. He says he wants to see the label. Instead, I praise his unique insights and understanding of the animal kingdom. I suggest, to celebrate said insights and understanding, Monroe allow me to take him to lunch. Then, I run a finger across his chest and say, "I always knew there was something special about you."

That last part is Dr. Farragut's suggestion.

Of course Monroe says yes. Of course he never bothers to check the label, which has been blank the entire time.

While we're gone Dr. Farragut sneaks into the Cryo Lab and steals some samples.

It takes Monroe a few hours to notice they're missing. Then he reports the missing samples, and, per protocol, Dr. Farragut calls for a facility-wide search.

Sample theft has been a major concern since the Rusty Torson scandal. Rusty was stealing Bengal tiger samples and then selling them to Chinese businessmen with virility issues. What those businessmen did with the samples is anyone's guess, but it's not something I care to think about.

We make a show of searching the entire facility. Then we get to Janet's office where, of course, we find the samples in her filing cabinet.

Janet tries denying everything, but Dr. Farragut cuts her off. He condemns her selfishness. He chastises her ability to play fast and loose with the future of the animal kingdom. Then he makes a comparison to a pirate on Noah's ark, which is ineffective, and, frankly, a bit much.

Finally, two guys from Control come in. They flank Janet and march her from her office. They don't even allow her to pack her things.

As she passes by, she doesn't say a word. She just stares at me the entire time. Right at me. Right through me. And even though her face doesn't move, doesn't display any emotion, I know that she knows.

Then the three of them turn the corner and disappear.

"Well," Dr. Farragut says, "I'm glad that ordeal is over. I, for one, feel better. Lighter somehow."

"Not me. I feel empty. Like I've been hollowed out."

"That's a kind of lighter," he says. "Look, did I say this would be easy? Or pleasant? No. But it's done now, and the important thing, the necessary thing, is to get over it and move on."

Maybe he's right. No, he's definitely right. I need to focus on the here and now. I need to think about my pending promotion and upcoming assignments. I need to find some solace in the fact that I am finally free from toads and frogs.

"So no more standing around on company time with that sad-sack face," Dr. Farragut says. "One of us still has a toad to Release."

Then he smacks me on the back and walks away.

Before I head down to Animal Enclosures, I go to my office and do some research on the Puerto Rican crested toad. Their population numbers are in free-fall. It's predicted that without serious conservation efforts, the toads will be extinct in less than a decade.

Though no one can say exactly why. There are no environmental factors threatening their habitat. No rise in predators. Their food supply hasn't dwindled, and, in fact, has increased in some areas. It seems that the toads have simply decided to stop mating.

The scientists are baffled. But maybe they're overlooking something. Something not as simple as mating or not mating.

Maybe the toads have looked at the day-to-day makeup of their lives, the pressures and responsibilities, and realized that they are no longer living, no longer thriving, but merely surviving. Merely enduring for some unknown reason. Maybe they're no longer hopeful about the future. Maybe they've realized that to experience love and happiness, to really let it in, is to leave yourself unguarded. To leave yourself vulnerable to betrayals and indignities and the inherent self-serving nature of others. And so maybe they've said, *thanks but no thanks. We are no longer interested in this world. We've had enough.*

Probably not, though. They're just toads after all.

I head down to Animal Enclosures. I walk past Duncan and he stares at me as if he'd like to claw my eyes out, and I think: *get in line, big guy.*

When I get to the toad I see he has slightly burrowed himself near the front left corner of his terrarium. His snout is pressed against the glass, and his cream-colored vocal sac vibrates at a steady, rapid rhythm. As I reach in to grab him, his golden irises contract, narrowing his pupils into fine, black lines. He looks like he wants to be left alone.

He looks like Janet did before they took her away.

As I prep him for Release, I think about how I got here. A choice was given to me. A choice about who I was willing to use, how much of them I was willing to take. Then I made that choice and justified the decision by saying it was part of a "greater good."

That's what I did.

God help me, that's what I do.

Far Rockaway

Julia Lichtblau

The last time I hit my mother, I was ten. It was Valentine's Day, the day before the annual conference that the Department of Education requires between teachers and parents of special needs kids.

My two worst enemies, twins named Augie and Julius, arrived at school that morning excited as two dogs who'd treed a squirrel. They pulled the other kids into a whispering, moving clump and looked at me over their shoulders. "She *psspss* . . . and . . . *psspss* . . ."

My father was on business in Singapore, and Mom was working on a big story for her newspaper. "I'm very tired, Amanda," she said at breakfast. "I need you to be my big girl. Make that my valentine."

I promised.

All morning, the kids whispered. "*Psspss*, she . . . *psspss* . . . and then *psspss* . . . Remember *psspss* . . . ?" I couldn't get back at the whisperers by chasing or pushing them because we could not go out for recess after lunch. A warm snap had followed a heavy snow, and the playground, sidewalks, and streets were ankle-deep in brown slush. The principal didn't want a school full of wet, sugared-up kids.

In Library, I heard Augie and a girl on the other side of the stacks. "You saw it?"

"For real. Me and Julius were helping out for the party. Mrs. Belcher went to the bathroom and left the file on her desk. We didn't touch it, I swear. It was, like, there."

"What'd it say?"

"Ee-Dee."

"Huh?"

"Emotionally Disturbed. You know, like psycho." Their mom was an aide who sat with the autistic kids so they must have learned the acronym from her.

My parents never said I was emotionally disturbed. As they explained it, I had "executive function issues." When I was younger, they put it this way: "Executive function is like the president of your brain. It tells you when it's okay to be mad and when it's not and to tell people you're upset in a nice way, so you don't get in trouble for some dumb thing. When your birth mother was carrying you in her tummy in Guatemala, she didn't get enough food or medical care. The part of your brain where the president lives didn't make all the helper cells it needs to do its job. We have to teach it to be a good president without helpers." This conjured a troubling vision of a man in a tuxedo roaming an empty mansion in search of people to give orders to.

I was waiting in the lunch line when Augie slithered by, carrying a big, oozing sloppy joe. It seemed to pulse like the red buttons that evil geniuses in movies used to blow up the world. I brought my hand up under his plate and clipped it. Red, drippy meat flew all over his shirt. A blob dripped off his nose. The lunch-room monitor marched me to the principal's office.

My mother was on deadline. "No, I'm sorry. I can't drop my story," she said on speaker phone. "And no, there's no one else. My husband's away." She could have called my babysitter, Esmeralda, who was three blocks away looking after my white baby brother, Joey, the miracle baby, who had arrived seven years after my parents stopped trying and got me instead. Mom asked the principal to put me on the phone. "You can sit on the bench until school ends. Wait 'til your father hears about this. Forget about any birthday party." My eleventh birthday was in March. I looked forward to my birthday all year long.

I sat on the bench outside the principal's office while Valentine's parties went on up and down the hall. I could hear music and laughter. There were treats in the office, too. Teachers came out munching heart-shaped cookies, holding them away from their nice clothes, sprinkling crumbs on the floor for the janitor to sweep later.

Right before the bell rang, the principal told me to go home. For five minutes, I had the neighborhood to myself. I jaywalked between two idling yellow busses.

"Hey, Amanda, I'm going to tell your mother," the crossing guard yelled.

"Go ahead," I yelled. "She's going to kill me, anyway." I cut down a side street. In the zones around fire hydrants where no cars were parked, I waded into the swollen gutters, though my boots leaked. By the time I reached our house, my socks were soaked, and my toes were aching with cold.

I kicked the thick wooden door of our brownstone. Esmeralda answered. I raced past her, up the stairs, leaving blobs of slush on the polished oak.

"*Nena, tus botas!*"

"I don't care," I called.

I'd known Esmeralda since I was two, when my parents had brought me from Guatemala. Her mother was my first nanny until she got a night job cleaning offices. Then Esmeralda took care of me in the day and her nephew at night. Her family spoke to me in Spanish and to Joey in English. They were Mayan, with long, straight jet black hair, curved noses, and heavy-lidded, almost Chinese, eyes. I was mixed—Spanish and Mayan. I had a pointy nose and round eyes. Esmeralda considered it unfair that I'd gotten rich parents. When I wasted food, she'd say, "*En*

Guatemala, tú comerías solo tortillas viejas y café negro." In Guatemala, you'd only get stale tortillas and black coffee.

I hated hearing how poor Guatemala was.

We rented out the parlor floor and lived on the top two. My father's study was in a tiny maid's room on the third floor. I wasn't allowed to use the computer without permission. The Internet was still new at the time and considered bad for children. Dad bought me educational game discs. My favorite, "Learning Circus," had a cartoon ringmaster who would announce the words as if they were a circus act. *Drum roll*: "Canteloupe!" Each time I spelled a word right, he chortled, "Hip-Hip-Hooray!" or "You are hot stuff!" and the tiger roared or the elephant trumpeted.

I turned on the computer, put my disc in the slot, and started racking up points. I started at the second highest level. Pathetic. Maintain. Performance. Signature. Ta-da! Ta-da! So the President of my brain hadn't gotten enough to eat in my birth mother's tummy. The Speller-in-Chief must have stolen all his food. She was brilliant. She understood the traps. When she made a mistake, she remembered and got it right the next time. I wanted to be a speller when I grew up.

Joey had woken from his nap. His room was next to Dad's office, and his high voice broke through the hurdy-gurdy music and sound effects of my game.

"Where's Manda?" he asked.

"Shhh, she do her homework. Djou can't bother her, Shoey," Esmeralda said.

She stopped in the study door holding Joey. "*Nena, cuidado. Cuando llega tu mamá, le voy a contar todo,*" she warned, and continued downstairs.

I might have laughed if I'd been older and not in a fury. Esmeralda never told my mother I'd done something bad if she could avoid it. She needed my mom to believe every day went fine because mothers fire babysitters who can't control their charges. As much as she hated me, she didn't want to lose this job. Mom paid better than other parents because I was so difficult. I knew this because I'd heard Esmeralda and the other babysitters comparing bosses. "*De verdad?*" they'd say when she told them she got so much extra for Christmas or a full week when she was sick. Sometimes she bribed me with candy to act nice so she could say, "*Todo bién, todo bién,*" when Mom asked how the day had gone.

And my mom, who'd majored in Spanish in college, would say, "*Ah, me alegra.*" Oh, I'm so happy. Mom couldn't fire Esmeralda because no one else would work for us without complaining about me and asking why she didn't try this or that, making her feel like a terrible parent, and eventually quitting. I remember hearing one of the other babysitters say her mother in Ecuador took a whip to a brother who talked back. Esmeralda had laughed. I was playing on the floor nearby with Joey. I caught her eye, and she looked embarrassed, as if I'd caught her, whip in hand. I never told my mother. I felt as if I, with my brown skin and black hair, belonged to their world when they said these things and had no right to betray them.

Outside the study window, night fell. Cold radiated off the glass. The Valentine's thaw had been a head-fake.

The front door opened downstairs. "Mommy, Mommy," Joey cried.

"*Buenas noches, señora, sí, todo bién, todo bién,*" Esmeralda said.

"Liar!" I yelled. "*Todo mal, muy muy mal!*"

"That's quite enough, Amanda," my mother called, adding in Spanish, "Yes, I know, the school called." Joey interrupted. My mom hushed him. Esmeralda said good-bye to him. Mom said goodnight to Esmeralda.

"*Buenas noches. Nos vemos, si Dios quiere,*" Esmeralda said, that superstitious Spanish good-bye. We'll see each other, if God wishes. For some reason, He kept wishing it, day after day. Why then had He made us hate each other?

The door closed. Mom and Joey were coming upstairs. Big foot, little foot, big foot, little foot. "What did you do today, pumpkin pie?" Mom asked.

"I played this much games." I envisioned him holding up his ten little fingers.

"Ooh. So many."

"Manda's in Daddy's office," Joey said.

"*Shhh,*" Mom said. "Come have your dinner. I'll deal with her."

The silverware clinked on dishes. Water ran. I hit the highest level. Monotony. Flabbergast. Petroleum. Melancholy. Psychology. The TV went on. Nick at Night. Mom must have plunked Joey down so she could turn to the ugly business of me.

She stood in the doorway. "Get off NOW."

"No." I hunched closer to the keyboard. "P-u-s-i-l-l-a-n-i-m-o-u-s."

"One, two—"

"You are simply AMAZING!" the ringmaster bellowed.

"Three." Mom leaned over and grabbed the mouse. Her freckled cheek and right ear with its pearl earring faced me. I cocked my fist and slugged, connecting on the dome of her cheekbone. She called out and fell forward, catching herself on the keyboard. The screen filled with error messages and scrolling rows of symbols. I shut my eyes and bicycled against the air, to prevent her from catching my ankles and dragging me off the chair. I was still wearing my snow boots. The social workers and doctors had taught her to pin me to the floor and sit on me, holding my wrists so I couldn't kick or hit. Nothing happened. I stopped bicycling and opened my eyes.

She stood out of range, hands over her face, the tails of her white silk blouse hanging out of her navy dress pants. She uncovered her face, and I saw the blue egg I'd raised.

"Maybe I'm the wrong mother for you," she said. "Nothing I do helps."

She turned, and I heard her walk toward her bedroom, which was at the front of the house, overlooking the street.

"What did you do to Mommy?" Joey stood in the study doorway. He wore his footie pajamas. The light from the frozen screen gave his pale face a blue caste. He looked like a baby alien.

"Go away," I said. "This is the bad peoples' club." He thumped away, his little padded butt wiggling. He still wore diapers at night.

The TV in the living room kept talking to itself. On my father's desk was a framed photo of me in Guatemala sniffing a frilly red hibiscus flower. The pistil had deposited saffron pollen on the end of my little brown nose. My father, who held the flower, was laughing. If they'd known, could they have given me back? In scary movies, evil children had spooky eyes. I looked cute, like billions of babies. When had I gone bad? I had been like this as long as I could remember.

I got up and walked down the hall to my mother's room. Joey's bed was empty. He must have been with her. I listened at her door. She was on the phone. "I spoke to the doctor. We've reached that point," she said.

I rattled the door knob. "Hold on, dear," she said. "Go to bed, Amanda. I don't want to hear another peep out of you before tomorrow."

The next day around eleven, the school secretary's voice on the intercom interrupted class: "Please send Amanda Frankel down to the office. Her mother's here." The kids looked at Augie—Julius was in the other fifth-grade class. He did that duck movement with his chin. Uh-huh, uh-huh. Toldja.

Mom wore jeans and a sweater, not office clothes. The place where I'd hit her cheek was still swollen. She'd put a lot of beige makeup on, hiding her freckles along with the bruise. "Come along, I'm double-parked." We didn't own a car, so I guessed she'd rented one.

We slid along the icy sidewalk.

"Are you getting rid of me?"

"God, no. Of course not." She wiped her eyes on her sleeve. "I'm taking you to a hospital on Long Island."

"What are they going to do to me? Will they stick those things on me?" I had had a test where they taped electrodes on my head once to find out if I had epilepsy.

"No. You're going to stay there until we figure out how to help you to stop acting the way you do."

"Can Joey come?"

"Yes. We'll visit, of course." Nothing was of course. Why did she say that? "Here." She pointed to a beige car.

The car was parked against a blackened, mushy snowbank. She forced the door open enough for me to squeeze in, buckled my seatbelt as if I were a baby, and handed me a tote containing my security blanket. I pulled it out and stuck a corner in my mouth.

I sucked on the fuzzy corner and imagined going back to Guatemala, where I would start over, and everyone would like me. We drove along Atlantic Avenue, up Flatbush, past the Jamaican beef patty places, the movie theater, Grand Army Plaza, down Eastern Parkway, past the Brooklyn Museum. Now most people on the street were Orthodox Jews, men in their caftans and hats, women in wigs and 1930s outfits. We were every-other-year High Holy Day and Passover Jews. Mom didn't even believe in God but when Esmeralda said, "*Nos vemos, quiera Dios,*" Mom would sometimes say things like: "Tell him I'd like a vacation, too." Esmeralda would smile her crocodile smile. I hated them both at those moments.

After a while, the Orthodox were replaced by brown and black people and their storefront churches, Iglesia de la Manantial, Eglise de Jésus. The streets became longer, lonelier, the traffic faster. The businesses were car repair shops, beauty salon supply stores, mini-storage facilities, soul food restaurants.

We turned onto the Jackie Robinson Parkway. Rush hour had begun. Traffic stopped and started, and my stomach couldn't take the lurching. "Mom, I feel sick," I said. "Stop."

"Where?" she said, gesturing to the concrete walls on either side of the road. "Use that bag."

The bag was only paper and gave way all over me. "Mom, help!"

"Oh, God, I'm so sorry," Mom said. "Here." She pulled a used tissue out of her pocket. The smell made me sicker, and we had to open all the windows. My teeth chattered from the cold wind on my wet clothes. Mom and I were both crying. "Just a few more minutes, I promise," she said.

It took another half-hour to reach the hospital. An enormous concrete sculpture consisting of one large red and two smaller blue circles stuck together, sort of like Mr. Potato Head, stood on the lawn. I guessed it was meant to make the sick people laugh, but the only funny thing about the place were the flocks of Canadian geese snacking on the lawn. My mom took my wheeled suitcase out of the trunk and pulled it to the Pediatric Inpatient Psychiatric Unit on the eighth floor. Someone buzzed us in.

The nurse flared her nostrils at the smell of vomit. "*Uy, mamita,*" she called to a lady pushing a cart of cleaning supplies. "Give this girl a plastic bag for her clothes. Amanda, I'll see if your room's ready."

The cleaning lady tore off a garbage bag from a roll on her cart. She patted her stomach and made a sad clown face. She was mixed-race, like me; her hair, which she wore in a coiled braid, was dark brown, her eyes round. She wore a badge pinned to her gray uniform: Yadra.

"*Gracias,*" I said.

"*Hablas bién el español!*" she said with exaggerated excitement, as if I'd made an entire speech.

My mother stood at the counter filling out forms.

"*Es tu mamá?*" she said.

My mom turned.

"*Buenas tardes, señora,*" the lady said, smiling.

"*Buenas tardes,*" Mom said, without really looking at her.

The doctor came out of her office and greeted us. "So this is Amanda. Welcome. I'm going to talk to your mom, then you can join us."

The other nurse was coming down the hall.

"Where were you born?" the lady asked.

"Guatemala."

"*Como yo,*" she said, widening her eyes at the coincidence. "Why are you here?"

"I'm sick." I patted my stomach.

She leaned close. "*Tu sabes,* this part of the hospital isn't for normal sick people."

"I know."

She frowned. "You very nice girl," she said in English.

"No," I said. "I'm not a nice girl. *Soy loca.*"

A boy about my age and a burly man with a red beard came down the hall. The kid jump-shot imaginary baskets over and over.

"Last warning, Matthew," the man said. "No jump-shots."

Matthew jumped.

"That's it. Back to your room." He took the boy's elbow. The boy slumped to the ground and lay on his back, kicking furiously. "You want to lose your movie, too?"

"Fuck you," the boy said.

The man started counting.

"*Ese es un loco,*" the lady said. "*Tu no eres así, verdad?*"

"*Sí, un poco,*" I said. I was kind of like that, except for the jump shots.

She tsked. "*No digas eso.*" Don't say that.

"Amanda Frankel," the nurse said. "Follow me." She showed me my room, and after I washed and changed, she took me to the doctor's office, where Mom sat in a big armchair, crying. I wedged in next to her. Mom sniffed. "Great. You washed."

The doctor, a stocky woman in a royal blue suit with a big fake-gem brooch on the lapel, pointed to a chair. "Sit there, Amanda."

I did.

The doctor beamed. "Do you know why you're here?"

"I hit my mom in the face."

"Why?"

"She messed up my game."

"Why didn't you use your words?"

"I wanted her to leave me alone."

"If you'd asked nicely, would she have left you alone?"

"No."

"What do you think, Mrs. Frankel?" the doctor said to my mom.

"Of course I wouldn't have left her alone," she snapped. Mom's flare-up at the doctor's stupid question made me think we might walk out together. But she didn't get up, and tears kept streaming down her face.

"How do you feel about being here?" the doctor asked me.

"Like a dog that pees on the furniture," I said.

"No, no, no, no." Mom covered her face, and I climbed in her lap and held her.

"Your mom has to go," the doctor said, after a while.

There were about twenty kids in the PIPU, as they called it. In group, the therapist asked how we ended up here. "I cut myself," said Jamila. "My uncle kept touching me down there so I cut my arm, and I was going to just let it bleed, but it hurt so bad I screamed, and a neighbor called the ambulance."

"That screaming was your way of asking for help. That's a good sign, Jamila. What about you, Amanda?"

"I hit my mother."

"That so? Why?"

"It pisses me off when she says no all the time."

Everyone looked at each other from under their hands. ("She serious or what?")

I called them assholes since all of them had done way worse stuff, and I lost my movie privileges that night.

The next session, the social worker started in with me. "What happens when you hit your mother, Amanda?"

"She sits on me. Or she holds my arms like Trevor." Trevor was the burly red-bearded nurse. I crossed them over my chest straitjacket-style and squirmed. That cracked everyone up.

"What do y'all think Amanda's mother should do?" the social worker asked the group when we settled down. "Jamila?"

She shrugged. "Mm-mm. My mama'd kill me if I touch her."

"She kill your uncle?"

"No, he's her big brother, so she couldn't."

"Antonio, what do you think her mother should do?"

"Hit her back."

"Why would that be a good idea?"

"Make her stop."

"That ever work for you, Anthony?"

"Sometimes."

"What would you do if your mother hit you back, Amanda?"

Everyone perked up, as if they were watching a prizefight in their minds—Amanda vs. Mom. What if my mom hit me? It worked for that babysitter's mother in Ecuador. Part of the problem was that my mother was a deer, and I was a tiger. A mother deer only thinks of protecting her meek little fawn. A tiger sees a mother deer and attacks. Her deer-ness brought out the tiger in me.

"I don't know."

"You'd let her hit you?"

"Maybe," I said, flinching at the thought of her hand coming down.

"And after? Would you feel that you were even?"

"I might break something of hers when she wasn't looking or take money from her purse."

"Then?" The social worker was working it.

"She'd punish me . . ."

"And . . . ?"

"We'd start all over."

"Exactly," the social worker said. "Y'all get that?" Everyone scuffled their feet on the linoleum.

My hospital friends' families had done terrible things to them. After my roommate's parents engaged her to a man in Pakistan, she stopped eating. One day, she told us in Group that her parents were going to send her over there once she started eating again. Even the social worker looked scared. What was my problem? Even I couldn't explain it. I had a black hole in me, and I wanted my mother or someone to fill it with something sweet. Chocolate or cherry syrup or M&Ms.

The therapist had asked my mother to bring the earliest picture they had, the one the agency had sent. In the picture, I was wearing a blue dress and brown baby shoes. A man's hand reaching in from beyond the frame of the picture held me steady. I was at least one, because I could stand. When I was little, my mom and I would look at the picture, and she would say: "Look at that face. You were so adorable, we wanted to eat you up." She would pretend to eat my arm like corn on the cob.

"What does the picture remind you of?" the social worker asked.

"I can't remember," I said. I lived with a foster family for two years, because the U.S. Embassy didn't believe my birth mother understood she was giving me up for good, and the adoption agency had to track her down in the mountains before they'd give me a visa. When they found her, she told the interviewer that she understood, my mom told me.

I woke to the smell of institutional cleaning products. Yadra's crew came early in the morning and cleaned the bathrooms, the halls, and the nurses' station. They cleaned our rooms when we were in class—the Unit had a one-room school—and the dining room after breakfast and lunch, when we had outdoor time in the fenced-in yard.

One morning, I went back to my room from school to get my baby picture for a class project, and I found her, mop propped against the dresser, looking at the picture.

"Nice goo' baby," she said in English. She pressed the picture to her chest and patted it, as if she were burping me before setting it on the dresser. She held up five fingers. "*Tengo cinco.*"

"Where are they?" I asked.

"In Guatemala."

"Who takes care of them?"

"*Mi papá.*"

"Where's their dad?" I asked.

She shrugged, showing her empty palms.

My parents said my birth mother had met a man at a fair one night and found out she was pregnant. When I was younger, I thought you could get pregnant from fairs.

"I have to get back to my class," I said.

She handed me the picture. "*Vas a ser una morenita bién hermosa.*" I was going to be a beautiful brown woman. I never thought of myself as a beautiful anything. I felt as if I should hug her. But I only said *gracias* and left.

Over Passover, my family came, and we did craft therapy in the play-room. I was helping Joey make a log cabin out of popsicle sticks. Yadra stood outside the door watching. I waved.

"Who's that?" Mom asked.

"A person," I said.

"What does she do here?"

"Oh my God. She cleans, Mom."

"How did you get to know her?"

"She talks to me. She's from Guatemala."

"Do housekeepers usually get involved with the kids?" she asked the play therapist, going into investigative reporter attack mode.

"Something wrong with that?" he said. He was Spanish.

"No," Mom said. "Just wondered if it was a good idea . . . you know . . ." The glue on Joey's popsicle-stick cabin hadn't dried, and I pulled the roof off to change the subject. Joey screamed and hit me.

"Is that typical sibling interaction?" the therapist asked.

"Yep," my father said, picking up the writhing Joey and carrying him out.

Each day, kids were discharged and new ones arrived. I had no idea there were so many crazy kids. It was kind of comforting because in my neighborhood everyone seemed perfect except Augie and Julius. The second week, the doctor said I'd made progress and could go home in a few days. "Happy?"

"I guess," I said.

Augie and Julius would call me psycho. Esmeralda would tell her friends I was *necia y loca*, while saying *todo bién* to my mother. Joey would tattle when I went on the computer.

That afternoon, I picked a fight with Jamila. We'd earned a movie, and she wanted to watch *The Nutty Professor*. I said she only liked movies with black people, and I was white and deserved to watch white movies.

213

"Racist!" She pulled my hair. We grappled. She was tall and had long arms. I curled up like a potato bug. An aide held her arms back and pulled her off me. Trevor, the big nurse, grabbed me.

"You brown, bitch. Brown like shit. Look in a mirror. Look at your ugly self."

"I'm going to kill you," I yelled.

Trevor tightened his grip. I bit his arm and left a purple half-circle.

Two nurses held me while the doctor gave me a shot in the butt. They carried me to a padded room, where I fell asleep.

I awoke in my room alone. My roommate had been discharged. The red display on the clock said 8:55. School had started. They'd let me sleep.

The door to my room opened, and Yadra came in, pulling her mop and wheeled bucket behind her. "*Qué pasó*? Are you sick?"

"I got in a fight, and they put me in the mattress room."

She closed the door and sat on my bed. She reached out a hand and stroked my hair, running her fingers through the tangles. My mother liked to do that when we had a good day.

"So why were you *necia*?" she asked.

"I don't want to go home."

"Don't you love your mother?"

"No."

"You have to love your mother."

"She's not my mother."

"*No digas tonterías.*" *Tonterías* means foolishness.

I smacked her hand.

"*Necia.* I go," Yadra said, in English. She stood up and took hold of her mop. She was very angry.

"I'm sorry. I'll never do it again."

She passed the mop very quickly over the floor—enough to leave a clean smell—put it in the wheeled bucket, and left. I heard the nurse ask her in Spanish what she was doing in there, the sign said "Staff Only."

She said she couldn't read English and was just doing her job.

I pulled my blanket over my face.

The nurse came in. "Rise and shine, honey. Doctor wants to talk to you about yesterday."

The doctor said I was acting out from anxiety, that it wasn't unusual for kids to have a setback before discharge.

The weather brightened, and crocuses sprouted out of the goose poop. From my window, I watched the patches of purple flush open and close up with the sun. I missed running and playing.

I didn't see Yadra the next day or the day after and hoped she hadn't lost her job.

The night before my discharge, I wrote her a letter saying I was sorry I'd been *necia,* and I hoped she'd visit me when I got out. Fridays, when I didn't have therapy, worked best. I wrote my address and phone number. I couldn't spell in Spanish, so I wrote my letter in English and gave it to the cleaning lady who took her place. They rode the bus together.

My parents wanted the doctors to keep me longer. But the hospital couldn't justify keeping me to the insurance company. "Bring her back if the behavior starts up again," the doctor told my parents, as if I were a car. She prescribed new medicines.

My mother signed the discharge papers. The doctor and the nurses hugged me and told me I'd done great. The security guard clicked us out.

Walking to the parking lot, my mom said, "There's that lady, your friend." She was waiting at the bus stop. I waved. Yadra crossed the street. "I got your letter," she said. "I'm so happy you are going home."

She kissed me on both cheeks.

My mother looked very uncomfortable. "What did you write?" Mom said, as we walked to the car.

"I said I was going home and thanked her for being nice."

"That's good. I'm glad you were so polite. The hospital really has done you a lot of good, after all."

I didn't say I let Yadra stroke my hair and it helped me.

The doctor told my parents that to break the cycle of frustration and explosion, I needed some autonomy. So my parents gave me my own house key and ten dollars a week allowance if I did chores. They praised me effusively when I did a good thing and let some bad stuff go.

The new freedom or the new medicine or maybe both made me trembly and anxious.

The first Friday after I got back was warm enough that we left our coats in a pile at recess. I went to the park after school with Esmeralda and Joey because I had no therapy or after-school activities. I joined some third-graders making the bouncy plank bridge move like an earthquake had hit, until the mom of a toddler yelled at us to stop and let her kid on. We hung over the railing, drooling spit blobs on the blacktop. I felt the beginnings of happiness. The week had gone well. No one had made fun of me. Augie and Julius left me alone. The teacher was nice.

Suddenly one boy, a classmate's younger brother, said, "Amanda, is it true you were in the loony bin?" A hot, electric flush came over me, like the injection for a contrast MRI, which I'd had of my brain. If this little squirt knew, everyone at school, on the whole playground, in the neighborhood knew. The adults had told the kids to be nice. That's why I'd had a good week. Soon Augie and Julius would start up bad as ever.

"You don't know what that means," I said.

"Do so. My dad's a shrink."

"What?"

"The nut house."

A ball bounced on the bridge, and the shrink's kid caught it.

"Hey, that's our ball," a boy called.

"Finders keepers," said the shrink's kid. He ran off with it, followed by the rest.

I ran to the monkey bars, climbed to the horizontal ladder and straddled it. How did he know? Had my teacher gathered everyone around and told them she had sad news, like when a girl in school got leukemia?

I scanned the playground. Joey was on the baby swings; Esmeralda was talking to her friends and pushing him. Esmeralda had told the babysitters, who'd told the moms, who asked their kids: "Is it true Amanda Frankel's in the loony bin?" I could imagine the babysitters sitting around our living room, whispering about me, while the white babies they pretended to love played on the floor. Pspss . . . *She's the worst kid in Brooklyn. And all those toys and that beautiful house. And she hits her mother so she had to go to the crazy place. No matter what our mothers did to us, we never hit our mothers.* Nunca nunca. La mamá es la mamá. *And all those people waiting for green cards so many years. How much do you think they paid for her? Psspss.*

The sky was pink and the air cooling. Soon, everyone would go home.

I let myself down and snuck out of the park along the dirt strip between the shrubbery and the playground fence. No *todo bién, todo bién, señora* tonight.

I ran the five blocks to my house.

"Hello," Mom called from upstairs.

"It's me," I said.

"I'm on the phone. I'll be down in a few minutes."

On Friday, Mom paid Esmeralda. On the hall table sat an envelope, the top tucked in, not sealed. I opened it. Six hundred dollars. I could go to Guatemala. I'd go back to my first mother and start over. I'd never hit her. *Nunca nunca.* I knew the order of the countries. Texas, Mexico, Guatemala. I'd go to Port Authority and take a bus. I'd ask the Spanish people where to go. I stuffed the envelope in my jeans pocket and went out as quietly as I could. Up and down the street, babysitters were herding kids home. Any second, Esmeralda and Joey would round the corner. They would come from the left. I ran right and turned at the next corner toward the subway. Grownups passed, minds still on work. *I have six hundred dollars, and you don't,* I thought.

The last block before the subway ran downhill. I picked up speed and charged across the street as the light turned red and dashed down the subway stairs.

I met Yadra coming out at the turnstile. We both stopped in surprise. People behind us yelled, "Move it." I turned and followed her back upstairs to the street. We stood on the corner by a Chinese takeout place.

She looked worried. "I came to see you," she said. "*Vamos*, I want to greet your mother."

Seeing her, I realized I'd made a mistake. I didn't want to know her outside of the hospital, where I was officially ED. I wanted to run home, lock the door, ask my mother to make Yadra leave. But I'd stolen Esmeralda's six hundred dollars. I couldn't go to Guatemala, either. I'd forgotten about my passport, which my mom kept in her desk.

"I can't," I said.

"Why?"

"I stole a lot of money."

We faced each other, brown girl and brown lady. More people erupted out the subway. The sky had turned that cobalt blue. My teeth were chattering. My nose running. I started to cry.

"Your mother will forgive you," she said.

"No, she won't." The thought of them only having Joey made me feel even worse, as if I'd died and was watching their life from heaven.

A police car pulled up across the street. One officer went into the Starbucks, while the other stayed at the wheel. Part of me wanted to turn myself in.

"Where were you going?" she asked.

"Manhattan." I'd seen homeless teenagers with their piercings, tattoos, blue hair, dogs, and cardboard signs in the village and Times Square. The police officer came out of Starbucks with two coffees and drove off.

"If you promise to behave, I'll take you to my house," she said.

The direst parent warning was don't go with strangers. Was she a stranger?

"Where do you live?" I asked.

"Fah-rahk-a-way-ee."

"Where's that?"

She had to repeat the name several times before I got it. Far Rockaway. I'd gone there with my family. A strip of city and sand at the end of train line. We'd had fun.

"Okay." I could sneak home and steal my passport tomorrow.

We rode one stop and changed for a Brooklyn-bound A train. It was full of European tourists going to JFK Airport, and their suitcases crowded the aisles. A lot of them were tall and blond. The train went unusually fast. The stations had odd names: Euclid, Kingston-Throop, Ralph, Van Siclen. The tourists lumbered out at Howard Beach. Almost everyone left was black or brown. The houses stood on piers and had boats in the backyard. We crossed a bridge. Far away, the Empire State Building stuck up like a hypodermic needle. The train turned, and we ran parallel to the beach. Huge apartment buildings looked like they'd been stuck there, like in Monopoly when you put a hotel on a property to catch people and make them pay you a lot of money.

We reached the end and went down to the street. I had never been to this part of the Rockaways. Where we went was empty and wild, except for the washed-up garbage, and you could still see the Empire State Building.

The area around the train had many doctor's offices. The old people were white and used walkers. Rap music boomed out of a passing car, and it looked as if someone had hooked up the wrong soundtrack. Yadra led me toward the beach. The wind was cold and strong. We crossed an avenue, passed two blocks of big apartments with guards and signs, and then turned onto a street lined with bungalows that looked cute from a distance but turned out to be wrecks up close. We walked to the end of the street. On one side was a low brick apartment building. We went inside. There was no lobby, just a hall. The only light was the red exit lamp.

"The elevator is broken," Yadra said.

We took the stairs to the fourth floor. She pulled out her key.

I didn't want to see her apartment. I'd seen Esmeralda's. Crammed with furniture, souvenirs, family photos, pictures of Jesus. "Take me back. I won't tell anyone you brought me here. I'll say I ran away. Please," I said.

"I have to go to the bathroom." She opened her apartment door and flicked on the light. It was one room. Six mattresses lay on the floor. "*Mi cama*," she said, pointing to the one covered by a fuzzy orange blanket. Mickey Mouse pointed his white-gloved index finger upward. "*Te gusta Mickey?*" she asked.

"*Sí*," I said.

A TV sat on a block of driftwood in one corner. Plastic milk crates held clothes and personal objects. Yadra took some clothes from a milk crate and went to the bathroom.

The window faced the backyard, but you could see the ocean if you turned your head all the way to the right. TV sounds came through the walls on both sides.

Yadra came out of the toilet wearing a limp purple turtleneck sweater over jeans, the first time I'd seen her out of her uniform. She looked younger and prettier. She'd let her hair down. It reached the middle of her back and had glossy waves from the braid.

"Can we go?" I didn't want to take my coat off.

"Give me a few minutes," she said. "I've been up since four this morning. Do you want a soda?"

I was very hungry. "Okay."

She brought me a can of Coke from the kitchen and knelt on her mattress. "Sit."

I knelt. I wanted to like her the way I had at the hospital, but I'd lost the feeling.

"Where are the others?" I asked.

"At work."

"Are they from Guatemala?"

"And other places," she said. "*Dios mío*. I'm so tired." She stretched out on her side and closed her eyes. I watched, not sure if she was sleeping until I heard little snores.

How would anyone find me here at the end of the world? Would they post notices in the subway? "Missing: Amanda Frankel, 11 years old, Hispanic. Black hair, brown eyes, height 4'6". Emotionally Disturbed."

I patted Yadra's arm. "Wake up. I need to go."

She sat up and rubbed her eyes. "I want to show you my family." She reached under the clothes in her milk crate and pulled out a photo of a gray-haired man and four children in front of a fountain. They were all very different looking.

"I thought you had five." I got off my knees and squatted like a racer.

"One more girl, yes."

"What happened to her?"

She examined her hands, turning them over, spreading her fingers.

Finally, she said, "*La vendí*." I sold her.

I lost my balance and spilled my soda over Mickey's face. I crawled across the mattresses to the door and tried to unlatch it. I was terrified that she'd locked me in, and I turned the knob the wrong way. "Let me go!"

"*Tranquila, tranquila*." Yadra unlatched the door. "Wait. You'll get lost."

I didn't wait. I knew to walk away from the ocean. But when I reached the big avenue, I turned too soon and wound up on a side street.

Retracing my steps, I ran into Yadra, hair blowing wildly in the wind. "Amanda, Amanda! *Vamos*."

My medicine had worn off. I could feel waves of strange energy, fear, anger, sadness, rolling through me. "Why did you sell your baby?"

"My father said he would send the others to be adopted. We needed money."

"Didn't you have a job?"

"I sold tortillas."

I imagined her handing over the baby, as if she were a package of tortillas. The picture was very sharp.

"How much did they pay?" I absolutely needed to know.

"Five thousand dollars."

"Wow."

"I gave it all to a *coyote* to bring me here." She pulled her shawl over her hair.

We reached the station. A train was arriving on the elevated track. I took the envelope of bills out of my pants pocket. "Here," I said. "You can buy her back." But I knew she'd never find that girl, any more than my Guatemalan mother would find me.

She looked inside the envelope. "I can't take this."

She was frightened of me now, of the trouble I could get her into.

The wheels of the arriving train squealed to a stop, and the doors opened. "Far Rockaway," the conductor said. The voice rang out over the neighborhood.

I pulled out three twenties. Was that a good amount? "Here."

She put the money in her pocket. "Go."

I went to the fare booth and gave the man a twenty. He held up ten fingers.

"Yes, yes."

He pushed a yellow and blue Metrocard and a ten through the mouse-hole shaped cut in the window.

The car was empty, except for me. I lay on the seat. The conductor passed, and I thought he was going to say something, but he went into his little booth, where I couldn't see him. The cold wind blew in the open door, making my teeth chatter. The door closed, and the car became warm. Someone shook me. I opened my eyes to see a policeman, squatting in front of me.

"What's your name?" he asked.

"Amanda Frankel."

"Where are you trying to get to?"

I told him.

"What the heck are you doing out here?" He looked at his watch.

"I went the wrong way," I said.

"I'll say," he said. "Come on. We'll drive you home."

He put me on the phone with my parents. "Thank God," my mother said. "Whatever were you thinking?"

I gave the policeman the phone. "She may be in shock or something," he said to my mom.

Joey was in his PJs, looking out the living room window when we drove up. I put my key in the lock, and his shrill voice announced my return.

When the police left, I lay down on the couch. It was short, and I just fit between the arms. My mother made me tuck my feet up so she could sit there, too. She rubbed my hip bone, as if she were polishing it. My father sat in the armchair holding Joey.

"Esmeralda said she'd told you to leave the park, and you started hitting her and ran away," Mom said. Joey wiggled out of my father's arms, as if he didn't want to hear.

"She lied. She lies to you all the time. I hate her, and I'm never going to do what she tells me," I said.

"Joey, did Amanda hit Esmeralda?" Mom asked. "Tell the truth this time."

"No," he said.

My mother sat up, hand on her forehead. "To think I believed her."

Hadn't I said "Esmeralda's a liar" a thousand times?

Still, my mother's anxious blue eyes asked: Could she manage without Esmeralda and the lies they told each other, and could she trust me not to hit her again?

"This is what happened," I said. "I was going to Guatemala, and I ran into Yadra, the cleaning lady. She took me to her house."

My mother sat up. "I knew it. I'm going to report her."

"Let her be," my father said. "She didn't do any harm."

My mom sat with her hands in her lap for a while. "I guess not," she said. "Something about that woman bothered me."

"Did she hurt you?" my father asked me.

"No."

My mother picked up the policeman's card and reached for the phone.

"Put that away," my father said.

"God, I hope this doesn't set us back to where we started," Mom said. "I don't think I could take it."

For several years, I kept expecting Yadra to pop up. I went to therapy at the hospital clinic for a while and eyed the cleaning women, who eyed me back. What's to stare at, *morenita*?

One day, in my junior year in high school, I saw her on the A train. She had a little girl with her who was looking at a picture book. I stood right in front of her, waiting for her to recognize me. I wanted her to see a kid wearing eyeliner, big glasses, jeans, and heavy black shoes like everyone else my age, first. I'm normal now, I wanted to say.

"*No lo creo*," she said, putting her hand in front of her mouth. I don't believe it.

"Who's that, *mami*?" the little girl said in English. She had soft brown eyes, but her face was delicate, less Mayan than Yadra or her children, or me for that matter.

"This is—I forgot your name," she said. "*Discúlpe*."

"Amanda."

She tapped her head. "How's your *mami*?"

"Good. How are your other children?" I said.

"*Bién*," she said. "*Todo bién, gracias a Dios*." She stroked her daughter's hair.

"*Me alegra*," I said. I was truly happy to hear it.

I wanted to ask Yadra questions but without upsetting the girl. Who was her father? Did she still live in that apartment in Far Rockaway? What did she know?

The girl looked up from her book. "I have two sisters and two brothers in Guatemala. But I've never been there. Where are you from?"

"Right here," I said. I pointed toward the end of the train and Brooklyn.

Ghosts

American Ghosts

Elisabeth Doyle

She took a job at the guesthouse, the decrepit remains of a French villa, not far from the South China Sea and the vast, undulating mountain range of the Truong Son. The mountains vaulted in the distance, ancient and foreboding, filled with the spirits of the dead, those who still traversed the steep jungle paths. Often, she could hear them; they roamed the hills at nightfall, awakened, calling to one another, searching for one another. And sometimes, at daybreak, as the mists of dawn began to clear, she would see them—tattered, weary figures, retreating.

Each morning, on her way to the guesthouse, where she would wash towels and bed sheets in a basin, she would walk down the dirt road, past the wooden home of her great aunt, open at the front. Past the modest home of the village wise man, the man who had taught all of them to read and write, his long gray beard in wisps, his clothing loose upon his emaciated frame. Occasionally, as she walked, she saw idle men on porches, farmers who had lost limbs while tilling their fields. Their hoes had struck a mine; the fighters had planted them all over this landscape but never bothered to retrieve them, so here and there were people without legs, without hands.

Not far away, in another village, there were people who were like another species altogether, their bodies stunted and twisted. The chemicals that had been used had caused this mutation, a new kind of human being, reptilian, with sharp claws and backward limbs, some of them without eyes or mouths. These people lived together in a kind of sanitarium, with others who took care of them, who did things for them because they could not walk properly with their misshapen legs or feed themselves with their talons. Sometimes groups of visitors would come to the sanitarium, to look upon the people and their terrible, disfiguring maladies.

So many chemicals and bombs had been dropped there, near the Truong Son Mountains, where the Ho Chi Minh Trail lay, where it snaked through the deepest jungle, undetectable to mortal eyes. The leaves and plants had evaporated, the coconut and banana trees had withered and browned. The chemicals had killed the animals, too; the corpses of monkeys and tigers rotted on the forest floor, emitting sickening, fruity odors as they decomposed. As a child, she had once come upon the body of a dying panther, wedged between two rocks. She had crawled into the crevice and cradled its huge black head, looked into its yellow eyes, and saw the pleading in them, the beauty that was beyond comprehension, and she was overcome with love and anguish.

All of the holy creatures were now gone from this place, for no reason they had caused or could prevent. Contrary to what she had been taught, she understood that the animals were the greatest and most beloved of all souls, the highest on the wheel, for what could be greater than to enter this world only to be subject to the will of men. And so these great souls, selected and most prized by heaven, made their compact, and came into the world with their heads lowered, in their regal and most vulnerable forms, to be slaughtered and sacrificed.

Sometimes, as she walked, she would pass the remains of the American base, not far from her village. She remembered it from her girlhood. Now, after many years, it was overgrown, and you had to look very hard to find it. In one area, you could see the bunker, with wide slats or turrets through which the machine guns would fire. In another area, an area that now belonged to a farmer, but he nonetheless let it remain covered with vines and brush, there was hidden a large cement block. From the block radiated something dark and sinister. Inscribed in its side was the word "Hunters." From this place, she remembered, men would move into the jungle, in the deepest nighttime, guided only by moonlight. They would walk silently, in single file, their weapons slung across their shoulders, their faces painted in a terrifying swirl of black and green. These were the deadliest of all the soldiers, moving in an undulating line across the jungle, coiling and uncoiling as a single creature, covering the terrain like a great serpent. These were no longer boys, no longer men; they had become dark spirits, they had merged with the shadow. They had learned the secret, of how to abandon their bodies and hover over the earth, released from all earthly tethers, from all that once bound them, governed only by a single instinct. What they had not yet understood was that this instinct is not truly at home in human beings, it would not withstand the scrutiny that would later come, would not reconcile with the conscience that would inevitably reemerge, when the moment had passed, when peace arrived.

She thought of these young men when she passed the former base, crumbling, decaying, when she saw the peaked look in the faces of the older villagers, the indelible grief and worry that lingered in their expressions. She wondered what their lives had been like, these boys, when they returned home, into the shiny airports, sterilized and with bright tile. She wondered if their families could look at them and know and see all that had happened, the places where their sons had been to, and whether they could ever recognize them again.

In recent years, these men had begun to return to her country. They were getting old now. Their bellies stood out in front of them. Their hair was graying. They wore gold wedding bands, many of them. Some of them brought their wives and children with them. She had seen a man like that in her village, once; her neighbors said that he was someone important now. He was with a child, a young girl. The girl hid from the sun in the jeep, with the guide, while the man stood and surveyed an open field alongside the river. He stood there for a long time, his hands in his pockets. He was dreaming of something that had happened there. The farmers in the opposite fields watched him, they were old men now, too. One of them raised his arms over his head, in some kind of gesture, and the man lifted his hand in return. They stood and held their arms extended toward one another like that for what seemed like a long time, with the river rushing between them, coursing, pulling down with it the memories and events that had happened there, releasing them finally into open waters.

When they put their arms down, there was something different about the day, about the light. The man turned and went back to the jeep, where his guide was waiting, smoking, and they drove away together, with the young girl waking up in the back seat and asking what had happened.

Another time, she'd met a man outside of the guesthouse, where she squatted with the laundry. This man was very different from the one at the river, she could see that right away. He had been back to Vietnam many times, he said; he visited once or twice each year. He spoke to her in Vietnamese. Why do you return so often, she had asked him. Ghosts, he said, his lip curling in a rueful smile.

She looked at the man and she felt sorry for him. She wondered if he had been one of the soldiers who would file out of the camp late at night, and disappear into the jungle. She could see in his face many lives, many lives taken. The bitterness, the sourness of death hovered around him; it exuded from his pores, like stale nicotine, like the stench of illness. He was not yet free of it. Beneath his shirt, she imagined a necklace of human remains.

I'll say a prayer for you, she told him.

She watched the returning soldiers when they appeared, wondering if she would ever see the ones that she remembered. For the most part, they were a blur, they had merged into one man, one American, with a few exceptions. She remembered one boy, he was especially young, he'd lied to the recruiter about his age. He called himself Harry. He was from the American South and spoke differently from some of the other men. His chest was thin and hairless, his face nearly hairless, his beauty almost feminine. She was only sixteen herself, at the time. Their village destroyed, her father dead, the family had moved south, to Saigon, to escape the horror of the countryside. There she lived with her ailing mother and younger brother in a small room on a dirty alleyway. Outside, each morning, an orphaned girl would wash herself in a mud puddle, weeping.

For money, she and her brother would gather rotting vegetables from the vendors, and then try to sell them, second hand. They sold the remains of half-smoked, discarded cigarettes and packages of chewing gum. Her little brother learned to navigate the teeming, dirty streets, his bare feet slapping at the pavement, tugging at the sleeves of the American men, plying them with the standard pidgin English, you buy, GI. At night, he would hold his stomach and cry with hunger.

She met the young soldier, Harry, in a bar on Tu Do Street. She never could have imagined such a place. The door opened to her for the first time, and a large man in jungle fatigues ushered her in. He wore dark glasses, even in the dim light, rendering him completely blind. He waved his arm at the room, as if in a grand introduction to the dark figures huddled together, groping. On the stage, she could see the women, half-naked, their expressions blank and vacant, dead. She could see the eyes of the men, as well, and she could see that they had been ruined by the excess, the availability. Once mothers' sons, now they would take the women and defile them in communal rooms— it meant nothing, it was a dark amusement, a distraction. The men did not think about, did not understand, why those girls were there; their circumstances, their horrifying poverty, their desperation. Later, the self-loathing, the drug addiction, the suicides.

She felt sorry for the girls. You could see them out on the street, calling to the soldiers from their places in the doorways, their hair piled up, their eyes done with makeup in the western style. Their ruined, unnatural beauty. She felt sorry for the men, too, for how would they ever again be able to find a place of tenderness within themselves; how could they go home and be someone's husband now, and look upon the bodies of their wives, without seeing the degraded

brown bodies of all the women that had come before, the women of
Tu Do Street.

She was sixteen when she met the young soldier, Harry, the boy from
the American South. It was her first time in that bar, sitting on a stool
in a borrowed skirt and blouse, out of place. He sat down beside her
and spoke in his funny voice, the sound of it rollicking, playful, like
water bouncing off stones. Listening to him made her want to laugh.
He had red lips and sharp white teeth, and a glowing yellow crew cut.
His eyes were a kind of crystalline blue, the kind that made her marvel,
how could a human being have eyes that color? They talked at the bar
for a while, over the noise, neither one understanding what the other
was saying. She could only understand, from his gestures, that he was
a radio operator, which he explained to her was called a Romeo. From
his pointing at the speakers and strumming, to the distorted, unnatural
sounds that emanated from them, she understood that he liked music.

After a while, they left the bar and walked down Tu Do Street. They
walked past the Continental, where journalists sat out on the terrace,
talking loudly and moving their hands. They traveled down past the
Caravelle, all the way to the Saigon River and the beautiful Hotel
Majestic, where they sat at the rooftop bar and listened to the muffled
sounds of the war, and saw the flares rising in the distance, like aborted
fireworks. He bought her a lemonade, and they sat together, with him
talking and talking, and laughing out loud sometimes, and she began
to take a kind of comfort in the lull and drone of his voice. Perhaps this
was all he wanted, after all.

Afterwards, they walked on Le Loi, the wide boulevard named for the
ancient king of Vietnam, visited by a great turtle on the banks of a lake.
The creature had emerged from the waters, massive and magnificent,
bearing on its back the sword that would be used to drive from their
country the Chinese invaders. They walked up the boulevard, past the
milk bars and the beggars, and entered a small pawnshop, where the boy
picked out a guitar and bought it for her. She felt humiliated in front
of the shop owner and the old women who squatted outside, watching
her. Her face grew flushed, and she tried to rush the boy out of the shop,
pulling at his arm.

Why so fast? The boy asked, laughing awkwardly. He did not understand; he had only wanted to buy her a gift.

After many hours, the crowded streets grew quieter. The boy followed her home like an expectant dog. It was assumed. She felt sick to her stomach; she wished that they could just keep walking, and she could imagine that perhaps he was a real boyfriend, and that nothing would pass between them at the end of the evening but a smile, a press of the hand, but that was not the world they were living in.

The next morning, when she awoke, everything looked different. What had once been familiar and comforting was now strange and distant. She no longer inhabited her body, she heard her own voice as if it was coming from another room, muffled, and she watched herself from very far away. The world was like a photograph with a dark tinge around the edges. She gave the guitar to a child in the street; there should be no trace.

She saw the boy once more, a few weeks later. He brought her French chocolates and tried to hold her hand as they walked beside the river, and then she never saw him again. She understood, after a while, that he had been killed. In fact, she had known, from the moment she saw him, that he would die. He was not the kind to survive a war. He was never supposed to be there, just as she was never supposed to be in that bar. They were not meant for war, and so one way or another it would consume them, and they would be devoured by it, churned into the endless stream of waste. She thought about herself and the boy, and how he had been born into a body in the United States, a white body in a safe country, and she had been born into this body, in an impoverished, ravaged land. She thought about why that was, and who decided such things, and how their lives and fates had nonetheless been decided together, by events that drew him from all the way across the world, in the stomach of a great jet, and moved them like pieces on a checker board.

One night, in a dream, she saw his death. It replayed in her mind like a newsreel, the kind she saw in the lobbies of the hotels. She saw him lying on a muddy hilltop, in the churned earth, amidst the sharp splintered trees, the destroyed remains of the forest. He and many other boys, some of them on their stomachs, their hands over their heads like sleeping children. Some of them were shirtless, shoeless, and she wondered why that was. She saw his beautiful boy's face, frozen now in anguish. She wondered what he must've thought about in those last minutes, feeling the life leave his body, seeping out into the earth around him, unstoppable. There would have been time for him to realize it, time to know, to understand: He would die on this mountaintop, across the world from his home, under the hard bright sky, the unrelenting light of Vietnam. In the final moments, the blue of his eyes became cloudy, covered over by a thick gray mist, an ethereal film. He was passing into the other world now, it was claiming him, and he held the images of his parents, his little sister, in his mind for a moment, sending them a telepathic message, *good-bye*.

The war went on. She continued in the bar, she took the men to the upstairs room. Sometimes the men just wanted to sleep with their head on her chest. One of them asked her to sing to him until he fell asleep. Some of them shot heroin into their veins in front of her, some of them wept, one of them tried to strangle her.

Over time, she began to numb herself with drugs, against the horror, the unrelenting terror and degradation, so that while her body was being used she could be elsewhere. She would rise up out of her body like a spirit, and look down on the bed below, at the strangers who were lying there. Sometimes she would leave the room altogether, floating out of the window or down the stairs to the street. There she walked among the other lost spirits of Saigon, among the ghosts of the colonial past, the young students taken by the French and tortured in the basement of the Surete, the murdered prostitutes, the starving babies, the maimed children.

She remained in Saigon for many years. She stayed in the little room on the alley, where the rats ran freely and human waste accumulated in the gutters. The orphaned girl disappeared after a while, like so many others, dismembered or sold into slavery. Sometimes she could still hear her weeping in the street, a phantom, endlessly mourning, washing her arms in a mud puddle.

She remained alone. She did not marry, it was impossible now. Her mother and younger brother died of typhoid, she kept pictures of them on the altar in her home, next to the photographs of her father and grandparents. There was another photograph that she kept, as well, not on the altar but in a small box, and she would take it out and look at it from time to time. The city rose up and changed around her: The shops on Le Loi now sold other things, the remnants of the soldiers, the cameras and watches and dog tags of dead or departing American boys. Piles of them were gathered in the windows, the things they left behind. The tourists started to come more frequently, and they would roam the city in their pale, awkward forms.

Tu Do Street was changed, as well. Like many other streets, it had been renamed. Its multiple incarnations tracked the history of the country. All of the bars were closed now, but she could still imagine them as they had been, the flashing neon lights, the blaring music. She could still see the soldiers strolling up and down in their tan uniforms, coming in and out of the clubs, and the girls waving to them from the doorways. If she looked up, to the upper windows of the establishments, she could see through the open windows, into the darkened rooms, and she was sure that she could see the shadows of girls, moving with the men behind curtains of sheets.

And sometimes she would see the real men, returned. Their khaki shorts, their cotton shirts, their baseball caps. Up and down the street they roamed, looking, holding a map that bore the post-1975 street names. The city was different now, but still its heart was the same, and they quickly honed in—this is it, hovering, pointing. She wondered what they remembered about their time in Tu Do Street, what they remembered about the girls they had known, whether they had ever come to understand. In their eyes, she could see a depth, a sadness, which made her believe that perhaps this was possible.

She never spoke to the men; she averted her eyes when she would pass them on the street, for fear of being recognized. She thought sometimes of the young soldier, and she imagined what he would be like now, if he had lived. She remembered sitting on the rooftop of the Majestic, with the flares illuminating the distant sky. Sometimes she allowed herself to imagine—what if they had met as boy and girl, in other circumstances; what if he had survived, what if she had returned to America with him, to his town in which people spoke like rolling rivers. She would think of him especially when she saw Vietnamese women, returned, with their American husbands. Plump and well-dressed in their older years, impeccably coiffed, they made the pilgrimage with their teenaged children in tow, children who looked tall and strong, healthy, with a limitless future in front of them. Her gaze would follow the children, yearning, her spirit rising up to walk behind them.

When she was much older, too old to be alone, her niece came for her, to take her back to their family home, the place of her ancestors, and she took a job at the guesthouse. Now, each morning, she walked down the dirt road, past the home of her great aunt, open at the front, past the old men who sat upon their porches with missing limbs. She would look up and around her at the mountains through which soldiers once patrolled, hunting one another, fearing one another. They lingered there, still—emerging from the mists at nightfall, the dead Vietnamese soldiers, the American ghosts.

Sometimes, as she walked, she would think about her years in Saigon, and all the things that had happened there. Sometimes she would think about one day in particular, her last day in that city, the day before her niece had come to retrieve her, to bring her home to this valley where she would spend the remainder of her life. On that final day, she had been walking in the teeming neighborhood of Cholon, near the market, when she saw something. Coming toward her, in the crush of people, was a man. He was tall, fully a foot taller than all the people in the crowd, and this is why she noticed him at first—his great, looming height, shocking. As he grew closer, she noticed his pale skin, the dramatic contrast with his black hair, which hung in long bangs across his forehead. She saw his tattered clothing, too small, so that his wrists showed bare and thin. She stopped and stared as he neared.

The young man had been made a half-wit, she could see, beaten and abused by the locals, who avenged their suffering upon these children, symbols of shame and subjugation. Many had been abandoned years ago, left alone and defenseless when the Northern soldiers closed in around the city, as dangerous liabilities in the new regime, evidence of fraternization. Someone had taken a brick to this young man's head, and now his eyes were vacant. And so he wandered the streets like a ghost, exquisite and otherworldly, haunting and reminding them.

She pulled herself into a doorway and watched as the man grew closer. Her mind reeled suddenly backward, moving awkwardly in reverse, off-balance, and she grasped at the doorframe to steady herself. As he came into focus, she saw him—and in a rush of shame and anguish her heart went out to meet him. The living dead, the war come back to her, and as he passed, like a blow in the stomach, beneath his long black hair, she saw his piercing blue eyes, his red lips, his sharp white teeth.

Disappearance

E. Farrell

"I n the wind, I guess."

At the end, an old voice, his own voice, a voice he recognizes but doesn't recognize, the words referring to himself as much as anyone else.

The beginning is in lostness, a disappearance—though Shrever didn't believe hikers ever really disappeared. Dozens went missing and were reported to his Fish and Game unit every year. Dozens were found. Most had made wrong turns or changed routes somewhere in the tangled skein of trails that wound through White Mountains—trails to views, to waterfalls, to solitude, trails to other trails. Some were injured, some wandered off the path (though rarely far), a few were found in motels, shacked up with mistresses, exploring topography of a different sort, even fewer turned up dead, more likely victims of heart attack or stroke than of accident or misadventure. But in dozens of searches of every kind no one had just disappeared.

This call had come in at four forty-five from the crew at the Appalachian Mountain Club's hut at Zealand Falls—*female hiker, Naomi Judson, reported missing.* Shrever got the details later as the summer sun set at the Zealand trailhead from Naomi's husband Jack, who had hiked out from the hut to meet him.

"She should've made it by early afternoon; three at the latest. We asked people coming in if they had seen her on the trail but no one had, not since last night on Guyot. It's like she vanished."

Shrever sized the man up. About six feet, relatively lean, greying hair, maybe sixty or a little older, wearing a light jacket over khakis and a polo shirt, newish mud-splashed hiking boots, carrying a small daypack. Agitated. Definitely agitated.

"So you weren't hiking with her?"

"No. No. This whole AT thing was her deal."

"She was hiking the Appalachian Trail? In segments?"

"No—through hiking. Since late March. I'm running support."

"Through hiking?" That at least bespoke an experienced hiker—a good thing for the circumstances. But something else was waking in his head, too; an alarm he didn't want to hear. "Alone?"

"No. I mean yes—the last few days. She was hiking with a friend of hers, Jan, Jan Hills, but she sprained her ankle on Moosilauke and couldn't keep going. I told Naomi to give it up, that it wasn't safe. But she wanted to try it. She'd come such a long way."

"It's hard to quit." Shrever had through hiked the AT himself, at twenty-two. Nearly six months of sweat, mud, tedium, and insects—but still a satisfying thing, one where you could say, 'I did that.' And one that could teach hard ugly truths, too. I did *that*. "If she got to Moosilauke, she's six-sevenths of the way home. At that point you can almost smell the barn."

"It's my fault. I should—" Judson interrupted himself, shook his head before going on. "What could have happened?"

"Lots of things happen, Mr. Judson. She made a wrong turn. She changed her route. She got off the trail. She twisted her ankle just like her friend did." He did not say, *Or she ran into someone crazy out there.*

Which could happen. Which he knew too well. *I did that.* "Chances are she'll turn up on her own but if she doesn't, we'll find her."

"Tonight? You'll find her tonight?"

"Tomorrow, Mr. Judson. There are a lot of routes to cover. I'll have crews on each of them at first light."

"But if she's hurt—"

"*Tomorrow*, Mr. Judson." Shrever cut him off. "It's wet out there and it's dark out there. And the first rule of search and rescue is don't create another rescue situation. She's experienced and she's well equipped—she'll be okay. We'll find her tomorrow. Now I need a picture if you have one."

"Yeah, sure." The man's hand shaking a bit as he reached into his pocket. "Right here."

The woman in the photograph on Judson's phone was short, trim, and ivory-haired. Wearing shorts, a tee shirt, and well-worn boots, she was squinting in summer sunlight, leaning on red trekking poles, and carrying a bright red backpack—a Kelty Coyote from the look of it. She had a look of competence that long months on the trail could give you, and an open, friendly smile.

"When was this taken?"

"Three days ago. Is that right? No, four—we were at a campground down in Woodstock. Then she went up to Eliza Brook, then Liberty Springs, then Garfield, then Guyot."

"Garfield to Guyot?" Judson clearly knew her itinerary but this seemed odd. "Isn't that kind of a short hop?"

"Yeah, she was gonna come all the way over here, to Zealand, but that Franconia Ridge traverse is pretty tough, and Naomi had heard that South Twin was a real bear."

Shrever chewed his lip a bit. What Judson was saying made sense but it wasn't what you expected from a through hiker. "When did she change her mind?"

"I don't know. She told me in Woodstock."

"And how was she then?"

"Fine. A little nervous about going solo, maybe."

That would be true. Being alone in the woods could work on you in funny ways, teach you things about yourself that you didn't want to know. Shrever shook his head at the thought, from an inner voice he never wanted to hear. "She didn't say or do anything unusual? Mention someone else she wanted to hike with or a problem on the trail?"

"You're not saying someone would hurt her, are you?" Head shaking rapidly, eyes closed as if to hide from some strange vision. "No. No. That's unthinkable."

Unthinkable. A false concept. You could think about anything, no matter how repulsive. In fact, the more abhorrent something was, the more it held onto your attention, like the thick body of a snake coiled on a sunny rock. To release that hold, to not see it everywhere, you had to force yourself to think about something else: the next quarter mile of trail, what you had in your pack for lunch, where your next resupply stop was, how you were going to live the rest of your life. Shrever knew, heard the echo of a strange familiar voice say '*I don't want to hurt you.*' He pushed his mind away from that to focus on the man in front of him, who was waiting for an answer. "It's not likely, Mr. Judson. But it's not impossible either. You don't recall her mentioning anything?"

"No. I mean I don't think so. I mean maybe Jan would know, her hiking partner."

"You know how to reach her?"

Judson seemed to be sagging a little, like a clothesline with too much weight. "I don't know. I probably have her number somewhere in the rig." He looked up at the looming mountains silhouetted against the darkening sky. "Naomi was looking forward to the ridge and the Presidentials."

Shrever nodded. She would be looking forward to it—these stretches in the Whites were some of the best hiking on the whole AT. "Where're you staying, Mr. Judson?"

"The RV is just down the road, at the Sugarloaf Campground."

"Okay. Look for that number. We'll put teams out at first light. You'll be with me if you want to go." Not the usual protocol but Shrever only planned to go back to Zealand hut; an easy walk. He hoped to find a hiker there who might have talked to Naomi at Guyot; he would relay anything he found out to the other teams by radio. "Be here at five."

"Okay." Judson turned to leave but turned around again after a step or two. "Hey? We'll find her, won't we?"

"Yes, Mr. Judson. We'll find her."

In the end Naomi Judson was found, and it did not take long. At dawn teams had started up four routes: Wilderness-Bondcliff, Gale River, Garfield, Skookumchuk, while Shrever and Judson headed back up the Zealand trail. The radio crackled while they were on the steep stone steps below Zealand Falls not long after the sun had climbed over the eastern summits. Shrever pushed the send button to acknowledge.

"Shrever."

"Sam, we've got something." The voice was Susan Rollins from the office below Cannon Mountain.

"I'm with Jack Judson now, Sue." A way of telling her to choose words carefully. "What's up?"

"Billy Legrand, the AMC guy from Guyot called it in." Shrever knew Billy, a fifty-ish neo hippy teacher with a ponytail and a long brown and grey beard who spent his summers in the mountains as a campsite caretaker for next to nothing. "Below Bondcliff."

Something, not someone. Below a cliff. *A body,* Shrever thought. Anyone who went off that cliff was not likely to be alive. "Need Medivac?"

"He didn't say."

"Well, find that out and tell him to secure the scene. He shouldn't move anything. And call Romeo."

"Okay, Sam, you got it. Out."

Jack Judson's face had gone as grey-white as a birch. "What did they find? Who's Romeo?"

"I don't know what they found, Mr. Judson. What I do know is that you'll need to wait at the hut." He let the second question disappear, like breath vapor on a cold morning. No point in telling Judson that he wanted the police called. "If it's your wife and she's hurt, they'll helicopter her to Dartmouth but there won't be room for you. If it's not bad, we'll walk her out. I'll radio over as soon as I know something."

"But the man didn't ask for a Medivac, did he?" Judson's hands were moving now, as if they were discrete creatures, touching first his brow, then his nose, then his chest, settling for a moment on his hips, finally grasping each other as if holding on was the only thing they could do.

"No, he didn't request that." Relief that he hadn't asked about Romeo again. "But we don't know what he found, do we?"

But Judson knew. He shook his head rapidly, spoke too quickly. "This is my fault, all on me."

The second time for that. Best not to let it drop. "What makes you say that, Mr. Judson?"

No answer, though, only a series of mumbled starts and stops like a sleepwalker's gibberish before he dropped his head and wandered slowly up the trail. Shrever left him on a bench on the porch of the Zealand Hut and picked up his pace on the section of trail that rose through the conifers behind it. A quarter mile on his radio crackled.

"Shrever."

"Sam—it's Kate. Sue asked me to check in." Kate Romeo was the major crimes investigator from the Twin Mountain state police barracks. A homicide, even in the national forest, would fall on her desk first.

"Thanks, Kate. We've got a body at Bondcliff. My hunch is you should take a look." That's all it was—a hunch. But it gnawed at him all the same.

"You don't think it was just an accident?"

"Could be. But, Kate, if it's who I think it is, she shouldn't have been on Bondcliff at all. And now she's dead."

A long pause told him that Romeo was mulling this possibility over. But when the radio spilled static into the air again, her mind was made up. "Okay, Sam. I'll call for the bird. Where are you?"

"Twinway east of Zealand. Be there in two hours, maybe a little less. And Kate? Could you bring some climbing gear? I've got teams coming up but I doubt that they planned on cliff work."

"Can do. I'll get there as soon as I can. You'll hear me coming."

That he did. Just before the Bondcliff Trail junction the steady *whump whump whump* of the copter's blades cut through the forest stillness, reaching full crescendo as the chopper's shadow passed above the treetops en route to the Bonds, now less than three miles away by trail, not even two on a beeline. He pictured it hovering in the sky, now a clear cerulean blue, imagined Kate Romeo tossing out rope, harnesses, and strings of protection hardware, finally letting the crew lower her in a harness on a swinging cable to the bare granite of the exposed summit.

Which was where he found her fifty-five minutes later, waiting with Billy Legrand. Romeo raised a hand in greeting as he climbed out of the woods towards the rocky height they stood on. When he reached them she pointed over the edge of the cliff.

"Down there."

Shrever stepped to the brink and leaned forward a bit to peer over. Eighty feet below, the twisted body of a white-haired woman lay in the talus at the bottom of the sheer rock face. Naomi Judson.

Billy Legrand spotted the phone. They were waiting for the first search team to arrive when the thin side of its chartreuse cover caught his eye, wedged between two rocks on a narrow ledge a few yards down from the top. Kate Romeo had the one of the team retrieve it before they all began rappelling down to the body. When she pushed the on button, nothing— the phone was as dead as Naomi herself.

"Whaddya think, Sam? She's taking a selfie and loses her footing, goes over?"

Shrever shook his head. Something was wrong with that picture. "I think she shouldn't have been here. She's a through hiker, she's just had three tough days, good days. She should be looking forward to seeing her husband. Why would she detour four miles out of her way in rough terrain?"

"Sometimes people are crazy, Sam. You know that. Maybe solo through hikers more than most people, huh?"

That was true, too true. Tiring days, an endless string of them. Alone, alone, alone. Whatever unloved part of yourself you thought you'd hidden away would emerge. That ugly thing stirring again in the muddy bottom of Shrever's memory—*I don't want to hurt you.* He pushed out words to elude it. "Did you see her leave, Billy?"

"No." Billy didn't said much but he didn't miss much either. "Heard something early, just before dawn. Coulda been her."

"Anyone else up and around early?" Romeo asking this time.

"Another through hiker up there on one of the platforms. Earworm, I think." Shrever and Romeo nodded at the odd name—AT travelers typically gave themselves fanciful trail handles. "Didn't see him in the morning."

"Thanks, Billy." The grizzled man moved away and hunkered down to stare at the green swell of Owl's Head rising from the valley floor. Romeo turned to Shrever. "What do you think, Sam?"

"Something's wrong, Kate." He bit back the thought that maybe his own history was the problem, and let his mind wander through the scant facts he had about Naomi Judson. "Something's missing."

The phone pinpointed the lost puzzle piece, the something that was not there but should have been—and raised another issue as well. Shrever and Romeo made that discovery when they met with Jack Judson to tell him that his wife was dead. After walking him through the initial shock Kate was able to ask him if he had a charger for Naomi's phone. He did—and when they powered it up, they found what they were looking for. A photo of Naomi on Bondcliff, the pointed cone of Mt. Garfield in the background surrounded by clouds tinged pink by a rising sun.

Standing outside the RV while Judson called his children, Shrever voiced the obvious question. "Who took the picture?"

"Yeah—too much distance for a selfie. Someone else was there." Romeo chewed her lower lip a bit, eyebrows arched.

"Something else—did you see this? It's the photo he emailed us of Naomi." Shrever held out his phone and Romeo furrowed her brow at it.

"What are you seeing there, Sam?"

"The poles. Where are her trekking poles? They weren't on Bondcliff, were they?"

Kate Romeo glanced up quickly. "No," she said, "they weren't. Think she left them at Guyot?"

"Possible. Not likely, though. Woman that size carrying a full pack coupla thousand miles, she's gonna love those poles. Lekis, I think—make 'em in Europe. Pretty pricey."

Romeo nodded. "So who are we looking for?"

Shrever paused, then spit it out. "Maybe this guy Earhart, or whatever his name was—I'll see if I can locate him, and maybe some of the other folks who were up at Guyot if Billy can give us names. But I wonder what you think about Jack Judson?"

"Judson!" Her eyebrows arched again. "Seems pretty broken up. Why him?"

"Before we found her he told me it was all his fault. Twice. Struck me as odd. And he would have had time to get in there if he had a headlamp. A longshot maybe but could be there's a backstory."

Kate Romeo chewed on that for a moment. "Okay. I'll see what I can find out."

What she found out did not quite rule him out. Their father had had an affair, a year ago or more; that's what their children thought Jack meant. No talk of a divorce but after that their mother had decided to walk the AT—as a part of her rebound. So his fault in that way. And there was life insurance—fifty thousand. But Judson's net worth was in the millions—he owned car dealerships—so money didn't feel like much of a murder motive. Maybe something had happened between them in Woodstock at their last rendezvous but there was no evidence of that. Their kids—now both in their late thirties—had talked to both of them then and hadn't picked up anything strange. And a long hike in the dark to meet her at sunrise? Not impossible but according to them he wasn't much of a hiker—liked golf better. But if not him, who?

Billy Legrand's register had names for seven people who'd been at Guyot with Naomi on her last night and between Fish and Game and Romeo's unit, they had been able locate four, two through hikers further up the trail and two who were locals. All of them had seen Naomi at the shelter, but none of them had seen her leave and so couldn't say if anyone had been with her. Three were unaccounted for—a vacationing couple from Philly who were presumably on their way home, and Earworm, the through hiker, whose real name hadn't surfaced yet. Was he the key? Shrever thought so; but Romeo, meeting with him at the state police barracks in Twin Mountain, was less sure.

"Why, Sam? We don't know anything about him. And there wasn't a fingerprint on that phone—not even Naomi's. Wiped clean."

"But what we do know is interesting—he was up there at Guyot, he left early, he's short, and no one has seen going north along the trail."

"Short?" Romeo studying the ranger's face. "Why's that interesting?"

"Naomi Judson was what? Five four, I think. Maybe five five. Her poles wouldn't be much good to a tall person."

"Okay." A barely perceptible head shake. "But we'll need some luck to find him—he could be a long way from here by now."

"Could be—but I'm thinking not. He didn't walk all this way to quit now. If he did, why pick up the poles?"

"You seem pretty sure he did."

Thinking, *yeah, I'm sure*; saying, "If he didn't, I'll apologize."

Romeo chortling at this. "Any thoughts about where he'd go?"

"If he came out, it'd be to Lincoln or Twin—maybe your people could ask around." Shrever looked past his counterpart toward the door. "We'll look in the Pemi. I'm thinking he'd bury himself in there for a few days."

"Really?" The Pemigewasset Wilderness was forty-five thousand acres of green space on the map; only a few trails laced through it. "Why?"

"That's what I'd do."

That's what I did. Two days, two nights on a flat patch by a stream in the Wild River watershed. Talking to himself, crying some, shouting curses at a waterfall, stewing in fear and regret like some crazed holy man in the desert.

"But this guy's not you."

Maybe he is. "Could be that none of us are so very different."

Romeo gave him a quizzical look, pauses a beat before speaking. "If he's off trail in there, he's gonna be hard to find."

"All the more reason to start looking soon."

Shrever's search criteria were simple: near water, not overly trafficked, reasonable access back to the Appalachian Trail. Assuming he'd moved away from Guyot and not back towards it, Earworm would have dropped down the Bondcliff Trail towards Lincoln. A topo map—likely he'd have one—would show him good terrain for laying low to the west around Owl's Head but would also reveal that getting there would take him close to another backcountry tent site near a waterfall, which would attract dayhikers the way milkweed draws monarchs. Would he know that? Probably. So it was more likely he'd turn west, deeper into the woods, where no one would see him. The Thoreau Falls trail was possible but Shoal Pond was made more sense—less used, a middle-of-nowhere kind of route, brooks close by, and not a shortcut to anywhere though it did connect with the AT at its top end. Shrever set his sights there, assigning teams to sweep the other trails that were possible venues for a fugitive.

"You're going alone?" Romeo watching him organize his pack, her eyebrows cocked skeptically. "Is that safe?"

"Kate, we both know there's not much chance I'll find him. And if I do see him, I've got a radio."

"What if he sees you first?"

"Give me some credit, Kate. He won't."

He didn't. Shrever retraced his path along the Zealand Trail, then continued on the AT towards Ethan Pond, working his way through the scree field at the base of the Whitewall cliffs before heading south into the broad valley of Shoal Pond Brook, finally dropping his pack fifty yards off the trail at the edge of a nameless side rill a bit more than a quarter mile below Shoal Pond itself. The muddy low places in the trail had not shown him any footprints headed north so if his guess was valid, all he needed to do now was wait. *Let him come to me,* Shrever thought.

Earworm didn't come the first day—but another hiker did. Nameless, faceless now after so many years, but familiar, a woman standing by a stream in the Wild River basin, near Evans Notch only a few dozen miles from where he sat now, a woman hiker alone like Naomi Judson, on a hot late summer day. Thirty years on and still he met her, had been meeting her for years. He had hiked down from Mt. Imp to the forest service campground, to meet a cousin who provided stove fuel, instant oatmeal, raisins, freeze dried chicken, beef jerky, honey roasted peanuts, brown rice, Tang, a small block of sharp cheddar cheese, six Granny Smith apples, and a letter from Ann, his girlfriend back in Illinois.

Which said *you've meant a lot to me.* Which said *you've been gone so long.* Which said *I've met someone else.* Which said *it's over.*

Then hiking back up the Shelburne Trail to the ridgeline where the AT twisted, curved and fell, then rose again like serpent writhing atop the ancient eastern mountains, crying, talking to himself, cursing—*fuck her, fuck her, fuck HER*—until the words ran out and all that was left was jagged, gasping breath. Recalling it, Shrever wondered what grip the trail had on him that he kept on walking instead of riding with his cousin back to the nearest phone to call Ann and make his case. Fear's grip, maybe. Fear that there was no case to make—wasn't that some of what had pushed him onto the AT in the first place less than a year into his first job after college? A fear of being conventional? Pinned down by a job, a wife? To prove something? *Fuck her. I'll show her*. And then the woman by the stream.

She was kneeling by the brook at the bottom of a short cascade perhaps twenty yards below the trail, kneeling in a shallow pool, wearing only panties, dipping water with a drinking cup and pouring it over her head, baptizing herself against the heat of the day. He should have stopped, looked, then kept on hiking. Why hadn't he? But the question he had been asking for more than thirty years still had no answer except the memory of his younger self dropping down the slope to where the woman was.

The music of falling water had masked the sound of his footsteps. He was only thirty feet away, maybe less, when she noticed him, standing suddenly in the calf deep water, crossing her arms to cover her breasts, a woman older than he was then, perhaps thirty, five six or so, and slim. She spoke with a note of panic in her voice, like a snared bird's frightened cheep.

"Don't hurt me."

In the moment he was confused. Or so he had been telling himself for years. What did she mean?

"I don't want to hurt you."

He was trying to reassure her. It wasn't a threat, was it? She seemed to think so. Trembling visibly, she said, "I'll do what you want."

He could have walked away then—should have. Why hadn't he? What was it in her trembling that had held him there, aroused and transfixed? The woman was crying then—not audibly but silver tear tracks marked her cheeks—a sight that somehow stabbed at him like a goad, enraged him. Why? No answer—not then, not now. But then and now, he can hear his own grating voice: "Come out here and take those off."

The woman did. Stepped out of the stream, stumbling a bit on the bank; hooked her panties down with her thumbs, stepping out of them, looking down, revealing a triangular brown bush a shade darker than her hair. In all of that an erotic surge of power and disgust.

"Turn around and kneel down."

How could he have said that? What had he been thinking? And the rest of it—dropping his pack, his hand tightening in her hair, the rough penetration, her sobbing wails, the quick climax—could he have done that? Now, sitting in a copse of birches with a view down the Shoal Pond Trail, it seemed impossible. But the man who did it had been with him every day since then, the moment a haunting he could not escape. *Kill that motherfucker. Him and the memory, too.* And the present case had hooks, barbs that tangled it with that distant one that wouldn't go away.

Earworm walked into this snarl on the second day of the search, the third day after the murder. On the first Shrever had set camp and waited, watching from a copse of birches a quarter mile from his camp and twenty yards from the trail with good sight lines up and down it. Nothing. Restless, troubling thoughts, an empty trail, and the sun moving across a broken blue sky. On the second, more of the same. Cool air of the morning, grey light silhouetting the eastern peaks at dawn, a yellow-orange sun ascending the sky's dome behind Mt. Carrigain.

And then singing.

"I'm going down that long lonesome road, babe . . . "

Off key, loud and getting louder.

"Where I'm bound, I can't say . . . "

A hiker coming into sight: a short, dark-haired, bearded man, maybe thirty, in shorts and a tee shirt with a sizable green backpack and red trekking poles, lifting his face to wail at the treetops. On a city sidewalk it would have drawn stares but Shrever knew his singing wouldn't be thought odd in the fraternity of distance hikers. The tedium of days required creativity—on his AT trek he had met a couple who hiked for days naked except for boots and socks just to stave off boredom.

"But good bye is too good a word babe . . . "

Motionless in his seat among the trees, Shrever let him pass.

"So I'll just say fare thee well . . . "

When he was thirty feet farther down the trail, Shrever slipped soundlessly out of the woods behind him.

"When the rooster crows at—"

"Earworm!" Shrever holding up his badge with his left hand, his right on the butt of his holstered service weapon as the man slowly turned and stood staring for a moment as if he were an alien beamed down from a saucer.

"Are you going to shoot me, Wyatt Earp?" The man's voice even; something like a smile appearing briefly in the beard.

"Not planning on it." Keeping his face as flat and grim as a grave marker. "But I do need to ask you some questions."

The man considered this for a long beat. "Am I, like, under arrest?"

"No."

"Okay, then. In that case I gotta be going." Earworm began to turn away.

"I don't think so." Shrever lowered his badge, raised his automatic, and began moving forward very slowly, actions that widened the hiker's eyes. "Now you are under arrest since you seem to want it that way. Put the poles down and kneel on the ground."

"For what? You can't just—"

"Wrong on that, mister. Put the poles down and kneel."

"I'm not—"

Shrever still approaching slowly, closing now to fifteen feet. "I can't call for backup out here, sir, so this could get very messy. Put the poles down and kneel."

"Fine, I'll answer—"

Ten feet, still moving forward, weapon up. "Too late for that now, sir. Put the poles down and kneel."

Earworm let the poles drop and stood defiant with his arms crossed in front of him as the ranger continued to come closer. At two feet Shrever turned slightly to his right, darted his left leg forward, hooked it behind the hikers left knee and yanked it back, sending Earworm sprawling backwards onto his own back. Before he could recover, Shrever had holstered the automatic and grabbed his left wrist, wrenching it counter-clockwise and forcing the smaller man to roll over as the arm curled behind him.

"Fuck you, you fuckaaaii—"

"Sir, I'm going to twist this arm until you reach your right arm slowly back here so I can cuff you. If I have to, I'll break it. Do you understand that?"

"Yes, you motherfuck—" Another twist. "YES!"

The hand came back and Shrever clicked the handcuffs on. "Do you see how easy that was?" His knee on the hiker's backpack kept the man pinned face down. "Now, you have the right to remain silent. If you choose to waive this—"

"Fuck you, I'm a lawyer."

"Really? Good for you. I'm taking that as confirmation that you understand your rights. Shall we get you on your feet?"

"Fuck you."

"Okay, counselor. Suit yourself." Shrever moved away from his captive and leaned against a leafy sapling. Breathing hard, shaking a little—now it hit him that it could have been him laying in the path, his own hands cuffed—which would not have been wrong once.

"Are you just going to fucking leave me here?"

Thinking, *Not a bad idea.* Saying, "That's up to you, counselor. Think about it as long as you like."

As it happened, not long. Earworm had spit a few more curses out and rocked back and forth helplessly like an inverted turtle before Shrever had tugged him back up to a kneel to him get his legs under himself, the pulled him to his feet. Up the trail to the side stream, up that to Shrever's campsite, the ranger following with the red poles tucked under his arm, the prisoner had muttered but not spoken. Now installed on a flat rock next to a quiet pool in the rivulet, hands still cuffed behind him beneath his pack, watching while Shrever rolled up his tent, finally breaking silence.

"So could you, like, loosen these? My arms are cramping up."

Shrever glanced at him for a moment as if considering the situation but did not answer, turning his attention back to his tent and its stuff sack. When it was stowed and clipped on to the bottom of his pack, he hunkered down and turned back to Earworm who was squirming a bit, rolling his shoulders and trying to tug his hands free.

"Don't think that'll help much. Probably make it worse."

"What would help would be for you to take the fucking things off. Or at least tell me what the fuck I'm under arrest for?"

Shrever looked him evenly, brushed an imaginary speck out of the corner of his eye, waited a beat, then two, spoke. "I think you already know."

Earworm returned a looks-could-kill glare but after a moment broke into a wide grin. "Wait a minute." His face was almost gleeful. You don't have a thing on me, do you? How could you?"

The prisoner's smirk flipped a switch that tightened Shrever's jaw and narrowed his eyes. Because what he said was true. Because there was nothing he could do about it. Because he had done it himself. But then Earworm's voice again in the back of his mind: *Are you just going to fucking leave me here?* Shrever tipped himself back off his haunches onto the ground, stretched his legs out, and smiled.

"I don't have much, counselor. I'll give you that."

"You don't have shit. No witnesses. Not a fingerprint, not a footprint. Nothing."

"Funny you should mention fingerprints. See, that's what made me sure. Because there were *no* fingerprints on that phone. Not even hers. What does that tell me? That someone wiped it clean before they dropped it off the edge."

"And you've got no idea who! Fuck you!"

Shrever ignored the taunt and smiled beatifically, looking past him at the glint of light on the water flowing behind him. "And yet you have her poles."

"The poles? Is that what this is about?" He laughed. "Fuck the poles. I found these next to trail and you can't prove I didn't unless I say otherwise. And why would I do that?"

All that was true—even if they could put him at the scene there was no way to say what had happened. But Shrever smiled again, suddenly and coldy sure of himself. The water was the answer.

"They say confession is good for the soul."

"Is it? I wouldn't know."

"But I do." He stood up and stepped across the small clearing to stand above the bound man. "See, I took a life once—didn't kill anyone but took a life just the same, just broke it where it was—and that's eaten at me for thirty years. Wouldn't want it to happen to you."

"What the fuck are you talking about?"

In lieu of an answer Shrever grabbed him by his hair with one hand and the side of his backpack with the other and flipped him back and to his right so that his chest and head were above the brook's pool.

"What are you doing? Let go—" The hand on his head pushed down and the words became bubbles. When it pulled him up again he was gasping and coughing.

"It just eats at you, reminds you what kind of man you really are. Just like a song you can't get out of your head, Earworm. How funny is that name now?" Pushing the face back into the water, pulling it out before it stopped resisting, listening to its retching.

"So what I want to know is why? Why. Did. You. Kill. That. Woman?"

"You . . . you're crazy . . . " Coughing more, struggling as Shrever forced his face close to the water again.

"Wait!" When Earworm's forehead touches the surface, Shrever eases up. "Wait . . . I just wanted . . . those poles . . . that's all . . . and no one, I got her to come with me . . . there was fucking no one . . . around. I don't know why. I don't know. Okay?"

Sam Shrever reached down to pat him tenderly on the cheek.

"See. Doesn't that feel good?"

"No. No. Fuck you. It doesn't feel good." Earworm sobbing a little now.

When Shrever spoke again, the words were clipped and distinct as if pronounced for a voice lesson or a play. "Looks like he was breaking camp but it's hard to say when animals scatter the bones like that. Maybe he slipped, hit his head, fell into the stream. Hard to say."

He pushed down again, pushed down both on his own past and on Earworm, this time with two hands.

"No luck, huh?" Romeo's cramped office at the State Police Barracks, looking out at rows of cars whose passengers were inside in a sterile waiting room, nervously awaiting their respective turns at a DMV driver's test. Shrever taking all this in thoughtfully, as if he was an alien just landed on Earth, thinking about his friend's comment a moment too long before answering.

"If there was any luck at all out there, all of it was bad."

Was that what it was? Maybe. Maybe just bad luck that Naomi Judson had crossed paths with Earworm. Maybe just bad luck that had brought him to Shrever on the Shoal Pond Trail, that there had been a woman by a stream so many years ago. Maybe.

"Where do you think he could be?"

And maybe not. But what was done was done.

"In the wind, I guess." The room cold as if a chill gust had just blown through. "Disappeared."

Borealis

Edward Hamlin

Daniel's come north in the season of mud. By day, the gutted back roads suck at his tires and paint the car with brown slurry, every crossroad a mire. By night, the frozen ruts take on a starlit frost that lingers well into morning. In this awkward season the sun's warmth is slow to make itself felt. If he lays a palm against the foundation wall it's as cold as bones in winter earth.

Midnight has passed with barely a whisper. It seems like weeks that he's sat by the leaking casement window and watched the cold come and go, the austere northern spring pinned down like a rabbit in a trap, but really it's been only a matter of days. His sense of time has been unreliable in the years since losing his wife and daughter. Perhaps it was only a month ago that he sat with Emily over morning coffee while she sketched her plans for the garden, Janie coloring in her dinosaur book on the living room carpet and the Oklahoma sun already bristling in the ivy. Perhaps it was only last night that Emily slipped out of her flannel nightshirt and woke him with a soft breath on his neck. Or perhaps it's all a decade ago. It's hard to be sure sometimes, especially this late at night.

Eventually Daniel abandons his post by the window and climbs the creaking stairs, feeling his way through the darkness to his warm bed, his second wife's breath a slow threshing, a rhythmic clearing of the day's undergrowth. The scent of sleep settles lightly into the narrow space between them. The bed is smaller than theirs at home, the sort that was in favor when the cottage was built in the 1940s, in the heady days after the war. It's possible that his first wife was conceived in it; Emily always believed so, having done the arithmetic and made certain reasonable assumptions. Her parents had slept there for years, after all, summer after summer, after long days spent on the lake, pressing as far into autumn as the weather permitted. It certainly isn't hard to imagine that Emily was the product of some chilly September night here, the woody bedroom more intimate for the waning of summer and the nickering of a fire in the grate, the narrow bed that much warmer.

It still astounds him that Lissa has insisted on keeping the old counter-sawn cedar frame, even knowing its history, its deep connection to her predecessor—keeping it out of fidelity to the house, she says, though he knows it's for his heart. And for Emily, too, wherever she may be now. As Daniel nestles under the blankets, his wife touches his hair, asleep but also aware of his presence, and rolls away. Somewhere out in the night, he hears an owl hoot twice and go silent, *one-and-two*, as if there were nothing more to be said about the night.

On the other side of the pine wall their daughter is talking in her sleep, the little voice confident even in its meandering. Daniel knows she'll have her stuffed Black Beauty in her arms; the starfish nightlight will be casting its glow across the woven rug, its five arms waving away the darkness. The murmuring ends abruptly with a grown-up sort of sigh, then, after a pause, begins again. What seemed a monologue now sounds more like a conversation. For a fleeting moment, Daniel wonders if she's talking to the half-sister her parents speak of only as a cousin who lives very far away—a *cousin*, they say, because it seems too soon to reveal more. But no: Janie is gone. In her short life she never knew this place, as dear as it was to her mother's heart. They'd always meant to bring her north, but it never happened, and then it was too late. If she's in the house now, she's found her way here through other means.

In the next bedroom, little Hanna is telling a convoluted story. Another pause, then a sparkling laugh: Who's made her laugh? Daniel stops breathing for a long moment, waiting, listening . . . then takes one even breath.

"No," he whispers into the chilly quiet of the bedroom. "She's out like a light. Just dreaming. That's all."

His wife stirs at the sound of his voice, drifts toward the surface for a moment and then sinks back, pulling her sturdy legs in closer. Daniel feels her tug at the sheet and releases a bit of slack for her. Lissa's a far better sleeper than he'll ever be. Meanwhile, Hanna burbles away on the other side of the wall, and for an instant he thinks he hears a second voice—another girl.

"*No*," he insists again. Daniel's discovered that he believes in ghosts only while drinking, which has seemed for some time now an excellent reason to stop drinking. His daughter is only dreaming. That's the beginning and end of it.

He lays a hand on his wife's hip, compact and reassuring even in sleep. It's this capable woman who's seen him through the worst of it. No one, he's certain, could have understood better what he's gone through, because her grief has been as sharp and dangerous as his own.

She's been there from the beginning, after all: Elissa Zacharias was the one who'd convinced her friend Emily to go out with him, years ago, and later to marry him. The two women had been as close as sisters since their college days, the shy Chicago girl utterly taken with her plainspoken Greek roommate. Lissa would go on to become a frequent guest in their home, a reliable and beloved fixture of Daniel's world, too—and then, in the terrible months after the tragedy, his only true confidante. That she should become his lover and then his wife was both strange and strangely right, just as it is strange and strangely right that they now sleep in the bed where Emily was conceived.

It doesn't matter what others think of the arrangement. Lissa put it best one evening in a Greek restaurant after sharing a perilous third bottle of wine with friends who would cease, later that night, to be friends: *Anyone who deserved an explanation is dead now, and the rest of you can go to hell.* On the subject of their marriage, Daniel and Lissa give no quarter.

Daniel shapes his body to his wife's, takes in her scent, gathers in a lazy breast, but she draws herself into a tighter ball, too deeply asleep to entertain his advances. And then he's gone too, carried off within short minutes, the house creaking quietly as the temperature drifts down its slow incline and the constellations stare down from on high.

In his dreams, that bright prairie morning of 1995 is more present, more urgent than any he's ever witnessed, the brute ground wave of the explosion still rolling under him five years after the fact. The fatal moment hangs in the night air like some catastrophic Wagnerian chord. Hours pass while he sleeps under its spell, oddly acclimated to its gravity, the dark pulse of it as familiar as his own heartbeat. And then he's awake again, vaulted into his new and millennial life, the Earth stilled and ready, a different wife and daughter still tumbling through dreams of their own. He takes inventory quickly: Yes, they're still there, breathing steadily, his daughter moaning a little with every outbreath. All is well.

As Daniel lies at the edge of the bed and studies the murky ceiling, guessing it's too early to get up, he wonders whether he's tried, unconsciously, to recreate the world that vanished on that April day. A loving wife, a little girl, this summerhouse in the north country—he's landed well, he knows, and on many days he's as happy as he's ever been. But there are times when he finds this second act suspect. What right does he have to be happy?

"Jesus, Danny, will you stop overthinking it?" his stockbroker brother demands. "You've been to hell and back—isn't that enough? Count your blessings, man. You deserve whatever happiness you can find."

But only a fool would think it's as simple as that. This is what Daniel tells himself, fairly or not. What can his brother know, or for that matter anyone else who didn't live through that April day in Oklahoma? So few can speak to him with authority.

It can't be much later than five in the morning. Daniel leaves the bed gently and goes to the window seat, pulling a blanket around his shoulders against the chill. Downstairs, the fire will be nothing but guttering embers. In the careful silence the kitchen clock ticks away. Out in the woods, he imagines, there are restive animals large and small, the meltwater creek slipping down through patchy ice, pewter-gray in the starlight.

Through the window overlooking the barn, he can see Saturn, large and in opposition, and to its south, balanced on the highest pines, a sharp crescent moon. The machinery of the universe clicks along. The gears of time and gravity mesh. It was Emily who taught him what little he knows of the heavens, Emily who'd drag him from bed in the middle of the night to observe some nebula or wispy comet through her father's old reflector, her hand on the small of his back as he leaned over the eyepiece. It was Emily, too, who nestled in his arms at the edge of the dock as the aurora borealis erupted overhead in great swaths of indigo and crimson. All that was celestial belonged to her.

By six, he's made coffee and taken up his post in one of the Adirondack chairs overlooking the lake, the cold brushed across the water like a painter's glaze. Through the chair's wooden bones he feels an ache reaching up to meddle with his spine. It's here that he'd sit with Emily's mother, Grace, on cool summer mornings, the two of them observing a monkish silence, listening closely for the first birdsong, the first shuffling of wings. As the light came on he'd steal glances at her, her profile stolid and peaceful, her gray-blonde hair caught up in an offhand twist, her chapped hands cradling a steaming mug. Already she'd be tucked into her overalls and Peruvian sweater, ready to take on the garden as soon as breakfast was done.

They were as comfortable with each other as two childhood friends, he and Grace. He'd never dreamed that a mother-in-law could be such a friend, and yet she was, unquestionably. To this day he's been unable to recreate the smoky coffee she brewed while the rest of the house slept on. When he'd creep down the stairs and nod to her she'd have his mug ready, five-thirty being their appointed hour. And then she too was gone, like Emily and Janie and his wry, talkative father-in-law, Bern, only the quiet mood of those early mornings in the Adirondack chairs lingering on, and the phantom scent of her irreproducible coffee.

The small lake, deep and narrow, has its own phantom history: Its basin, they say, is the divot left by an enormous chunk of glacial ice, long since vanished. For years Emily's family speculated on whether their well water could be traced back to the original glacier, whose gradual collapse was said to have filled the aquifer beneath them. Now Daniel wonders whether there is still some trace of the old clan dissolved in the waters below. He's nearly certain there is. He's felt the touch of Grace and Bern, Emily and Janie on his skin while swimming in high summer, has tasted them more than once. He can't be simply imagining it, nor does it repel him. It's not a matter for science but for the heart.

Come June, on Emily's birthday, he'll swim the two-mile perimeter as she used to do, reenacting the annual ritual in her honor. When he enters the cove where he scattered her ashes he'll feel, as always, that he is in some way passing through her, anointing himself with her. The little cove is a spawning ground for bass and splake, its long reeds a busy nursery, the water warmed by the business of life; she too is alive there, in ways he doesn't quite comprehend. The elements of her body have carried on, certainly—her phosphorous and carbon and calcium incorporated into the bodies of walleye and splake, into grasshoppers and the killdeer that pluck them from the air. But it's more than this. He feels her presence in the cove, her intelligence, something more, something crisply self-aware.

On this cold morning, the fifth anniversary of Emily's death, he feels closer to her than ever. Still she embraces him in these quiet ways. Janie, too, and Grace and Bern—the whole lost tribe, all of them somehow inhabiting the waters before him and the house where his second family, his second life, sleeps.

"Daddy!" says the bright voice behind the hands. "Pancakes! With *blueberries*, Daddy."

Hanna doesn't know yet that there was once another little girl who stood behind this same father and covered his eyes in just this teasing way. She's heard of a distant cousin named Janie but can't guess how intimately that other girl was woven into her father's life. She is Daddy's only girl. In her trusting heart there has never been another.

Janie would be eight years old, had she survived. They've debated when and how to tell Hanna that Janie was not just a cousin but a half-sister who is gone forever now—gone along with her mother, Emily, who was once married to Daddy. It's a salvo of revelations that even an adult would have trouble withstanding. Already Hanna's noted the portraits of mother and daughter high up on the bookshelves and has begun to ask questions. The two faces hover in her mind as a mystery to be solved. For some time now, her mother and father have dutifully sifted through the varied advice of pediatricians and psychologists and other parents who've lost children to violence—experts all—and have been assured that at three she's still too young to understand. Or perhaps her parents are the ones who aren't ready for the difficult conversation. Perhaps they just haven't found a way to begin.

How can they possibly explain to Hanna what happened to Janie and Emily in far-off Oklahoma City, a place she's never heard of, on that April day two years before she was born? They barely understand it themselves. The official accounting, of course, is no help at all. To know the bomber's motives—to delve into his shadowy association with survivalist militiamen hunkered down in camouflage not far from this very cottage, for example—is to understand nothing of how that April day gutted them. Nor can it explain this placid morning by the lake, these joyful little hands covering his eyes, this scent of sleep and cherry toothpaste tucking itself into the crook of his neck. "Daddy," she insists, "come inside and make *pancakes*. Mommy's up!"

Daniel catches the wriggling bundle of his daughter and squeezes her, lifts and tickles and kisses her until she squeals. He is grateful in every way that she's come into his life. Everything eases in him at once. Hanna slips around to stand between his knees, exactly the right height to meet her seated father's gaze, and regards him soberly, as if a serious conversation about breakfast is long overdue. It will be months yet before his own skin is as dusky as the little arms she wraps around his neck; it's her mother's Greek skin she's inherited, and her straight dark hair, so thick for a child's, so different from Janie's airy blonde curls. Daniel catches a wayward strand between his fingertips, tucks it behind an ear, waits for her ultimatum.

"Daddy," his daughter says, and lowers her chin gravely. At times she's a perfect mimic of her mother. "It's freezing out here. Come inside and make pancakes. And don't forget the blueberries this time. Or *else*."

It's a day filled with the slow and companionable business of opening the house for the season. Mother and daughter have busied themselves with dusting shelves and whiskey-barrel planters and the mulched-over garden, uncovering one winter burrow after another, the bottom layer of dead leaves stiff with frost. As for Daniel, he's spent much of the day contending with a balky pump and a burst irrigation pipe down in the clay and cobwebs of the crawlspace, which is accessible only through an exterior trapdoor. Just sawing through the rusted padlock was half an hour's work. After shoveling a desiccated vole from its midden he examined the pump like a surgeon, palpating the casing for winter cracks, tracing the electrical supply in search of insulation gnawed by mice, priming and repriming the standpipe, cycling the motor on and off to catch it in the act of failure. All the while the scent of Michigan earth filled his head, familiar and welcome, the rooty hillside erupting into the crawlspace to hug the old house's walls.

The sensible thing would have been to call a plumber—there's one just down the road, a tight-lipped Vietnam vet they hire to shovel the roof in winter—but tending to the simple machinery of the house is part of Daniel's northerly ritual, his boreal labor, gratifying in some way that's grown more important to him over the last few years. For a history professor to succeed in repairing a well pump is no small victory, after all. Through a hundred mistakes, some of them costly, he's gradually learned how to clean the flues and pilots of the gas heaters in the mudroom and barn; to drain the pipes in the fall; to redo the perilous cloth-wound wiring improvised, long ago, by some other overconfident male. He tends to the house as if it were an elderly relative, sensitive to its needs and limitations.

By four, he's discovered the hairline crack in the pressure line, drained the system and soldered the wound closed, primed the pump with lake water. With his daughter standing at the kitchen sink under orders to stamp her feet whenever water flows, he's tested the repair through a half dozen pump cycles, convincing himself it will hold, then turned his attention to the broken irrigation line. By suppertime his jeans are as filthy as a gravedigger's, but he can vouch for the health of the house's circulatory system. It's been a day's honest labor.

When he goes upstairs to wash, the scent of grilled salmon is already in the air and the sun is down. His wife and daughter are setting the table before the picture window that looks out over the lake, having lit slender candles against the darkness.

"We went down to clean up the beach this afternoon," Lissa says as they eat. "You wouldn't believe the driftwood that's washed in. It's like a shipwreck."

Daniel says, "It's a tough winter up here. Sometimes they even get the remnants of gales off Superior. The weaker trees just can't take it." His daughter has dissected her salmon into a hundred pieces as if searching for a missing diamond. "The dead stuff's mostly birch?"

"All birch."

"Birch is fragile. You won't see too many maples down."

"We picked up what we could, but we left some big pieces for Daddy, didn't we, Hanna? I think the *chainsaw* may be called for." Lissa's eyes flicker across the table at him, flick away. "I know Daddy'll be disappointed to hear that."

Like his plodding education as a plumber, Daniel's fascination with the chainsaw amuses them both, though she tends to hover nervously by whenever he uses it. The irony is that her own work as a marine biologist— on hold now while he plays out a fellowship in Chicago, far from any sea—has left her far more at ease with machinery than he'll ever be. His Lissa is as much sailor as scientist. She's repaired bilge pumps, five-thousand-dollar underwater cameras, transponders extracted from the hides of migrating whale sharks. But here in Michigan she indulges him.

"Mommy said we can make a bonfire!" says Hanna, setting her fork down decisively.

"Is that right, sweetie?" Daniel says.

"Yes!"

"Why not? But not until you finish your salad, young lady."

After dinner, they leave their dishes in the sink and walk down to the beach by flashlight, Hanna bobbling between them, each mittened hand clasped in one of theirs. On the opposite shore, there's not a light to be seen. It's very early in the season, a good month before the summer residents come north; the mud is too much of a nuisance by day, the danger of nighttime freezes far from past. Toward the east end of the lake, a jagged sheaf of ice as broad as a house still drifts on its own, now and then issuing a low thud as another crack rives through it.

They wouldn't be here themselves had they not decided to pass the fifth anniversary of the attack at the cottage, in Emily's private heartland. It seemed a way of honoring her, though they would have been hard pressed to explain why. All they knew was that they needed to go north, and so in April they'd packed Hanna's pink suitcase and loaded the car with a week's worth of groceries and set off through the South Side's dreary gauntlet of soul food kitchens and caged-in currency exchanges and grimy mosques, powering on through the sulfurous funk of Hammond and Gary until they surfaced on the eastern shore of Lake Michigan and pointed the car north, the atmosphere gradually clearing and Hanna dozing away the hours as they drove and drove.

Now Daniel stands on the beach with his flashlight and surveys the damage the winter's done. His girls have built a waist-high pile of birch branches and anchored it with a jagged section of trunk, the white bark curling away like shavings from a huge carpenter's plane. Just down the beach at the Thompsons', four heavy dock sections, disassembled and stacked for winter, have been flung toward the water, a fifth having floated off and come to rest twenty yards downshore.

"Take a look," says Lissa, pointing the flashlight deep into the bleached switchgrass along the slope that climbs to the house. The narrow beam reveals an upended birch, its base a tangle of grayed roots grasping at sand and clay. "Isn't she a beauty? We left her for you."

The bonfire is fast and bright, bark peeling from the birch debris and going up in glowing pirouettes. They sit on the breakwater log with Hanna bundled in a blanket between them, smoke snapping back and forth as a faint breeze plays on the lake. Their little girl has already drifted off to sleep, the heat of the blaze reaching down into her bones, her dark little head tucked under her mother's chin. Daniel is drowsy too: He could sleep right where he is, in fact, huddled here with his two girls, the firelight carrying him off.

"Danny?" Lissa whispers, careful not to wake their daughter.

"Yeah?"

"Do you feel like they're here with us?" With a snap, the fire throws an ember onto the sand at their feet. "I don't mean like ghosts."

"Then what do you mean?"

"I don't know, exactly. It's almost like . . . we're them. Is that crazy?"

It isn't crazy, and there's no need to say so. She knows. So much goes unspoken between them. Of all the things Daniel cherishes about his marriage, this is what he cherishes the most.

"You know what I wish, though?" she continues.

"What?"

"I wish Janie could have experienced this place. I wish she could have swum in this lake and sat on this beach, just like this. With Emily, of course. And Hanna." She strokes her daughter's head, draws a gentle finger across the fine little jaw. "Although—"

Lissa gazes past the fire into the indistinct night, careful as ever on the topic of Janie. Despite her intimate connection to them all, she is careful not to insert herself into Daniel's memories of his first wife and daughter. Even little Hanna has no place there. And yet sometimes she forgets her diligent caution. Sometimes the past bleeds into the present, even for her. "All I mean to say is, I wish Janie could have come here with her mother and father. Could have had moments like this."

"We couldn't bring her. We just couldn't. You need to trust me on that."

"I didn't mean it as a criticism, Daniel." The black eyes narrow, a trace of annoyance in them. He hadn't meant to sound defensive. Under his sheltering arm his daughter fidgets, sighs, resettles.

He tries to explain again. "We wanted to bring her, but once Bern died it didn't feel right. This place was always about the two of them, you know? Bern and Grace. Grace and Bern. One never came up here without the other. When Grace was left alone in Chicago we didn't know how to think about this house anymore. We didn't know if we'd ever come back, or if she would. Not to mention the prospect of a seventeen-hour road trip with a toddler. Grace was the one who pushed for renting the place out for a couple summers—I guess it was a way of avoiding the hard questions, of putting it out of her mind. So we let it be. It was the best decision we could make at the time."

"I know, Daniel. I get it. I'm not saying it was the wrong decision. I just wish Janie could have come. Could have experienced this at least once in her life. That's all I mean. She missed so much."

They sit in silence for a while, the scrappy birch quickly exhausting itself, the fire beginning to smolder and cast off lazy plumes of smoke. Soon it will be time to shovel sand over the coals and go back up to the house. With the fire failing, they become aware of a damp cold coming off the lake, and at the same moment pull the blanket more tightly around their daughter, their protective instincts in perfect synchrony. Over the top of the little head, Daniel kisses his wife slowly, the lemon tang of the salmon still in her mouth, but she's holding back, her tongue dormant and heavy. Talk of his other family can do this, he knows, even when she's the one who's started the conversation.

"I hope you know," Daniel whispers after a time, "that I always *wanted* to bring Janie here. So did Emily, God knows. She held off on swimming lessons because she wanted Janie's first swim to be in this lake, not in some YMCA pool. Does that give you some idea?"

Lissa leans forward and tosses a wind-stripped branch onto the fire, keeping her own counsel. Daniel peers out into the night where there is nothing to see. He's in no way a mystic, but lately he's opened his heart to certain possibilities he once scoffed at. "But it could be you're right," he says when the silence grows too long. "Maybe they're here somehow. What do we know? Maybe Janie's here."

With a shudder their daughter wriggles free, the drunkenness of sleep still on her face but her eyes sharp and bright. "Janie's here?" she demands. "Janie's here!"

Lissa's hand finds Daniel's under the blanket and squeezes it hard. Neither of them can think what to say. Into the breach their daughter rushes. "I *heard* you say it," she declares. "I heard you!"

"You were only dreaming, sweetie," her father protests.

"I was *not*. I heard you say Janie's here."

"You know what I think?" her mother says. "I think it's way past someone's bath time."

Daniel lifts Hanna to her feet and rises. With a petulant look, Hanna breaks free and stamps off toward the waterline, kicking up sand. "I want to see Janie!" she whines. "Cousin Janie and Aunt Emily!"

"That's enough, young lady," Lissa says curtly, but Daniel can hear the quaver in her voice. With a piece of discarded birch bark Daniel shovels sand over the remains of the fire, the smoke going up in a twisting veil, and swinging their peevish daughter between them they mount the steps up the hill.

It's his wife's turn to give Hanna her nightly bath. As he does the dishes he can hear them talking soberly in the bathroom off the den, but he can't make out the words. The mood shifts just as he's standing the last dish in the drying rack: A squeal of delight escapes into the house, a splash, then his wife's voice, chastening but plainly relieved. Somehow she must have eased Hanna's fixation on the absent Janie. He knows she'll brief him privately at the first opportunity, so that mother and father can speak with one voice. If the story's changed, he'll need to know it.

Daniel pulls on his heavy parka and steps through the sliding door onto the deck, turning off the kitchen lights as he goes. On this anniversary of Emily's passing he cannot go to bed without consulting the stars. He needs a few moments in their silent company, a few moments to reflect.

This was Emily's ritual over a lifetime of summers up north. If the night was clear, she'd take his hand and lead him to this same railing, nestling her back against his chest and pulling his arms around her like a welcoming sweater, a pair of spotting binoculars slung around her tanned neck. After the drab Chicago winters with their amber skies she could never get enough of the spectacle above. She hungered for it. An overcast night could leave her out of sorts for a good part of the following day.

With the winter constellations gone, the spring stars are out in force. Thanks to Emily, he knows a few of them and scans the vault above to get his bearings. As always, the first thing is to locate the old signposts. High in the southern sky he easily spots Regulus, the front paw of Leo. Then Polaris. And to the southeast, Arcturus. There was a spring night long ago when Emily swept her binoculars down and found Arcturus reflected on the still surface of the lake—a celestial signature on the waters—as if the lake were the mirror of an enormous, open-air telescope. She talked about it for days. There were stars burning in the water that night. It was a strange fact but a fact nonetheless.

Daniel can't recall the name of the constellation where Arcturus lies but remembers it's meant to represent a plowman. He tries to trace out the figure in his mind and he might have it or might not—all he remembers is that Arcturus is meant to be the knee. Emily was a natural at spotting constellations, lightning-fast at grasping the gestalt of the skies, but on most nights the exercise only makes him feel inept. Nevertheless he tries. On his slow crawl across the heavens he identifies three more constellations and a planet, though he'd only be guessing if asked to name them.

It is as he's puzzling over the eastern sky that a bluish light flickers at the outer edge of his vision. By the time he shifts his gaze it's gone; there's nothing there but a starfield, static and cold. But then a soft indigo plume folds across the northern sky and vanishes just as quickly.

"Hanna!" he calls out, then slides open the glass door and calls out again. "It's the northern lights! Come and see."

His little girl has seen the aurora borealis only once in her life, squealing in the gravel driveway the summer before as the skies danced and billowed with green. She'd prattled about it for days, too young to understand how the sun could have wind and how that wind could blow green clouds across the sky. They'd been charmed by her efforts to puzzle it out. Perhaps now there would be another teachable moment. Daniel hears his wife and daughter talking excitedly inside the house, bundling up. "Hurry, guys," he says. "You never know how long it'll last."

By the time they're all assembled on the deck, Hanna buried in her mother's big coat and her mother shivering under a blanket behind her, the heavens have gone utterly still.

"Daddy, where is it?" Hanna says. "Make it come back!"

Daniel suspects it's over, that the moment has passed. But then Lissa kneels behind their daughter and points toward the northern horizon. "There!" she says. "Did you see? It's blue this time, not green."

The three of them stare at the northern quadrant, barely breathing. "Where exactly did you see it?" Daniel asks.

"There," she says, pointing to a spot just below Polaris. Daniel scans the sky and lets his eyes pass slightly out of focus to heighten his peripheral vision, a trick Emily taught him. If she were here, she'd be squeezing his hand in the dark.

It's Hanna who spots the next irruption, this time to the northeast. "I see it!" she cries, "I see it!" And there it is: an indigo sail flapping languidly across the Big Dipper, as if catching the faintest of breezes. It's not much as auroras go, but it's enough to thrill Hanna. "Daddy! I can see the wind!"

"That's right, sweetie," he says. "It's the wind blowing in from the sun, remember?"

"Mr. Sun is *sleeping*, Daddy."

"Well, he must be snoring pretty hard then."

"Daddy?"

"What is it, sweetie?"

"Can Janie come over? I want her to see. Where's Janie?"

Daniel senses his wife stiffening under her blanket. When he looks down at her, kneeling behind their daughter, there is a trace of panic in her eyes. Out by Polaris, meanwhile, the sky is a loose flux of blue, the aurora shifting from velvet to vapor and back again.

"Where's *Janie*?" Hanna demands.

Her parents negotiate silently behind her back, her mother widening her dark eyes and shifting her gaze toward the heavens inquiringly. Daniel shakes his head. But Hanna is ahead of them. Pointing at the blue lights in the sky, she says: "Look, Mommy. It's Janie's dress!"

Daniel sees his little girl's logic instantly. The picture of Janie that Hanna knows best is the one in the bedroom bookcase—a picture of his first daughter kneeling in a cornflower-blue dress among fallen leaves, her blonde curls luminous in the late afternoon sun. At this moment the dress lies folded in a plastic bin in the attic of the Chicago house. The memory of it clutches at Daniel.

"Maybe you're right, honey," Lissa tells her daughter. "Maybe Janie—"

"Don't," says Daniel.

"What, Mommy?"

"Maybe Janie's up—"

"Don't, Lissa."

Daniel stares at his wife and she at him, her gaze suddenly defiant, their daughter distracted by the heavens.

"It's stopping," Hanna says in a small voice. "No more blue."

She's right. The display seems to be over for now, the stars restored. Daniel breaks his wife's gaze and turns his back on the lake, heading inside. "It's time for bed," he says abruptly, climbing the stairs to the bedroom before either of his girls can say another word. He leaves it for his wife to stoke the fire for its long haul through the night. He needs to subtract himself from the situation until he gets his bearings, until his thoughts make more sense. He's angry, but whether at his wife, at himself, or at the callow killer who robbed him of Emily and Janie five years ago, he cannot say.

"That wasn't very kind of you," his wife says after Hanna's tucked in and she's slipped into bed. They lie on their backs, unable to look at one another, arms crossed atop the covers. "Snapping at me like that and storming off. It wasn't the Daniel I know."

"I'm sorry," he says. "It just wasn't—"

"Wasn't the right time? To have the big talk with her?"

"That's part of it."

"And?"

"And it wasn't the truth. Janie's not up in the sky, and we shouldn't say so."

"Oh come on, Daniel. Hanna's three years old. You can't always tell a three-year-old the literal truth."

"But you were going to tell our daughter that Janie was in *heaven* if I hadn't stopped you."

"Can you really think of a better explanation?" Lissa takes an exasperated breath. He doesn't need to look in order to see her expression: the tightly sealed frown, the arched brows, the sharp unwavering gaze. At times like these, her staunch Greek mother is plainly in evidence.

"So," he says, "you can still believe in heaven after Oklahoma City?"

"Heaven? I never believed in it. Who's the scientist in the family, Daniel?"

"Plenty of scientists are believers, Lissa."

"Oh, give me a fucking break!" She kicks at the blanket as if it's made a sudden grab for her feet. "Besides, it's not about what *we* believe, Daniel. I don't think you get what's needed here. At all."

"Hanna doesn't need to hear another fairy tale. That much I know."

"Oh? Do you really?" she says. Then, as if instructing a child: "Sometimes fairy tales are best, Daniel. Especially for little girls."

As her scold hangs in the air, it occurs to Daniel that if it were Emily and not Lissa lying beside him, the argument might have followed exactly the same course. Intimate as she was with the firmament above, her love for the heavens as uncomplicated as any child's, Emily too might have favored the softer explanation. Perhaps he's missing the point. Perhaps his two wives know best.

And yet—and yet.

"Look, Lissa," he says carefully. "Janie's dead. Emily's dead. Five years ago today. It's a fact. Nothing we can say will change that."

A silence settles over the small room, a stillness of deeper consideration. Motionless as a dead man, he can feel his wife's slow respiration through the tiny nudging of the sheet. In the next room, Hanna fidgets in her sleep, the old bed frame creaking. After some minutes Lissa's legs shift lazily under the covers, signaling a change in the weather.

"Daniel," she says finally, and rolls toward him, laying a hand on his chest. "I know you're in pain. I don't mean to minimize that."

"It's not about my pain, Lissa. What about Emily and Janie? What about their pain?"

"Daniel, stop. We've been living with this for five years now. We've been over and over it. It goes nowhere, remember? It can't be solved. It's done."

"Which doesn't mean we tell Hanna some lie about what happened to her sister, does it? Tonight of all nights. Tonight we need to be honest about what actually happened. That's all I'm trying to say."

Her small hand makes a fist on his chest. "So what *are* you going to tell your daughter, Daniel? That some crazy guy parked a truck with a fertilizer bomb in front of the Federal building and blew up Emily and Janie? You can't tell a little girl that."

"Do you actually think that's what I meant? Is that the kind of a father you think I am? Jesus, Lissa."

But in fact, he has no idea what to tell his daughter. It needs to be the truth, somehow, but the truth has never seemed more impregnable. It cannot be scaled, cannot be attacked, cannot be surmounted in any way he can see.

His wife sighs and lays a hand on his cheek and turns his head gently toward her, kisses him. "You're a good man, Daniel. I hate to see what you put yourself through sometimes." She threads her fingers through his, squeezes his hand. "But I'm not saying let them go. I would never say that."

"I can't," he manages, his heart unruly in his chest, the room too cold. "I can't let them go. I don't want to."

"You shouldn't."

"But I'm not living in the past, either. You know that."

"I do."

"Sometimes it scares the hell out of me, being in this house, in this bed, with Emily all around." He feels his wife stop breathing. "I'm sorry. I shouldn't be saying all this."

He waits for her reply, and waits. After a long while she guides his hand to her hip and tucks her body into his, the scent of smoke in her thick hair and her dry lips on his neck.

Later, Daniel dreams that the bonfire on the beach has reared out of its smoldering and stalked up the hill toward the house. He awakes with a start, the raw buzz of crisis in his limbs. For several long minutes he lies in the darkness telling himself it's a ridiculous worry, but the fact is he didn't do much to extinguish the remains. At a certain point it's clear that sleep won't return until he's put his fears to rest. And so Daniel slips from bed and creeps down the stairs and finds his heavy parka thrown over the sofa, cast off during his angry march upstairs a few hours before. At the back door he pulls on his winter boots and feels around in the darkness for the black flashlight. Moving as quietly as he can, he slides open the glass door and lets himself back onto the porch and closes the door behind him, leaving the house to its dreams.

Down on the beach the fire is nothing but cooling embers, but he douses it again, kicking sand loose and scooping it up with his bare hands. It's not a night to take needless risks; the world has already spun far enough off its axis. If he'd thought to bring a bucket, he could have dipped water from the lake and smothered the fire once and for all, but sand will have to do.

When his work is done Daniel sits on the breakwater log and gazes out across the static lake. Somewhere in its depths there is life: Somewhere below the thermocline the old bass hang quiescent, powered down, waiting for spring to catch on in earnest. Come June there will be dragonflies skimming the water at dusk, killdeer shrieking, young splake nipping at the surface, and in the long evenings the loons stretching their cries across the water. It will all come to pass, given time and turn of season.

But tonight the lake seems devoid of life, a mirror reflecting the even icier heavens above. As he gazes across it Daniel sees what Emily once saw: Arcturus pricking at the still waters, and a little way past it Regulus, perhaps even Polaris. He's certain of it. The brightest stars have dropped anchor. He wishes Emily were here to share the moment, to revel in the perfect symmetry of sky and water. If she were here he would kiss her, the heavens his witness.

Daniel stands to get a better view, and as he straightens to his full height the lake erupts into blue flame. In an instant the starry reflections are scorched away. At first he's completely baffled, but something in the sinuous play of blue seems familiar, and then he has it. Above him an aurora the color of Emily's eyes is dancing across the northern sky, brighter and more sprawling than any he's ever seen, its magnificent lungs pumping as it cavorts among the watchful constellations. The plasma races across the heavens in great swooping gusts, unstoppable and joyous—yes, he thinks, unmistakably joyous.

Daniel stops breathing for a long moment, the spectacle almost too much to take in. The atmosphere itself is indigo, prismatic, cleansed. He stands alone between the burning sky and the burning lake, his hands blue as a Hindu god's and the tang of birch smoke on the air like a rogue incense. Somewhere behind him, somewhere up the hill, his wife and daughter are sleeping through it all, unaware that the sky has exploded, that the Earth is no longer the Earth of the day before, that he is no longer who he was when he bid them goodnight.

Daniel opens his eyes before he realizes he's closed them. He cannot guess how much time has passed. The lake lies before him like a glass plate now, Arcturus and Regulus and Polaris just tiny flaws in the photographer's emulsion. When he looks up into the sky the aurora has vanished without a trace, its blue dissipated into the frigid ionosphere high above, its dance no more than a memory. The heavens are just as they were before, dull and silent as a deserted theater: harmless. It is as if the bright apocalypse were only a dream. As midnight passes, Daniel plunges his cold hands into the pockets of his parka and mounts the uneven steps toward the house and his daughter's room, choosing his words by the more fragile light of stars and galaxies, some long since extinguished and others but newly born.

Left Center Right

Victor Barall

I n a crowded bar on the rue Valette, not far from the church of St.
Etienne Du-Mont, an American soldier of perhaps twenty-one is
sitting at a small, rickety table with three of his comrades in arms.
The olive green of their standard-issue uniforms, which had provided
some small semblance of camouflage in the forests and fields through
which they have slowly, painfully, made their advance, here, against
the dark wood and the blue and crimson tablecloths, makes their presence particularly conspicuous, which is a fine thing because there is
no need, for the moment, on this night, for them to hide. On the contrary, here the idea is to be as present as possible because they are what
they were told they would be if they lived to see this day: conquering
heroes, Goliath-killers, liberators, and all around them, the ecstatic locals

are shouting and saluting them and buying them drinks. The soldier wonders where it all came from, this liquor flowing so promiscuously, this wine uncorked bottle after bottle. Could it be, he wonders, that they had had the foresight to send their spirits into hiding, to secrete these flasks and magnums in church cellars and deserted farmhouses, in anticipation of the day when, once again, there would be cause for celebration? The soldier empties his glass and no sooner does he return it to the table than it is refilled.

All around him there vibrates the deafening roar of Parisians making merry, like prisoners released, en masse, from the penitentiary, or children under quarantine given a clean bill of health and sent into the open air, and at the soldier's table, too, moments before, they all had been shouting at once and slapping each other's backs, but now, a quiet has abruptly descended over his group because one of his comrades has let slip out the words they all in the back of their minds have been thinking: "If only Camminetti could have been here to see this." Moods can change so swiftly among drunken men, the soldier muses; one minute, they are on top of the world, the next they are ready to begin bawling. This mood, too, will pass, the soldier thinks, as soon as they are drawn into the next toast, or the accordionist by the bar picks up the tempo, but right now, each of them is immersed in his own thoughts of the future and the past.

The soldier remembers a favorite saying of his dead, horseshoe-playing grandfather—"Almost only counts in horseshoes"—and he thinks how true it is. Almost doesn't count in war, that's for goddamn sure, as Camminetti's example goes to show. You come through it all with hardly a blister, and then, *and then,* when it's all over but the shouting, you go and get a little careless and walk through the wrong door, and then it's all over, just like that, all over but the weeping. The soldier wonders whether, even now, it's all over, or whether, as the terrible rumor would have it, after the mop-up operation in Europe, MacArthur will grab them all up for the Pacific War. Now *that* war, rumor has it, makes this war look like fun and games.

The soldier's best buddy, Halliwell, rises unsteadily, jarring the table and overturning his chair. Pulling himself up to his full height to see over the heads of the patrons filling the narrow aisles, he locates the latrines deep in the interior. "Oh, the hell with it," he says, lacking the patience for such a strenuous, obstacle-ridden journey, and promising he'll be right back, he slips through the door into the street. In his absence, the soldier notices for the first time the woman sitting against the wall at the table directly behind the still overturned chair.

She is sitting alone, just her and a shot glass of honey-colored liquid and a leather-bound notebook in which she is writing rapidly with a jade-green fountain pen. She must be about forty-five or so, the soldier estimates, forty-five or fifty, tops, and not bad looking at all for a woman of her years, although a bit on the short side. A woman, in the soldier's opinion, should at least come up to a man's shoulders.

The soldier wonders what she is doing here, so solitary in the midst of this orgy of fellow-feeling, and he is impressed by the sense of dignified apartness she projects, the serious, composed air she radiates, the boundary about her person that everyone feels obliged to respect. She seems like a member of a certain species of widow, the type of widow who will never marry again, who will retreat into a houseful of servants and receive no offers, and again he wonders why she has come here and whether she is writing of this world or some other.

Watching her pen move so quickly across the page, watching her cover the blank sheet so effortlessly, as if all the thinking has been earlier accomplished and all that remains now is the mechanical task of setting it all down, the soldier remembers a letter he has been meaning, for some time, to write. In war, there is a letter they call the "Dear John" letter—a letter from the sweetheart back home announcing that it's all over. Sometimes it reveals that there's someone else and sometimes it doesn't, but either way, the bottom line is the bottom line. The soldier has had occasion to read more than a few of these letters, thrust into his reluctant hands by their unhappy addressees, and the soldier thinks that all in all he has commiserated rather well, having had a sure sense of when to be sorrowful and when to be incensed, but above all, what he has been struck by in these letters—what he has thought about often but never expressed out loud—is their horrendous timing. What a terrible thing to tell a man in the middle of a war, when already he's half over the deep end; it's the kind of news to make a soldier take all kinds of unnecessary risks, and he is glad his girl has had better sense than that, which doesn't make it any easier to write the letter he has been meaning, for some time, to write.

In going over in his mind the words he wants to use, it occurs to the soldier that, their timing aside, these letters have the force of logic all on their side, for war, he thinks, is the great divider of man from man, and even more, of man from woman. "Dear Anne," he intends to begin, "What I have to say is not an easy thing . . . ," and then he draws a blank because what he wants to say is something he only vaguely understands himself. War, he thinks, will have changed him, will have left its imprint on his character, on his outlook; war will have insinuated itself into his heart in ways, at present, he cannot possibly specify, but which, nonetheless, he is certain will have made him someone different from the person he was before, someone different from the person who loved the girl he loved before.

The soldier can envision that he will pick up exactly where he left off, that he will go right back to the college in Connecticut and make all the right contacts and go on to make large sums in an office downtown and return in the evenings to a large house in the country, but even so, it will be a different life, the soldier thinks; it will be a life requiring, for a comrade, a different girl from the one who knew him when. War is like hell, the soldier thinks, because once you go, you never come back, even if you come back.

A blast of fresh, cool air ushers the soldier's buddy, Halliwell, back into the bar. In the brief interval between his entrance and the moment when he picks up his chair and resumes his seat across from the soldier, the solitary woman looks up finally from her writing and, meeting the soldier's glance, she raises her glass to him, her expression conveying a grudging gratitude, and perhaps something more. But that is all he has time to read into it before the woman disappears behind his buddy's broad torso.

"Geez, that felt good," Halliwell says, and he begins to relate a story the soldier isn't sure whether to take at face value. "So I go outside, and I'm near to bursting, and I walk around the corner into this alley where there ain't no people, and I unbutton my flap and pull out my thing and I'm doing my business, minding my own business. There's this penny glinting on the ground and I'm taking my best shot and I'm making it jump, I'm making it dance, and then I hear footsteps.

"I look up and see this pair of *mam'zelles*, arm in arm, coming towards me. *Tres jolie*, believe you me, ooh-la-la. They're coming towards me, laughing it up in that language of theirs, I can't make out a word they're saying, but I can feel Old Honest Abe stirring in my hand and now he's trying to wash the moon right out of the sky.

"So all at once these two dames see me, standing in the shadows, and they stop in their tracks and begin to whisper. Then one says to the other, real loud so I can hear, and in English, '*I* will if *you* will.' And they look me up and down and start to giggle and then they run back to where they came from.

"And if I hadn't been 'indisposed,'" Halliwell says, employing that catchall euphemism popular in movies of the preceding decade, "if I hadn't been 'indisposed,' believe you me, I woulda gone after them, believe you me, 'cause they say there's no tail like French tail."

The soldier is less than completely inclined to take this claptrap at face value because, being a man himself, he knows that men will talk this way amongst themselves and that mostly it's just talk—all talk and nothing doing, although, he has to admit, the fact that nothing happened does lend the story a certain credence most such stories lack. In any event, as he joins in the general levity, the soldier feels a stirring in his own abdominal region, and lifting himself from his chair, he announces that he, too, will be right back. But unlike his friend Halliwell, the soldier, even after years of war, even after years of watching and being watched by other men in the performance of the most bodily of functions, has not shed entirely every shred of his former sense of decorum, and so he heads not for the front door, but for the pair of doors down at the other end of the long, narrow room. As he ducks beneath a low-flying flag, the soldier experiences a wave of dizziness and he has to grab onto the back of a chair to steady himself. He is drunker, he realizes, than he had thought.

The soldier nudges his way through the throngs of patrons squeezed against one another like the passengers on a downtown train at rush hour, and comes to a full stop as he waits for a dancing couple, seemingly oblivious to the massing of bodies, to whirl past him. He resumes his difficult march, two steps forward, one step back, and a hundred excuse me's, and with a feeling of relief, he begins to unbutton, pushes open the door, and staggers in.

It is an old bar, a bar still possessing its original fixtures, the soldier surmises, as he enters the dark, malodorous room with its drain in the center of the floor and nothing else—its drain in the center of the floor and nothing else but the small, solitary woman from the next table over. She is crouching over the drain and glaring at him from her crouch, and her eyes are registering him with an expression of undiluted disgust, and the soldier in that instant realizes, with a shiver, that he has walked through the wrong door, and, stammering an apology, he executes a clumsy about-face and makes his retreat as quickly as the congestion will permit, but not very quickly at all.

"Hey, what took you so long?" Halliwell demands, and with a grin and a wink, the soldier responds, "I met a girl," and as they pound him across the back and ply him for details, the soldier senses, with disgust and with relief, that the letter he for so long has been composing in his head is a letter he never will write.

:: :: ::

Just behind the Palais de Justice, inside a *salon de thé* on the Place Dauphine, a man approaching seventy is settling himself at his favorite table close by the window. It has been an unusually warm day for late June, and he is glad to be able to take off his jacket, which he hangs carefully over the back of the empty chair opposite him, so that when he sits down, it is as if he is sharing the table with a younger or older or merely a less substantial version of himself.

The beautiful young woman who waits upon him Tuesdays, Thursdays, and Sundays emerges from the inner room, smiles at him sweetly, and asks after his health as she regularly has done ever since the day when, in a moment of weakness he has come to sharply regret, the man divulged to her the existence of a minor heart condition that sometimes gives him pain. He is perfectly fine, he replies, he has never felt so well, and indeed, he says, there is nothing he was capable of at the age of thirty that he is incapable of at present. "Oh?" the girl asks, with a slight elevation of the eyebrows, and the man is pleased to think that perhaps he has recovered fully the ground he thought he irrevocably had lost, that perhaps she is receptive after all to the full range of possibilities hinted at in his declaration. "And what would you like?" she asks, her brows still arched and her eyes merry, and she takes down his order on an unlined sheet of paper in a leather-bound book.

The young girl re-emerges from the room in the back, and with lively step, returns to the man's window table, on which she places a pot of tea blended with bergamot, a cup and saucer, and a sliver of peach *tarte*. As she fills his cup, left-handed, she reaches her right hand behind her and pulls from her taut apron string that morning's issue of the *Neue Freie Presse*. Although the man has lived in Paris for decades, he remains more than casually interested in the life of his native city, and the proprietor of this establishment, to which the man comes every day like clockwork, has assumed the responsibility of seeing to it that with his tea, the man receives his daily infusion of Viennese intelligence.

"*Et voilà!*" the girl says playfully, laying the crisp paper on the immaculate white tablecloth, and just before again disappearing through the heavy curtain at the back of the shop, she flashes him another dazzling smile.

The man has the room all to himself, and lighting his old meerschaum pipe, he soon finds himself in the midst of a thick aromatic haze—a haze that grows thicker with his every exhalation. It is early afternoon, that hour of the day when he has seen to everything that must be seen to, when he has concluded, slightly fatigued, his walk along the river, and when, sitting at his table in this shop smattered with vases of flowers and cluttered with *ancien régime* prints and thick with pipe smoke, his attentions drift freely from one to another among the chambers of memory in which reside the many women of his life: the few he loved early, all those he loved later, and, alas, the last woman he will ever have loved.

For although he feels there is much life in him yet, he knows that to love yet again would be ridiculous. Indeed, even that last time he had come perilously close to making a fool of himself, and it had required the young lady's good sense, supplementing his own, to prevent that result from occurring. A man, he reflects, may grow old with grace; he may remain slender and erect of carriage and keep his dark eyes from clouding with cataracts and his silver beard perfectly groomed and free of weeds, all of which he has done, but there is something irreducible about age, and there comes a time when one must call it a day if one would not be ridiculous: There comes a time when the deliciousness of memory is the only consolation that remains to the lifelong bachelor, such as at some moment he must unalterably have become. The man knows all this, and although he is fully persuaded by the logic of the proposition, still, he resists its application to himself, for there is life in him yet, he thinks, and a courtly foreign gentleman of substantial means and wide experience is not without his appeal, even to a woman in her first flowering. Even putting those considerations aside, isn't it in the bachelor's essential nature, just as it is in the hunter's, always to be embarking on the next chase?

The man wonders when it had been that he had made his bed, when it had become too late to change course, and settling upon a particular moment, he decides, substituting a puff on his pipe for a sigh, that, alas, it had become too late too early—too early for him to have known that, thereafter, he would have no other option, and too early, in fact, even had he known, for him to have been persuaded that he should arrange matters otherwise. He had been thirty, if he remembers correctly, thirty or perhaps thirty-one. It was just shortly before he had begun that period of bootless travel in Asia and the Americas, just thirty years of life behind him when he had found himself, wavering of purpose, walking first in circles and then in straight lines, pacing up and down before the great oaken door, perspiring in his high collar, and at last lifting his hand to the great brass knocker in the shape of a double eagle. Not that he is certain, even now, that, had he his life to relive, he would have chosen to marry, but certainly, he has to admit, there are times when regret tinges his outlook, times like the present, when he finds himself alone and feels less than perfectly well.

The man sips his tea and unfolds his newspaper, holding it open before him at an angle such that, glancing over its upper margin, he can make a study of the young girl who, when he was looking elsewhere, had rejoined him in the shop's front room and situated herself with her back to the room's back wall. She is reading from a slender book, and making a show of great seriousness, is jotting down her thoughts in another book, perhaps the very one in which she had recorded his order. She is all seriousness, as is he, but the truth of the matter is that they are playing a sort of hide-and-seek: He is giving her his attention during those stretches when her head is lowered, and she too, is engaged in considering him during those stretches when his attention is taken up with the goings-on in Vienna. But it is in the nature of such a game that it reaches a moment when its players find themselves face-to-face, eye-to-eye, and knowing well how to grasp such a moment, the man asks, "What is it you are reading?"

The girl blushes and looks into her lap, in effect conceding that it is he that she was reading. But anxious not to be taken for a simple creature, anxious not to be seen playing all her cards at once, she gets up from her table, strides quickly across the room, and thrusts the volume into his hands. It is a volume of Maupassant, an author with whom the man has a passing acquaintance, and he remembers in particular a story about a set of earrings, presumed to be false, which turn out to be the genuine article; a story about an impecunious husband who is forced to conclude that if the jewels are true, then it is his departed wife, whose memory he reveres, who was false. The man flips through the pages with satisfaction because he knows that a young lady is what she reads, and he is glad that this young lady is filling her head with thoughts of romance and all its exquisite twists and turns.

"Ah, Maupassant," the man murmurs, handing back the book. "Unfortunately, our translators have failed to do him justice," he says, and after a brief, calculated pause, he adds, "Perhaps our difficulty has been with the subject matter. In matters of the heart, you should know, we are light-years behind you."

"Oh, I doubt that that is true," the girl quickly demurs, as he knew she would, but the truth of the matter is that it is precisely her nation's great love of the sport of love that, so many years earlier, had drawn him so powerfully to it.

"And what is it you are writing?" he asks, knowing that, after his last question, this time he will not catch her off guard, knowing that when, again, she colors slightly and looks away, this time she is only pretending to be caught out.

"Perhaps I am writing about you!" she abruptly declares, looking him, now, full in the face, showing that she, too, can play at this game, and having made this false confession, she turns on her heels and, pushing aside the curtain, passes out of sight.

The man pours out some more tea, finishes his pastry, relights his pipe, and resumes his perusal of the newspaper, and soon, too soon to have seen it coming, he finds himself among the branches of a delicious-smelling peach tree, heavy-laden with fruit, and as he climbs from branch to branch, tugging at the fruit, it occurs to him that while each fruit is, indeed, a peach, nevertheless each has its own particular shape, its own particular texture, which it does not quite share with any other of its type, and each has its own particular arrangement of hues, which it keeps entirely to itself; and as he climbs from branch to branch, tugging at the fruit, it abruptly dawns on him that whether he is tugging at the branches or the branches are tugging at him is very much an open question, and as this dawns on him, he opens his eyes and the girl is standing over him, pulling on his shirtsleeve.

It takes the man a moment or two to recover himself, and once he does, it registers on him that during his absence of indeterminate length, the room has been radically transformed. Where before his empty jacket had been his only steady companion, now he is surrounded by the bustle of customers, some sitting, some standing, and all talking excitedly in this tongue of theirs which, even after so many years, is still nearly incomprehensible to him until such time as he has fully awakened and had a chance to switch over. More alarming is his discovery that, during his probably only brief absence, he has made a thorough mess of things: Some of the pages of his paper are sitting in his lap, others form two haphazard piles, one on either side of his chair, and his pipe, still smoking faintly, is now lying on the floor, a short distance away.

"*Monsieur*," the girl pleads, pulling on his sleeve, her tone and her expression betraying a flattering degree of concern, but a degree of concern which, unfortunately, is not nearly sufficient to fully dissipate the man's feeling of humiliation.

"I beg your pardon," the man says, not knowing what else he can possibly say. "I must have overexerted myself. The heat, you know."

But the girl seems not to hear him at all, as if the urgency of her own message has sealed her ears. "*Monsieur*," she repeats, trembling, "your heir-apparent is dead."

"I beg your pardon?" the man asks, because at first all he can think is that he is childless and has named no heir.

"In Sarajevo, *Monsieur*. The Archduke has been shot. The Archduke and his wife. In Sarajevo."

"*Mein Gott,*" the man whispers to himself, and instantly he feels a twinge of pain in his left shoulder.

"*Mademoiselle*, I believe I better be going now," he says matter-of-factly, trying to maintain an air of calm, an air which he instantly betrays as he hastily gathers up his scattered pages, lunges for his pipe, puts on his coat, and struggles with his billfold. He knows he had better be going, for there are so many things that he must see to, and soon, he senses, all too soon, this people he has loved so well will be calling him their enemy and they will be right.

The man pulls open the curtained door and steps outside, and as he turns toward the Palais de Justice, he looks in through the window glass in order to catch a final glance at the last woman he might ever have loved, and just as he does so, he sees the handsome young man he had not before noticed, and he sees the young woman of his ambitions planting a kiss on the young man's cheek.

What is right is right, he thinks, with sadness and satisfaction, and wistfully he wonders whether he ever was truly the holder of the cards, or whether the truth of the matter is that they all merely let him think so. What is right is right, he thinks, as he hurries along, a hand to his chest, and it is right that this is the man she should marry, and with sadness and satisfaction he senses that soon, all too soon, in a matter of months, her husband will be dead.

:: :: ::

Just off the Parc Monceau, in the rue de Lisbonne, a man of about thirty, a scarf loosely looped around his neck, is sitting at one of the half dozen outside tables flanking a small café. Sipping a coffee and fiddling with an unlit *Gitane*, he is considering the few sitters at the other outside tables and following the progress of the occasional pedestrian as he waits in the orange glow of the late afternoon sun for his *petite amie* to make her arrival. He is intending to inform her that she is no longer, in the future, to be his *petite amie*, and although he has rehearsed just what he intends to say and is firm in his resolve, and although the prospect does not induce in him feelings of guilt because he has given thought to what is best for her as well, still, he is not looking forward to breaking the news because he knows it will come as unexpected and will cause her distress.

There may even be a scene—not a loud, rancorous scene, no loud, harsh words or slamming of silverware, but a quiet scene, quiet but just as apparent to onlookers, who have a sixth sense for these sort of things. A single large tear will form on the lower lid of her right eye—always her lead eye as far as crying is concerned—and will hang there, defying gravity for the longest time, catching the light and reflecting all the world, like the convex mirrors certain Flemish Old Masters liked to hang on the back walls of their paintings in order to provide a minute reflection of everything not shown in the depicted scene itself. The tear will hang there until, finally, she will ask if he has brought a tissue, and when, after fumbling in his pocket, he admits that he has not, one of these several onlookers, no, two or three, will each rush forward with a handkerchief. "I'm sorry," she will say, sorry for the embarrassment she is causing him, knowing that above all else he hates a scene.

The young man has observed quite a few of these scenes himself, being a frequent café-goer; quite a few of these scenes of suddenly lowered voices, and hands withdrawn suddenly from other hands, or extended toward other hands in a new, tentative, exploratory manner, and faces looking away from one another and forks fidgeting with *pâtisseries* for which there is no appetite, and yes, he, too, more than a few times, has felt like offering up his handkerchief but has resisted the impulse. He has never understood why people choose to make their farewells in public places, and yet here he is. Perhaps, he thinks, he is merely obeying an unwritten rule of social life, a rule nobody has ever understood or even contemplated but which everyone, unthinkingly, automatically, has felt called upon at some point to honor. Perhaps then, he, too, is merely doing what must be done, but perhaps, he thinks, he, like so many others before him, is trying to avoid a scene; perhaps he is counting on the public setting to inhibit any impulse on the part of his *petite amie* to resort to words or gestures that privacy would most certainly permit.

In which case, he realizes, he has acted in vain, he has merely substituted one type of scene for another, and he wonders, now, as he waits, whether he has chosen the wrong type of scene, for in contriving to inhibit her, he will also have inhibited himself, and, in fact, he will have inhibited himself the more, because, try as she might, she will be unable to fully suppress her feelings, whereas he, the initiator of this event, will be obliged to contain himself and will be left, as it were, the odd man out. Certainly, if his experience as an observer is any guide, he *will* be the odd man out: At some point, not very many minutes after her arrival, when no more words can be spoken and with her *tarte* untouched and her coffee undrunk, she will rise from the table and very quickly stride off, not looking back, and he will be left sitting, the focus of all stares, and will have to remain long enough to keep up the pretense that nothing has happened, nothing at all, and that their stares are entirely misplaced. Not that anyone will be deceived: They will shake their heads, almost imperceptibly, and perhaps someone will make those nearly inaudible little clucking noises, and those of them who form a couple, however troubled a couple they form, will reach for each other's hands and clasp them in reaffirmation of their bond.

The young man wishes his *petite amie* would come so he could get it over with, for although he is not so very young, he has had very little experience in what he is about to do. In fact, it now occurs to him that in those instances in which infatuation did not, as if by magic, evaporate simultaneously on both sides, invariably he has been the one to be let go. Not that a vaster experience would be too helpful, he realizes: These matters can never be pleasant, and not even Casanova's experience could have been so vast as to have provided him with a foolproof method of determining, on any future occasion, what the other's reaction would be.

At the table to the young man's right—a little round table like his own, hardly large enough to contain a pair of saucers, a sugar bowl, an ashtray, and the cardboard pyramid advertising an obscure brand of liqueur—sit an elderly husband and wife, a pair of Americans on holiday, pausing here to catch their breath, exchanging few words, their view of each other completely obstructed by the *International Herald Tribune* the husband is holding open before him. "Listen to this, dear," he utters from time to time, and then he proceeds to inform her of what they are missing back home. She meets his piecemeal offerings with a series of noncommittal murmurs, absorbed, as she is, in the copy of *Paris Match* she is holding at arm's length, having, the young man gathers, left her reading glasses in their hotel room. In this manner, the young man imagines, they have passed all but the very beginning of their life together.

At the very beginning, he supposes, there had been an element of passion between them, for even now, in their late sixties, it is possible to see them as handsome and to infer that, forty years earlier, they must have been objects of beauty, each for the other. But it had not lasted long, that mutually passionate interest, having been replaced on the one side by children and on the other by mortgages and promotions and games of golf, and for a long time now, several decades at least, they have occupied different worlds, they have separately occupied the same space, the same breakfast table in the Dutch-tiled kitchen, the same spacious living room with its view of the sky through the trees; several decades of his reading the newspaper while she paid the bills, of her doing the crossword while he mixed a drink, exchanging few words, comfortable, to be sure, in each other's presence, even fond, still, each of the other, but with a fondness verging on and passing easily into indifference. Neither quite knows, and neither cares to know, what the other is thinking or feeling or fears.

At the table on the couple's other side, slowly sniffing a brandy and rapidly writing in a leather-bound notebook with unlined pages, there sits the ancient lady the young man privately has designated "Madame X," the tiny old woman with whom, for some years, the young man has shared the café, but with whom he has never spoken. That she is a widow he surmises from his never having seen her with a similarly statured counterpart, or, for that matter, with anyone at all, although still she wears a wedding band. Regrettably, over the period of their co-patronage, she has grown smaller and smaller, so that now she is scarcely taller than the small, gray-bearded dog sitting quietly, politely, across from her. From time to time, the old woman looks up from her writing and softly speaks to the dog in a secret language he seems to have no trouble understanding.

In days gone by, the young man recalls, the dog used to sit at her feet, like a protector or an acolyte, or like a friend who held her in the highest esteem, but of late, he has taken to sitting at the table with her, watching her ardently from beneath his thick gray eyebrows, registering with his dark brown eyes her every gesture, and indeed, with his air of self-possession, with his dignity and his beautiful, rigid posture and his perfectly trimmed whiskers, the dog might be taken for the lover she took in the early years of the century, the wealthy gentleman over three times her age, who, if he continued to remain acquainted with good fortune, would have expired just days before the outbreak of the First World War.

"Listen to this, dear," the American utters, but unbeknownst to him, sitting behind his newspaper, his view of the world limited to the pages spread open before him, his wife has soundlessly pushed back her chair and gone inside, no doubt to locate what in the United States, the young man remembers, is sometimes called the "powder room," the room where women go to apply fresh powder to their cheeks and fresh paint to their lips and to rub fresh perfume on their wrists. She will not be pleased with what she finds there, the young man is certain, because it is an old café still possessing its original fixtures; she will not be pleased with the dark, malodorous room with its drain in the center of the floor and nothing else, and perhaps when she returns, she will lodge with her husband a mild complaint, and he, speaking in a tone she has rarely heard, but which, she suspects, may be more common in his discourse amongst men, will remind her that he had been present in the city at the end of the war, and he will relate to her, for the first time, how in the midst of the victory celebrations, more than a little inebriated, he had mistakenly wandered into the women's toilet of the bar where he had been carousing, and how what he had found there had been entirely pleasing and much to his liking and perfectly suited to his masculine anatomy. He will emit a little chuckle and she will frown, but will quickly recover herself, for he had been a soldier then, and no, they had not yet married.

But that is still in the future and the past, while in the here and now, unbeknownst to the American, absorbed, as he is, in the news of the day, his wife has abdicated her wrought-iron throne, and the small, gray-bearded dog, quick to spot the vacancy, has jumped down from his seat across from the old, old woman and clambered up into the foreign lady's chair. Friendship endures, the young man thinks, but lovers are fickle, always receptive to opportunity, always ready to exchange the known for the unknown, the captive for the quarry.

"Listen to this, dear," the American utters, and then he proceeds to read a few lines aloud—a story, so far as the young man can make out, concerning a candidate for the presidency and his extramarital activities. What a difference, the young man reflects, between the United States, where a politician may not have a mistress, and the Republic of France, where, of course, he must.

"Are you listening, dear?" the elderly tourist finally inquires, its having at last struck him that he has failed to hear his wife's customary acknowledgement that she is according him at least some small fraction of her attention. Still failing to hear the least emanation from behind the wall he has erected, at last he lowers the paper and discovers the new face his wife has put on. The dog gazes at him ardently, and the young man, too, watches the American's face, as it makes its brief journey from shock to dismay to relief. The old man lets go a laugh as he realizes with pleasure that his wife, whose every curve and fold he had thought he knew down to its minutest detail, is, yes, still capable of surprising him.

The young man finishes his coffee, uncrosses his legs, and consults his wristwatch, and he realizes, first with relief and then with dismay, that his *petite amie* will not be coming. And the old, old woman glances across at him, restores the cap to her ancient, jade-green fountain pen, and closes her notebook.

Biographical Notes

Victor Barall ("Left Center Right") was born and raised in the Bronx and currently lives in New York City. Victor is an attorney who for many years has worked in public service. His other stories have appeared in *The Greensboro Review*, *The Quarterly*, and *Lettre International*.

William E. Burleson's ("Fox") short stories have appeared in numerous literary journals and anthologies to date, most recently in *The New Guard* and *American Fiction* Volume 14. Burleson recently published *Tales of Block E*, three stories set in 1979 on a downtown block that has seen better days, and is currently serializing it on his website. In addition, he has two novels in develop-ment: *The Avenue*, which picks up where *Tales of Block E* leaves off, and *Ahnwee Days*, the story of a small town that has seen better days and the mayor who tries to save it. Previous to writing fiction, he had published extensively in non-fiction, most notably his book, *Bi America* (Haworth Press, 2005). For examples of past work and more information, visit www.williamburleson.com.

Josephine Cariño ("Old as Rain") holds a degree in English with a minor in music from East Carolina University in Greenville, NC. Her poem "Postlude" was a finalist for *december Magazine's* 2015 Jeff Marks Poetry Prize, and was subsequently published in its 2015 Fall/ Winter issue. Most recently, her haiku "Calligraphy" won second place in the 2016 Myong Cha Son Haiku Contest at West Chester University in West Chester, PA. Josephine is currently attending North Carolina State University in Raleigh, NC for her MFA in Creative Writing.

Joe Dornich ("Endangered Animal Release Specialists") is a PhD candidate in Texas Tech's creative writing program, where he also serves as Managing Editor for Iron Horse Literary Review. In addition to writing, Joe is also taking a mail-order course in veterinary medicine. His mailbox is often filled with sick kittens.

Elisabeth Doyle ("American Ghosts") is a lawyer and writer who lives in Washington, DC. She holds a Masters of Laws degree (LL.M.) in Global Health and Human Rights from Georgetown University Law Center, where she focused her course of study in areas including peacekeeping, refugee issues, and war crimes, and performed her graduate independent research on the topic of genocide prevention. Her first collection of short fiction, *War Stories*, was published in 2013 to strong reviews by *The Washingtonian* and *The Philadelphia Review of Books*, among other venues. Her second collection of short fiction will be completed in 2017.

Elizabeth England ("Bruised People") is a recipient of a 1998 New York Foundation of the Arts Fiction Fellowship, and her stories have appeared in the *Nebraska Review, North Atlantic Review, Berkshire Review,* and *The Connecticut Review.* She won Ohio State University's *The Journal*'s 2007 short story contest as well as *Inkwell*'s 2001 short fiction competition where the winning story was nominated for a Pushcart Prize. An excerpt from a longer piece appeared in the 2011 issue of *FictionNow*. Most recently, her story "First Girl" was reprinted in the *Writers Studio at 30* Anthology, published by *Epiphany*, Spring 2017. A content strategist as well as a college consultant and essay coach, Elizabeth teaches spinning on the weekends, lives with her husband and two college-age children in New York City and spends any free moment honing her craft.

Edward Farrell ("Disappearance") is a child of the Midwest and a present resident of the great Commonwealth of Massachusetts. A sometime ditch digger, retail manager, salesman, international executive, teacher, chaplain, student, consultant, security guard, orderly, father, husband, poet, singer—he is a full time human being. His fiction has appeared in *The Mississippi Valley Review, Pigiron, The Furnace Review, The Crab Orchard Review,* and *Euphemism*.

Mike Goodwin ("It Formed a Heart") recently earned his doctorate in English at the University of Southern Mississippi's Center for Writers in Hattiesburg, Mississippi. Born in New Jersey, he grew up outside of Philadelphia before moving around western Pennsylvania. His poetry has previously appeared in *Slab* and *Radioactive Moat*.

Yen Ha ("Her Dentist") is a principal of Front Studio Architects in New York City. She is a maker of spaces, stories, drawings, and dinners. Her writing has won both a Top 25 finalist and honorable mention in *Glimmer Train*'s Short Story New Writers Contests and has been published in *Chicago Quarterly Review, Kentucky Review, The Minola Review,* and *Crack the Spine.*

Edward Hamlin's ("Borealis") *Night in Erg Chebbi and Other Stories* was selected by Pulitzer Prize finalist Karen Russell as winner of the 2015 Iowa Short Fiction Award and went on to win the Colorado Book Award. Edward's work has also been recognized with a Nelligan Prize, an NCW Short Story Prize, two Pushcart Prize nominations, and other honors. A New York native, Edward Hamlin spent his formative years in Chicago and now lives in Boulder, Colorado. For more information, see www.edwardhamlin.com.

Kenneth John Holt ("Spring Beneath Silence") is a writer of fiction working from his native city of Los Angeles. He attended private schools before embarking on a twenty-year career in filmmaking that had him travel the world. Interests include religious and philosophical studies along with art and music. Beginning submissions in June of 2016, Holt is off to a good start his first year by being selected as a finalist in two fiction contests. In addition to contributing to American Fiction 16, TulipTree Publishing chose his story "A Beer in Bastille" (humor category) for their 2016 *Stories That Need To Be Told* Anthology.

Robert Johnson ("The Devil's Age") holds an MFA from the University of Iowa Writers' Workshop. In October 2015, his story "Bird Fever" won the Marguerite McGlinn award for fiction in *Philadelphia Stories* magazine and was subsequently nominated for a Pushcart Prize. His stories have also appeared in the online magazines *Wag's Revue* and *Winning Writers.* Johnson was a finalist in *Glimmer Train* and *Pinch Journal* contests in 2015 and in *Narrative* magazine's Winter Fiction Contest in 2016. He attended Bread Loaf Writers' Conference in 2015 and 2016.

Julia Lichtblau's ("Far Rockaway") writing has appeared in *The American Scholar, Blackbird, The Drum, Superstition Review, American Fiction* Volume 13, *Narrative, The Florida Review,* and *The Common,* among other publications. In 2015, she was finalist for the Dana Award for Short Fiction, the Kore Press Short Fiction Contest, and short-listed for the Fish Story Prize. She's been a finalist twice for the American Fiction Prize, won the Paris Short Story Contest, and earned second prize in the Jeanne Leiby Chapbook Contest. She is book review editor for *The Common* and covered international finance in New York and Paris for *Business Week* and Dow Jones Newswires for fifteen years. She has an MFA in Fiction from Bennington College and lives in Brooklyn, New York.

Deena Linett's ("Mirrored Reveals") newest books are *Translucent When Fired: New & Selected Poems,* from Tiger Bark Press, and a novel, *What Winter Means,* winner of the Grassic Short Novel Prize from Evening Street Press, which follows two prize-winning novels in the '80s. Her short fiction, poems, and essays have appeared in a variety of magazines including *The Massachusetts Review, The Georgia Review,* and *The Bellevue Literary Review.* "Mirrored Reveals" appears in a collection of short stories, *Here & Elsewhere,* which is circulating.

Corey Mertes ("Sidney's Sound") grew up in the suburbs of Chicago and received his bachelor's degree in economics from the University of Chicago in Hyde Park. He earned a Master's of Fine Arts in Film and Television Production from the University of Southern California and a law degree from the University of Missouri-Kansas City, where he was Editor in Chief of the law review. His short stories have appeared in many journals, including *2 Bridges Review, Green Briar Review, Sundog Lit, Valparaiso Fiction Review, Bull: Men's Fiction, The Prague Revue, Midwestern Gothic, Poydras Review, The Doctor T.J. Eckleburg Review,* and *Hawai'i Review.*

Tatjiana Mirkov-Popovicki ("Snow Angels") is a writer, visual artist, and electrical engineer living in Vancouver, Canada, where she emigrated from Serbia twenty-two years ago. Her story "Snow Angels" has earned an Honorable Mention in *Glimmer Train*'s 2016 March/April

Very Short Fiction Contest. She is the winner of the postcard section of the Federation of British Columbia Writers Literary Writes 2017 contest.

Tamar Schreibman ("Forgive Me, Father") is a former magazine editor and freelance writer whose fiction has been selected as a finalist in numerous literary contests, including *Glimmer Train* and *Salamander*, and as a semifinalist in the Raymond Carver Short Story Contest. Schreibman studied fiction at the Writers Studio in New York. This is her first published story. She lives in Vermont with her husband and sons.

Steve Trumpeter's ("Puro Yakyū") fiction has appeared in *Sycamore Review, Hobart, Jabberwock Review, Chicago Quarterly Review*, and others. He teaches fiction writing at StoryStudio Chicago and co-hosts a popular quarterly reading and music series called Fictlicious. Find more of his work at www.stevetrumpeter.com.

Eric Vrooman's ("Meredith's To-Don't List") short fiction has appeared in *The Kenyon Review, The Cream City Review, Passages North, Monkeybicycle, Hobart, Twelve Stories, Paper Darts*, and *Ninth Letter*. He is the recipient of a Minnesota State Arts Board Artist Initiative Grant and a SASE/Jerome Award. He lives in Minneapolis and teaches at Gustavus Adolphus College.

Mark Williams's poems have appeared in *The Hudson Review, The Southern Review, Open 24 Hours, Rattle, Nimrod*, and the anthology *New Poetry from the Midwest*. Finishing Line Press published his long poem, "Happiness," as a chapbook in 2015. His fiction has appeared in Indiana Review. As in his story "One Something Happy Family," he once thought a young woman's shout of "I love you!" was intended for him. He lives with his happy family in Evansville, Indiana.

About New Rivers Press

New Rivers Press emerged from a drafty Massachusetts barn in winter 1968. Intent on publishing work by new and emerging poets, founder C.W. "Bill" Truesdale labored for weeks over an old Chandler & Price letterpress to publish three hundred fifty copies of Margaret Randall's collection *So Many Rooms Has a House but One Roof.*

About four-hundred titles later, New Rivers, a nonprofit and now learning press, based since 2001 at Minnesota State Univerity Moorhead, has remained trued to Bill's goal of publishing the best new literature—poetry and prose—from new, emerging, and established writers.

As a learning press, New Rivers guides student editors, designers, writers, and filmmakers through the various processes involved in selecting, editing, designing, publishing, and distributing literary books. In working, learning, and interning with New Rivers Press, students gain integral real-world knowledge that they bring with them into the publishing workforce at positions with publishers across the country, or to begin their own small presses and literary magazines.

New Rivers Press authors range in age from twenty to eighty-nine. They include a silversmith, a carpenter, a geneticist, a monk, a tree-trimmer, and a rock musician. They hail from cities such as Christchurch, Honolulu, New Orleans, New York City, Northfield (Minnesota), and Prague.

Charles Baxter, one of the first authors with New Rivers calls the press "the hidden backbone of the American literary tradition." Continuing this tradition, in 1981 New Rivers began to sponsor the Minnesota Voices Project (now called Many Voices Project) competition. It is one of the oldest literary competitions in the United States, bringing recognition and attention to emerging writers. Other New Rivers publications include the American Fiction Series, the American Poetry Series, New Rivers Abroad, and the Electronic Book Series.

Please visit our website: **newriverspress.com** for more information.